"COME HERE, KIRSTEN."

The deep sensuality of his voice sent a ripple coursing through her. With her back to him, she wriggled into a clean shift.

She did not hear him until his breath grazed her neck.

"I am not accustomed to being disobeyed."

"And I am not accustomed to having to obey."

She faced him, chin raised, her eyes glowing with a savage inner fire. He returned the steady gaze, his eyes boring into her, probing her very soul. "Say the words, Kirsten," he whispered, his finger grazing against her temple. The slight touch of his hand sent a warm shiver through her. "You know what must be said." She nearly swayed with the intensity of her feelings, for the anticipation of his touch was unbearable. "Say the words!" His voice broke with huskiness.

"I am yours to command, my lord."

"Nay! Not to command. You know the words."

She tried to look away, but he shook his head decisively as he tilted her chin and studied her face. "Say the words!"

"I am yours—to love."

"Forever."

"Forever."

He brought her fingers to his lips for a light kiss and then to the drawstring at her throat. She tugged and the chemise fell to her ankles. . . .

"Drama, passion and history merge in a breathtaking tapestry of medieval romance. Powerful, engrossing entertainment from a new author."

—*Romantic Times*

Firebrand's Lady

CARYL WILSON

POCKET BOOKS

New York   London   Toronto   Sydney   Tokyo   Singapore

An *Original* Publication of POCKET BOOKS

POCKET BOOKS, a division of Simon & Schuster Inc.
1230 Avenue of the Americas, New York, NY 10020

ISBN: 1-4165-0699-3

This Pocket Books paperback printing September 2004

10 9 8 7 6 5 4 3 2 1

POCKET and colophon are registered trademarks of Simon & Schuster Inc.

Cover art by Donald Case

Printed in the U.S.A.

Acknowledgments

Many thanks to Linda Lael Miller for the benefit of her insight; to my agent, Irene Goodman, for her professional expertise and assistance; and a special thanks to my editor, Caroline Tolley, who has guided me along each step with patience, intelligence and wisdom beyond her years.

Prologue

1050

Maude squinted through the autumnal night mist in search of the enshrouded moon. Three days, with its waning! It bode ill for her child, Glenna, who lay twisting on her pallet, caught in the throes of childbirth gone awry.

Maude had seen others in her score of years as midwife for the Village of Retford. The child presented breech. She would have to turn the babe, or risk losing them both.

She brought a pigskin pouch from the folds of her coarse woolen kirtle, untied the braided thongs, and sprinkled columbine seeds into a wooden bowl, then crushed them under a smooth stone.

Maude feared for her daughter. Glenna, a fragile child of only thirteen summers, could not withstand the rigors of childbirth. The midwife cradled the girl's head on her forearm, trying to force the vile-tasting liquid between her parched lips.

"Mother?" Glenna rasped, her words slow. "Shall I die for my sins?"

"What sins? 'Twas not in your power to deny your lord."

"Will I lose my babe? I want the child, bastard though it may be. If it should die, I would not want to live."

"Hush!" Maude placed her finger over her child's irrever-

1

ent lips for fear that God might hear her despair and strike her down. "God will understand," she said, more to convince herself. "Naught shall happen to you or the babe." She caught the beads of sweat with a rough cloth before they trickled into Glenna's eyes.

"Promise me!" the girl urged.

Maude was reluctant to say her nay, lest she abandon all hope. "I promise that you shall hold the child in your arms when you awaken."

At that declaration, Glenna slipped into a troubled sleep, but Maude could not begin her work in earnest until later, when Alyson, her elder daughter, returned.

Alyson set her basket on the table and warmed her hands at the crackling fire as Maude poked about and drew out a flask. "Wine from Father Jerome, bless his soul." She mixed the wine with the crushed columbine seeds, and the potion was ready. "Glenna shall rest easy this night, but I fear for her. So frail, and the head—too large."

"You are the finest midwife in all of Andredeswald," Alyson assured her. "Have you not presented Lady Astrid with two strapping sons, and another due any day?"

"With her Viking blood, she is well made for birthing."

Alyson sat in a chair by the hearth and watched the smoke drift in a gray curlicue through the thatched roof of the wattle-and-daub hut. Her mother would save them both. She was sure of it. She had the gift. Glenna was—

Her thoughts were interrupted by the clamor of men-at-arms and horses' hooves pounding the dirt road to the secluded hut.

The animal skins in the archway were flung back and the room filled with men wearing Lord Wulfrid's colors.

"You know me?" a giant of a man, at least two heads taller than the women, asked gruffly.

"Aye," Maude acknowledged. "You are Lord Wulfrid's housecarl, Cedric."

"Ready yourself. My lord commands you to Retford Hall to attend my lady's birthing."

"But 'tis not time—" Alyson began.

"My own daughter has need of me," Maude insisted.

"Yon Alyson can continue your work here," Cedric grumbled.

"But my Glenna—"

"Dare you imply that your daughter is more important than your lady?" The giant looked perplexed. "My lord would not overlook such impertinence."

Maude wanted to remind him that Glenna's babe was also a child of Wulfrid of Retford, but she held her tongue and sighed resolutely. "Take your men and wait in yonder copse while I gather my herbs and medicinals and instruct my Alyson in the girl's care."

"Hasten, Maude," Cedric warned gruffly through thinned lips. "You know the measure of my lord's impatience."

"Aye. Well I know it."

Soon Glenna's concerns were replaced by those of Lady Astrid of Retford, but whether lady or cottager, the fear was the same. "Am I to die, Maude?" Lady Astrid asked as she clenched the midwife's hands. "Will the child—"

"The child is fine. Feel how it moves."

"But 'tis not time!" Lady Astrid watched with concern as the midwife examined her, but would not allow herself to be comforted. "I do not want to die."

"None of us do, my lady. Now, try to remain calm. You are in no danger."

"But 'tis so different this time," Astrid mumbled. Maude kept the reason to herself as doubt etched deep circles under Astrid's eyes, and as dawn approached, she howled that she could not bear the pain one moment longer.

"Here. The flower of forgetfulness," she whispered as she slit the stems and squeezed the contents into a horn of water from the nearby spring. "This shall ease your discomfort."

As Maude held the horn to Lady Astrid's lips, the young woman sipped the bitter liquid greedily.

Later, when the servants inquired for their lord, they were assured that their lady fared well. The door, however, remained bolted as the midwife performed her work, opening only when Alyson brought news of Glenna's child. At dawn, as the mother slept, the child's cries pierced the silence.

"Glenna shall heal well," Alyson said.

Maude breathed a deep sigh in reply. "Yes. God provides."

3

Chapter **1**

1066

Morgana! Sit at your task!'' Father Jerome tapped the table.

"I hate Norman French! I hate it!'' The maid hung out the chapel window, elbows akimbo and legs off the tile floor, and turned to bask in the warmth of the midsummer sun. "You promised you would let me out for a bit.''

"Nay! 'Tis the pond that beckons. How many times must I repeat, girl, that you must not swim in the pond alone any longer. More strangers travel in our midst each day. You are comely. Has your grandmother never explained what can happen to a young woman unattended?''

"You yourself told me that God is always with me,'' she said slyly.

"Of course I did,'' he sputtered. "Yet even God yields to a man who, while exercising free will, forces himself upon a fair, sweet maid.''

"How will Norman French help me in that situation? No is *non*. Why need I know more?''

"Should Duke William land upon our shores, as King Harold expects, you will thank me for this forced instruction.''

"Learning is for the nobility and clergy, not for the granddaughter of Retford's midwife.''

4

"Glenna may have been your mother, and bastard you may be, but you are Lord Wulfrid's daughter, too. I take both your education and your safety very seriously. Now—" he pointed to her chair—"I have a *chanson de geste* that I am certain you shall enjoy."

"I would more enjoy practicing with my bow. Should the Normans or King Harald Hardrada land upon our shores, my archery would stand me in better stead than my command of Norman French."

"A woman who knows her conqueror's language is at an advantage. Already you read Latin proficiently, when most women and men cannot read at all. Think, girl, what value 'twould be to be able to understand an enemy who underestimates you. With your quick mind, you are a natural spy. Leave the fighting to those more suited. You shall survive by your wits, not your might."

Morgana sighed as she opened the book. Father Jerome could enforce this slavery to her studies, but he could never end her dreaming of summer days and cool waters.

Blaise, Vicomte de Rouen, stood atop the grassy knoll, helmet in hand, an imposing yet unassuming figure. As he fixed his attention on the valley below, his chin set grimly, bespeaking an obstinance that his men had learned never to question. The gold in his eyes flickered with interest. The edge of the great forest that the Saxons called Andredeswald bordered on the Village of Retford. To the other side was a wide lake said to be well stocked with trout. This was to be his prize. His square jaw tensed visibly.

"No unusual movement in the village, *mon seigneur*," said Sigvald, his second-in-command, who towered above Blaise by nearly a head. With shoulders straining against a leather byrnie, he looked every inch the Viking he was— muscular, almost handsome, if not for a scar across his right eye where he had been near blinded in battle. The eye had healed, but a hardness had covered the man's heart. Blaise was ever thankful that Sigvald was his man, and not his enemy, for when aroused, he gave no quarter.

The wind whipped a shock of black, silky hair across Blaise's forehead and into his eyes. "My hair must be shorn," he grumbled. " 'Twill yet cost me my life, for all that it grows like a weed."

"The village houses at least forty families. They have cleared about two thousand acres from the forest. There is a water mill at the east edge. By all accounts, Edward and Harold spent many a day hunting in yonder wood. Your falcons will no doubt net a prize."

"We are a short distance from Godwinson's estate?"

"Aye, *mon seigneur*. The village is well settled."

"As long as there is a blacksmith, for my friend here has limped this last half day." He leaned over and stroked his horse, Reynard.

Sigvald dismounted and handed his reins to Blaise. "The people of Retford should not see their new lord enter his demesne on a lame steed."

"I have been blessed with your wisdom and friendship these many years since my father commended me to your care." Blaise eased off his horse. "What else is there in this godforsaken wilderness?"

"A beekeeper." Sigvald grinned. "I got this from a peasant by the side of the road." He handed Blaise bread soaked in honey and a hunk of cheese. "Methinks you—"

"I know," Blaise chuckled, " 'twould not do for me to be hungry when we arrive." Blaise sunk his teeth into the cheese.

"These whey-faces have done well by the West Saxon king," Sigvald said. "All of England has grown fat and lazy on peace."

"Before this year—possibly. But the defense of England has taken its toll. My spies tell me that the West Saxon fyrd had been at the ready for months along the coast, until they were disbanded just before we landed. They lay in wait for us, but King Harold's traitor brother, Tostig, commanded his attention first when he joined forces with the Norwegian King, Harald Hardrada, the Landwaster. The stores are low. We have much work ahead of us."

"The village has suffered little damage. Not like Hartley—sacked and burned. Methinks Christian D'Arcy has too much taste for violence." Sigvald sighed.

"D'Arcy is a fool," Blaise agreed. "He was too quick to put Hartley to the torch." He shook his head. "But then, he never has been known to control his appetites, be he satisfying his craving for power—or a woman. I should have been more insistent in my opposition when William forced D'Arcy back into my service with the guarantee of his own demesne. No doubt I shall have to remedy yet another predicament of his making."

"Aye! Retford fairly bursts with villagers from Hartley seeking refuge. Many of the men have fled to the forest."

"Any word of Lord Wulfrid of Retford?"

"Killed with his two sons, Brent and Edgar, at Stamford Bridge."

Now it was Blaise's turn to sigh. " 'Tis probably for the best. Retford has been spared because no lord was here to raise arms against William. Any children at home?" Blaise added as an afterthought.

"A golden-haired, freckle-faced lad of about ten, and one daughter, Lady Kirsten, rumored to be as beautiful as a delicate rose—tall, long of limb, and willowy, with hair the color of scarlet ribands."

Blaise detected hesitation in Sigvald's voice. "What more?"

"They maintain that she has been stolen by the Viking, Eirik Godricson."

"That is absurd. Eirik of Dubh Lin travels the sea trading goods, not stealing helpless women."

" 'Tis claimed they were betrothed, and that, when Lady Kirsten disavowed the betrothal, Eirik attacked the Convent of St. Agnes and took her away."

"Do you believe this claim?"

"The convent is undamaged. Mayhaps Lady Astrid, fearing for her daughter's virtue, has hidden her away with the sisters."

Blaise had the same thought, and if it was true, he could not allow this ruse to go unquestioned. Gullibility would make him easy prey to those who would undermine his authority. William had bade him hold this place well in his name, and a mere woman would not threaten his work with her cunning deceit. "I must needs ponder this, for my actions now will set the tenor of my rule amongst these people." He adjusted the reins of Sigvald's horse and started down the slope.

At Retford Hall, the conversation dwelt on the same subject—the disappearance of Lady Kirsten. Lady Astrid and her housecarl, Cedric, had spent long hours debating the matter, for just when Cedric thought they had agreed on a course of action, Lady Astrid would change her mind.

"My lady, the Norman scouts will have reported to their leader by now. We must decide on a plan."

"What think you, Cedric?" Lady Astrid inquired. "Will they see the truth in my words?"

Cedric shrugged. A graying, weary, war-horse, he knelt before his mistress and took her hand in his. "The word has spread like wildfire, my lady. Many have fled to the forest. The Normans are just without the palisade."

Lady Astrid remembered how, little more than a fortnight before, she had awaited Eirik Einar, son of Godric, Jarl of Dubh Lin, with much the same apprehension. Eirik had come to claim his bride, her daughter, Kirsten.

Why had Kirsten run from Eirik to the sanctuary of the convent? It made no sense to Lady Astrid. The betrothal had stood for over two years. As a bride-price, Eirik had commissioned forty long-swords—two inlaid with gold and richly chased and gilded—and delivered them to Lord Wulfrid on the eve of King Harold's battle with Harald Hardrada. Indeed, Eirik's men had fought valiantly alongside Lord Wulfrid at Stamford Bridge, helping to defeat the Landwaster and save England, only to lose it to Duke William of Normandy.

Lady Astrid made a solemn prayer of thanks that Retford had not suffered as had the women and children of Hartley, who now camped in makeshift dwellings within her palisade.

Eirik had foretold King Harold's ultimate defeat, for when he had taken his leave, the king was leading a forced march of his battle-wearied men to meet the Bastard at Hastings. It was rumored that even the Church had abandoned the Saxon cause, for Duke William had schemed so well that he had secured the blessings of the pope, and now carried the papal banner.

When Lady Astrid had first heard from the fishwife that Duke William's men had harried the towns along the southeastern coast, she held her chin straight, determined to face adversity with grace.

"I wept when I thought of Lady Kirsten in Ireland with Eirik," Lady Astrid confided, "but 'tis preferable that she be the Viking's honored bride rather than some Norman's whore." She swallowed. "I shall wear the jeweled brooches that Lord Wulfrid gave me when Kirsten was born to greet my new lord."

Cedric motioned, and a serving girl hurried to do her bidding. Within the hour, Lady Astrid sat in Lord Wulfrid's chair, clad in a gown of the finest blue and red silk, her hair secured with ruby hairpins. She would greet the conquering forces with dignity, and pray that she could yet save Retford from the torch.

To leave such a task to a woman! Yet no noble men had returned. The housecarls had fought valiantly, but had been cut down like wheat in the fields. The exhausted Saxons had been no match for William's men, who had been on horseback, well rested and supported by a wealth of archers. Many had heeded King Harold's call—fierce fighters the equal of or better than the Norman hordes, men who had fought for a higher purpose than riches, not mercenaries gleaned from the dregs of Europe as were William's men. And yet, they had been defeated.

Defeat was a word she would never understand. As the only daughter of a fearsome Danish thane and a noble Saxon lady, she had been weaned on intrigue. Her marriage had been arranged before the pious King Edward had come to power from his exile in Normandy. She had held no illusions about her husband, a proud man with an unparalleled weakness for women, who used his position to coerce those weaker than he into doing his bidding. With full knowledge of these shortcomings, she had loved him all of their married life.

Her fortunes as Wulfrid's wife had been intertwined with those of Harold, whose father, Godwin, was the most powerful of Edward's earls. It had pained her to flee her Wessex home for Ireland with her children when, in 1051, Godwin's family was banished.

Godwin had returned within the year victorious due to Harold's invasion forces. Wulfrid had fought with Harold, harrying the Somerset coast at Porlock, wresting power from Edward. With the passage of years, Harold had become the king's greatest supporter. Edward himself had named him "Duke" when he had granted him the charter to Worcestershire.

How now, Lady Astrid wondered, could she battle this plague that spread with swift feet upon her land, consuming it? With guile, for that was the only weapon of a conquered woman.

The clopping hooves of neighing steeds and the clang of mail and weaponry grated against her sensibilities. Lady Astrid sat frozen to the seat of authority that Wulfrid had occupied, absently pressing her flaxen hair under the head-rail that identified her as a married Saxon woman. She straightened her back, lifted her chin, and dug her nails into her tunic as she awaited the confrontation that would surely come.

Men, fully armored and swords drawn, poured into the hall, forming an arc around the entranceway, ever watchful as their leader strode into the hall to stand directly before Lady Astrid.

Cedric kept to her side, hand on his dagger, determined to protect his mistress with his dying breath.

The Norman knight's eyes darted swiftly around the great hall. He was attired completely in black, but his shield was white and gold, with a flaming gold torch in the center. Blaise de Rouen—the "firebrand" of Duke William.

"Astrid of Retford?" a man-at-arms asked, drawing her attention.

"Yes, wife to Lord Wulfrid, Thane of Retford."

"Thane of the worms, you mean," the fearsome knight replied, his one blinded eye taking on the aspect of an eagle.

Lady Astrid winced as the callous words washed over her like iced water. She would have swooned had she not Cedric's strength to draw upon. "I stand corrected, sir knight."

"Aye, you will stand, Astrid of Retford, and kneel to your *seigneur,* Blaise, Vicomte de Rouen."

Lady Astrid would say or do nothing that could be interpreted as an act of defiance, for the Norman dogs would seize any opportunity to ravage Retford and lay waste the work of her lifetime. When she started to rise, Cedric moved forward, hand on his sword hilt, but she motioned him back, her pleading eyes speaking volumes of concern for her people.

She knelt to Blaise, her eyes leaving his golden gaze to glare at the etchings on his helmet—flames of fire surrounding a cross. This murderer pillaged under the sign of the cross?

"Do you yield Retford to my control, or must I take it by force of arms?" Blaise asked, speaking fluent Saxon.

"Has anyone raised a weapon against you or your men?" she replied.

"You shall address my master as *'mon seigneur,'* or 'my lord' in your godforsaken tongue," the man-at-arms insisted, watching Cedric's every move.

"Very well, my lord." Though a model of obedience, Lady Astrid heaped curses upon their immortal souls, even as she smiled graciously. Such swine would never break her unfettered spirit.

"Sigvald, disarm her man," Blaise said quietly.

"Am I to be denied protection then?" Lady Astrid asked.

"Sigvald will be all the protection you will need, woman. Even I would think twice before daring to question his might."

As Sigvald relieved Cedric of his dagger and sword, Blaise removed his helmet and scrutinized the hall. "How many villagers have we?"

Lady Astrid noted that, even with the grime of war upon him, the viscount was a fine specimen. "The tally changes daily."

"Perhaps an approximation."

"I must study our reeve's report from last spring." At Blaise's approval, the ledgers were brought.

He slumped carelessly in Lord Wulfrid's chair as Lady Astrid took the seat below the dais and began poring over the ledgers. This hall was not as well appointed as most Norman halls, he noted, but having spent many a year in this ill-starred country as a lad, he had expected as much.

"Wench!" Sigvald bellowed. "Some wine."

"No wine, my lord," one of the kitchen girls replied.

"Our wine stores are depleted," Lady Astrid explained. "We have ale or mead."

"Ale then." Blaise nodded to Lady Astrid to continue her work. Although he appeared engaged in other matters, he kept one ear on their conversation.

"Where are your children, woman?" Blaise asked casually, noting the meaningful glance that passed between the woman and her housecarl.

"My two eldest sons lay hacked to pieces near York . . ." She paused. "My youngest son is abed with fever, and my daughter, Kirsten, has been taken to Ireland by her betrothed, Eirik Einar, son of Godric, Jarl of Dubh Lin."

Blaise slammed down his horn, and ale spilled across the table, wetting her books. Lady Astrid straightened, but did not retreat from his implacable, unnerving visage as she calmly wiped the ale with a kerchief produced from her sleeve.

"I marvel, woman, at your ridiculous attempt to deceive me."

"My lord, I have no reason to deceive you," she replied with barely controlled annoyance.

"Indeed!" He nodded toward the archway where one of his men balanced her youngest son, Gareth, on his shoulders. " 'Tis a miracle! The bloom of health has returned to your lad's cheeks, and the child has quit his sickbed to play at the edge of the wood with his dog."

Lady Astrid reached for her son, but Blaise motioned her back and beckoned Gareth to him. "Do not fret, little mother," Blaise assured her. "Even a Norman would not harm an innocent child." He removed his gauntlets and touched the back of his hand against the boy's forehead. "The fever has abated as suddenly as it commenced."

"My lord, if you do not believe me, mayhaps the good sisters can convince you," she continued in exasperation.

"Beware, woman! Do not compound your falsehoods. Only your daughter, sitting at this table, will persuade me of your good faith." He removed his mantle with measured indifference, then Sigvald loosed the ties of his hauberk and drew the heavy mail over his master's head to hang upon a nearby oaken post.

"I wish to clean the stench of death from my body. Where is the lord's chamber?"

Lady Astrid nodded toward the upper level. "I have moved my belongings to my daughter's chamber."

"Good, for when I find the maid, she shall have no need of it."

Lady Astrid silently thanked God that He had delivered Kirsten from this Norman warlord.

At the top of the stairs, Blaise hesitated and faced her. "You have until we sup this eventide to produce the girl."

Lady Astrid bit her lower lip as she watched him disappear, then slammed shut her ledger and removed herself to her chamber, accompanied by Cedric. "This rigid and exacting Norman has placed me in a difficult position," she pronounced as she traversed the length of the bedchamber to the window. "As I cannot possibly produce my daughter, we must flee. Gareth must be kept safe."

"Aye, my lady. I will make the arrangements." Cedric turned to leave.

"Take heed! His man, Sigvald, keeps close watch on us."

"The Norman bathes now. We will have no better opportunity to escape."

As feared, it was the ever watchful Sigvald who discovered their flight. He had gone to Lady Astrid's chamber at Lord Blaise's request to invite the woman to dine with Blaise and his knights. When he was unable to find her within the hall, he realized, much to his chagrin, that she and her housecarl had fled.

"Mon seigneur!" The door flung wide on its hinges to slam against the wall, sending Blaise leaping from his bath, sword in hand and poised for defense, the actions of a seasoned knight. "She has escaped," Sigvald advised him.

"Lady Astrid has dared to defy me? And the child?"

"I know not how she did it. She stole him from his chamber while my man stood watch at the door; they have fled to the wood."

"Does she not realize that I hold her lifeblood in these hands?" He squeezed his fist and slammed it upon a nearby table. A sudden, thin chill hung on the edge of his words as he hurriedly rubbed his flesh dry with a flannel cloth warmed at the fire. "Witless woman! To flee into the night like a winged bat." Sigvald handed his lord a clean chainse, chausses, and a leather tunic.

"Who knew?" Blaise asked as he buckled his mail and pulled on the gauntlets. "The maids? the kitchen wenches? Her—"

"All claim innocence, *mon seigneur.*"

"I shall test the truth of their words," Blaise replied as Sigvald placed the helmet on his head. "This woman truly believes that she can flee me?"

Sigvald shook his head, unwilling to explain the foibles of women. He had soldiered all his life, for Blaise's father, his brother, and then for Blaise. There was no explaining women. Their only worth lay between their legs.

"I have never been here, Cedric. What place is this?" Lady Astrid shuddered in the eerie stillness.

"We are near the hut of Maude, the midwife. You will be safe with her while I go to Brigstoc to arrange passage to Ireland."

"Methinks we cannot cross to Ireland now. Only a fool would brave the Irish Sea in November."

"Then to Wales."

"My husband accompanied Harold to Wales to put down Prince Gruffyd's rebellion. The Welsh will murder me and my child."

"God's bones, my lady!" Cedric halted his horse in frustration. "You set me a task at each turn. I know not where we will go, but I will protect you."

"Is there anywhere that I could be safe with the Norman scourge upon the land? Is this not what Edward the Confessor foretold on his deathbed? My Lord Wulfrid recounted King Edward's terrible dream to me when he returned to our chamber in London from Thorney Island. 'Within a year and a day of his death, our cursed land will fall to the enemy to be harried by fire and sword.' "

"Yet Edward commended his wife, Harold's sister, and the Normans who lived in England—his very kingdom—to Harold. It was undisputed. That is why the witan voted unanimously to uphold the deed."

"William the Bastard claimed Harold's oath of fealty."

"An oath not freely given, or given when he had not the power to give it. Harold could not gainsay the witengemot. They would have no Norman bastard duke as King of England. Harold was king by acclamation."

Lady Astrid knew the truth of his words, but the most strange events of the past year had shaken her faith. She was not by nature a superstitious woman, and yet, when the fiery-tailed comet had overshadowed the land, Edward's prophecy had come to mind. Was it only in April, on the eve of the festival of the Greater Litany, that the hairy star had first come, to hang over England like a cross of fire for seven nights, a presage of doom? That was the last time she saw her lord, Wulfrid—the last time she felt his strong body against hers and in hers.

Lady Astrid followed Cedric through the wood, determined not to fear the night's sounds. She tightened her fur cloak about her, and her jewels banged against her knee. The Norman had not had time to plunder her caskets and trunks, but she had left him a token payment—mere trinkets in comparison to the treasure she carried.

They skirted the pond to a clearing near the place of stone monoliths once inhabited by the Druids. "'Tis an eerie place, Cedric." One ancient oak had a horrific face carved into it. "Mark this tree," she whispered as she pointed to a hollow section at its base. "It shall hold my jewels."

"What mark, my lady?"

"Thor's hammer, to guard the future hope of Retford."

Cedric worked quickly lest anyone observe them. With a piece of slate he stripped back the bark and scratched the hammer directly above the hole. When he was done, he carefully laid the leather bag in its new resting place.

"Let us hasten away, my lady."

They mounted their steeds and made for the old woman's hut.

As the uninvited guests burst in upon Maude, the old woman backed up against the hearth, eyes widening in fear. Lady Astrid barely recognized her, bent as she was with a crippling of the joints.

'Twas Lady Astrid and the housecarl, Cedric, Maude thought. *He* had come for her when the girl was born. And

15

they had a young boy with them. That must be the one they call Gareth. Alyson had been called for that one, for by that time, Maude had suffered an ague that had left her hands useless.

"Cover your windows, woman!" Cedric ordered as he pulled the skins over the openings, and looked to the hearth.

"Fear not. We have no wood to burn. Come! Sit!" She motioned to a nearby stool.

Lady Astrid sat near the cold hearth, bone-weary, and Gareth lay down next to her on a pallet.

"Your burden weighs upon you," Maude noted.

"Aye, old friend." Lady Astrid shivered with chill and fatigue. "How have you fared?"

"Well enough, my lady." Her thin form and haggard appearance belied her words.

"Your lady no more, I fear." The old woman offered her a strange liquid. "What is this?"

"It shall calm you, and help lift your spirits."

As Lady Astrid sipped, the cool brew warmed her. "How are your daughters—Alyson, and Glenna?"

"Alyson puts the food on our table, more often than not. Glenna has been dead these nine years past."

"Your loss sorrows me. I know what it is to lose a child." Lady Astrid fought her melancholy. "Cedric, mayhaps we should try the coast—a ship to cross the sea to Ireland—to my daughter, Kirsten. She is all that is left for me, besides my Gareth here. If we stay—"

"We cannot risk capture. The Norman scum means to do you harm if you cannot produce your daughter. He will never believe that you do not hide her away."

Lady Astrid fought to maintain a fragile control, but her voice quivered with unshed tears as she searched for a response.

"I am sorry, Mother," Gareth cried miserably. "Were it not for me—"

"Gareth, the warring of knights is not your fault. Yes, it was wrong for you to disobey me and go outside the palisade." She tousled his hair. "But you are a child yet, and I did not explain to you the importance of following my orders. Now, lie back and rest. We can ill afford your fever returning. 'Tis not you I blame.'' She covered the child, humming until he fell asleep.

"Make no excuses for the boy, my lady," Cedric spoke gruffly. "Sooner than you wish he will be a man, and must learn to accept responsibility for his behavior."

"His days of childhood are almost ended. Let him continue for as long as God wills it."

Maude pulled Cedric aside. "What is this that you speak of, man?" Cedric explained the horns of the dilemma upon which Lady Astrid stood poised. "Take heart, my lady." Maude patted Lady Astrid's hand. "Things have a way of working out."

"Normans overrun our village, you old fool! Bah!" Cedric waved her away with a negligent hand.

"Will he punish my people when he realizes that I have fled?" Lady Astrid wondered aloud.

"Nay! He will think himself well quit of you. Retford is a rich settlement. He shall gain more by gentle coaxing than violence. Besides, if he planned on laying waste the village, he would have already done so."

"Lie down and rest, my lady," the midwife said as she pressed her backward onto the bed. "Let the potion do its work. Fate has taken a hand in all of this, and there is nothing more to be done for the moment."

As Cedric covered his lady with his woolen mantle, she grasped his hand, loosening her grip only when sleep came to claim her.

It was the voices that brought her back through the cobwebs of nightmares. There were two of them in peasant garb. Alyson! The years since Gareth's birth had taken their toll, for her hair was white, her skin rough and spotted.

"Lady Astrid has come to visit," Maude said calmly. Alyson looked swiftly from her mother to the hooded figure by the door. "You remember my Alyson. And this is Morgana. She lives with Alyson, in the hut behind my own." The old crone's palsied hand beckoned the girl to her.

"Grandmother?" the girl questioned, obviously reluctant as she inched forward.

Lady Astrid, her mind a tumble of confused thoughts,

inclined her head to one side. The girl's face lay shadowed, yet her voice *was* vaguely familiar.

"What is it, Grandmother? Why are these people here?"

" 'Tis the day of reckoning, girl," Maude replied. Alyson gasped, and Lady Astrid and Cedric looked to each other. What mystery was this? Maude reached up and tugged the girl's hood to her shoulders, revealing a mass of red-gold curls.

"Kirsten! By the rood! What are you doing here? How did you escape Eirik Einar?" Lady Astrid leapt from the bed to draw the frightened girl into her arms, but the girl shook herself loose, and searched the old crone's face. "Grandmother?" A tense silence enveloped the room.

"Lady Astrid, this is not your daughter, Kirsten; 'tis Morgana."

"But that—that cannot be. She is the mirror image of my daughter." She remembered the gossip about Wulfrid and the midwife's daughter, Glenna. "Glenna's child?"

Maude shook her head in the negative as Alyson prostrated herself at Lady Astrid's feet. "Forgive us, my lady. 'Twas not my mother alone. I aided her in . . . in . . ." Her voice trailed off.

Cedric yanked Alyson up by her arm as Morgana, unused to such violence, moved backward. "What say you, woman?" Alyson fell into a crying fit, unable to continue.

" 'Tis my fault, and mine alone," Maude said calmly. "I forced the girl to act as a dutiful daughter. Sit, and I shall explain."

They sat by the hearth. Maude's voice shook as she recounted her foul deed. "The night that you birthed Kirsten, my Glenna birthed her own child—also a babe of the loins of Lord Wulfrid."

"Then this *is* Glenna's child?"

"Nay, my lady, 'tis Lord Wulfrid's child, but you are her mother."

Lady Astrid's heart threatened to stop beating and her breath came in painful gulps, as if squeezed from her.

"My lady, please do not fail us now," Alyson begged. "I have lived so long with this deed. Do not deny us our moment of soul cleansing."

"That night," continued Maude, "I was desperate. Glenna's only hope for a live child was if I should deliver her. But yon Cedric came from Lord Wulfrid, insistent that I leave the girl to attend your birthing." She licked her parched lips. "I knew that I would return to a dead babe, and possibly a dead daughter.

"Right after you gave birth to Morgana, my suspicions were confirmed. Twins! When Alyson came with the news of Glenna's dead babe, I was grief-stricken and angry. Why had God given you two healthy babes, whilst denying my Glenna her one? Alyson had insisted that Glenna would heal, that it was the will of God, but I would not see. Lord Wulfrid was selfish. Alyson could have helped you birth your babes, but he would hear none of it. So I determined to give Glenna what I had promised, a babe to press to her bosom for however long she would live."

"Twins?" Lady Astrid remarked quietly.

"Aye. Long, strong lasses, with red-gold hair, each a mirror of t'other. I dosed one child with the sleeping potion, and she slept well."

"You stole my child from me?"

" 'Tis not that simple, my lady. I was possessed by a demon. Alyson tried to dissuade me, speaking of what I already knew—your kindness to the villagers, to us. In my grief, I was unmoved." Maude wept silently, large tears streaking both cheeks. "You, after all, had another child, and Glenna had none. Having never suspected that you had borne two babes, you would never mourn her loss. Alyson tried to explain that Glenna could start anew without a bastard child, but I was convinced that she was ruined for marriage anyway. No one wanted Lord Wulfrid's leavings. The only happiness for Glenna lay in her having her own child."

"I remember staring at your still form," Alyson continued the tale at her mother's pause. "Dread crept inside me like some unseen animal. It was so easy. Your servants gave us two baskets of food for our services. We fed the contents of one to the hounds, and hid the sleeping infant inside. Your ladies were so busy fawning over you and the child, no one noticed as we crept from your bower, our sinful deed hidden within the folds of muslin."

Throughout the telling of the tale, Morgana had remained

silent. Then, when the truths that the last few moments had revealed assailed her, she turned to the two women whom she recognized as family. "Aunt Alyson! Grandmother! What does this mean?"

"Morgana, the blood of two noble houses surges within you. You have brought me nothing but joy these sixteen years past. But much as it pains me to say so, I speak the truth. I am not your grandmother, nor Alyson your aunt. Glenna, God rest her soul, was not your mother. Only one in this hut has any blood claim to you—Lady Astrid of Retford—your mother."

When Lady Astrid rose to go to the girl, Morgana raised her hand, her eyes wide. "Stay! 'Tis not true! Tell me that you lie!" Maude shook her head. The girl whimpered as if a hurt animal and flung herself through the door, her hair whipping on the night air, inattentive to the cold or the danger that beset her at each turn.

Cedric made to follow, but Lady Astrid held him back. "She needs a moment to ponder the import of what has been said this night." She sat down on the edge of the bed. "We all need a moment."

"She will go to the high place," Alyson assured them. "She will seek the counsel of the gods of the oak and the stone, as did the Druids of old."

"Ponder she may, but only in this hut," Cedric insisted. "The Normans will be scouring the wood for us, and if she is taken unawares, who knows what harm might befall her."

"Go to her, Cedric. Bring my child back," Lady Astrid pleaded. When he had left, she turned to the midwife. "My heart is sadness and hope. You have deprived me of my child these many years. To be brought up as a cottager, when she was the daughter of a thane much loved by both King Edward and King Harold—"

"My lady, I can do naught about the passage of time. The girl was well tended." Maude took Lady Astrid's hands. "She even reads and speaks Norman French. She is bright. She has studied with Father Jerome, who believed her to be Lord Wulfrid's daughter by Glenna. I have taught her about herbs and medicinals. She shoots a bow and handles a dagger better than half the fyrd. She can survive in the forest, if need be. She even swims like a fish."

"Has she known who her father was then?"

"Aye. No sense in taking both parents from her."

"You give me my child when I am feeling most bereft of children. For all my dreams of reaching Ireland, I doubt that I shall ever leave England alive; I must face the harsh reality of defeat."

"Perhaps God has shown you a way to save Retford. The Norman wants to see your daughter, Kirsten. Morgana is her image and would suit well. As for memories, 'tis not unusual for one so distressed at the recent turn of events to suffer forgetfulness."

"Nay, Maude!" Astrid said. "I must try to escape with my children, for should the Norman dog sniff around the girl, 'twould be the end of her. He is full of himself and exceedingly handsome. As tall as Morgana may be, he is a full two hands taller, and built like a war machine with a coldness of heart to match. There is no chance that the Norman would let so ripe a flower go by without trying to pick its bud, especially now that we have tricked him." Gareth stirred. " 'Tis best that the child has slept, for he will know naught of what has transpired."

Lady Astrid cradled her surviving son's head.

Morgana sat in her place. No one would find her here. She could think upon what she had heard with only the ancient gods as her witnesses.

She was heedless of the chill night and the wind whipping at her cloak, as her mind reeled with confusion.

Lady Astrid's child? Not Glenna's child? No kin to the women she had called grandmother and aunt?

Mixed feelings and thoughts muddled her brain until she was in a tumult. A child of the nobility, and not the bastard spawn of a rakish thane of King Harold? A child of a mother and father properly wed?

Years of pain washed over her as she remembered the faces of all who had called her bastard. All for naught.

And her mother. Not that pitifully fragile young girl whom she barely remembered but had loved so desperately these years past. Not the girl, but a strong, stately woman.

Tall—like her. Hair the color of spun gold with a flaxen hue, but eyes just like hers, a fine sea green.

She had grown up in the wild wood when she could have grown up a lady. She would have worked at the art of needlepoint. She would have been taught the workings of a household in preparation for her marriage to a fine lord someday.

If William's men had come, as the foresters claimed, did it really matter if she be Saxon noble or cottager—rich or peasant? The rich would lose all to the invaders anyway.

Loss! She had lost her father without ever knowing him. Brothers, too! All dead except for one boy. And a sister— a twin—taken to a foreign country against her will.

A raw and primitive grief overwhelmed her. As she stood embracing the clouds and screaming her pain on the night wind, an owl swooped down to whisk the sound away with its piercing wail.

The old ones would protect her. She had come to this place of worship to entreat them many a time. On this stone, where it was said virgins were slain in Druidic rituals, she had been at one with them. They would strike this pain from her heart.

Night birds ascended the sky in unison, wings flapping hurriedly as if to escape the devil himself. Something, or someone, had frightened them.

She crouched down on the rock, feline in her movements, and searched for some sign of an intruder.

When a twig cracked, a spasmodic trembling attacked her limbs.

Chapter 2

Mon *seigneur*, our scouts report movement ahead, on that large stone perched atop the mound.'' Sigvald pointed to the place. "Mayhaps outlaws await to strike a blow?''

"Lend me your torch,'' Blaise ordered. "I go alone. Take the men and cover both flanks. Once you have surrounded the place—'' he motioned—"then move in from the rear.''

"My lord, if you are injured—''

"If I am so easily laid low, mayhaps another *should* be lord, eh?''

"But a knight of your abilities—''

"Sigvald! I refuse to be thwarted by this rabble.'' Blaise urged his mount forward as his men dispersed to either side. Reynard, sporting new protection on his hooves, moved stealthily through the forest and up the hill, stopping at the base of the high rock. He sniffed the night air, whinnied, snorted softly upon the wind, and refused to move.

"Ah! You smell it, too!'' Blaise remarked. All was silent, but his inner sense told him that danger lurked nearby. His eyes scanned the darkness. The wind whistled through the trees, but it was not in the trees that the coward had chosen to hide. Too simple! Too obvious! The smell came from

23

the high place, a vantage point from which the scoundrel could efficiently pounce upon his unsuspecting prey.

Pig dung. A fitting smell for serfs. But if this one chose to pit himself against Blaise, he would sleep beneath the mud of the pigsty for eternity.

Morgana pressed flat against the stone, fighting the fearful images in her mind, her pulse erratic. She was certain that he could hear her blood rush through her veins. A wave of apprehension swept through her, even as the cold stone cut into her belly and breast.

It was one of *them,* the Norman marauders who had come to plunder her land—perhaps the very one who had killed her father and brothers. No doubt he had soaked English soil with the blood of her people. She wrapped her cloak tightly around her body lest the wind whip it up and betray her. Why was the Norman stopping there? And where were his men?

Blaise continued forward, his senses attuned to the slightest movement or sound. His men skirted the rock to cut off the coward's retreat. Upwind from the peasant, he sensed that he was near. Reynard whinnied and danced skittishly as pebbles rolled from atop the boulder, showering the Norman knight.

With her ear to the stone, Morgana could hear vibrations. She glanced over her shoulder stealthily, and saw their helmets first. As they advanced to stand only twenty feet from her, poised, their weapons in their hands, Morgana skidded forward on the rock, bloodying her knees until she reached the edge. The devil himself awaited her below, his fiery dragon's eyes visible on each side of his nosepiece, impaling her in his steady gaze.

"Come down, wretch. You dare lay in wait for me?"

Morgana did not move. Behind her the men advanced slowly, obviously enjoying the moment.

"Come down, or I shall slit your gullet and feed your guts to my dogs."

True to Father Jerome's teachings, Morgana pretended to not understand him. He repeated the words in Saxon, adding several vile epithets. His men closed in, propelling her forward in a moment of recklessness to leap upon the Norman knight with a fierce battle cry.

24

She nearly succeeded in unhorsing him. She looked for a vulnerable place in his armor, and finding none, aimed for his groin somewhat short of the mark. He easily parried her thrust and flipped her back, his fist grazing her jaw in a slightly lopsided movement.

Morgana fell heavily to the ground, but recovered as the swift blood surged through her body. Fear drove her as she circled him, the blood pumping so swiftly through her heart that it would surely split asunder.

The fearsome devil-knight drew his sword. "Saxon swine," he spat as Morgana leapt at him with a cry, lunging with bared teeth. He sidestepped her easily and slapped her on the backside. She rolled over twice, and was knocked unconscious with the hilt of his sword. She lay sprawled upon her back on the ground—senseless.

"Saxon pig!" Blaise spat contemptuously as he stood, sword poised, above the silent figure.

"Hold!" Cedric shouted, as he vaulted into the clearing. "Stay your assault, my lord, I beg you."

"The varlet attacked me. He has reaped the whirlwind."

Cedric lay his body across Morgana's silent form. "Hold your assault, lest you kill the one whom you seek."

Blaise paused. "What say you, man? Impossible!"

Cedric whipped the hood back to reveal Morgana's gold-red, bloody curls. "My lord, this is my lady's child."

Blaise leaned forward and parted her cloak. Bathed in moonlight was a young woman with hair that had loosened to cover her like a fur pelt. Silent. Clothed in a beggarly shift. But definitely a woman.

Within seconds his men were beside him. "Light the torches," Sigvald ordered, as Blaise knelt, his cheek upon her face as he checked for breath.

"My lord?" Cedric inquired.

"She barely breathes." Blaise looked again at her garb. "A girl she may be, but not who you claim. Her clothing is that of a serf. She smells like a pig girl."

"She wandered into a sty. Here." Cedric lifted his foot. "I myself have lately wandered through the same place." Blaise wrinkled his nose. "As for her clothes, she wears the garb of the woman who hid her, my lady's midwife,

Maude. Look upon her, Norman. Do you not see the fine line of her mother's chin? Is this a serf's face?"

Indeed, the girl was more than passing fair, even garbed as she was. "And when she opens her eyes, they are the color of the sea, like her mother. This is my lady's daughter—Kirsten." It was only a partial lie, Cedric reasoned, a calculated risk to save the child's life.

"Take her to Retford Hall, and call for that priest, Father Jerome," he ordered. "He claims to know the girl well. He will tell me the truth of your words."

Cedric shook his head, uncertain that this was an auspicious turn of events. Father Jerome would most likely know or suspect that this was not Kirsten, but Morgana. Would he give away the ruse? Yet how could he explain this complicated story to the Norman who already believed them to be iniquitous liars?

There was no other choice.

"Look upon this girl, Father. Do you know her?" Blaise pointed to Morgana, who lay unconscious.

Father Jerome looked from Cedric to Blaise, then to Lady Astrid, who knelt at the girl's side, bathing her head with cool cloths. What was Morgana doing at Retford Hall laying upon Lady Kirsten's bed? he wondered.

"Kirsten! Can you hear me, child?" Tears of anguish fell unheeded as Astrid gently cleansed the lump at the back of the girl's head.

"Indeed, I know her," Father Jerome nodded, now confident that he understood the game afoot, and mentally praising the intelligence of his star pupil. "She is Lord Wulfrid's child. I swear it upon my immortal soul."

" 'Tis done then," Blaise nodded. "I am well satisfied." He turned to Astrid. "Were you fool enough to think that you could hide her from me? You cannot escape me."

"Nor did we try," Astrid insisted. "We went to retrieve my daughter."

"I have no way of proving the truth or falsity of your words, but beware! In future, you shall be closely guarded. Should you again try to flee, I will hunt you down and display your head on a pike at the entrance to my hall."

Astrid swallowed. He appeared to be a man of his word. "I understand, my lord."

"Here is Cedric, with the midwife—your healer in these parts, I am told. She may tend your daughter, though I am tempted to leave the bitch to die for daring to attack my person. But 'twould be a waste of fine flesh." His eyes roamed over Morgana's partially clad figure, punctuating his words.

Astrid shot him a withering glance as she covered the girl from his frank appraisal. "She is delicate, and cannot take another such injury."

"I was not thinking of injuries, woman. I was thinking of something more suited to her female form."

"Whatever injuries you inflict—"

"Injuries *I* inflict? Madame, the girl attacked me, and I believed her to be an outlaw. Had she revealed herself to be a maiden and your daughter, she would not be in this predicament."

"Of course, my lord." The defiance in Astrid's eyes told him that she blamed him nonetheless.

He cursed beneath his breath, glowered at her, and strode from the bedchamber, only to turn at the threshold for a last word. "Be thankful, woman, that in my magnanimity I have chosen *not* to cast the lot of you in chains."

Astrid mumbled, but turned her attention to Morgana, who had murmured a weak groan.

Morgana gasped, panting in terror. A demon, tall and straight, and covered with the mail of a knight, stalked her dreams, mace and sword in hand. As she sped through the marshes, the bloodied hands of unseen faces reached from the muddy blackness to rip at her legs and kirtle and wind themselves in her red-gold curls. They were jackanapes of the hound of hell.

An arm's length behind her he moved with an easy grace through the marsh, crushing the supplicating arms beneath him as he swooped down upon her to mar her skin where his icy gauntlets touched.

Her screams rent the night air to echo in the stillness. "Morgana! Morgana!" She trembled as his hoarse whisper broke the silence and his burning golden eyes—

"Morgana! Wake up, child! 'Tis only a dream."

Morgana fought the nightmare, half in anticipation, half in dread. Though her eyes were open, it took a full moment to orient herself. She had no idea where she was, but it was warm and sweet-smelling. "Grandmother?"

"Morgana, girl. You gave us quite a fright." Bony, familiar arms enveloped her, crushing her against a breast long ago flattened, yet still able to comfort. "You are safe, child. Safe in the home of your mother, Lady Astrid."

From the foggy haze of her memory, Morgana recognized the woman who came from the shadows by the window. When and where had she seen her before?

"My child! My God! I feared that he had injured you sorely." She turned to Maude. "She will be all right?"

"Aye! A bit battered, mayhaps, but she is a strong lass and shall soon be on the mend." Maude turned back to Morgana as Astrid took her hand. "You can hear me, Morgana. Do you understand my words, child?"

"Nay. My head aches so. What has happened?"

"We will talk later. Take a spoon of this brew." Maude administered the thick liquid, laid Morgana back against the pillow, and motioned Astrid aside.

As they spoke, Morgana tried to remember how she had come to this place. Finally, too exhausted with the effort, she drifted into a half sleep, awakening only when all rushed back to her in painful remembrance. They claimed that this woman with brows drawn together in an agonized expression was her—

"Mother?" Morgana sat straight up.

Astrid left Maude's side and grasped Morgana's hand. She bent and kissed it gently, then laid her fingers against her cheek and forehead.

"You are my mother?"

"Aye, your mother true," Astrid replied, tears blinding her eyes and choking her voice. She turned to a small table by the bed, and lifted a large linen cloth. "Maude has washed you a bit, but I would like to bathe you, if I may?"

Morgana nodded and Astrid arranged the bathing. All about her, figures moved to a marked cadence, until Astrid assisted Morgana into the bath's soothing waters. She recognized the scent, for she had often picked these very flowers and herbs on her carefree jaunts into the fields and wood. Would she ever be able to do so again? she wondered.

Her hair was a mass of snarls, but Astrid worked tenderly to clean the injured area, which yet oozed blood. Alyson readied a poultice, and Maude administered a potion to dull the pain, for the wary girl was bruised from head to toe from her encounter with the Norman. As Astrid rummaged through two trunks in a corner of the chamber to find fitting garments, Morgana lay upon the featherbed on a clean sheet of fine linen.

A serving girl pulled a coverlet of wolf pelts around Morgana's shoulders. Morgana pressed her chin into the fur as she watched the fire dance. This was the most beautiful chamber she had ever seen. "Where am I?" she asked Astrid, when she returned with clothes flung carelessly over her forearm.

"This was your sister's bedchamber," Astrid whispered. "The Norman lord has taken the chamber that I once shared with your father."

"Is he the one who attacked me in the wood?"

Astrid nodded as she helped the girl to sit up. "He claims that you attacked him, but then, he is a cold, prideful ass, and one may expect nothing better, I fear." She turned to the maid. "Away to the kitchen, girl, and bring Lady Kirsten a light repast."

After the serving girl had gone, Morgana spoke. "Kirsten? Is that not my sister's name?"

"Aye. Taken away across the Irish Sea by her betrothed. We have had to play a game with the Norman. Lift your arms." She placed a linen shift over Morgana's head and tied it around her neck. "He thinks that you are Kirsten."

Morgana tried to swallow, but her tongue was thick and heavy and her lips were plastered with some kind of salve. "May I have some water?"

Maude poured water from a pitcher into a wooden tumbler. "You have had very little liquid, lest your brain swell from your injury. Though the time of danger has passed, no doubt it still aches."

"It pounds like the blacksmith's hammer," Morgana assured her, greedily sipping the refreshing liquid.

"Maude and Alyson have been here since we brought

you from the clearing. I have asked them to stay, but the Norman has ordered them to leave as soon as you are conscious." She braced Morgana against her and draped a kirtle of emerald green brocade over the shift. The deep plunge of the neckline fell between jutting breasts to a narrow waist, and slits on each side allowed for free movement. A roc, or supertunic, of gold brocade was then attached at each shoulder by emerald brooches to fall in loose folds to the knees until Astrid clasped a jeweled girdle around Morgana's waist and bloused the roc. The wide, bell-shaped sleeves revealed the long, narrow sleeves of the kirtle, embroidered at the cuff with golden threads on silk. The same embroidered pattern circled the neckline and hem of the roc. Morgana could only stare in awe.

" 'Tis lovely work," she noted. "I know nothing of such niceties. Were I to try my hand at needlework, no doubt 'twould look no better than that done by a kitchen wench."

"By the grace of God, there shall be many days for me to teach you. Mayhaps you will find it not to your liking. Kirsten always thought it deadly dull, and from what I have heard of your pursuits and interests—"

Astrid led Morgana to a nearby chair, and fit stockings of lightweight wool onto her chilled feet. "I have never worn stockings," Morgana said as Astrid removed a pair of leather shoes from the trunk. Morgana had worn only round-toed, pull-on canvas shoes. These were pointed, with a thong of leather that passed through loops around the ankle and led to two buttoned straps on the vamp.

Morgana was unmarried, so she wore no headrail. Astrid plaited her hair and piled it high upon her head, fastening it with emerald and gold hairpins.

"You are ready now," she said, admiring her work.

"Aye, but for what?"

"To meet Blaise, Vicomte de Rouen, the new Lord of Retford, may God damn his soul," Astrid said calmly.

"Did I hear my name?" Blaise asked from where he stood at the threshold. "Ah, Lady Kirsten of Retford has returned from her foray into the nether world, I see." Though he spoke to Astrid, he gazed relentlessly at the woman-child before him.

Morgana was thankful that she sat, for her legs weakened

at the sight of him. She had not thought him this tall from her perch on the stone above him. As he leaned against the doorjamb, his careless stance emphasized wide shoulders that tapered into a trim waist and slim hips. There was a strength inherent in his face. His hair, too long for a Norman, was black and silky straight, with a slight graying at the temples. Although she had been told that the Normans were clean-shaven, a couple of days growth shadowed his jaw.

"Blaise, Vicomte de Rouen, Lord of Retford, at your service." He stood before her, dressed in solid black with eyes glowing golden like the devil's own, and made a mock bow. Morgana wanted to spit in his face, but thought better of it and remained immobile. He fingered a tendril of hair that had loosed itself from her plait to lie across her cheek. Beneath the tendril was a violet-blue bruise. " 'Tis a pity to mar a cheek of such fine alabaster." She smelled drink upon his breath. Because Father Jerome had said that a man under the influence of drink was often unpredictable, she refused to rise to his bait.

Blaise continued to stare at Morgana in mock amusement as he spoke to Astrid. "I have sent your man, Cedric, to assist my men outside the palisade. He shall help us gather food, so that none will be unduly taxed."

"To take any food from those who starve is to unduly tax," Morgana said quietly.

"And what would you have me do? Starve my men? Take care, girl. Do not further test my patience merely because I have allowed your mother free rein of the household in deference to her former position." He surveyed the chamber. "Too many people in here! Out! The lot of you." He waved the servants and visitors away. "Aye, you, too, mother hen. Do not worry; I shall not slaughter the chick." He nodded toward Astrid and then toward the door. When she made to protest, his eyes darkened dangerously.

"I am ever your humble servant, my lord," Astrid replied in false acquiescence as she bowed and left the chamber.

Blaise circled Morgana's chair. "Twisting and pulling your hair like that does not hurt this large bump on your head that I have heard so much about? Come! Show it to me.''

She lifted her hair and pointed out the spot, low and to the right, where the skin was broken. His fingers pressed gently into her shoulder to move her forward. "This cannot be comfortable for you." He slowly withdrew the pins from her hair, until the red-gold tresses tumbled carelessly down her back to capture the firelight in their bronze glow. "You are not what I expected to find in the wood," he said huskily.

"Nor are you, sir knight, I assure you." She wondered if her voice betrayed her fear.

"I see that they have brought you food. Come sit by the fire and eat."

"I am not hungry," she replied too quickly.

"Nonsense! You have forgone solid food for more than two days. Sit and eat!" His words, though spoken in soft, velvet tones, were edged with steel. "Your lord commands it."

"Lord Wulfrid is my lord, and after him, King Harold."

Blaise's brows drew together in an affronted frown. "Has no one schooled you in either proper decorum or political events?" He sighed, as if required to perform a disagreeable task, and in a voice of quiet consideration, he asked, "Has no one informed you of the death of Lord Wulfrid and King Harold?"

Morgana flinched. She would never know her father, a man seen from afar, yet never approached by his bastard daughter. She now regretted her whims of pride. Mayhaps if she had approached him—

Blaise rose and stood looking down at her intensely, touching her trembling lips with one finger. His voice was low, yet seductive. "I am sorry about your father's death."

"Are you, Norman? You sleep in his bed, eat his food, and order his women around like the lowliest slaves."

"Aye!" he acknowledged. " 'Tis because I am still very much alive, and soon to be the lord of these lands by right of arms." Again he leaned over her and grazed her cheek with one long finger, as if a sculptor studying his model.

She seethed with anger and humiliation as she whipped her face out of his reach. "Please do not touch me, sir

knight." A muscle quivered at his jaw and there was a
lethal calmness in his eyes as he studied her intently. Then,
with maddening arrogance, his eyes raked boldly over her.
He granted her an approving nod. "Forgive me, demoiselle.
I meant you no harm."

"I beg of you, sir knight, leave me. I am wearied by all
this talk. My head aches so—"

"*You* are weary," he replied in disbelief. "I have had no
more than snatches of sleep for three days while you lay
barely conscious on yon pallet."

"You cannot blame me for that. If your guilt—"

"*My* guilt, demoiselle? What have I to feel guilty about?"

"Why, your thoughtless attack upon my person."

"Nay, mistress, in that you are misguided. I merely de-
fended myself. It was *you* who attacked *me,* an act for
which I have yet to find a fitting response. You were frightened, 'tis true—"

"Frightened!" Her fury threatened to choke her if it was
not released. "Of a Norman pig?"

"Hold your tongue! Your mother has spent long hours
pleading your case. I have promised her to overlook your
violence on this occasion, but this continued insolence—"

"Overlook? I have not asked that you overlook a thing,
brave knight. You war upon women and children; you lay
waste to Hartley and steal from the people the very wood
from their hearths and bread from their mouths. I pray,
do not overlook my one act of courage in defense of my
people."

Disconcerted, he crossed his arms and pointedly stared
at her. "Your mother had led me to believe that you were
a mild-mannered doe, yet I knew, in my heart, that you
were a shrieking she-wolf. A temperament such as yours
cannot be hidden away for long." He smiled humorlessly
as he remembered her attempt in the wood to unman him.
"Even now she tries to convince me that you are addlebrained from the blow to your head, but as confused as
you may be, 'tis clear that you are a shrew."

She rose and made a mock curtsy. "I beg your pardon,
sir knight. I agree with you, of course. Do with me what
you will; I am your lamb to slaughter."

"Enough!" As he slapped her on the backside, she rolled

away in a liquid motion and crouched like a cat ready to pounce. Yet he, in a lightning-fast leap, pounced first and subdued her until she was sprawled upon her back, all limbs pinned to the floor. "I have done none of the crimes you have laid at my door. I fought by Duke William's side, 'tis true, but there was no dishonor in that. 'Twas my feudal duty to bear arms for my liege." When she tried to turn her head away, he held her face so that she was forced to look into the molten depths of his eyes. "I came directly to Retford from Hastings. I have killed no man, except in battle. I swear it to you.

"As to the people of this village, you are misinformed. If they have no wood in their hearths or bread in their bellies, 'tis because they accompanied your father in battle and neglected their duties at home."

"Can you hope to escape your evil deeds by blaming the conquered?"

He stared at her, shocked that the young woman who had only recently lain at death's door could find such strength to vex him so. "My head fairly pounds with stale drink and your mother's insignificant chatter, but an argumentative lass that insists on a battle better left to men— that is truly absurd."

Morgana twisted in his arms, trying to arch away from him and free herself, but he held her too tightly. One hand gripped her wrists over her head, while the other insinuated itself under her back, molding her soft curves to him until she felt every contour of his body. A disturbing reaction caused icy fear to twist around her heart.

His mouth moved toward her, and she expected anything but the whisper-kiss he gave. His lips brushed her brow, leaving her weak and confused, as his manhood pressed against her.

"I yield, my lord." He stiffened above her and groaned, as if reluctant to stop. "I beg quarter, my lord."

"For a price—a kiss, freely given."

There were no alternatives under the circumstances. She nodded her assent.

His mouth covered hers hungrily as he freed her wrists and brought one huge hand to rest lightly on her cheek. The kiss was slow and thoughtful. He traced the fullness of her lips with his tongue, then opened her mouth to explore its soft recesses. Each place he touched burned as if consumed by fire. He made his way down the hollow of her neck, plundering each inch of skin along the way. Her senses reeled as she was transported out of her self.

She was not aware exactly when her arms circled his neck, but the realization doused the flame of her girlish passion and she struggled.

He hesitated and rolled away, his body still evidencing his obvious attraction to her. "Forgive me. I have been too long without a woman. You have my word that I shall not try to kiss you again."

Morgana wondered how she, barely a woman, could arouse such lust.

When his ardor had cooled sufficiently, Blaise faced her. She stood near the door, poised for flight.

"Do not worry, little dove. My word is my bond. Yet 'twould be wise of you to accede to my wishes. You appear well enough to leave this chamber. You shall be my guest at dinner. Methinks I need a rest until this meal. I am strangely weary."

Morgana averted her face until he quit the bedchamber, when she exhaled sharply. Astrid returned, locking the door behind her. "I will not allow this deception to continue. Your life is in jeopardy. Your honor—"

"My honor is intact so far, Mother. 'Twas only a kiss he took, though he may soon seek more. But—" she turned to Astrid—"if truth be told, the battle with him was no less than with myself." Astrid understood her meaning. "When Father Jerome taught me the game of spy that I could play at should the Normans conquer England, did he ever truly understand what would be required of me?" She searched desperately for an explanation, as Astrid enveloped Morgana's hands in her own to impart her strength.

"No one would expect it of you, Morgana. I would never ask such a thing. This man—"

"He desires me. I can sense it. He is like a wild animal stalking his prey. Is this the only way, Mother? Must I lose my soul to help my people?"

"Nay! We will escape—"

"There is no escape. I have never known such power,

such strength of purpose. I look into his eyes and I see the flame that burns in him, the determination of a man who takes what he wants. Nay! For the good of all, I must continue to be my sister, Kirsten.''

'' 'Tis sure peril for your immortal soul.''

"I will edge as close to the Norman firebrand as possible without getting burned. 'Tis what I was trained for—to glean information. They say that a man in his passion will grant his love any boon.''

"Morgana! Take care! Do not make so bold—''

"Bold? I fear him as I fear the devil. There is a hardness in him that I have never known in another, and yet—a tenderness, too.'' Morgana lapsed into her thoughts. "Do not concern yourself, Mother. 'Tis only a game to take a measure of the man. If truth be told, I suspect that he is no match for me. I shall control him by this passion that he strives to hold in check.''

Astrid shook her head, feeling not one whit of Morgana's confidence. "Careful, Morgana, lest the flame of that passion devour you.''

When Morgana entered the great hall for the afternoon meal, she sought him out, her eyes drawn to his as if by a magnet. He sat upon the dais. If it was possible, he was even more handsome clean-shaven. His hair had been shorn in the Norman fashion, which Morgana did not find particularly attractive, yet she *could* more easily see the clear-cut lines of his strong profile.

He was dressed again in black, this time velvet with gold silk edging on the cuffs and hem of his tunic. Even in this crowd, his presence was compelling.

Morgana and Astrid sat at a table far from the Norman and his men. He halted the conversation and motioned her to his table, to the seat next to him. This had been her mother's former place, no doubt. "Go, girl. 'Tis not a point of which to argue,'' Astrid insisted as she went to sit nearby with Sigvald.

Morgana feared that, by her habits, she would reveal her true identity. She knew naught of the ways of the nobility. Yet if she did all in moderation, it would probably go well with her.

The meal proceeded at a slow pace as the Normans

gulped freely of the mead and ale. This was a small contingent, she knew, for the majority of the men were stationed outside the palisade where they could wreak havoc on the village if need be.

"Settle a point for us, Astrid of Retford," Blaise said jovially after half the meal was done. "My friend there, Sigvald, claims that women can hold land in England if there is no male issue."

"Not with the coming of William, I venture," Morgana quipped.

"A foolish notion, anyway." Blaise scowled as he glanced at Morgana's plate. "Is there something wrong with the food, or do you have the appetite of a bird?"

"Nay, 'tis good enough," and much better than she was used to. "I am not hungry."

"Not hungry? You have eaten less than yon falcon there in the last few days." He pushed a horn toward her and called for some ale.

"Birds eat twice their weight, I am told." Her witticism was met with loud guffaws, and even Blaise smiled slightly.

"Your monkish ways have caused you to lose your manners, *mon seigneur,*" Sigvald suggested as one of the kitchen wenches poured ale into Morgana's horn.

Morgana cocked an eyebrow and exchanged glances with Astrid. This was interesting information indeed.

"I was the second son of four," Blaise explained. "By right of primogeniture, my older brother inherited my father's lands. I entered into the duke's service to gain a fief, but turned away from a soldier's life for the peace of the monastery."

"How, sir knight, did you come to this road then?" Morgana asked.

"I was pressed into service by circumstances. My older brother died last January, and William insisted that I put the Church behind and take up arms for him again. I thought to appease him temporarily; after a few months I would hand over the fiefdom to whomever of my brothers could best keep it. Then, when William spoke of invading England, there was no turning back. I was already out of favor for leaving his service."

"You could not have turned him down?" Morgana asked.

"One does not say 'nay' to Duke William. Stronger men than I have died for less. At the very least, my lands would have been forfeit and my family held in disrepute."

"But to walk away from your vow of holy order?" Morgana was shocked at this possibility.

"I was never ordained."

"I see." She was silent for a moment, but with the impetuousness of her youth, a thought flitted through her head and was out of her mouth before she could call it back. "Then that explains how you were able to so cavalierly rape and murder women and children at Hartley." As she tore a leg off the game hen on her trencher, the occupants of the hall stood frozen in a stunned tableau.

"I have told you that 'twas not I that ravaged Hartley—"

"And put it to the torch," she continued as if she had not heard him. "You are their leader, and must accept responsibility for their actions."

He spoke in a murderous low whisper. "Do you care naught for your life that you would put it in such peril, demoiselle? One word from me, and they would be on you and your women like hounds on a fox." Angered that she continued to ignore him, he grabbed her wrist and forced her eyes to meet his. "It has not been easy restraining their ardor. Look about this hall. Your ladies have been treated with the utmost courtesy. Should you continue to test me sorely, mayhaps I will grant my men free rein. Is that what you and your women prefer, a few Norman bulls in your bower?"

"Damn you to hell, butcher of Hartley," she responded sharply, abandoning all pretense of acceptance of him as her lord as she wrenched free. "You believe overmuch in your prowess, Master Bull, but all I see is an ox without ballocks."

When he slammed down his horn, his outcry unleashed a wildness within her—blood lust and a need for vengeance. So much had the last few days cost her, for she would never again be free of cares. Caution had replaced youthful joy; and all because the Normans were vicious, warring bastards.

He frustrated her attempt to bolt from her chair. "Hold fast, little bitch! You think to humiliate me in front of my men, then thwart my retaliation?"

"That depends on how heavy a punishment you believe that mere insolence warrants."

"You question my manhood and you call that mere insolence?" he spat through clenched teeth. "Mayhaps you have been too comfortable here at Retford. Mayhaps you need to fully understand the extent to which you have fallen." He removed his dagger, stabbed it into the wooden board, and began to unbuckle his girdle.

"What are you doing?" she asked as a cold knot formed in her stomach. The great hall was thick with expectation.

"My lord, please! *Mon seigneur!*" Astrid tried to rise, but Sigvald restrained her.

Blaise swept the table clean in front of him and jerked Morgana toward him. He forced her back across the boards. "You have questioned my manhood for the last time. I shall prove the lie of your words. 'Tis what you want, is it not? No? Then what does your quick wit have to say now, wench? Will you beg for quarter again?" These last words were smothered on her lips, as he covered her mouth hungrily and she was forced to endure his punishing kiss. She whipped her head to and fro, but it was impossible to escape his cruel ravishment, nor did his mouth soften after a time, for this kiss was meant to send the message that he would break her at all costs. "What will you do now to stop me from taking you here, if I wish, demoiselle?"

She tasted blood on her lips as his emotionless voice chilled her. As if to reinforce his question, his hand inched up her calf. She grasped his forearms, and the muscles hardened beneath his sleeves. As he reached her thigh, his expression darkened. He was not going to stop. This was no longer a game. Did he not realize that, in trying to humiliate her, he was forcing her to react in the only way she could?

Morgana lifted her other leg, pressed it against his chest, and pushed him from her. It was unexpected, and for a moment she gained the advantage. She ignored the warning voice in her mind as she rolled away, ripped the dagger from the wood, and lunged at his throat.

He marveled at her fluid movement, even as he parried her thrust and was cut at a minor depth on the forearm for his troubles. The dagger glanced across his neck and down his chest, leaving a thin red line in its wake. A quick slap on her wrist, however, and the dagger slipped from her hand to fall with a heavy thud.

Sigvald was out of his seat in a lightning flash. He ripped his muslin shirt and wrapped the strip around Blaise's forearm. "Take the wench from here and put her in chains!" he commanded as the guards subdued Morgana.

"Hold!" Blaise's voice thundered throughout the hall and echoed from the rafters. He bled profusely from the surface cuts, yet stood as if unscathed by her attack. "You, madame," he pointed to Astrid, "have neglected this bitch's training. No manners! Understands naught of a woman's behavior or deference to her lord." He turned back to Morgana, who struggled against her captors like a wild she-wolf.

"You need taming, a task that I shall gladly take upon myself. Remove her to my chamber."

"No!" Astrid pled. "She is innocent."

His lips curled back over his teeth. "Innocence has never hidden itself among a temperament so vile and bloodthirsty. You have not watched your daughter closely enough, madame. Having witnessed her behavior, I doubt this supposed innocence." He looked to Morgana. "What say you, girl?"

Morgana refused to answer.

"Tell him, child," Astrid insisted, but Morgana merely glared in defiance.

The great hall broke into raucous laughter as Astrid remained stock-still, shocked by Morgana's refusal to speak.

"Remove her!" As Morgana was dragged up the stairs, he turned to Astrid. "Your daughter has washed up well, woman. I shall no doubt enjoy her."

"There will be no joy in this vile act. You shall find no rest this or any night. You were a man of God. How can you force a child to submit to such cruelties as you will surely press upon her?"

"Must I tell you yet again, I am not ordained."

"Because of William's intervention."

"This babble will gain you naught." He shrugged. "What care you, anyway? Your daughter and I are well met. Better me than some villein in the wood. She will be paramour to a lord of the realm."

"I would rather see her with the lowliest cottager, my lord, if of her own choice."

"Then you are a fool, madame. Your England is gone. Your power is gone. All that is left for you is to hope that I do not tire soon of your daughter."

She persisted as he mounted the stairway. "As your leman, she will be an outcast. Her dalliance in your bed will cost her dearly; she shall hate herself—"

"Silence, woman!" Sigvald said as he drew her back. "Do you not see that he must have her? She is in his blood."

"But 'tis his loneliness," Astrid explained quickly. "I can understand that. 'Tis a need for rebirth after weeks of death and destruction." As she turned back, Blaise had nearly gained the top step. "Despite her refusal to speak, she *is* innocent."

"You claim that your daughter shall be shamed, yet you continue to speak of this matter in my hall for all to hear."

She scurried up the steps to him. "I do not seek to shame my daughter, my lord, but to save her from shame. Marry her!"

"What say you?" Shock fused Blaise's eyebrows.

"Marry the girl. A wise strategy, if you mean to hold this place. She is well loved as the daughter of the former lord. You can consolidate your strength, and your child, born of the old and new blood, will—"

"Hold! Your pleas are useless. I shall marry no woman. She will be my leman, treated with the full courtesy of a wife, *if* she pleases me."

"Courtesy? Her people will show no deference to the enemy's whore."

"Then her people are fools, for she may be their only hope."

Chapter 3

Morgana was locked into his chamber, apprehensive about what she had wrought and about what punishment the Norman madman would settle upon her.

The door swung open to admit Blaise de Rouen. His retainer, Sigvald, followed a pace behind with two fearsome knights, but Blaise read Morgana's bewilderment and ordered them all away, securing the latch behind them.

He seated himself near the fire on a wolf pelt. "Here is a comb that I have brought you. 'Tis made of the finest ivory. Unbind your hair, and I shall comb it for you." When she stood unmoving, his brow raised and a half smile twisted his handsome face. "Demoiselle, do you yet dare to defy me? Where do you find the strength to do so?"

"I do not understand."

"Aye, you understand full well," he replied, rising. "Should I assist—"

She backed away and removed the pins. "I will do it myself, please, sir knight." Her voice was now satiny and pliant. He tossed the comb to her, and as she pulled it through her hair, he raised the black velvet roc over his head, and methodically began to unclothe his body.

"So that is the way of it." She nibbled upon her lips.

His chainse opened at the neck to reveal a broad chest covered with silky sable hair. "Aye, and too long in coming, methinks. For days I have watched you, barely conscious. Can you fathom how alluring you are while asleep?" He stood before her. "Not as delightful as when awake, I grant you. I cannot recall when a woman has captivated me so, like a spider coaxing the unwary fly into her web." His large palms framed her face.

When her chest constricted and her breathing quickened, she arched away lest he take note, but she knew that he persisted in disrobing by the subtle sounds he made. She started when his breath grazed her neck. He neither moved nor spoke as she shifted from foot to foot, but his lips brushed her cheekbone. "Have you ever seen a stallion mating with a mare? He nips her on her neck, like so—" He demonstrated this love bite as he wrapped his arms around her slight waist and jerked her against him.

When he spun her around to face him, she remained absolutely motionless at the sight of his bare skin, her eyes staring up into his golden depths, refusing to go lower. His dark brows arched mischievously. "One would think you had never seen a naked man, demoiselle."

She could not deny it. Truly, she had tended naked men, but never did they have such shoulders nor such long, sinewy arms. Never had their hair been so thick and straight, smelling of herbs, yet manly. And never—never had they elicited a response such as this from her.

He unclasped the emerald brooches at her shoulders, and the garment fell in loose folds at her feet.

"Hold, Norman!" Her tiny fist jammed against his breastbone. "You think this just payment for a scratch?"

"A scratch?" He encircled her wrist and straightened her fingers, then dipped them into the furrows at his neck and arm and wiped them across her lips. "You drew blood, demoiselle. Good men have died for less, I assure you."

"And my penalty shall be a moment's dalliance with you?"

"I have more than a moment in mind," he replied with a perverse smirk as he reached for her. When she evaded him and bolted for the door, the mirth abruptly left his eyes. "What game do you play at now? This is no doubt a diversion—but for what purpose? Beware, witch! Should you goad me into battle, you may yet be conquered—again.'' He mocked her as he doffed the chausses and breechclout and pitched them aside.

His manhood stood out in obvious arousal. His intent was clear. ''You would take me without bonds of marriage?''

''The last man needed no marriage vows.''

''The last man?'' Screams of frustration rose from the back of her throat. ''You boar's ass—''

He lifted her against him, his massive body a study in feline grace as his lips nuzzled her forehead. ''I will not ask who he was. I care not. If truth be told, he has done me a service, and if I knew his name, I would reward him. Mayhaps your Viking lover, Eirik Einar.'' He paused, then held her away from him and asked, ''Was it him?''

She kicked at him, punctuating her anger with words. ''Think what you will. 'Tis not my place to say you nay. In my reduced circumstances—''

He inched her toward the bed.

''Who am I to be now? Your slave? Your serf? Your whore?''

When he pitched her onto the bed, she rolled away, eluding his grasp and shaking her head in defiance as she searched for an alternate route of evasion. ''Nay, little bird! There is no escape this time,'' he taunted.

She fell to her knees, her head bent. '' 'Tis yet daytime, my lord. 'Tis not meet. I beg of you—''

''Ah, so now 'tis 'my lord' and now you 'beg.' '' He circled her, but her head remained bowed. ''Do I think you tamed only to be stabbed in the back at the first turn of my head?'' He hoisted her up by her shoulders and brought her to rest against him as he effortlessly discarded the remainder of her clothing down to her shift. When his long, slim fingers insinuated themselves into her neckline, her hand stayed his groping.

''You do not understand.''

''I understand that your body shall bloom under my careful ministrations.'' He kissed the pulse spot on her neck. ''I should not wonder that you will be as full-breasted as your mother after a time.'' At the mention of Astrid, her cheeks flushed. ''Now, there is an exquisite woman prac-

ticed in the ways of men. I have noted an appreciation in
Sigvald's eyes that I have not seen for countless years.
Mayhaps she would welcome my man to her bed."

She ripped herself from his clutches. "You make me ill,
Norman dog," she spat through clenched teeth.

"Tsk! Tsk! Such anger in one so fair." He cornered her
in a thrice. "Jealousy? Do you fear that I will seek out
your mother in your stead? She is a comely woman of fine
bearing and good stock. There is a certain lushness in her
gestures, an intelligence in her speech—" He put a hand
on each side of Morgana, framing her head against the wall.
"Mayhaps it is your mother's bed that I should seek."

"These thinly veiled threats have a purpose, so cease
your prattle and speak your mind."

"I want you in my bed—willingly. I have never forced a
woman—indeed, have never *had* to force a woman. I want
you to accept me in your bed as your lord, and your lover."

"I—I cannot." She was alternately pale, then fevered.
"You are a—"

"Guard your tongue well," he warned, "for I shall brook
no refusal." He lay among the wolf pelts and beckoned her
to him.

Did she truly have no recourse? Yea, he was in control
of Retford now, but was there no one to aid her? Outside
the palisade, the cottagers and villeins toiled, heedless of
the changes that the merciless Normans had wrought. Not
so for her. Her life had been so simple. Why must this duty
fall to her?

The village was bathed in sunset's violet glow, and the
daylight grew shorter as winter approached. She thought
for a moment, then turned to him. "What day is this?"

"All Hallows' Eve."

"Samhain. Yes—" she nodded thoughtfully—" 'twould
be so." She walked to the opposite side of the bed, averting
her gaze. "I will not oppose you, if you make two
promises."

"I am determined to have you, promises or not. But, as
I prefer you willing, I will listen to your requests. If they
are something that I can readily concede—"

"Whether you are satisfied with me or not, you will
never coerce my mother into anyone's bed. Agreed?"

"Agreed, though if your mother takes a liking to Sigvald, that is their matter." This promise was easily given, as he had never truly considered taking the mother in the girl's stead. "The second promise?"

"You will wait until the sun is down to take me."

He almost snickered, but as she was deadly serious, he complied. "But you will lie with me until that time."

She nodded and whirled away from him to hide the salty tears that lined her cheekbone. She licked the wetness from her lips, frozen by a knock on the door. "Enter," he called.

A servant slipped into the chamber with a bottle and two horns. "Lady Astrid bade me bring this mead to you and Lady Kirsten so that you may toast."

He nodded his assent as she handed over the larger horn and filled it to the brim. "No doubt 'twould relax Lady Kirsten."

The girl handed Morgana the smaller horn, winking as she did so. Though Morgana wondered at her actions, she sipped the mead, hoping that it would indeed lessen her vexation.

After the girl left and he had downed the contents of his horn, Blaise motioned to her. "Remove your gunna."

Morgana, her back to him, disrobed and wriggled beneath the wolf pelts. His thigh was hard as stone, and though her taut breasts tingled and her skin ignited where they touched, she shivered.

" 'Tis cold in here," he said, misreading her. "I shall build us a fire to last the night through." As he labored at the hearth, she yanked the wolf pelt up to her chin and scrutinized his every move, fascinated at the rippling of his muscles as he worked. He knew his power and relished it. Of that she was certain.

"Did your father snare the wolves that make up that coverlet?" he asked. She nodded, not really knowing whether he indeed had. He pointed to a pure white skin in the middle. "White wolves are rare."

"I have never seen a white wolf, but 'tis rumored that one stalks Andredeswald." She sighed. "Of course, I have my own white wolf in this bed."

He threw back his head and let loose a great roar of

laughter. "Am I truly a wolf, demoiselle, or are you merely frightening yourself needlessly?"

"I do not fear you, Norman," she insisted as she straightened her backbone.

"Aye!" He shook his head. "I sometimes think that you have not the sense to fear anyone or anything."

"Except my dreams. In a dream not long past, I was a Celtic priestess preparing virgin sacrifices for the gods of the trees, the stone, and the sun."

"Even in your dreams you blaspheme, girl."

"Why? Because I follow the ways of the Druids? You should fear them. You took me from the high place. The old ones saw you, and shall avenge me."

"And what were you doing there when I found you—offering yourself as a sacrifice to save your people?"

"Do I not now lie in your bed?"

A restive chill raced through him, but he was not one to be dissuaded from his desires. "Your very words are heresy. Have you no fear when you utter them?"

"Why, my lord? What more could happen to me?"

He stalked her. "You could be burned as a witch. Are you a witch, little one?" He stared into the fathomless depths that were her eyes.

"Are you a wolf?"

One side of his mouth curled in amusement. "By the gods, you are charming. I like quick wit and intelligence. You would have made a fine mate were I interested in marriage. You are not a silly wench like some, but a Valkyrie. Aye! The challenge of your taming shall keep me from boredom for many a day—and night—to come."

His fingers caressed the sides of her breasts, luxuriating in their supple smoothness as if they were chiseled from alabaster. He ringed their peaks, and they grew firm, entreating. She held her breath and bit her lip, loathe to let him see what excitement she found in his embrace.

As his lips approached, there was a strange quivering of fear, anticipation, and wonder deep in her belly. She could react to anger, and the pain of rape, but how could she be expected to deal with his gentle consideration?

He is not your husband, she reminded herself. He is your enemy! Your conqueror! Yet the warnings grew fainter as his tongue invaded her mouth. A fluttering began, as if a flock of birds were entangled within her, as his fingertips flicked across her midriff.

He stroked the line of her hip, and she heard a subdued sob, realizing only after a moment that it was her own voice. Moisture rose to the top of her skin as she melted in his arms.

When his fingers insinuated themselves between her thighs, she tensed. "Open for me, little love. Once you have lain with me, you shall never desire another." His words did little to allay her fears.

"Nay, my lord! Nay!" He crushed her mouth and her protests, dashing all hopes. She squirmed, but he lay over her, stilling her progress.

He devoured her, draining her soul from her body. No words were spoken, for no words were necessary. From the beginning of time, men and women knew inherently how to perform the love dance with no necessity of words.

"The sun is down, demoiselle. 'Tis time." He was heavy, but she had presumed that he would be, as tall as he was and muscled as if hewn from a giant oak. His hair fell into her eyes, and she angled away from him. "Hush!"

His husky voice enthralled her. She had never been with a man in his passion, and the strength of its command over him stunned her, for he was truly weak at this moment.

"I shall give you joy of which you have only dreamt." It was evident that he wanted her not only to tolerate him, but to welcome and desire him. It was important to him, for what reason she was not quite certain. Mayhaps it had to do with his own pleasure.

"Come, my love," he coaxed as he inclined toward her, his splendid eyes strangely glazed.

She wondered exactly what the deed involved. It had always seemed natural enough to the animals, but then, so did childbirth. The human animal never did anything by half measures.

He drank from her sweetness as if he were thirsty. As one leg insinuated itself between her thighs, his knuckles pressed at the small of her back, until she was more or less at one with him. His hardness rammed against the gate of her woman's place, and she knew instinctively, as she raised to meet him, that all was lost. She was ill prepared for this particular fight.

But then, neither had reckoned with Astrid. Having laced the Norman's drinking horn with a powerful drug, she bided her time in a secret passage behind the tapestry until he fell asleep. No doubt it would be any second, she assured herself, but as matters progressed, she feared that it would not be soon enough, and determined to act.

She stole out from her hiding place and, wrapping an unused candlestick in her roc, firmly knocked the Norman on his crown.

As he slipped into unconsciousness, Astrid shoved his body aside and plucked Morgana out from under him. "Make haste! Friends await you at the edge of the wood." She gathered Morgana's clothes and stuffed them into a bag, then flung at her the shapeless dress that she had worn to Retford Hall. "Quickly!" she entreated. "You shall have little enough time to secure your hiding place. I have sent word on ahead with Gareth. A party shall await you on the lake shore. There." She directed Morgana to the window that faced a side of the palisade not usually well protected because it was bordered by a small lake.

"He will ill treat you when he discovers that we have fled. He has already threatened—"

"He will do naught to me, for I am locked in my chamber right now with a sentry at the door. He has his code of honor. He shall not harm me without proof."

"He will know," Morgana insisted. "Come with me! I beg you!"

"He may *suspect*," Astrid began as she sat Morgana in a chair and plaited her hair, "but he will *know* nothing, for he shall be slumbering until early morning, I warrant." She threw a fox-lined cape around her shoulders and led Morgana through the tapestry. "I have given this much thought. I cannot leave my people to bear my burden."

"He will scour the countryside for me—"

"By tomorrow it will be too late. He will never find you in Andredeswald." She kissed her on the forehead and hugged her to her breast. "Now, make haste! Go with God, my darling child."

Once outside, Morgana was met by a farmer and the

miller. They helped her into a rowboat, pushed it into the water, and began the crossing.

A moment of regret washed over her. The Norman was a magnificent animal, and would have made a fine lover. From the first moment that she had seen him astride his devil horse, his fiendish eyes glowing on each side of his nosepiece, she had foreseen that he would be her downfall. Now that foreboding grew even more potent, and as the boat glided away from Retford Hall to freedom, she had to fight the urge to turn and seek him out.

Gareth tarried along the shore with a third man she could not identify. Though they hastened her from the boat, she was tempted back for one last gaze. She would stock her memory for the long years ahead with every rock and timber of her mother's home.

She surveyed Retford Hall. The torches along the perimeter were ablaze as if wildfire had spread.

"Come, my lady! Let us away." The miller tugged at her arm, but Morgana held back, her eyes seeking out the bedchamber window overlooking the lake where she had stood mere hours before. The chamber was now bright, and *he* was silhouetted in the window. Though he could not possibly see her, she sensed his gaze boring through her to her very soul.

"For the sake of my wife and babes, let us away, my lady," the miller beseeched her.

"Take me to the stone," she said resolutely.

The three men grumbled among themselves. " 'Tis All Hallows' Eve," the miller said. "There will be feasting. The fires and music shall lure the Normans to that place first."

"Gareth is to be taken far away, into Andredeswald, but I go to the sacred place. Do you help me, or do I go alone?"

When they arrived at the place where she had first met Blaise de Rouen, there was indeed feasting, wilder and more pagan than she had imagined. As a maiden, she had never taken part in the celebrations of years past, but this year unseen forces had beckoned to her. The night fog rose around her in spirals, and once in the clearing, she could see naught of what lay beyond. The trees were strung with shafts of wheat. Dolls with shrunken apple heads had been carved of wood and girded together at the waist where their sexes met. Men with horrific masks undulated lewdly with women until, in the frenzy of the moment, they both ran off into the wood to fall upon the ground together seeking wanton bliss.

As Morgana made her way atop her stone, savage music pierced the night, driving even the owls to seek refuge. The villagers had laid out offerings of fruits, vegetables, nuts, grain, and small animals. Morgana made a place for herself on the stone and sat in their midst. Removing her shift, she smeared animal blood across her breasts and abdomen as the voices chanted in ritual and all joined hands around her to prance in wild abandon.

Clad only in her mantle, Morgana danced upon the stone, her body swaying to the rhythmic drums and flute. As a lull fell upon the revelers, she proceeded, oblivious of the expectant hush, twirling, enveloped in the exhilaration of the moment, around and around and—

She was wrenched against *him*. Nay! She need not see his face, for she knew well the size—the texture—the very scent of him. He waved his torch around them, and she saw that they were alone—that all had fled into the wood.

"Loose me, hound of hell!" she commanded.

He wedged the torch in a place nearby and shed his fur cape to lay it upon the rock. He unfastened the tie of her cape in a fluid motion and let it fall to her ankles, never relaxing his hold upon her wrist.

The fog had formed thick gray walls around them, hiding them from prying eyes, until she could see naught beyond the stone.

"Loose me, fiend!"

He took note of the blood markings upon her body. "It has not developed as you planned it, has it?" With bruising fingers, he gripped her upper arm to shake her. "Did you think that you could elude me?" He laid her back upon the mantle, his body holding her down.

"Nay!" she growled.

"Are you expecting your lover?" His question was a whispered caress in her ear. "Have you lain with him? And what is this on your breast—blood of the sacrifice? Are you a pagan priestess or a Christian girl?"

"The old ways—"

"The old ways are evil." His eye twitched as he traced the outline of the blood on her nipple. "But God forgive me, witch or no, I desire you even as you repel me." His lips upon her throat were insistent. "This is human blood or animal?"

"Ram's blood."

"Devil's blood." He booted the offerings into the darkness, cleansing the rock of all but their bodies. He had sought her without his armor, and was out of his clothing in scarce moments. "Is this where the Druids made love to their priestesses?"

"I would not know. I was not there."

"Were you not, witch?"

"I know what I am. Your words cannot change me."

"Aye! I know what you are, too, vixen. Your appetite has been whetted by this night's entertainment, as has my own." His lips trapped a nipple, and when he rolled it around his tongue like a sweet berry, a craving flourished deep within her. He knew what she needed, and his palm pressed into her mound in a circular motion.

Her thighs opened to him spontaneously as he murmured love words into her ear. His fingers gently insinuated themselves between the folds of her sex, and she moved against him, no longer averse to his fondlings. When he lay over her, she flexed her back, wanting to prolong the enjoyment of each and every sensation.

She was jolted back to reality by the pain. It was not unendurable, but merely extended to the very depths of her soul—a pain of loss. Yet when he would hold himself back, she rose to meet him, binding him to her in an iron grip of arms, legs, and lips.

She perceived his shocked disapproval as he swore an oath. "Lie still, my love. Grow accustomed to the feel of me within you, and the discomfort shall soon fade."

"Nay!" she sobbed. "This pain shall never fade."

He kissed her into silence. "It shall, I promise, to be replaced by the most wondrous miracle. Trust me—"

"Never, you son of a demon. I hate you." Yet her body

had a mind of its own, as her legs clamped around his waist.

"Give over to me, little love." Unable to hold himself in check, he tore into her to the hilt, exacting a moan from her. She was ready for him, in body if not in mind, for her arms stole around his neck and she met his thrusts, gripping his manhood at each plunge.

"My beautiful sacrifice. Who could have known how you would inflame me? I am bewitched."

They moved as one, each listening to the pulsating rhythm of blood rushing through one heart to be answered by the blood of the other's heart. Each body moved in cadence with the other—probing—probing—

The moment of satisfaction, when it came, wrested such a response from her that she nearly swooned. Never having experienced such rapture, she was unprepared for the reality of its wonder. Each inch of her skin was alive—consumed by the power of that incredible and divine euphoria. He drove into her relentlessly as she muffled her screams first with the back of her hand, and then with his lips, until a blinding flash of light—myriad countless stars—crossed her eyes as he filled her with his seed. She drifted off into a dreamless languor, unaware of the weight of his body upon her.

Twice more that night they rushed to that point of welcome forgetfulness. Toward dawn the mist parted, and they watched the sun rise upon the horizon, she in the crook of his arm, protected and possessed. They spoke not a word, each respecting the other's need for reflection. Had the old gods ordained this night? Morgana wondered, for from the moment she had breached the palisade of Retford Hall, she had admitted to herself that her flight was in vain. She could never escape him—except possibly in death.

His lips scraped her temple, a bare hint of a touch, as he stood and drew her to her feet, wrapping her into his fur-lined mantle. Sigvald appeared, seemingly from nowhere, and Blaise handed her down into the retainer's stiff arms.

The tranquillity persisted as they rode toward Retford, she perched on the saddle in front of him, and Sigvald at their side. As they skirted the hall, Morgana grew skittish, but he gentled her, uttering soothing words until she lay once again at peace in his arms.

As they ventured forth through the palisade walls, he barked orders to his men for food and a bath. Astrid watched from her window, concern etched in her frown, then flew from her bower and down the stairs to bar their ascent. Blaise rebuffed her as he carried Morgana to his chamber and laid her upon his bed.

When the servants had left, he removed the mantle. Her body was covered with the remnants of sacrifice, and her thighs were stained with her own virgin blood. Blaise heard a gasp, and saw that Astrid stood frozen at the door, aware of all at a glance.

"Begone, woman, or I shall have you flogged for your part in last night's little adventure." He shoved her through the door and barred it behind her.

When the wooden tub was ready, he bathed Morgana tenderly, brushed and braided her long hair, and laid her upon his bed, where she promptly dozed.

When Morgana awoke, she noted that he, too, had bathed and the tub had been removed. He was slumped over on a bench by the window, one foot on the floor and the other bent and resting against the wall. Her heart pounded in her chest at the memory of the sinew of those limbs.

As if sensing that she had roused, his eyes snapped open and he turned toward her. She blushed with the shame of her thoughts as he arose. His aspect was tortured, bleary-eyed, and as he came closer, he smelled as if he had freely partaken of a horn of mead.

She averted her gaze, but he pried her chin up until she faced him.

"Why, girl? Why did you this?"

"What have I done?"

"You led me to believe that you were used to the ways of men, and yet I discover the lie of those words this past night."

"I never responded to you, my lord, neither yea nor nay. You assumed my lack of innocence because you wanted me and there was a fever within you that would not be denied."

"Verily, I am beguiled, but you shall never convince me that this was not part of your mother's plot to force our marriage."

"My mother has no such plot—"

"Indeed, demoiselle! Then why did she suggest as much as I climbed those steps to come to you yesterday?"

She was taken aback for a moment. "Mayhaps she thought to discourage you from forcing me into your bed. How would I know my mother's purpose? 'Tis impossible to understand my own mind."

"The truth!"

"You would never be her choice of husband."

"Mayhaps the Viking, Eirik, would have suited. Did you invite him into your bed, too?"

"If I had, you would know of it by now." She fought back the tears at the corners of her eyes.

He sighed and pressed upon his temples. "Aye. I would no doubt be the first to know," he admitted. "Forgive me! My head aches. Come! Eat! The food sits overlong."

"May I have my mother to tend me?"

"I think that lady has done quite enough. Later, when matters are arranged between us."

"I do not understand. Arranged?"

"I think that you do," he stated meaningfully as he pushed a strand of hair back from her forehead.

"We made an agreement, Norman. One dalliance, and I would be released."

"Even had I made such an agreement, I do not believe that the contract would stand, even in your shire court. I have a lump on my head as evidence of your breach."

"You mean to keep me then?"

"I have spent the night lost within your body, trying to appease my demons, and yet—I want you still. Though untouched, you knew intuitively how to play my body as if it were a lyre and you the troubadour." He seemed disturbed at her dejection. "Dearling, I want more than the distractions to be found inside your woman's place. We are joined in spirit, Kirsten—welded together more effectively than any blacksmith or priest could have joined us. I have acknowledged this. Why can you not do likewise?"

"I cannot—" A suffocating sensation restricted her breathing.

"I am your lord. 'Tis my right."

"And if I say you nay, would the monkish man take a lady against her will? St. Blaise, debaucher of virgins."

He sat at the edge of the bed and pressed her back into the wolf pelts. "What know you of me and my ways? Do you understand how I crave you?" She shook her head in denial. "What did you expect from me? I am a flesh-and-blood man, not a saint." He bounded from the bed and kicked a stool to bounce off the wall. "My God, girl, must you vex me so?"

"I implore you, let my mother tend me, so that I may put her mind at ease."

He thought on this, then nodded his assent. "Mayhaps the woman can impart some wisdom."

As the door was unbarred, Astrid swept into the chamber. Sigvald dragged her back, but Blaise motioned him away.

Astrid's breath caught in her throat and her heart hammered. "You shall be all right, my child. He shall not hurt you again."

"Indeed, after the first time, it did not hurt her at all," Blaise said. "She will fare well."

"My lord, are you suggesting that this shameful behavior will continue?"

"I swear that I never believed her a novice, or by Christ's cross, she would have remained unsullied. 'Tis too late now for regrets."

"I swore as much, but you declined to believe me. Leave us now."

"You will tend her in my view, madame. She does not require overmuch. I have bathed her."

"What has she done to you to be so ill used?" She glared at him with somber, reproachful eyes, then spoke to Morgana in a soothing tone. "Forgive me, my child. We should have fled to the convent. I should never have brought you here."

" 'Tis my fault," Morgana said, lowering her gaze in confusion. "I have yielded all to him with very little struggle."

"Nay! 'Tis not your fault," Astrid persisted. "You could not have hoped to fight him and win."

"What is all this?" Blaise asked.

Astrid beheld her ravished daughter, and struggling to maintain a conciliatory manner, confronted their captor. "The deed is done. Now all must be put to right."

"Not again, madame!"

"Under the circumstances, you *must* marry her."

"Marriage to a Saxon?" His guffaws grated against her sensibilities. "I would not marry her were she a fine Norman lady, never mind a girl who would stab me with nary a second thought. I have no need of a wife. I have had my one experience with the institution of marriage."

"You are—married, my lord?" Lady Astrid panicked at the possibility.

"The woman is dead," he replied solemnly.

Morgana's pride was seriously bruised by his words. "I would not marry you, Norman pig. I despise you!"

"Yes, you showed me how much last night." His features hardened behind this angry retort.

Morgana colored crimson, and curses falling unrestrained from her lips, she tried to pick up a candlestick to fling at him, but Astrid moved it from her reach.

A devilish grin transformed Blaise's eyes. "I understand how difficult it is to recollect those moments when you cried out in your passion, so I will overlook this outburst and see to my horse." He nodded to Astrid. "Your daughter is commended to your care, madame. See that she is schooled in matters that you have clearly neglected. Had I not been a patient lover, she would have taken the bedding with much distress."

"You want me to school her so that she may entertain you as your leman?"

"Nay, madame, so that I may please her."

"I shall never be your paramour, you Norman son-of-a—"

Astrid cupped her palm over Morgana's mouth as Blaise hastily retreated.

Tears of indignation trickled from Morgana's eyes as Astrid stroked and patted her back. " 'Tis my own weakness."

"Hush, child! Do not blame yourself. He is no doubt a proficient lover."

Morgana could not explain that her pain came not in the act of deflowering, but in the intense elation she had experienced in his arms. "Is this the way between a man and a woman?"

"I found great joy in your father's arms. I would not wish any less for you. When you marry him—"

"I shall never marry him!"

"As his wife, you will hold much power."

"He does not want me to wife."

"Then we must make him want you, as he shall if he believes that you do not want him."

"But I truly do not," she sputtered, bristling with resentment.

"Then you shall have no trouble feigning disinterest, shall you?"

Blaise did not return until that evening. "Have you eaten?" he asked as Sigvald removed his chain mail. Morgana nodded imperceptibly.

He dismissed his man and disrobed, watching her shadow dance against the wall in the firelight. She was clad in a pink linen gunna edged with braid and tied at the neckline with satin ribands. Her hair had been plaited, then wound around her head and secured with bone hairpins.

She ignored him, as if she were in the flame, she *was* the flame, now dancing, now shooting off into nothingness, now brilliantly ablaze, now vanishing—

She jumped as he pressed his thighs against her, his hands on her shoulders. He did not move, but she sensed his eyes raking her back. One finger traced a path down her spine, and her breasts grew tight. His fingertips skimmed her sides as he nipped at her earlobe.

I will win at this game, she thought. I will make you want me as you have wanted no other. I will make you love me. And when you do, I will take your heart, shred it to pieces, and feed it to the wolves. You will be mine one day, Norman, and then, watch out for your soul. I will chew it, spit it out, and walk away with nary a regret.

She closed her eyes, swaying from the intensity of her anger. He spun her around to face him, as if he had read her mind, and braced her against him until they were thigh to thigh. He inhaled sharply at the contact as he locked her into his embrace.

"What we have shared—it is more than the physical loving."

"Aye! It was a raw act of possession."

"It was unique," he insisted. "You are meant to be mine—forever. Never run from me again, dearling. I vow on pain of death that I shall never—never release you."

A hot, exultant tear trickled down her cheek.

Chapter 4

Morgana awoke to urgent whispers. In the predawn light, she could make out the outlines of Blaise and Sigvald, while below, in the courtyard, the cranking of wheels was followed by the shouts of men-at-arms.

She fairly ached to stretch, but instead lay inert and listened. All for naught, for the clamor outside easily drowned out the Normans' voices.

She stole a one-eyed glance at Blaise. He leaned against the doorjamb, his buttocks tight and muscles bulging from his sturdy, hair-covered legs. He did not care that he was naked. As he shifted, she watched the play along the corded muscles of his back, and cursed him when he took a position behind Sigvald that restricted her view.

Unexpectedly he shut the door and turned to her. Her eye snapped shut, but not soon enough. She heard his throaty chuckle as the bed moved under his weight.

"What is this, Kirsten? Mock modesty? I know you are awake. You need not cast furtive glances at my body when I am more than willing to reveal all." He reached for her hand and moved it toward his manhood, but she abruptly broke his hold and bounded from the opposite side of the bed, pelt and all.

Though her movement was brisk and showed remarkable grace, he leapt across the bed like a mountain cat and pinned the fur under his foot so that she bounced back against him. He lifted her over his head, flung her back onto the bed, and tickled her mercilessly. In moments she was trussed up within the bed linens like a cooked game hen. She thrashed around on the featherbed and, with a supreme effort, loosened her face and hands. Feathers cascaded around her. He was over her, a glint of humor in his eyes as his fingers drew the sheet away to expose her breasts. She opened her lips to protest, but his mouth came down hard upon her own, stifling her speech. When she thought that her lungs would burst, he raised from her.

"Good morrow, fair maiden. Ah . . ." His mouth fell in a frown. " 'Tis penitent I am, my lady love, but you are a maiden no more. Well—" he shrugged, chuckling—"we must take advantage of that turn of events at another time, for my engineer and workmen have arrived to begin rebuilding Retford."

"Rebuild? There is naught to rebuild at Retford."

"Mayhaps not to your mind, but for a Norman, there is much work to be done. Your mother yielded because she could not hope to defend against our might in a hall of wood."

"My mother yielded because, with none left to defend our village, her people would have been slaughtered."

"I will hold this land for William," he said confidently, "but to do so, I must build a new hall of stone on a motte, so that we are not murdered in our sleep. Look around you, girl. 'Twould be simple enough to burn us out. A few well-aimed arrows hit this timber, and this chamber becomes a death trap." She shivered at the thought. "Do not fear. I will protect you," he said seriously. "I swear it."

"From who? You are the one that I need protection against."

"If only that were so. But there are others with less scruples than I, who would think naught of sampling your body and slitting you from throat to navel at the climax." She shuddered at his words.

"Is that any different from what *you* do to me?"

" 'Twas not what you said last night. Clearly not—"

"You are a bastard!"

"You confuse me with my liege. But be forewarned, girl. William would kill anyone who named him such. He is easily offended where *that* word is concerned."

"There are many things that I would call Duke William, and bastard is the least of them."

"Sheathe your talons, little eaglet, for if you do not learn soon, 'twill be a hard lesson for the future."

"Learn what? To bend and scrape and play the daunted maiden to a man that I shall never recognize as my lord? To play the mare to your stallion in this bed?"

"Indeed, a little more of the daunted maiden might serve you well. As to the other, that is something you need not learn. You have a natural talent."

Before she could rail at him, he vaulted from the bed, snatched up his clothing, and withdrew.

Morgana bolted the door behind him and pressed her naked body against the huge timbers and iron pegs. He had a disturbing sense of humor, yet at times was the most serious man she had ever met. Either way, he was infuriating.

Clean clothes had been laid out on a chair near the window. As she donned her shift, the preceding night's evil washed over her. Her cheeks stung and her nipples hardened. He was right; her acquiescence had urged him onward. What if she had fought him? Mayhaps—

"Kirsten!" Her mother's voice was followed by a light tapping at the door. "Kirsten!"

Morgana unbarred the door and opened it a crack. "Send for Alyson."

Astrid pressed her way into the chamber. "My God! What is it? Are you hurt? Unwell? Did he harm you?"

Morgana turned from her. "Nay, Mother. I just want to speak with her. Please! Send for her."

"Morgana, if you will just—"

"Mother." She met Astrid's probing gaze and clutched her hand. "I beg of you, send for Alyson."

" 'Twill be dark when 'tis time for her to return home."

"She can sleep here."

"But the Norman—"

"He will grant me this, I assure you. Fear not, Mother. 'Tis only her wisdom I seek."

Astrid left to do her daughter's bidding. Morgana watched Blaise jesting with his men in the courtyard below. As Astrid related the request, his smile faded and he glanced up at Morgana in the window. Those golden eyes held her motionless as Astrid continued to speak. He finally nodded, then summoned one of his workmen. After they spoke, the man gathered a party of five others and an extra horse, and headed out into the wood.

When his questing gaze returned to Morgana's window, she whirled away, her rapidly beating heart bursting in her breast. As she knew he would, he returned to the chamber within minutes.

"You are ill?" he inquired. She shook her head in the negative, not trusting her voice. "Then why do you send for the healing woman?"

"I have a question for her, but 'tis not for your ears, my lord."

He looked as if he wanted to shake her, the pulse at his temple beating wildly, but instead he left the chamber, slamming the door behind him as she sat to await Alyson.

She did not have to wait too long, for Blaise, concerned for her well-being, had sent his ablest horsemen to fetch the woman.

Morgana sat Alyson before the window and held her hand, their gazes locked, and put the question to her.

"Why would you think such a thing, Morgana?" Alyson asked as she shook her head in disbelief.

"Is it possible?" Morgana insisted.

"Yes," Alyson answered. "You need be with a man only once, if the cycle of the moon is right. But, Morgana—"

"It has happened, Alyson." She clutched her belly. "I knew last night, on that stone—I knew the exact moment that it happened."

"Morgana! 'Tis your lively imagination. 'Tis not likely—"

"I know, I tell you!" She crumpled upon her bed, inconsolable in her despair. "If I carry his child, I will be bound to him forever."

"Morgana," Alyson said as she brushed wisps of hair

from her face, "your mother waits without, fearful that you are ill."

"Your word that you will keep this secret from her."

"Aye! In truth, there is naught to be said. But what am I to answer when she asks?"

"Tell her that I miss you and Maude. 'Tis true enough."

"This, also, may upset her."

"Tell her that you have brought me a potion for my nerves, to help me rest."

The midwife nodded. "And Lord Blaise?"

"Damn him to hell! I care not what you tell him."

The door swung open, squeaking on its hinges, to reveal Blaise and Sigvald. "Have this door oiled. This place shall fall down around us before the new hall is built." His eyes were dark and assessing as Alyson curtsied to him and attempted to slip away.

"Hold!" he ordered, and Sigvald barred her exit. "What need you with the midwife?" he asked Morgana.

"I posed a question to her, and she responded. That is all there was to it."

"And what was this question?" He eased her chin up, forcing her doelike eyes to meet his gaze. "You will tell me this question."

"My lord! Please!" Alyson gasped.

"And you will go to hell!" Morgana retorted, kicking him in the shins. He quickly restrained her, and as she struggled, Alyson flung herself at Blaise and seized his forearm. "Remove the healing woman and detain her below. If I get no answers from this one, I shall get them from the other." His voice was taut with anger. "This I vow."

The color drained from Morgana's face. "I cannot," she mumbled.

"Since you have trouble speaking the words, pray that the midwife has more sense. If you think to continue your plotting—"

"I do not plot."

"Do not bother to deny it. Lies fall from your lips like ripe cherries from a tree." He hurled her from him. "Clear the hall. Bring me some wine from the kegs that arrived today—and bring the midwife. She will speak, or she shall feel the lash upon her back this night."

Blaise watched Alyson closely as she took the seat before him. He motioned to one of the kitchen wenches, and the girl poured a light, fruity wine and handed the horn to the midwife.

"I am waiting for you to speak, demoiselle."

Alyson swirled the liquid around. Was there no way to solve the matter other than to tell the Norman the truth? Well, what would it matter, anyway? If the girl was not with child, she soon would be, for Alyson had taken the measure of the man, and he was not found lacking.

"Why did she summon you today?"

"My lady's maidenly modesty has sealed her lips. 'Tis not a subject to speak of with a man."

"More riddles?"

"No more riddles. My lady asked me about something that she felt last night." She paused.

"Continue."

"It embarrasses me, my lord."

"Flaying the skin from your back would embarrass me, but never doubt that I shall do it should you continue thus."

"She told me of your lovemaking on the rock, in the holy place."

"There is naught holy about that place. 'Tis as pagan as the old gods for whom she dances."

"Something happened inside of her. 'Twas a dramatic feeling—akin to, and yet separate from, the coupling itself."

"Aye!" he mumbled as he brushed back his hair. "I felt it, too."

Alyson paused, unnerved. " 'Tis assured then."

"What?"

"My lady is convinced that, last night, upon the great stone, life was conceived within her."

The sharp intake of his breath confounded her. "She cannot know this."

"Only time will tell, my lord, but you already know the answer, do you not?"

"I pray that you have not burdened your lady with these thoughts."

"My lord, 'tis her mind that believes this, not my own.

She is attuned to the changes in her body, and is convinced that last night you planted your seed within her."

"And is she a field or a woman? The field knows when it is planted; the woman—"

"Would you say that a woman knows naught of her body?"

"I do not want her with child."

"You should have thought of this before you laid with her."

"I will not be lectured to by a serf." He considered her words, discounted them, and slammed his palm upon the table. "Pray, lady, that your mistress does not carry a babe while she sleeps in my bed. I cannot father a child, and if she were to conceive, it would surely mean that she has lain with another, and then she would never leave her bower alive."

"Morgana, are you addlepated? First the midwife, and now this deception? He has you watched every moment."

"I must go, Mother. My people need me. I can aid them."

"Your life would be forfeit should the Norman find out."

"This message was delivered to Father Jerome this afternoon." She clutched the parchment to her chest. "He gave it to me at dinner. 'Tis from one who calls himself the 'Black Outlaw.' Word has come to him by a friar in the wood that I was trained by the priest, and that I live at Retford Hall. I cannot deny his request for aid."

She handed the crumpled missive to her mother, but Astrid pushed it back. "I read very little—the reeve's report, and not much else."

"It asks that I come to the pond at dawn with food and clothing."

"He is at least straightforward in his requests."

" 'Tis rumored he is a man as bold as his seal. Do you recognize it?"

Astrid glanced at the seal etched in wax—a two-headed dragon crushing the serpent of death beneath its clawed foot. The paper fell from her trembling fingers and she sat, distraught, upon the stool near the hearth. "This is a cruel joke. It cannot be." She repeated the words to herself, over and over.

"Do you know this person?"

" 'Tis *his* seal. No doubt about it. But does he hold it still, or has someone stolen it?"

"Who is *he?*"

"Your brother, Brent."

"My brother is alive then? 'Tis wonderful news! He shall help us leave this place—shall lift the burdens from our shoulders. I prayed, but never truly hoped—" Morgana's mind raced like the swiftest steed. "He will know what to do about these witless curs." She hugged her mother, and the woman awakened from her shocked stillness.

"Aye!" Astrid agreed. "He is a strong, courageous fellow, and he shall surely help us find a way to escape these beasts. No doubt Gareth is in his keeping now. 'Tis good that at least the child has escaped, though if I have to endure many more of Blaise de Rouen's black looks because we succeeded in removing Gareth from his control, I shall scream."

As Astrid took on a faraway look, Morgana knew that she recalled her family in the days before Stamford Bridge—before the Viking Eirik kidnapped her sister—before the Normans seized her very existence.

"He *will* help us escape, Mother. We *will* go to Ireland, to my sister. Her new husband cannot fail to repay your graciousness of the past."

"If we must needs flee, then Ireland should be the place. Still, we cannot hope to go before the spring, for even the most able sailor would not cross the Irish Sea after the equinox."

"We can delay until spring. Then we shall leave this place, and you shall be happy once again." Morgana kissed her mother's wrinkled brow. "I give my oath on it."

They embraced, and Morgana marveled at how close she felt to her mother, as if they had never been separated.

Though Morgana was closely watched, when dressed in the proper clothing, she looked like just any other of Hartley's castaways. It was therefore a simple matter to leave Retford Hall at dawn to meet her brother dressed as a cottager on her way to pick herbs.

She recognized him immediately from Astrid's description. His long, dark hair was black as a raven's wing, and curled around his forehead in an almost classic style to fall down his back in long waves. His profile bespoke strength—and rigidity.

He clasped her in a bear's grip, practically throwing her into the air. "Look at you! I am gone less than six months and I return to a woman grown."

He was nearly as big as the Norman warlord, but with a face all planes and angles. His perfect noble beauty was marred by a red scar that led from temple to lip. His cheek had not quite healed properly, changing a boyish grin into a mocking leer. Still, his eyes glinted like black jewels.

"How have you fared, girl?" He held her away from him, his eyes clouding as if he feared the answer. "I had heard that you were kidnapped by that Viking who sniffed around our halls these two years past."

"Is there a place where we may speak privately?" she asked as she glanced around at his men.

"Aye, though I must stay near, for I await a girl from the hall, Morgana by name. Come. My men shall bring her to us."

He led her through the wood to his hut. It was hastily built and met only his basic needs. It made Maude's hut look like a palace.

He put his arm around her shoulders, and she turned to him. "I—I thought that Father Jerome must have told you."

"Though he has transmitted my messages, I have not spoken directly to Father Jerome. Told me what?"

"I am not Kirsten. I am Morgana."

His hand fell away and his mouth gaped open. "Have the events of the last few months addled your brain? Mayhaps this injury that I had heard about?"

"Listen! I *am* your sister, but I am not Kirsten. She *is* in Ireland with the Viking." She sat before the hearth and explained the circumstances of her birth.

He considered this new information carefully before replying. " 'Tis too amazing, little sister, but mayhaps this was ordained by God many years ago when fate cast the die." He hesitated. "You are a gift to our cause, Morgana, for you can help as no other. You are a spy, well versed in the Norman language. You can even read it. And you know Latin. The Norman reads and writes both. You can gather much useful information. God has a special purpose for you, Morgana."

"You sound like Father Jerome. I find it difficult, brother, to believe that God wants me to whore for the Norman scum."

" 'Tis not what I ask of you. Not whore, but spy, as you were taught. As his leman, none will approach or question you. You will be close to him, and he will underestimate you—a mere Saxon woman. The warrior knight would not conceive that you dare to plot against him or that you would attempt to undermine his rule to any great extent."

"He will burn down Retford, as he did Hartley."

A glazed mask covered her brother's ebony eyes. "He is not the lord who torched Hartley." Morgana was about to probe the matter, but Brent held up his hand. "Now is not the time to speak of these things. The pain is still fresh in my heart. Besides, Hartley is my concern. It has naught to do with you and the Norman warlord."

"You cannot *want* me to stay with him?" she whispered.

" 'Tis not what I want that matters, but what must be done." She turned away in frustration, but he drew her back to face him. "Morgana, in another time I would slit his belly for daring to touch you, but this is war. The conqueror will have what he wants—*you*. Why not use his lust as a weapon against him?"

"I came to ask you to help us leave England. Mother and I. We can go to Ireland—"

"Not before the spring."

"Then Wales. We can escape to Wales."

"Would you gamble Mother's life, and your own? The Welsh hated Godwinson. Would you put her into the hands of those who may take her head and do things that the Normans could not fathom?"

"There must be a solution that will save me from this hated Norman's bed."

"Morgana, please—"

"You do not understand, brother. His touch degrades me—"

Caryl Wilson

"You underestimate me, Morgana. Does another man know better than I about the degradation of Saxon women at Norman hands?" His cold tone chilled her. "They have taken my land, killed my brother, raped and murdered—" Morgana put her fingers on his lips to stop his harshly spoken words, but he gripped her as if her touch were fire. "We do what we must do to survive." He was distant now. "All I ever wanted was to marry my ladylove and raise a hall full of children at Hartley. We are all of us made to do things that we had rather not do. At least you are alive to grace your Norman's bed. Alayne and I were to be married on Michaelmas. Now she lies in the cold ground."

The breath caught in Morgana's throat. "I did not know Lady Alayne, but all have spoken of her sweet, gentle disposition." She sighed resolutely. "I shall do as you ask."

Brent put his arm around her shoulder and clasped her to him. "Blood wins out, Morgana." He handed her a horn of warmed mead. " 'Twould not be meet for you to take ill. Come now. You shall meet my men—do not tell them your true identity—and tell them all that has happened at Retford Hall."

The conspirators sat for hours quaffing horns of ale and plotting and scheming to thwart the Normans. She entered the conspiracy eagerly, drawing back slightly when he spoke of avenging her family by murdering the Norman lord, Blaise de Rouen.

He walked her to the edge of the forest, and she stood on tiptoe to plant a soft kiss on his cheek.

"Take care, little sister."

"I shall." She burst into tears as his arms enveloped her and his lips brushed across the crown of her head.

"Be most careful to never let the others see your tender feelings for the Norman." He held his hand up to fend off her excuses. "I detected your reluctance to plot his death, though you tried to hide it."

"I hate him. I wish that one of them *would* slit his throat. Verily! I hate him!"

"Nevertheless, whatever your feelings, you must keep them secret, for one slip of the tongue could cost us everything, be it with the Norman or my men. Do you understand?" She nodded. "I will avenge your honor, Morgana.

70

The Norman warlord will pay a high price for the use of your body—his life.'' She shivered as if thrown in a lake of icy water. The unemotional tone of his voice and the dead gaze in his eyes unnerved her. Whatever her brother had been like before the Normans had come, his true identity was lost forever in what he had become.

"Where is she?" Blaise bellowed from the top of the stairs. He had returned to Retford just before dusk, and had gone straight to the bedchambers. He had quickly realized that she was not at Retford Hall.

"Where is who, *mon seigneur?*" Sigvald asked.

"Lady Kirsten." Sigvald shrugged. "Bring me the Saxon woman—Astrid."

Before Astrid could be located, a rider came with news that Kirsten of Retford had been found near the wood, and was being escorted back in the company of his men.

Blaise doubled the watch around the village, and now sat in a fit of pique, sipping wine in the great hall, one long leg on the table, the other slung over the side of the chair. Astrid, by his command, sat impassively in a nearby chair.

A cacophony of voices and animal sounds announced her coming. He recognized her screech long before his men dragged her into the hall. It was obvious that she had been forced to return, for they hauled her through the doors, kicking and screaming a string of curses, her teeth clamped onto Sigvald's forearm like a lamprey. Sigvald swatted her away as if she were a troublesome fly. "She was dressed in these clothes. That is how she avoided the sentry's watchful eye," Sigvald brusquely informed him.

A guard grabbed the squirming girl, and at Sigvald's motion, unceremoniously dropped her onto her bottom. Morgana sprung off her heels like a wildcat and clawed the guard's face, drawing blood.

"By the rood! Kirsten of Retford, is there no keeping you from those pigsties?" Blaise twisted his nose in the air. "What do you find in there of interest?"

"Your men chased me into the sties."

"But where were you?"

" 'Tis none of your affair. Am I a prisoner, to be treated

so?" She tossed her head, and clumps of dung flew all about her.

Blaise stared first at her and then at his men scraping the muck from their faces, and at their disgust, burst into loud guffaws. He leaned back in his chair and grasped his gut as if injured, and roared with laughter.

The splatters had reached at least six of the men, for all around her now smelled like pig manure, she realized as Blaise's infectious laughter banished her cold resentment. Determined to maintain her haughty demeanor, however, she bit her lip to suppress a giggle.

"My lord, if I may attend to my daughter." Astrid rose from the table.

Blaise waved her on, and continued to chortle. Morgana climbed the steps, followed by her mother. "Hold!" Blaise called out as she reached the top step. "I have not forgotten my unanswered question."

"I would never underestimate *you*, my lord," Morgana replied mirthlessly.

Morgana explained to her mother all that had transpired during her meeting with the Black Outlaw in the wood.

"What can my son be thinking? Does he know that you shall be subjected to that man's unwanted attentions at his whim?"

"The Norman has not been near me since that first night."

"He has been at Hartley, and all over our land with his mapmakers. If he has kept from your bed, 'tis only because he slept outside the keep these three nights past." She sighed. "Sigvald has watched us closely."

They paused at an impatient, familiar knock, and Blaise entered with servants carrying the wooden tub and steaming water scented with dried rose petals.

He banked the fire, then sat on a nearby cushion to watch the flame. He was deep in thought, and clearly he had no intentions of leaving.

Blaise assessed her frankly. "You are quite an eyesore."

"If your men had not dragged her through—"

Blaise shuffled Astrid toward the door. "Out, woman! I am sick to death of your meddling."

Astrid faced Morgana, who nodded her assent, then dropped the bathing linen on the trunk and left, slamming the door behind her.

"I prefer to stay." He walked toward her, yet veered away at the last moment to lie across the featherbed. "You ran me a merry chase, demoiselle. I was certain that you had escaped, despite your mother's conviction that you had merely gone to the forest to pick herbs for your medicines. By the way, where are these herbs?"

"Ask your men. Could anything have survived their jostling?"

"Why this clothing?" One brow rose as he pointed to her attire.

"I thought it best that none know my identity."

"I disagree. If thought a serf, you may be treated as a serf. You expose yourself to unnecessary danger, little dove."

"Are you saying that a Norman soldier might think twice before raping a lady, but will think naught about a serf?"

"I am saying that you will catch your death if you do not get out of those wet clothes."

"I will bathe when you take your leave."

" 'Tis not your choice, demoiselle."

She pursed her lips in defiance, but his expression clouded in angry response. She shot him a withering glance, and lifted the shapeless shift over her head. The intake of his breath echoed loudly in her ears, and when she could see him next, the opaque gold of his eyes and the color in his cheeks no longer bespoke anger, but passion. Despite her limited knowledge of men, she had too soon learned to read this particular man.

Blaise rose from the featherbed and strolled toward her, a spark of some indefinable emotion flickering in his golden gaze. She fought to control her breath. Was this what it was like for the animal to be stalked by the hunter? She stepped back on unsteady feet, and when he stood a hairsbreadth from her, she ground the dung-caked shift on his chest.

Blaise swore a startled oath, and before he could whip the filthy garment from him, Morgana had slid like a sprite into the tub, arms crossed over her breasts, and knees to her chin.

Blaise strode toward the fire with the shift, but thought better of it and went instead to the door. "Sigvald," he shouted impatiently. "Bury this—this thing—far away from the hall. And these—" he removed his clothes "—are to be laundered forthwith."

Morgana averted her eyes from his naked form, but did not have to wait long to find out what he would do, for he dunked her into the water, held her down, then ripped her out, sputtering, her arms flailing in all directions. "See what has arrived from France with my workmen. Soap." He rubbed foam on her nose, then quickly cleansed her hair and scrubbed her skin until it was nearly raw and tingling.

"There!" he exclaimed in obvious approval of his efforts. "Passing fair work, if I do say so myself." He wrenched her from the tub and dropped her none too gently on the rushes. "My turn."

When she wiped the suds from her eyes with the back of her hand, she saw that he had taken her place. "What are you doing in my tub?" She flinched at Sigvald's knock, and yanked the bathing cloth around her just as he entered. As Morgana sat near the fire and dried herself, Blaise ignored her, humming a bawdy tune that she had heard that very morning beneath her chamber where the soldiers slept.

A serving girl pulled a comb through her hair, then braided and pinned it. She tried her best to spurn Blaise, but one ear cocked as he rose from the tub and ordered it removed.

"Come here, Kirsten." The deep sensuality of his voice sent a ripple coursing through her. With her back toward him, she wriggled into a clean shift.

She did not hear him until his breath grazed her neck.

"I am not accustomed to being disobeyed."

"And I am not accustomed to having to obey."

"I allow you these little unimportant eccentricities when we are alone. When you have seen men trying to push their guts back into their bellies, you learn what is important. But never contest my word in front of my men. I must keep their respect to command their loyalty, and if you do anything to threaten that, I will come down on you with such wrath, you will pray to die. Never doubt that I hold your very life in these hands." At the finish, his lips burned a path behind her ear and along her collarbone.

She faced him, chin raised, her eyes glowing with a savage inner fire. He returned the steady gaze, his eyes boring into her, probing her very soul. "Say the words, Kirsten," he whispered, his finger grazing against her temple. The slight touch of his hand sent a warm shiver through her. "You know what must be said." She nearly swayed with the intensity of her feelings, for the anticipation of his touch was unbearable. "Say the words!" His voice broke with huskiness.

"I am yours to command, my lord."

"Nay! Not to command. You know the words."

She tried to look away, but he shook his head decisively as he tilted her chin and studied her face. "Say the words!"

"I am yours—to love."

"Forever."

"Forever."

His right hand united with hers, then his left, until they formed the symbol of infinity—of handfasting.

"Swear it upon your immortal soul."

She thought of her family, and tried to draw back, but he held her fast, his eyes compelling her to speak. "I—swear it upon my immortal soul." Forgive me, God, she whispered inside her mind.

He brought her fingers to his lips for a light kiss and then to the drawstring at her throat. She tugged and the chemise fell to her ankles. Their eyes remained locked. "You have given your vow. We are bound for eternity in God's sight. The pledge is given and the contract shall be sealed."

He gripped her almost violently to his chest. She twisted, arching her back away from him, but he lifted her until she could feel the pulsating shaft of his manhood against her woman's place. "You are the wife of my heart and soul, Kirsten. We need no further ceremony—you and I. 'Twould not be any different."

Chapter 5

Sir Guy de Boulogne, Blaise's diminutive though talented architect, leaned across the trestle table and pointed a nubby finger to a section on the parchment. "The lay of the land is perfect. Here," he continued in a nasal voice, "we will dam this lake, dig a moat around the perimeter, then loose the waters so that they flow into the moat. This keep shall remain standing until we have built the other. Where we are now will be the outer bailey. The earth from the moat will form the mound, and upon that mound we will build the donjon."

"You have done well. Show me the design of the keep."

The small man unrolled a second parchment. "Six levels. Below ground—the dungeon in which you may chain up the village rabble or anyone else in need of imprisonment." Blaise looked at Morgana meaningfully.

Although she pretended disinterest, she heard each word uttered and kept one eye on the parchments. She must study these plans, must know the strengths and weaknesses of each entrance to this new keep. Brent would want this information.

"The well is here, on the first level with the storage chamber and the soldier's quarters. Here is your personal guard's quarters, and this—" he nodded toward Morgana "—a chapel for your lady."

"Methinks the bitch has little use for chapels," Blaise opined, smiling at her. Seething inside, she returned his smile.

"On the next level is the great hall, with a height of two levels so that the smoke can find its way out."

"Build many windows. I do not wish to choke to death over my meals."

"Aye, many archers' slits, so no enemy may creep in, but air may pass out. On the top level are the sleeping chambers for the family members, visitors of rank—"

"I shall need a separate chamber—not merely a partitioned area—with an adjoining solar."

"Aye, *mon seigneur*, 'tis evident why." He nodded toward Morgana. The man assumed that the space would be filled with children. Morgana sipped her wine to hide her blush.

"You have surpassed yourself, Guy. The duke will be well pleased, as am I." He rolled the thick parchments, tied them together with a length of leather, and tossed them onto the table. "Have you seen the rock quarry that my men discovered nearby? 'Tis like a gift from God."

"Aye! There is enough stone for the keep, and then some."

"More wine! Let us drink to the success of our venture, for we break ground tomorrow."

"But the weather, *mon seigneur*," the little man protested. "Mayhaps we should wait—"

"We cannot afford to wait. Even now my scouts advise that the survivors of Stamford Bridge and Hastings assemble in yonder wood. We must fortify immediately." He leaned toward Sigvald. "Many refugees from Hartley will work if it means shelter, freedom, and safety. Each dawn you shall call every able-bodied man in Retford to the hall. They will work with our men, and receive an extra measure of food daily for their efforts."

"Are you sure they will come?" Guy asked.

"They cannot refuse. They need the food. Their bellies will lead them here."

Their discussion was interrupted by the clatter of horses'

hooves, and a sentry entered and knelt to Blaise. "The duke's men, *mon seigneur*."

Morgana's ear perked up, though for the sake of deception, she pretended to know naught of what was being said by the Normans.

Blaise rose and went to meet the duke's messenger. "Good hail, Sir Roland!" Blaise slapped him on the back, and Sir Roland, whipping off his helmet and gauntlets, winced, and hobbled like a lame horse to the nearest bench. "What news?"

"A horn of ale first, Blaise de Rouen. My throat is parched with the dust of too many roads traveled."

Blaise called for cloths to cushion the man's seat, then brought the man to the dais, where his mail was removed. "Ah!" Sir Roland sighed. "If not for the calluses on my arse, I should be bloodied; I have been in the saddle so long."

A serving wench flashed the knight a smile as she laid a trencher of food and the ale before him. Roland lay back in his seat, and pinched the maid's plump buttocks. She grinned widely in response. "These girls are not as lovely as those in Normandy, but when you have done without for as long as I have, their beauty grows immeasurably." Sir Roland tore off a beef rib. "We have matters to discuss. Clear the hall."

"Sir Roland is Duke William's messenger," Blaise explained in the Saxon tongue to Morgana. Thinking quickly, she slammed down her wine, rose, spat upon the floor, and strode toward the steps.

Roland stopped his chewing midbite. She was a beautiful and lively piece, but overly proud, and no doubt in need of some effective training. None who valued their life dared to offend the duke's man. The girl was obviously a moonling.

"Hold!" Blaise's voice shook the walls around her, but she picked up her skirts and hastened up the steps, heedless of his bellowing.

She heard his horn slam upon the table, then hit the wall near the stairway. He caught up with her in the bedchamber.

"Demoiselle, you will return to the table and entertain William's messenger, or so help me, I shall have you flogged until every inch of skin on your back oozes blood."

As she formed a reply, he held up his hands. "I swear it, Kirsten."

She was elated that she had so effectively manipulated the outcome of the matter, for instead of sending her away, he would now force her to stay for the meeting. She walked back and sat in her chair in stiff dignity.

"Continue." Blaise motioned to the messenger. "The girl does not speak Norman French."

"My Lord Vicomte de Rouen, your liege lord, William, Duke of Normandy, bids you remember your oath to him."

"What would the duke have of me?"

"While 'tis true that William has ordered the harrying of almost all towns in Sussex and Wessex, he specifically exempted Hartley and Retford, the fief of the thane, Wulfrid. Lady Astrid is much loved by the queen, King Edward's widow. You have no doubt heard what happened at Hartley?" At Blaise's nod, Roland continued. "The duke has ordered Christian D'Arcy removed from power. You are to quell any uprisings. Should you bring peace and acceptance to Hartley, the duke shall add the lands to those of Retford. You shall be well favored by William should you accomplish this."

"D'Arcy shall be greatly displeased, for he thought to gain his own fief. As my former vassal, he will not wish to again serve me, nor do I want it so. The duke does me great honor, but—"

"You have not taught that young pup well, Blaise. The village offered no resistance, I am told." Sir Roland shrugged. "And to burn it without first removing the food stores—the man's an idiot." The servant girl brought a slab of roasted pig, and Sir Roland gnawed it with nary a pause. "He is to be underlord to you. You have your work cut out for you if D'Arcy is to be a worthwhile vassal to the king."

"The king?"

"That is the second part of my message. Although William has not yet brought London to its knees, he vows that, by Christmas Day, the witan will beg him to take the crown. William wishes to be surrounded by his loyal vassals so that none may challenge his right to rule England ever again. He therefore expects you to attend his coronation.''

"He is sure of this outcome, then?"

"As the spider is sure that the fly in his web will make a fine supper." Sir Roland chuckled. "Do you know anyone who has dared say 'nay' to William—anyone alive, that is?"

Blaise glanced at Morgana. "Do I take my lady?"

"William has asked for her by name. Seems she was a godchild of the old king. He has bid you escort her family."

" 'Tis good. The witch is like a spirit who walks through walls. I dare not go farther than Hartley without fearing her escape."

"Methinks she leads you around by your prick, Blaise. Watch out she does not cut it off."

The hall broke into loud whoops of laughter, which Blaise joined in good-naturedly, sobering only when he realized how close to the truth the man had come. He rose, picked up his plans, and beckoned Morgana. "Sigvald, make preparations. We must leave in haste if we are to make Hartley before nightfall."

Once in their chamber, Blaise explained only that he had been called to Hartley. He told her naught of his new obligations, William's coronation, or their possible trip to London. He would be gone for a few days, and she was to be confined to the hall. If she should disobey him, his fury would be boundless.

As soon as he left the palisade, she sent for Father Jerome. "No doubt you have many sins to confess," Sigvald agreed as he sent a messenger for the priest.

When Father Jerome came, she showed him the plans for the keep. "Bring a quill, and ink, and some leather, so that we may reproduce these plans for my brother."

"You have done well, Morgana. Very well indeed!"

The next day he brought what she had requested. She began the project, careful to keep her door barred at all times under the guise of doing penance. The task was completed within three days.

When she again sent for Father Jerome, however, she was informed that he had been called to Hartley to administer to soldiers injured in rebel attacks. Refusing to be hindered, she and her mother hatched a plan quickly implemented when night fell.

Astrid came to her bedchamber, dressed in a plain gown and a hooded cloak. They traded clothes, and disguised as her mother, she left her chamber and hid in her mother's chamber until most of the men slept. She then tied clothes to her body to make herself look thicker around the waist, and donned a peasant shift. She dusted her hair with powder to dull its appearance, and rubbed ashes on her face.

No one noticed as she waddled from the hall outside the palisade, for she looked much like one of the farmwives taking refuge within the perimeter of Retford Hall.

She was greeted with caution in Brent's camp, for she had fooled even his men, so perfect was her disguise. "I have something for you," Morgana told her brother as she removed from a belt at her waist a large herb bag that she had fashioned from the leather on which she had copied the plans. She dumped its contents, pulled out the drawstring, and laid the leather flat upon the ground. "See." She held her torch directly above it. " 'Tis the new Norman donjon. 'Tis to be built right next to our present keep." She explained in depth the meaning of each line and curve.

"You are a miracle, sister," Brent exclaimed when she had completed her explanation.

"Do you have enough now? You know his planned fortifications. Will you reconsider letting Mother and—"

"Not talk of escape again, Morgana? Not when we are so close. You must know that no escapes are possible now. Take courage, girl. Look at what you have brought me. You know the movements of his soldiers. You know his very thoughts and plans. You must know now how truly important you are to our survival."

"But he draws me to him, closer—closer—"

"Morgana." He tried to placate her with gentle words. "I know that you cannot sleep with the man without having some tender feelings for him. But hold your heart back. If the others were to find out, I cannot be responsible for what might happen. They might harm you as a traitor, despite your many good works for our cause. The Normans should be overthrown by spring. Then," he assured her,

"I shall deal fairly with this man. After all, 'tis D'Arcy who has earned the full measure of my wrath."

"Christian D'Arcy!" Morgana exhaled deeply, as if cleansing her lungs of filth. "My God! He comes to Retford Hall, as underlord to Blaise."

Brent slammed his fist against a nearby tree, excitement evident in the opaque onyx of his eyes. " 'Tis a stroke of good fortune—the hand of providence at work. God has put him in my path, to meet my justice when the time comes. He laid waste to Hartley when none raised a finger against him. He raped and murdered my betrothed, Lady Alayne." He drew in a deep breath, faltered a moment, then whispered her name, softly, and spoke as if he were in another place. "Alayne. He will pay, my love. I will cut off his hands and his manhood, and lay them across your grave to rot."

Morgana was anxious to escape her brother's disturbing presence. War had no doubt wrought fearsome changes in him. She tried to imagine him as the man her mother insisted he had been—with a sense of humor and a tender, artistic soul. That man was long gone, replaced with one obsessed with vengeance.

Morgana tried to extricate herself, for his fingers had tightened around her shoulders during his reverie. He released her only after she called his name three times.

"Hasten, Morgana, or the sun will be up before you reach the hall. My man will escort you to the fields. Here." He handed her a jewel-encrusted dagger in a leather sheath. "Tie this at your thigh, and put it to good use should the need arise." She nodded, and he gave her a basket. " 'Tis a suckling pig. Should anyone stay you, pretend 'tis the night's fare. Godspeed, little sister." He kissed her forehead. "Give Mother my love."

Love? Did he truly have any left to give? she wondered as she made her way along the edge of the field. She cocked an ear for the birds. This dawn was a somber moment—gray, misted, and exceptionally cold, even for November. She clutched the coarse woolen mantle tighter as the wind wound round her in an ever-increasing crescendo, seeking out every hole in her garment through which to blow mercilessly. And the dampness. Maude's joints would be swollen on a day such as this.

She chose to cross the common field that had lain fallow that planting season. It sat between an autumn wheat field and a spring barley field. Most of the wheat had rotted before it could be harvested.

The screech of a hoot owl rent the still dawn. In the near distance a tree full of birds took flight, their trilling sending shivers up her spine. The hairs on the back of her neck rose, for the place had an evil, ominous feel about it. Yet she saw no one on the horizon.

She plodded across the field, switching arms every few steps because of the weight of the basket. She felt a pulling in her back. The pig smelled like the sties she had found herself in of late, and oddly enough, it reminded her of *him*.

As she traversed the narrow brook, she slipped upon a too smooth rock, twisted her ankle, and sunk into the water, soaking her cloth shoes. It was a chore to hold on to the pig, and if she were not a good Christian, she would have dropped the ungrateful wretch and let it drown. With provisions reduced as they were, she could never waste food, even if still on the hoof. Those who camped inside the palisade would feed well on the meager animal.

On the embankment, she tripped over a root and tumbled onto the ground, skinning her knees. The pig squealed and wriggled from its wrappings. It ran her quite the chase, first in one direction, and then the other, until she flung herself on it to hold it down, paying no attention to the draft on her legs where her skirt had risen.

"Damn you, pork ribs!" The piglet continued to struggle as she gripped its two back legs, then one leg, then the tail. "Be still, you fool!" She crawled through the bracken, her cheek mercilessly scratched and bloody. "You shall definitely be roast pork this night, acting this way."

"Zounds! Not bad thighs for a pig girl."

Shock paralyzed Morgana as she released the squawking animal and rolled over to cover her legs, releasing the dagger from its sheath in the process. Norman soldiers, barely six feet from her. Where had they come from? Where had they been hiding? Had they seen her come from the wood?

"Come here, wench!" one rasped with a throaty chuckle.

She strove so hard to maintain her freedom that she fell back into a bramble bush, screamed, and lashed out at her attackers with the dagger. She bloodied two before one dropped her to her knees, where three men held her at the points of their own daggers.

One man approached, prodded forward with ribald jests and raucous laughter. She could not see his face, but on each side of the nosepiece, the ice blue of his eyes splashed her like a cold wave. He picked up her dagger and scrutinized it carefully. " 'Tis not a pig sticker, wench. 'Tis the weapon of a noble thane. From whom was it stolen?"

"I do not speak your language," she countered.

The man understood this, either because he knew Saxon or had heard similar words recently. He reached for the hem of her skirt and made to lift it.

"Loose me, sir, lest you be the instrument of your own death." Her deadly serious demeanor arrested his movement.

"That Saxon tongue grates against my ears," he said.

"Aye! An ugly language!" said another who held her immobile. "What does the wench say, *mon seigneur?*"

"You certainly are impertinent for a pig girl," he continued in Saxon. Morgana sighed in relief.

"I am not a pig girl," she sputtered. "I am—" What could she say? I am the whore of Blaise, Vicomte de Rouen. I am his leman.

"Yes?" the leader asked, one brow cocked in expectation.

"I am Lady Kirsten of Retford."

The knight gaped first at her, then at his men, replacing momentary speechlessness with a cynical snicker.

"My God! Quite the tale, pig girl," the knight continued. "Throw her into the brook and let us see how 'her ladyship' washes up. I bet my purse she is lovely under that ash."

"Loose me, or meet your death at the hand of my lord, Blaise, Vicomte de Rouen. I am his leman."

"What? Blaise's bitch! The man never did choose well, but he would never consort with a swineherd's daughter."

"The wench needs to be punished." This from yet another of his men. "And from where do you suppose she filched this dagger? 'Tis Saxon, no doubt."

"If you do not believe my identity, take me to Retford Hall and inquire."

"I would rather take you to yon meadow—"

"Nay, Christian! 'Tis best we take no chances on angering your overlord."

D'Arcy! A warning voice whispered in her head. This was he. She knew it in her bones. All that her brother had said about this man crashed her awareness, and a trembling began in her legs as unbidden images crowded her imagination.

"Be still, you fool!" he countered. "Girl, if you think to deceive me, 'twill not turn to your advantage. Such a ridiculous story. Not even Blaise would fall to such depths as to make such as you his mistress. You shall not escape me at Retford." His voice softened. "Welcome my attentions now, and I shall set you free, for if I bring you to the hall, there will be no escape for you. And your attack—"

"My lord, the attack was in defense of my own person. Nay! I do not wish to escape. I shall be pleased to prove the truth of my words."

The knight teetered on the brink of a decision. Finally he nodded his assent. "I will play this game, pig-maiden," he whispered to her as he drew her to him and loosed her belt. The stuffing fell from her until the drab clothes hung on her slight frame. "That is more like it," the knight muttered. "Come! You shall ride with me." He led her toward his horse, who drank at the nearby brook, and lifted her as if to seat her. He instead dropped her into the swirling water and reached down to rub her face. The creamy skin shone through. "First you must clean yourself. Ah! See! She *is* beautiful under that muck."

Morgana seethed with anger and humiliation, but held her feelings in check, for she would catch her death of cold if she did not soon return to Retford and bathe in a warm tub.

She arose from the water and shook off the sopping wet mantle. "Leave it!" D'Arcy ordered. He wrapped her into his own mantle and lifted her onto his horse. As he turned to converse with his men, she positioned herself on the saddle, grasped the flanks with her muscled thighs, gripped the reins, and kicked the horse's belly twice. Before the men could discern her intent, she bounded up the embankment at a fast clip, toward Retford and safety. She would not chance becoming D'Arcy's next victim.

Hoofbeats closed in on her, and without looking back, she knew that it was he. If she could get through the palisade, mayhaps—

He was almost alongside her now. She leaned into the wind, and dug her heels harder into the horse's belly. Never losing her sense of purpose, she rode the animal straight through the iron gate as it opened to admit her.

As she reined in the horse, he pulled up beside her and yanked her off the animal by her hair. Once upon the ground, he bound her hands with a long rope and dragged her toward the hall, heedless of her cursing and screams loud enough to awaken the dead. At the gate, the sentry stood motionless until D'Arcy crooked his finger in the struggling girl's direction. "Come here, man! Know you this girl?"

The bewildered sentry studied Morgana's state of dishabille, recognizing at once her foul mouth. "Aye!" he said. " 'Tis the former lady of this hall, Kirsten, daughter of Wulfrid."

"And is she Lord Blaise's bed-wench?"

"Do not answer that impudent question," Sigvald bellowed from the entry to the hall. As he strode toward them, Morgana detected a new wariness in D'Arcy. "How did you leave the hall, my lady?" He sniffed the air. "Ah! Dressed as a pig girl—" he raised one brow "—again."

"Mayhaps your lord should pay closer attention to his bed-wenches. I found this one fresh from the arms of her lover."

Because he spoke Norman French, she could not shout the falsity of his words. She refused to hear one more slimy insinuation, however, and fled to her chamber, where Astrid had arranged for food to break her fast, and a clean change of clothes.

She could only peck lightly at her food, and finally, in exasperation, Astrid pushed it aside. "Come here and I shall comb your hair," Astrid said, "and we shall talk."

Morgana sat at her mother's knee. "What am I to do? Blaise will think me unfaithful."

"Possibly. But you cannot speak the truth. You cannot betray your brother and those who follow him in the wood. Of course, 'tis your choice—"

"Betrayal is not a choice," Morgana agreed quietly. "My head aches! Betray my own flesh and blood, or have my lover think that I play him false—that I am a wanton? Yet I must lie to Blaise. Oh, why does it hurt so?"

"You cannot be thinking about whys now, girl. Trust me, and set your mind at ease." Morgana slipped into a clean shift. " 'Sblood! You are a mass of bruises."

Preoccupied with her dilemma, Morgana ignored Astrid as she fetched a stone jar. "This is a healing unguent." She gently massaged some into the bruises. "Leopardsbane."

"Uh-huh," Morgana responded absentmindedly.

"What preys on your mind now?"

"How will the Norman react? And how shall I behave toward this D'Arcy until Blaise's return? I must assist my brother. How—how—how?" She hid her forehead in her arms.

"So many worries to burden such young shoulders." Astrid stroked her neck.

"This D'Arcy is his underlord. He will believe him, whatever lies he tells." She paced to and fro, the fury growing within until she might burst. "I shall never let him enslave us! I swear by the holy saints!"

"You are really quite pleasing to the eye."

Morgana whipped around to face Christian D'Arcy. It was the first time that she had seen him without his helmet. Whatever she had expected, it was not this strikingly handsome young man. Though he was lean, he was easily capable of crushing a mere girl within his muscular arms.

He carried himself as one possessed of a ruthless charm. When he grinned, she could discern perfect, white teeth.

A shaft of sun came through the window and struck his hair until it gleamed like burnished gold. No man had a right to be so—

"Beautiful!" he remarked again, clearly astounded by the difference in her appearance. " 'Tis quite easy to see why he is attracted to you. But why were you pretending to be a pig girl in the wood? Who were you awaiting?"

" 'Tis not meet for a gentleman to intrude upon a lady," Morgana said firmly, stifling a barely perceptible waver in her voice.

"You are clearly no lady. My men have the gashes to prove it." He turned to Astrid, who glared at him from the corner. "Leave us."

Morgana met her mother's eyes, silently beseeching her to solve this irritating problem before D'Arcy courted bloodshed.

"I do not speak twice, madame."

Astrid nodded in assurance to her daughter, and left the chamber in a huff of exasperation.

Morgana wrapped herself in her mantle and sat in a chair by the fire to dry her still damp hair. He strode toward her and lifted the strands to hold them against the fire. "Look how your hair catches the glow from the fire." She whipped her hair away and bolted from the chair, but he raised his hands in truce and moved to the fire, kicking the embers until the flames burned a bright red. "I shall make no further movement toward you."

"Why do you pester me?" she finally asked.

"Because you fascinate me." The deep sensuality of his voice sent an immediate warning to her. "Does he keep you satisfied, Kirsten of Retford, or would a more lively bedding be to your liking?"

"My lord Blaise is all that I would want—and more," she replied somberly.

"Well, then, he must be doing well if he has managed to cower one such as you. But I think not, or you would not be skulking around outside the village, lying in the grass with some peasant. He cannot be doing too well."

"I have lain in the grass with no one, sir knight, and I take offense at your suggestion that I have."

"He must be a special man, the one that you met." He cocked his head to one side. "Mayhaps I should rid my friend of the rascal."

"No!" she exclaimed a little too quickly. "My lord is already displeased with your deeds at Hartley. You should not further anger him. Duke William holds Hartley, and

Blaise is William's man. Next time it may not be your fief you forfeit, but rather your very life. Heed me, D'Arcy. I was goddaughter to William's kinsman, good King Edward. Any action against me or my people would be ill advised."

"You have a quick mind, Kirsten of Retford." His half smile changed to a scowl. "I do not appreciate women who do not know their place." His scathing glance discomfited her. " 'Twould give me great pleasure to teach you your place—great pleasure indeed."

"My lord Blaise's instructions were quite clear," Sigvald bellowed from the doorway in his low, gruff voice, Astrid smiling in his wake. "No one is to enter this chamber but my lady, her mother, and her servants."

"A pity you did not do your duty so diligently this morning, Sigvald. Mayhaps then the girl would not have slipped out from the compound to meet her lover."

Morgana kept her counsel. The less said, the fewer lies to be explained, and less chance of being caught.

"Surely you wish to break your fast, *mon seigneur* D'Arcy," Sigvald continued. "Come!"

D'Arcy glowered at Morgana, but she turned her back on him.

"Come! You think overmuch of these brainless women." Sigvald successfully drew D'Arcy out of the bedchamber, but returned shortly thereafter. "You will bolt this door at all times," he ordered Astrid brusquely. "You will take all meals with your daughter in this chamber. You will both keep to your bowers until *mon seigneur* returns. Is this agreed?" Morgana nodded. "Know this, Saxon. I will not kill a Norman knight merely because an empty-headed girl cannot behave herself."

Christian D'Arcy examined the chamber that was to be his for the duration of his stay at Retford, or until the new keep was built. He had been told that the elder son of the former lord had slept here. Comfortable, but spartan by Norman standards. At least it had a soft featherbed upon which to sleep. Because his men had burnt down Hartley Hall, he had been forced to sleep on a bed of straw.

His belongings sat on a nearby table, and his chain mail hung on a hook. The mail should go to the blacksmith for repairs and cleaning. Near the fire, next to a tub with steam curls rising from it, a young woman awaited him. His lips parted in a wicked grin. "Come. Help me undress."

The woman was plain but buxom, and her eyes twinkled when she spoke. He liked that.

"What is your name?" he asked as he disrobed.

"Elvina."

D'Arcy moved effortlessly about the chamber, unashamed as the girl's eyes froze upon his naked form. His features were so perfect as to make him almost too beautiful for a man. His thick, yellow hair fell in a cap of ringlets. Still, there was a certain isolation—a certain unapproachability—as if he would let no one in.

As he descended into the hot water, each tensed muscle was lulled into soft security. He lay back, his head temporarily pillowed upon the wench's lap, and looked at the smoke-blackened rafters of the ceiling, searching for shapes amongst the black gloom. Why would William wish to be king of a country such as this? he wondered. The women were whey-faced; the men were vicious fighters, true, but their strength had been cut off at Stamford Bridge or Hastings. Why be king of a land so lacking in culture and refinement?

He was especially angry that William had forced him, through his oath of fealty, to come to England—had seduced him with promises of a bright future and a fief of his own. Yet the duke had sent Blaise to wrest it from him before he could even build a proper keep. He had fought valiantly for William, and this had been his payment—to be stripped of his lands and made underlord once again to that pompous bastard.

Why Blaise, of all men, when he had spent years trying to escape Blaise's iron grip?

Why, indeed? Gisele had foretold that their lives would be intertwined forever. Gisele, with her hair hanging loose and spread across her back like the most precious sable; Gisele, as she rode him, and loved him, and drained every ounce of strength from his manhood. Faithless Gisele, his one and only true love, who had gone from his bed to that of his overlord, to work her wiles, to seal the marriage vow and gain Blaise's fortune and power.

And what had the fool done? Rejected her when he had found out about her deceit. Granted, it had taken several years, for he had been easily duped.

And now it was too late.

"You are so stiff, my lord!" the servant girl murmured as she massaged his shoulder blades, his neck, and worked her way down each side of his backbone.

"A tribute to your voluptuous beauty," he replied with a naughty grin, as he rose to prove the truth of her words. "Come to this bed, and I will show you how stiff." He lifted the giggling girl, who quickly put her arms around his neck as he buried his lips between her breasts.

Outside the chamber, Sigvald and Astrid nodded to each other. No words need be spoken. Their plotting had worked. The maid would keep the randy lord occupied, at least until the morrow, when Blaise would return.

"I have saved your daughter's skin today, but who shall save her from *mon seigneur* Blaise on the morrow?"

"There is no need for you to tell him—"

"I must tell him. Would you rather that he hears the words from the mouth of that braying jackass?"

"You are right."

Sigvald, overcome with a sudden desire to protect this woman, caressed her cheek lightly. "I shall try to undermine Lord D'Arcy's charges. *Mon seigneur* knows him to be a liar. Mayhaps he will not believe him."

Astrid's cheek suffused with warmth. "Thank you."

Sigvald was in awe. She had not moved away from his touch.

D'Arcy was well pleased with the wench. He even slept in her arms for a bit, until hunger prodded him awake. "Girl!" He slapped her bare bottom. "Fetch some food for your lord."

Elvina reluctantly rolled over and slipped from the bed and into her shift. He had to admit—she had been a lively piece. "And the good wine—not that pig vomit Blaise gives to his soldiers."

While she was gone, D'Arcy pondered what had come to pass. Mayhaps it was not as bad as it had appeared on first impression. This situation could prove very interesting. He was in Blaise's home. Blaise would be away from the hall, at Hartley for a time, and he would be here with Blaise's woman.

What better way to wreak vengeance upon Blaise for Gisele than to take Blaise's woman? If he really did value the girl—even if he did not value her—his pride would be dealt a serious blow.

But D'Arcy knew that he would have to handle her gently. This was no servant girl, despite her words and deeds. She was proud. She would have to come willingly. He would have to pretend sympathy and consideration—even when he wanted to throw the wench upon the ground and rip into her with his manhood.

Bestow attention upon her with a gentle hand, and she would come to him. They all did. Gisele did. Yes, that would be most satisfying indeed!

Chapter **6**

He returns!'' Astrid paced to and fro by the chamber window. ''I see his firebrand, and the crimson and purple of Lord D'Arcy's gonfalon. Half of the men wear D'Arcy's colors.''

''I should be abed. 'Tis late! He would not expect me to await him.'' Morgana yawned. ''He will eat with his men. If I am already asleep when he comes to bed, mayhaps—''

Astrid gathered her belongings. '' 'Tis best I quit this chamber before he comes. No need to draw your bolt.''

''He would only tear the door down.''

After her mother had left, Morgana regretted not having asked her to stay. Alone, there was so much in her thoughts to torment her. She must be careful not to reveal her brother's identity or her knowledge of Blaise's language. So much to remember. So much to fear! So much required of a young, foolish girl.

As Blaise's men filled the hall below with boisterous, drunken guffaws, Morgana realized that she could not sleep until he had come to her and they had spoken about D'Arcy's lies, though they were truly not lies, for it could have looked as if she had met a lover in the wood. Of course, she would never admit this to Blaise.

As the hours passed and he did not come, she wondered whether anyone had even told him about her trip outside the palisade. He had forbade her to breach the palisade without an armed guard. The serf's garb she had worn had put her in danger—as he had warned. He would no doubt take great pleasure in reminding her of that.

She had expected confrontation. Mayhaps he would even hit her. Men were known to react with violence when angered.

In the wee hours of the morning, Morgana crept from her bedchamber to the top of the stairs to study him from the shadows. He was alone. The trestles had been dismantled except for the lord's table; knights lay sleeping, strewn along the floor of the hall like rushes. In front of him, stuck into the table, was the jeweled dagger that D'Arcy had wrested from her. Brent's dagger!

She inched backward into the shadows, but he sensed her presence and looked up toward her. She pressed her back against the damp stone wall, determined that he not know that she was there. When she heard his tread upon the stairs, she fled to their chamber.

She pressed her hand upon her chest to quiet her pounding heart as she slipped into the bed and turned away from the door to try, unsuccessfully, to act as if she were asleep.

"Your breathing is too ragged. Why do you pretend sleep?" he asked as he fitted his torch into a bracket on the wall.

He removed his clothes and crept into the bed beside her, smelling of leather and sweat.

"You stink of horses. I had a bath prepared for you hours ago, but it has gone cold."

"I am weary. I shall bathe in the morning."

She expected him to reach for her, but he lay beside her on his back, his hands locked under his head. When was he going to let her know what he was thinking? "You smell of stale wine," she added.

"I could smell of stale women." He pushed her flat upon her back, his eyes dark and cloudy. "You failed to answer. Why pretend sleep?"

" 'Twas not pretense, my lord."

"More lies! I saw your shadow upon the wall."

"I thought mayhaps you were unwell."

"You do not give a tinker's damn for my health." He brought forth the dagger and held it up to the firelight. "Where did you get this?"

" 'Twas mine."

"Lie upon lie upon lie. I have had your possessions cataloged and the weapons confiscated. This is not yours. Indeed," he continued, " 'twas not in this hall last week. And 'tis not a woman's weapon, but a man's dagger."

"I found it in the wood."

"Ah! We are closer to the truth, yet still you skirt around it. You came by the weapon in the wood, but you did not find it. 'Twas given to you by your lover." Though outwardly calm, his voice betrayed his barely bridled anger.

"I have no lover but you, my lord. I swear it."

Curses fell from his mouth as the anger swelled within him, and his rage grew so unwieldy that he swooped down on her like a falcon, and buried the dagger into the bed by her head. Morgana leapt from the bed, but he was too shrewd for her. He subdued her beneath him in an instant. "Would you escape your punishment, faithless wench?"

"I am guiltless, my lord. I beg of you!" She squirmed, but he clamped her tightly, cutting the flow of blood to her limbs.

"Then why run away?"

"You are not yourself. You frighten me."

"The innocent need not be afraid."

"There are those who would lie to serve their own purposes."

"Such as Lord D'Arcy?"

"Aye! Lord D'Arcy came upon me with his men like skulking fiends. I had no idea who he was, or what he was about. I merely protected myself."

"When Lord D'Arcy happened upon you, you were in your lover's arms, so close that not even the Holy Ghost could fit between you."

"Nay! 'Tis not true. I met no one in the wood."

"You left the compound, and were observed at the edge of the forest. If you did not meet a lover, then what were you about?"

"I purchased a piglet to roast for you upon your return. 'Twas a surprise, after your recent journey."

"Where is this piglet?"

"It escaped when D'Arcy's men—"

"How convenient! You were confined to this hall, and yet you left, even after you were warned of the consequences?"

"I am a free woman. Would you confine me like an animal?"

"You are a conquered woman. I would confine you for life if 'twould suit my purpose."

"Confined to this bed to be your whore?"

"Aye! If I wish it, that is how it would be. My whore, and mine alone, until I chose otherwise. I would kill anyone who sought to challenge me." He lifted from her. "Remove your shift."

She cradled her head in her trembling hands, then raised her face to his and, with dignity, whispered, "No."

"Not tonight, Kirsten. You would not dare to say me nay tonight. I will not be turned away while you give yourself freely to another." A thin chill hung on the edge of his words.

"I am not a whore," she countered icily, "and will not act one for you, or anyone else."

Blaise set her upon her feet, and ripped the garment from her body. "Did D'Arcy or his men touch you?" She shook her head in the negative. "Then your lover must have inflicted these bruises. They have the imprint of his fingers."

Morgana, remembering how Brent had clutched her arms, blushed, and averted her eyes. "I have no lover."

"You go to a man who inflicts pain upon you? Is that your preference—pain?"

"You do not believe me, so why should I continue to answer your questions?"

"Because at this moment, you will do or say anything to save yourself from my wrath." He thrust his fingers between her legs. "How many countless others have lain between these thighs?" Her limbs stiffened. "How many will vie for the right to call themselves 'father' should you produce a child?"

"Hold your words, my lord, I beg of you." She tore herself away with a choking sob. "Say no more, lest you say something that can never be forgiven."

"Forgiven? Do you think that I care to be forgiven? If not for this heat within my body when I am near you, I would leave your bed, I swear it. But you have bewitched me, pagan bitch. You are in my blood, a sickly craving.''

"I pray you, do and say no more to estrange me."

"Estrange you? You would have to be mine first. Despite our handfasting vow, you are no more mine than you are D'Arcy's. Will he be the next one to crawl into your bed, begging your favors?"

"You have never crawled, my lord, nor have you begged."

"I take what I want. But what of D'Arcy?"

"My mother has attended me, in this chamber, since his arrival. If you do not believe me, ask your man, Sigvald."

"You think to lull me with these words. You act the sweet maid, always under her mother's watchful eye, yet we know differently, do we not?" He scanned her body critically. "Come to bed, Kirsten. Show me what you have learned from your lover."

Morgana raked long furrows into his cheek.

"Vicious bitch!" he spat contemptuously as he wiped the blood on the back of his hand. They struggled, but he easily subdued her and lay her upon the bed, her wrists gripped in his hand and stretched above her head.

One knee pressed between her thighs, and Morgana bucked like an unbroken colt. "If you take me this night in anger, you shall find no pleasure in the act."

"I am the conqueror and you are the vanquished. There can never be other than this between us." There was an odd sound in his voice—not anger, but resignation. And regret. They were enemies. That would never change. Even should she grow to love him, they would always be enemies.

"If you take me, I will never again come freely to you."

"Give over to me. Yield," he whispered thickly in her ear.

"You have hurt me to the depths of my soul. If you must needs have me, I cannot stop you. You are stronger than I. But there will be no pleasure in it, I vow."

He paused, then rolled away from her and stared at the flame of the torch, exhaling deeply. "You are fortunate that I am weary. One of these days you shall issue that empty challenge—"

He rose and shook his head, then looked at her intently for a moment and strode to the door. "There are others who would willingly meet my needs." He ripped open the door. "Go! Sleep with your mother."

Morgana remembered how easily the servant girl, Elvina, had gone to D'Arcy's bed. He was right. Many would freely choose to be his mistress. In this very hall, Saxon women lay by choice with Norman knights. Astrid tried to keep her unaware, but she was not blind.

Under his watchful eye, Morgana dressed in a new shift from her trunk, and drawing her mantle about her, left the bedchamber and started down the hall. Behind her he stood at the top of the stairs, naked, calling for a serving girl and hot water for his tub.

"You do not stay to bathe your lord?" D'Arcy murmured from the shadows.

She shoved past him, but he followed her toward her mother's chamber.

"Trouble in Eden?"

"You would know, my lord D'Arcy. 'Twas of your making?"

"I told him nothing," he insisted. "Ask his man, Sigvald. I have known Blaise for many a year. He has a vile temper, when aroused. Gisele—that was his wife—Gisele was always wary when he was in these moods." He blocked Astrid's doorway. "I took pity on you, and told him nothing. Mayhaps one of my men—"

"Let me pass."

"Do not be angry with me."

"Let me pass!"

"For the price of a kiss."

"I may have been called whore this night, but that does not make it so."

Astrid opened her door, and Morgana slipped under D'Arcy's arm into the chamber.

"You stray, my lord D'Arcy," Astrid chided in a stern, disapproving voice. "I believe that is your chamber, over there."

She slammed the door before he could respond.

Morgana stood by the window, cocking an ear toward the frivolous laughter of the wench that carried upon the night wind.

"Come to bed, Morgana. There is naught to be done now.

He will see matters differently in the morning. Most men usually do."

Despite Astrid's best efforts, Morgana was unable to sleep, for she could hear *him*—could hear their low voices, his and the serving girl's. What could they have to talk about? The girl was a dolt. Would they prattle about onions and boiled beef? Would he dare to make love to the wench in the same bed where he had lain with her? Why were they laughing? Was the wench able to even understand his wit?

Unable to stay away, Morgana tiptoed down the torchlit hall and stood outside his door. Fortunately D'Arcy was nowhere to be seen as she pressed her ear to the door. She could hear nothing.

"May I help you, my lady?" a low, sweet voice asked. Morgana recoiled in embarrassment, and heat stole across her face. It was one of the kitchen wenches.

"What are you doing creeping around, girl?"

"Lord Blaise has asked for mulled wine."

"I see," Morgana replied, lifting her chin. "Well, I shall take it in to him. You may seek your bed."

The young girl was uncertain, but handed her the wineskin and left the hallway in haste.

Morgana breathed in deeply, resolved to maintain her control as she slipped into the chamber. He sat near the fire, reading, covered from the waist down in a bathing sheet as Elvina massaged sweet oil into his back. "I do not know much about the Romans, my lord," she said, "other than that they were in England many years ago. Ah! Here is your wine." Elvina's smile faded as she realized that it was Morgana.

Morgana placed her index finger to her lips, and handed a full horn to the girl. Blaise laid down the book, took the horn from Elvina, and quaffed its contents with nary a pause. Morgana glared at the girl, and inclined her head toward the door. Elvina hastily quit the bedchamber.

"Ah! 'Tis good. Mayhaps now I shall sleep."

Morgana took Elvina's place. She rubbed the almond-scented oil in her palms and continued to rub first his back, then his neck. Blaise laid his head in her lap, eyes closed, and sighed in contentment. "Your touch soothes me, wench. So much more gentle than that of your mistress." Morgana inched down his chest. He had only a cloth thrown across his waist, and she noted that his manhood grew beneath its folds. Her breath caught in her throat, and he chuckled.

"Take it in your hand, girl. 'Tis hard as marble for you."

"Take it into your own hand," she sputtered, bristling with indignation as she poured the warm oil over his manhood and stood up, dropping his head to the floor with a dull thud.

"Kirsten, sweet," he murmured as he caught her near the doorway. "I knew 'twas you from your scent—the herbs in your hair. I wondered what you were up to and how far you would go." He loosened the tie of her gunna.

"I—I wanted to speak with you," she lied.

"Speak! You do not want to speak," he muttered into her hair as he drew her gown down over her hips to fall at her feet. "We have spoken enough this night." He probed between her legs with his slick, wet fingers and she groaned. "Your desire betrays you." He molded her against his muscled thighs as one hand loosed her braid. Her hair fell like a mantle around them both as he lifted her, rising hard against her.

At first his lips barely skimmed across hers, but then, as he forced them open with his thrusting tongue, his kiss grew more insistent. Her tongue shyly entered to taste of his hidden sweetness, even as his large palm pressed her buttocks. She moved against him, grinding her hips into his until he moaned. He bore her to the soft bed and, with a lust-filled growl, laid her among the pelts, her hair fanning out in red-gold wonder.

Morgana sensed that primitive need growing within her, overwhelming her as he covered her body with his. When she thought he made to leave her, she rose with him, forcing him back into her arms. He gentled her with tender endearments. "Lie back, my darling, and enjoy what you are feeling." His lips brushed across her breasts, suckling first one rose-colored peak, and then the other. She shivered as a familiar tension twisted her abdomen and her skin prickled. His tongue slid a fiery trail down her hip and thigh, stopping at her knee. "What is this?" He grazed lightly over the scabbed area.

" 'Tis nothing." She concentrated on the sensations and ignored the pain. "I fell."

His searching tongue found the bend of her knee, and she gasped as he licked inside with quick, fluttery motions. His hand followed the line of her leg in perfect symmetry with his mouth, until lips and fingers met near her mound.

He drew her to the edge of the bed and knelt between her thighs. She had no idea of his intent, and once he made it clear, it was too late to say him nay, nor did she wish to do so. He knelt in front of her, hands on each hip, and drawing her close, slanted his head to her until his hot breath was replaced by the light press of his lips against her soft, red-gold triangle. Her eyes swept open as she tried to push him away, more fearful of this intimacy than of any other he had heretofore pressed upon her. Yet he laced his hands in hers, and held her fast as his tongue searched the depths of her, parting those other pink, honeyed, pouting lips.

Though she sought to elude his kiss, she merely furthered his intent. He sought out, and found, the core of her desire, erect and quivering, and lightly flicked over it and took her within his mouth.

Morgana thrashed upon the bed. "What are you doing to me?" This new form of loving took her so quickly to the precipice that she was certain she would fall over and fail to exist evermore. But though her mind knew that she should escape this torture, she found herself lifting to his questing tongue, inviting him to enter, to take her further—and beyond.

Waves of ecstasy overwhelmed her as his tongue elicited a shuddering response until she could not hope to repress the screams that tore from her throat. And still he wrested from her rejoinders to his heady passion, pausing only to cover her and thrust inside again and again, driving her over into the chasm of life-death. As he filled her near to bursting with his seed, she wrapped her legs around him tightly and surged in rhythm to the mating dance. Then, from her unconscious state, he knew that she had died the little death—and he was jubilant.

When she awoke, Blaise lay to her side, his manhood still erect within her. She held him at arm's length, spent and wearied. "Please, my lord, no more."

She separated herself and rolled away from him, staring, unseeing, at the last flickerings of the firelight. What had she done? She had allowed him to perform the most intimate acts imaginable—had degraded herself as he enslaved her to his desire.

"Why do you move away?" he asked as she sought the far side of the bed.

Caryl Wilson

"Is this how you have chosen to punish me—to humiliate me?"

"Humiliate you?"

"You made love to me as one would make love to a camp follower."

"Why? Because I loved you with my tongue?"

Her face flushed to crimson. " 'Tis evil. 'Tis the devil's fiery kiss."

"My name—Blaise—means fire. Now you know just how easily and deeply you may get burned."

"This shall never happen again. 'Tis too much! Never will you do this again."

He bound her to him and bit her neck lightly. "Aye! This, and more. Despite my hasty words spoken in anger, your vow to me is binding. I will have this—and much, much more. What is it that you fear? Is your lover in the wood less imaginative? I would have thought this coupling would have put you in mind of him."

Tears coursed down her cheeks. "Will you accuse me at each turn? I have no lover, and I will not change my story, even should I have to repeat it a thousand times."

"That is what it is. Just a story. I do not believe you, Kirsten, and when I find the man, he is dead. There will be no tears, no begging for forgiveness; nothing shall sway me."

"And what of me?"

"What do you expect? Do you want me to beat you so that you can hate me? I will not help lift your guilt. I gave you my heart—"

"When? You gave me this!" She circled his manhood. "Never your heart."

"I called you wife, and you were faithless at the first opportunity." He rolled away from her.

"Please, my lord! You must believe me—"

"Never again. You have made your choice. You chose your lover in the wood. You are no more to me than my leman. 'Twas your choice." He rose from the bed and clothed himself in his breechclout.

She sat up and drew the pelt to her chin. "Nay! In that you are mistaken, my lord." Ice spread through her as she rigidly held her tears in check. "You actually believe that we have choices."

102

Chapter 7

Each day came and went much like the one before it. After the first snow, Morgana managed to press back from her thoughts the pain that gnawed at her heart and concentrate on the work to be done at Retford Hall. And there was much to do, for the displaced villagers of Hartley drained Retford's resources daily. Blaise was right, of course. If they could survive this winter, the hunger in their bellies would not be quite so bad next year. The crops would be sown and reaped, and the villagers' lives would revert to normal.

Father Jerome regularly brought news from Brent of William's advances north and west—of burning and pillaging that had brought even the English church to its knees. William had been repelled in London, but had taken Winchester, and even yet pushed northward, toward Mercia. All had fully expected the northern fyrd, which had arrived late to assist at Hastings, to protect the West Saxons who fled north—to fight against William. Yet when the moment came, the only earls left in England, Edwin of Mercia and Morkere of Northumberland, good King Harold's brothers, took their men and went home. This had not prevented William from harrying southern Mercia, for he wanted no men at his back when he went, three divisions strong, to take London from the north.

Though Brent refused to admit defeat, Morgana was a student of history. She saw that the further defense of the country was doomed. All that was left for her was to flee to Ireland. It was all she thought of—her plan to leave Blaise.

Her mother and Father Jerome were right. Mayhaps 'twas best that this breach existed between them, for had she grown to love him, it would have made it more difficult to leave when the time came.

So she doubled her efforts to assist her brother and his followers. The daily exploits of the Black Outlaw gave her people hope. She overheard Blaise's men speak of him in the hall, some opining that he was not a man at all, but a vengeful demon. His feats were legendary. He fought with crude Saxon weapons, surely no match for the Norman knights, and yet—he scored victories at each turn, small to be sure, but victories nonetheless.

Morgana watched from her window as the English horses, corralled below, were walked in a circle.

"What if it does not work?" Astrid asked.

"It must work. We have thought of everything. Do not lose heart now, Mother. Tomorrow, just before dawn, one of the men will loosen the rope—and Brent will take care of the rest."

Brent needed the horses. Blaise had no use for them. Norman mounts were war-horses—larger and stronger to carry an armored man. Indeed, they were themselves armored. The English mounts were left in the corral to soften and waste away. Brent's men would feed and care for them—ride them until they were strong and useful again. "He knows that you are being watched, and cannot meet with him," Father Jerome had said. "If you would help, put the contents of this vial into the keg of wine for the evening meal. They will sleep like the dead, and those who do not will be too few in number to make a difference once the horses are loose."

Morgana yawned. "I should have stayed abed a bit longer. I have not been able to sleep, so anxious am I about the outcome of this plan."

Worry lines creased Astrid's brow. "I have sent for food to break your fast—"

"Nay! My stomach is in knots. I could not eat a thing. Later, when it is over—later I shall eat."

"Then lie down. I will stay and watch over you. You must rest."

Despite her anxiety, Morgana drifted off into a dreamless sleep the moment her head hit the pillow.

It was late afternoon when she awoke. She dressed hastily, and reached the kitchen while the evening's repast was being prepared.

"How goes the dinner this night?" Morgana asked as she traversed the kitchen.

"On schedule, mistress," the cook said, beaming.

"What do we eat?"

"Roast fowl. Squirrel—"

Morgana suddenly felt faint and her stomach lurched. Not now! Not again! Not here! She was not going to be sick here, was she?

"Are you all right, my lady? You look a bit pale. Sit, and I will get you something to drink."

While the cook rushed around the kitchen looking for herbs to soothe her stomach, Morgana poured the contents of the vial into the barrel of wine. She perceived eyes upon her, and turned to see Elvina's brows furrowed with confusion. Would the girl tell the Norman?

Elvina acted as if she had seen nothing as she filled the pitchers to brimming and brought the wine to the waiting knights.

Morgana, relieved, sat down to take a breath. When the cook returned with chamomile tea, she was asleep across the table.

Blaise returned to Retford in the pink dawn of the next day. The builders worked slowly at both Retford and Hartley, for it was cold and his men had to daily contend with small parties of bandits from the wood. No open fighting, but irritating thefts.

He wanted to stay near hearth and home—near her. Fewer men came from the village, despite the offer of food, and until these very cold days were over, he would not be able to accomplish much. So he had left half of his men at Hartley, and returned to wait out the snow.

Matters between them had not improved appreciably. Yet he was drawn to her. Though the strain between them was evident, she spoke whenever he approached her in conversation. And she was a wonderful listener. She wanted to hear all the details of his work—his very thoughts on all kinds of subjects. She understood him as very few men had. For instance, when he had talked with her of the peace he had found in the monastery, she had understood. "Simpler lives are always more peaceful," she had said. "When one takes on rank and privilege, one takes on responsibility—and responsibility is a heavy burden."

She still refused to bed with him, and he would not press her. Though he wanted her body more as each day passed, he had decided not to force her. He had awakened passion within her. She would come to him soon enough. Of this he was certain. Until then, he could bide his time, as long as she continued to speak with him, smile into his eyes, banter with him. It was enough—for now.

There were the other things she did for him—seeing to his comfort, planning his meals, mending his chausses and chainse. And she could play music. Some nights, before bedtime, he found her plucking the strings of a lute, and softly humming.

She appeared different—calm. Why? he wondered. Was it because he no longer made demands on her? Was it because she lay with another when he was gone?

Blaise pushed away these thoughts. She had done no more to appear faithless, and he would know, for she was closely watched. Indeed, the only one she saw besides her mother was her father confessor, though what she had to confess, he did not know. Mayhaps the priest was her lover. 'Twas not impossible. He had spent time among monkish men, and could attest to the fact that even God's chosen could behave in a lascivious manner on occasion.

Bah! He brooded needlessly.

He approached the hill where he had stood looking down upon Retford that first time. It appeared somehow different to him. Mayhaps because the land was now familiar. He was almost home. Home! It surprised him that he thought of it that way after only one month. Yet, as each day passed, this temporary place to rest his head became more his home.

Something was wrong. A cloud of dust led from the village into the wood. The rebels? Would they dare to attack when he was away? "What better time, you fool," he chided himself. "Kirsten!"

His men pulled up alongside as he bolted down the side of the hill into the valley. They rushed headlong after him, heedless of the peril.

The ride to Retford was the longest of his life. What if they had harmed her? How would he live with himself? Had they pillaged the storehouses?

A thousand questions plagued him—a thousand fears niggling at the back of his mind. And at the root of all, he thought only of her.

The postern gate was open. He entered the palisade warily, expecting rebels to jump out at him from each hiding place. The sentries lay on the ground, and upon closer inspection, he realized that they were not dead, but asleep.

The hall was unusually quiet. Except for a few servants, Sigvald, and a small complement of men, most of the diners, male and female, lay asleep across the trestles.

"What?"

"The Saxon horses, *mon seigneur*. They were stolen. It appears that the men were given sleeping potions. Just before dawn, the rebels made their move. I was certain they planned to attack the hall, and fortified it as best I could. But they took only the English horses."

"Where is Lord D'Arcy?"

"Abed with a maid, *mon seigneur*."

"The hall was his responsibility. He shall pay heavily for this stupidity."

"Verily, the man is a fool, and a pitiful excuse for a knight, but there was no way to tell in advance."

"He was to watch this hall. You all could have been poisoned. He is responsible for security, and if it was breached, and someone was let in—"

" 'Twas someone already in the hall, *mon seigneur*."

There was a lethal calmness about him as he inquired, "Who?"

"The Lady Kirsten was seen in the kitchen last night."

Raw hurt glittered in his golden gaze as Blaise strode from the hall, taking the steps two at a time, heedless of the weight of his mail. He flung the door of the chamber open, and was surprised to see that she was still abed.

Astrid sat in the corner, doing needlework. Clearly she had not drunk the wine.

"Is she asleep?"

"Aye, my lord."

"Leave us!"

It was evident from the tone of his voice that he would brook no refusal. Astrid rose, dropped her needlework on the chair, and left quietly. Outside the door, Sigvald motioned her down the hall. "You cannot save the girl from his wrath now. Go to your bedchamber, and pray for her."

Morgana lay upon her bed, like an angel, her hair unbound and forming a fiery halo around her.

"Wake up, you treacherous bitch!" He shook her until her eyes opened wide with fright.

Morgana sat up, awake and ready to do battle with him. "Are you addlebrained, my lord? To what do I owe this ill humor?"

"The horses."

"The horses? What horses?"

"Do not pretend innocence with me. I know that you put an elixir in the wine. Do you deny that you were in the kitchen?"

"I often go to the kitchen." Who told? she wondered. Elvina? The cook?

"Who was it?" He dragged her from the bed and pressed her against him, the mail cutting through the linen into her belly and breasts. "Was it your lover in the wood?"

"You hurt me, my lord."

"By God's blood, demoiselle! Do you think to play me false at each turn and have me merely look the other way? What have you done with the horses?"

"The horses again? I have done nothing with the horses."

"I swear that, should your next answer be less satisfactory, I shall lock you in the cellar until you find the truth."

"I think not, my lord."

"You think not!" He grabbed her forearm and flung her toward the door. "You think not! Then you are a fool. I am William's man first. Do you understand that? William's man first, and I would kill each and every one of his enemies."

"Would you kill me, I wonder?"

"Do not tempt me. Even now my eyes wander to that slim neck of yours—'twould so easily snap—"

"You would not murder an innocent."

"You are not innocent." He cornered her and pressed her against the wall. "And I sometimes wonder if you ever really were."

"You—are—hurting—me," she said through clenched teeth, abandoning all pretense of compliance.

"I will do more than hurt you if you do not tell me about the horses."

She spat full in his face, tossed her head, and eyed him with cold triumph. "I will tell you nothing."

"Mayhaps, instead of solitary time in the cellar, you should be flogged for your insolence."

"Indeed! Do it yourself. 'Twould no doubt give you great pleasure."

"Save yourself, Kirsten," he cajoled, his tone a little softer. "Tell me of the damned horses. It cannot matter now. If the rebels have horses, they can move faster, do more damage. Is that what you want—for this warfare to continue because a few rebels will not yield to William's rule?"

"I cannot tell you of the horses when I know nothing."

He shook her with fury, then flung her to the ground and called Sigvald to bring him the lash. "I will get to the truth, one way or another."

Astrid appeared as if from out of nowhere and knelt before Blaise in supplication. "Please, my lord—"

"Get up, Mother!"

"My lord, you cannot do this thing," Astrid implored as Sigvald brought the whip. He sensed the situation and took the woman's arm to drag her away, but she summoned an inordinate amount of strength and tore loose from the Viking. "My lord, you would not kill your child, would you?"

Blaise gave her a sidelong glance of utter disbelief, his expression like one who had been slapped in the face. "What say you, madame?"

"She carries your child."

He shuddered and drew in a sharp breath. " 'Tis true?" he asked Morgana.

There was a roaring din in Morgana's ears and she suppressed a need to faint, holding on, breathing deeply. Her mouth unable to form the answer, she nodded.

"Remove Lady Astrid," he said in a voice that held no vestige of sympathy or caring. When they were alone, he ripped Morgana's shift open at her neck, and it floated down around her. Her breasts were indeed swollen, the nipples larger, the color slightly darker. There was no other sign.

"Whose is it?" he asked with deceptive calm.

A sensation of sick desolation swept over her, as she gave a choked, desperate laugh and whispered, "Mine."

"Who is the father?" he repeated with contempt.

"I will not answer that question."

"You seek to protect your lover, when he has left you to face me alone?"

"There is no lover!"

"The man in the wood. Do you forget him that easily?"

"I have no lover but you."

"You lie, still?"

"You are riddled with sickness, in your mind and your soul. You know naught of me—"

"I know of women. 'Tis enough. And I know that it cannot be my child."

"Why?"

"Because I am incapable of fathering a child."

Of all the answers he could have given her, surely this was the one she least expected. She laughed, hysterically, and he wondered whether her wits were sound. "Well, my lord Blaise, for whatever reason you may have believed that to be true, I can say, without doubt, that you are indeed capable. I carry the proof here—" she covered her abdomen with one small hand "—within me. Your child." She stood proud, glorious in her nudity. "But your denial of me is no surprise. You have accused me of wrongdoing since the moment we met. I care not what you think any longer. 'Tis *my* child, and it serves my purposes that you should deny its parentage. You shall have no part of my child." She laughed humorlessly as she knelt to pull the shift back up and over her shoulders. "And to think that I actually feared that you might take my child from me when you cast me aside. Now I know that it will never happen. I thank you, my lord."

He did not answer her, but called Sigvald to remove his mail, then dismissed him. He removed his clothing and motioned her to the bed.

"Nay!"

"Nothing will again keep me from your bed, especially not this child."

"I expected no less from you, my lord. You are not a man who considers anyone else before your own needs."

"When the babe is born, it shall go to the village, or to the wood—I care not where—to be suckled."

"I choose to suckle my own child."

"I will send the child from you, demoiselle, even so far as Normandy. There will be no reminders of your whoring in this chamber."

"If you send the child from me, I shall kill myself."

"Nay, you will not. As long as you are alive, you will hope that I shall change my mind."

"I shall kill you if you would stand between me and my child—"

"D'Arcy is my underlord, and should anything happen to me, he shall stand in my place, at least for a time. Kill me and become D'Arcy's whore? I think not. He enjoys inflicting pain on his women during lovemaking, I am told. But then—mayhaps you would enjoy that."

"Some are adept at inflicting pain upon the body, while others are masters of inflicting pain upon the heart and soul."

"And still others, like you, are adept at meshing the two." His fingers parted the torn material and caressed her breast. He was rewarded with an almost immediate response. He again pushed the material down, and she did nothing to stop its descent. His fingers slid sensuously over her bare arm, then tenderly traced the line of her cheek and jawbone. His arm curled around her waist, and he lifted her to his kiss, hard and searching, until she capitulated and gave of herself freely to drown in his passion. He swept her into his arms, cradling her, not certain if he wanted to kill or protect her.

"I meant our reunion to be a loving one, and I will not

be cheated. Come to my bed willingly, Kirsten. Please me, and mayhaps I will let you keep the babe when it is born."

Morgana told herself that she went to his bed because she must maintain her position as spy. She must give him no indication that she planned to escape. Besides, her body could not stop its traitorous response when he touched her. And it *had* been so long since he had touched her, and being only a human being, she could not hope to fight away such a demon. And finally, it was the only way to protect her child.

But no matter what she told herself, she never admitted that she loved him. She never could love him. Never! Never!

When it was over, and they had reached that moment of rapture together, she cried—loud, wracking sobs, her whole body shaking as she clutched her knees to her chest.

"What is it, love?"

"You would not truly take my child from me?"

"I must think upon it." He sighed.

" 'Twould kill me."

"I promise, I shall think upon it. Rest now."

"Do not take my words lightly. I would kill for the child."

"Do you have no shame—no fear? Are you so certain of my need of you that you think to play me for a court jester without any response from me?"

"The only feelings you have for me are here." She grasped his manhood in her hand. "You desire me, but you do not love me. You are an empty vessel."

He had meant to speak to her of love—to confess how he yearned to be with her, how his soul united with hers when they lay in each other's arms. 'Twas not only her body. He wanted more. He wanted everything within her— her very being. 'Twas what he was willing to give her— what he had meant to give her when they had traded vows.

But then the horses—and the babe—had intruded. Although he may forgive the horses, his pride would not let him forgive her infidelity, even as he crushed her beneath him again, driving into her mercilessly to brand her as his possession, trying to erase all thoughts of another lover from her memory, and from her body.

And yet, even as he spilled his seed within her, he wondered whether it was possible that the girl told the truth—possible that the child was indeed his. If so, had it been conceived on All Hallows' Eve, upon that pagan rock, as the midwife claimed? And was it his child, or the devil's own?

Nay! It could not be his babe. His seed had never sprouted within his wife, despite the many times he had bedded her. Gisele had not conceived a child until her affair with D'Arcy.

Nay, the girl lied to protect herself. She would pay for her faithlessness. He would continue to take her at his whim, but he would never show her love, and never again trust her.

Chapter 8

May I gather evergreens to adorn the hall for the yuletide season?" Morgana asked.

"Have one of the servants do it," Blaise replied negligently as he pored over his ledger. "We will be in London for the holy day, anyway."

"I wish to do it myself, to lighten the burden of those who have no homes this year. 'Tis customary to open our hall to the peasants for Christmas festivities. Besides, I need fresh air. I need to walk. You keep me to this hall like a prisoner."

"Indeed, you are a prisoner, demoiselle," he replied lightly, as if it were nothing to concern herself with. "I thought that you realized that." He turned back to Astrid. "I need an accurate accounting for the duke. How many families were at Hartley prior to our arrival?"

"Prior to your invasion, you mean," Morgana quipped.

Blaise glared at her, and nodded to Astrid to continue.

"As Thane of Hartley, Wulfrid ruled over approximately thirty-two families. Twelve cottagers."

"Cottagers?"

"Skilled men, such as the tinker. Two millers. The beekeeper." She paused.

"The villeins that farm the land—how many?"

" 'Tis difficult to account for Hartley. Each man holds about twenty acres of land; a couple close to thirty acres. Some sow their own land; others tend land already sown. Each family used to have a team of oxen, a milk cow, six sheep—"

"Yes?"

"But this is how it was. I have no idea how it is now, since you give me no information, and I am not allowed to go out into the countryside or travel to Hartley. Some are at Retford, some in the wood, and some may have—died."

He sighed and closed the ledger. "This will have to do. What would happen upon a man's death?"

"My lord husband would regain the land. More often than not, he returned it to the family, provided the deceased had heirs who could work the land. If you would let me go into the countryside, you could give Duke William an accurate accounting. I could take a party of your men with me."

"And I could go along to gather evergreens to deck the hall," Morgana added.

"This smells of a trick."

"No trick, my lord," Astrid said. "I swear it."

Blaise looked carefully at Morgana. She did appear pale, her eyes lifeless and dull, ringed by large, bluish circles. He knew that she still vomited often, and had not regained her appetite. Mayhaps some air would prove beneficial.

"Do not make me regret my approval—this time."

Blaise picked Sigvald and five of his most trusted men as her escort, and all was quickly made ready.

"I did not think that he would let us go," Astrid mused as they trotted toward the wood.

"Bah! He believes me tamed, for I have been too ill to fight him—nor do I have the stomach for it these days."

"Where will he meet you?"

"Father Jerome said that Brent would be tending sheep." She scanned the edge of the wood. "I see only two men— a hunchbacked shepherd and an old woodcutter." Morgana neither nodded nor pointed for fear she would give herself away. "Could it be he?" Astrid shrugged, and Morgana called over her shoulder to their escort. "I wish to go to the wood over there. I see lovely holly bushes with ripe red berries.'' Three men split away to accompany Astrid, while two stayed with Morgana.

As Morgana drew closer, she could see that the hunchback was indeed Brent, and the old man—Cedric! Her mother would be disappointed that she had missed him.

Cedric came toward her. "May I work for you, my lady?'' he asked.

"Get out of the way, knave!'' one of the guards grunted as he lashed Cedric's hand away from the bridle.

"Wait! These men can assist me.'' She turned to Cedric. "Come! I see an especially lovely tree just ahead. Bring your ax.''

"What are you doing here?'' she asked when they were a sufficient distance from the men as to not be overheard.

"I escaped and joined your brother.'' He nodded toward Astrid, who rode in the opposite direction. "How fares my lady?''

"She is a strong woman. She fares as well as can be expected, under the circumstances.''

"Aye!'' he replied, his admiration evident. "And you. You are sickly?''

"I am with child.''

"I suspected the moment that I saw you,'' he replied gravely.

"We are leaving on the morrow for London, so I will not be back before Christmas. I wanted to see Brent—to tell him the news.''

Cedric stopped at a pine tree and started chopping down boughs. "You go to London with Lord Blaise? Why?''

"William expects to be crowned king.''

"The witan—''

"He thinks he has the vote of the witan. The queen has sworn him fealty. Bishop Stigand backs his claim. Edwin and Morkere will not challenge him.''

"William is a proud, unyielding man. You best remember that in London.'' Brent made his way toward them, dragging his foot behind as if deformed. "Do not tell your brother that you go to London. He may attack Retford in the lord's absence, and then we would have a bloodbath the likes of which you have never seen. I hear D'Arcy's men are at Retford."

"Both D'Arcy's and Blaise's men, under Sigvald's command." Morgana opened her arms, and Cedric lifted her from her palfrey. There was a cold severity in his eyes.

"If you tell Brent that you travel the road to London, he may attack. You may meet with harm."

"My brother would do nothing to put us in further danger," Morgana insisted, forcing a half smile.

"Then think of Retford. Should he attack Retford, your mother could be killed."

"She comes with me to London."

"Then your people. For the love of God, there are those who follow your brother whose families were murdered at Hartley, or whose sisters and mothers were raped and beaten by Norman knights and soldiers. We do not want to repeat the terror of Hartley. Keep your counsel, Morgana. Do not tell him about London."

"You are wise. But to lie to my brother—" She hesitated as Brent reached them. "How fare you, brother?"

"Our efforts come together slowly," he replied, staring from her to Cedric as if he knew something was afoot. "Soon we will have our men trained—our arms forged. Even as we speak, our quivers fill with arrows. The forest is bounteous."

"You *will* wait until spring?"

"Aye! Come spring, the lord of Retford shall feel our mighty vengeance. Damn!" He shuffled off to return a sheep that had wandered away, as a good shepherd would, for there must be nothing unusual in his behavior to alert the guards to his real identity.

As Cedric quietly studied Morgana, she shuffled her feet and picked with her toe at the fuzzy moss. "Brent does not know about the child?"

Morgana shook her head, her eyes pleading with him to maintain his silence. "I think it best to keep it to myself for a while."

"And he does not know how you feel about the child's father."

"I hate the child's father," she said, her eyes dark and insolent.

"I saw your face when Brent spoke his name; I did not see hatred mirrored in your eyes."

"Aye!" she admitted. "He suspects that I care for the man. But I do not—"

"I have the wisdom of many years behind me, girl. But does it not bother you that he is the enemy?"

Her bitterness spilled over into her voice. "It injures me sorely that he is a Norman, mayhaps the very Norman who wielded the sword to cut down King Harold."

"Then 'tis easier for me, I guess. I believe that fate and luck cut down King Harold. The duke had luck with him, not God. Many coincidences fell his way, and he was smart enough to use them all to his advantage."

"I remember the day that the hairy star appeared. 'Twas Easter week. We had feasted overmuch in the village. Some of the young men had gone with the thane—with my father—to watch the coast. I was in the wood that first night. The oak trees had begun to bud with new leaves. I had climbed upon a birch, for they were already a beautiful, vibrant green."

"I was on the beach at Thorney Island, with your father. The comet appeared like a ball of fire with the devil's tail. We all waited for it to touch upon the earth and burn us."

"We huddled in Maude's hut, certain that we would be cinders at any moment."

"And then, as the hairy ball went away, Tostig, Harold's jealous brother, tried unsuccessfully to take England for his own." Cedric sighed. "They sent him running with his tail between his legs to the Scots."

In places where the trees were not so thick, the wood, except for the evergreens, was bare in its wintry beauty, the ground covered with a carpet of snow. Tree limbs reached out like skeletal fingers, crystals sculpted by a gifted artisan.

A large sliver of ice fell. " 'Tis too warm now. Mayhaps I should go back, before I am injured."

"Brent expects to speak with you."

"I have a yuletide gift for him."

As Morgana sent Cedric to the men to leave one basket filled with evergreens and holly, Brent walked toward her and took the other to fill it.

"Inside is a fine cloak that Mother wove for you. I noticed when we last met that your other was tattered." She removed it carefully from the basket, let it fall to the ground, then pushed it under a bush. " 'Tis of a thicker wool, and edged in squirrel."

He mumbled a thank you and took a fit of coughing.

"You are ill? Why did you not send word? Are you being tended?" For the first time she noticed that the circles under his eyes were not from carefully applied ash, but were real.

"Aye! Your friends, Maude and Alyson, take good care of me." He coughed again, and it took longer to control this time. "Alyson tells me all about your life. Is it very difficult for you?"

"I do what I must."

"It pains me to think of you lying with him. It rankles me all the time—"

"I made my own decision. I chose to spy for you, and you must admit, it has been a fruitful association. How are the horses?"

For the first time, he grinned. "They do well. You *are* indispensable." He hesitated, his eyes coming up to study her face. He regarded her for a moment. "Why have you not told me of your trip to London?"

She stared wordlessly across at him, her heart pounding. "I have my reasons, Brent."

He nodded doubtfully, his jaw set, his eyes slightly narrowed. "You do not trust me, do you?"

" 'Tis not that—"

"I made a promise to you," he interrupted her vehemently. "My word is my bond. I gave my word that I would not attack before spring, after I have arranged safe passage from the country for you and Mother."

They discussed the matter in great detail in hushed, accusatory tones, and he once again assured her that, should she keep secrets from him, she would risk compromising their relationship.

"Go, now, before they wonder." He glanced at the mantle hidden under the bush. "Tell Mother that 'tis exquisite work, and I thank her for it. It shall keep me warm over these chill winter nights." She turned to go, but he stopped her. "Morgana. Keep your ears open, especially around William. Take a measure of the man. We must know our enemy." Brent looked in the distance at a rising cloud of dust. "Horses. Soldiers. Someone approaches. Quickly! You must go."

Morgana returned to where Blaise's men stood and handed them the other basket just as D'Arcy rode up with a small complement of men.

"I thought you were restricted to the hall, my lady." His eyes quickly brushed over her, but spent an inordinate amount of time on Brent. "Who is that fellow? He looks familiar."

"Just a shepherd. A sad man, bent and deformed."

D'Arcy appeared to be weighing her answer. "Did you enjoy your outing?"

"Very much."

"You did not gather much holly."

"The trees are covered with falling icicles, and I decided not to risk injury."

"By all means," he agreed, "you must protect yourself and the little mite." D'Arcy observed that Brent had shuffled off into the wood. "Are you not concerned that Blaise will accuse you of meeting your lover again?"

"I have no lover. Besides, if he is jealous of an old man and a hunchbacked shepherd, he deserves his fears."

" 'Tis curious, but that shepherd has the same coloring as the man I saw you with the last time."

"You are becoming a boor, sir knight," she responded nonchalantly.

"Should I remark on the resemblance to Sir Blaise?"

"I do not give a bloody damn what you do. Your saying does not make it so." She made to walk around his horse, but he cut her off. "I care not what you tell him, Lord D'Arcy. Now, move your horse out of the way, so that I may return to the hall. My feet are wet, and frozen solid, and if I do not reach the fire soon, they will fall off from frostbite."

He swooped down and, in one quick motion, gathered and lifted her up into his arms to place her onto the saddle in front of him.

"I would not want that to happen." There was a maddening hint of arrogance about him that burned her.

"Please let me down. I prefer to ride my own horse."

The contempt in her tone sparked his anger, but there was a lethal calmness in his eyes as he urged his destrier toward the hall. One arm stole lightly around her waist, and she was shocked by the impact of his gentle grip. He sat so close to her that heat emanated from his body. His breath on her neck chilled her, and she inhaled sharply at the contact of his thigh against her leg.

"Are you comfortable?" he inquired.

"More comfortable than the poor wretches in those huts. They have lost husbands, fathers, and sons—there is no one to protect them, to gather food, to chop wood for them."

"If you seek to prey upon my guilt, demoiselle, do not bother. I have no guilt. The English pigs may freeze, for all I care." She tensed. "They raised arms against William. Your whole country has suffered much for its stupidity."

" 'Tis because of this attitude that you are underlord to Blaise, instead of ruler of your own fief. He understands the value of a pair of hands tending the fields, while you would cut the hands off."

D'Arcy's men snickered as he halted outside the gate and removed his helmet. His brows drew together in an angry frown, as if he wanted to beat her, and yet there was something else in his face, a look of anticipated triumph, as if he had decided he would have her, and it would be only a matter of time.

And he had decided this, and more. As he rode into Retford, he forced a lighthearted smile, as if all were right with the world, and he was in the company of his ladylove. But deep within, he vowed that he would win her from Blaise, by fair or foul means. Then he would humble her at his leisure, take her down from her proud and haughty stance to her proper level. He would show her what it meant to be a conquered race. She had certainly not learned it gracing Blaise's bed, for she continued to rule the household, continued to act the lady of the manor.

Yes, he would grind her into the ground under his heel,

and when he was done, she would not be fit as bone meal for a dog.

As they rode through the gate, Blaise watched her from the entranceway of the great hall. D'Arcy—with Kirsten? D'Arcy's hand around her waist?

His heart hammered in his chest as he noted D'Arcy's thigh rubbing hers.

"Get her down," he muttered tersely to his retainer, who went to greet her.

D'Arcy lifted her from the saddle and laid her gently into his arms.

The men carrying evergreens followed her into the hall. Inside, she was drawn immediately to the blazing bonfire whose flames licked high, almost to the blackened rafters. Blaise drew D'Arcy aside. "Why do you hover over my woman?"

"She was chilled. I thought to return her before she took ill." A perfectly reasonable explanation, Blaise knew, but D'Arcy was not a reasonable man. "Besides," he continued, "I thought to bring her back before she escaped with that fellow of hers."

"What fellow?"

"She thought to trick me. They are clever, those two, but I recognized him. Pretending to be a hunchbacked shepherd—'twas almost humorous."

Blaise clenched and unclenched his fists, suppressing the desire to thrash D'Arcy soundly for his insinuations. And yet—she *was* capable of such treachery. He knew that much about her.

As Morgana supervised the placement of the greenery, she kept one eye on Blaise and D'Arcy as they talked intensely in a corner near the stair. Suddenly Blaise shrugged and strode to the dais. The hall was dark in the firelight, for the torches had not yet been lit. In the shadows, Blaise lifted a drinking horn to his lips, his eyes over its rim regarding her in a speculative gaze.

"Come!" he motioned to Morgana. "Join me."

She removed her cloak and hung it on a post. "Did I not find some lovely holly?" she asked.

"Where have you been?" His face was an enigmatic mask.

"Why—to the wood, to gather evergreens. You yourself gave me permission."

"I shall ask only once more. Where have you been?"

"My lord, you said—"

"Did I say that you could meet your lover?" He grasped her wrist and drew her closer to him. "Did you tell him of his child?"

She ripped her hand away from his grasp and slapped him. Then, in horror at her action, she fled to her chamber to fling herself upon her bed. When he spoke so viciously, she wondered how she could have ever thought he might possibly care for her. Her tears turned into loud sobs as she rolled herself into a ball. There was a heavy feeling in the pit of her stomach. "Poor child! Not only a bastard, but fathered by an unfeeling brute." She rocked back and forth, until merciful sleep claimed her.

She awoke to a darkened bedchamber, except for the fire. She lay naked beneath the pelts. Someone had undressed her with such a gentle hand that she had never awakened. Then, as a strong, muscled arm stole over her waist from beside her, she bolted upright in the bed.

"Lie down, dearling," he murmured soothingly. "Rest."

"I thought that we were to leave this night for London?"

His body tensed. "Is that what you told your lover? Does he wait to ambush us on the road?"

"You are insane! I could not kill the father of my child, enemy or not."

"I would be comforted, were I the father. Remember, they are your people, Kirsten, not mine. They would never hurt you, but would not think twice of murdering me."

"They would not exactly reward me for being a Norman's whore. But not to worry. No one will bother us on the road. I would not put my child's life in danger."

There was a long silence.

"So he has assured your safety. D'Arcy told me of your meeting. Every step you take, you are watched, you know. Your lover's disguise was original, but useless."

"D'Arcy lies," she responded matter-of-factly. "Why,

when you have no use for the man, does he suddenly speak the truth where I am concerned?"

"I know the signs of infidelity when I see them—the whisperings, the secret trysts, the silent smiles—"

"There are no marriage bonds between us. Should I have another lover, 'twould not be infidelity."

He raised on his elbow, his brow arching in a scowl. "You forget our vows? You forget the words we spoke—the joining of our hands?" His fingers slowly curled into her hair. "The Church could not bind you any closer to me, Kirsten."

"I would never marry you in the Church," she said with conviction.

"You would do anything that I ordered you to do," he challenged.

"Not anything, my lord. You forced one vow from my lips, but you would never be able to force the marriage vow in front of a priest."

"You would jump at the chance to bind my hands in God's house."

"You dream, Norman. I would be wife to *anyone else* but you."

"Be thankful, love, that you are mine, or you might be in the wood right now, freezing and scraping for food. They *are* starving—your people. When they should have tended their fields, they were traipsing across England doing false Harold's bidding. Now they pay for their shortsighted behavior."

"Why do you tell me of this suffering when you know that I can do nothing?" she asked in a choked voice. "Do you not realize that each time I think of these things, I draw farther away from you? You are a stranger to me, a lover who can never be my love."

"And what would you do instead? Kill me? Go ahead!" He ripped his dagger from its sheath and forced it into her hand. "Slit my throat, and I am replaced on the morrow, with someone less willing to feed your starving poor. My knights, fierce fighters, are reduced to foraging for deer in the forests while the rest of William's forces plunder and rape your country. My men chafe at the bit. They would prefer gleaning the countryside and filling their pockets with your Saxon gold to sitting around here.''

"You have already sent most of our goods of any worth to fill William's coffers."

"And I have left much in your mother's possession. Ask her. Do you think me a fool? I know that she has hidden her jewels. I know that there is much more than the few meager pieces she has offered me. Have I pressed her for them?"

"Why do you tell me this now? Do you hope to gain favor with me, merely because you have shown a modicum of human kindness? Can any conqueror be kind? You kill our sons and brothers, and take our daughters to warm your beds."

She turned away, but he placed a restraining hand on her forearm. He cupped her chin and searched her upturned face. "What are you saying?"

She leaned into him, her face tilting toward him. "If you would win my favor—release me."

He let out a long, audible breath and shook his head in the negative. "I am bewitched by you," he whispered, his low voice edged with passion, laced with fire. "I would give you anything if you would come willingly to me—in love. I would give you jewels—and fine silks to wrap around your breasts." His fingers grazed against her, but she tried to move away from him to the edge of the bed.

"I want only my freedom."

"You know that is the one thing that I cannot give you. 'Tis not mine to give."

" 'Tis not? Is there another who forces you to bed me? Nay, my lord, 'tis your decision alone. Let me move back into my own bedchamber, with my mother. Let me come to you of my own accord, if I wish it, and if not—''

" 'Twould take so little to make you happy?''

" 'Twould be a start." He mulled it over. "Can I not carry my child in peace for the rest of my time?''

Unspoken pain was alive, glowing in his eyes in the firelight for a brief moment. "I wish I could do what you ask, but I cannot." His lips brushed her brow. "Desire for you boils through me. I am obsessed with you." He eased her down gently, his eyes compelling her to submit to him. "I do not know how to stop what I am feeling. I have tried, Kirsten," he said in a harsh, raw voice. "Believe me, I have. I have promised myself that I would cleanse you from my blood, but when I see you, or merely think of you, my whole being fills with a need that can only be quenched in your arms."

She swore that she would not respond as he covered her body with his own. Yet as his hand seared a path up her thigh and across her abdomen, and his fingers searched for those places which aroused her to exquisite pleasure, she knew that she would not be able to fight him.

There was something greater than either of them, that drew her to him. It was a hunger—a need that refused to be foresworn. It gnawed at her each moment that she was away from him. It haunted her thoughts, her dreams, her very existence. Stronger than obsession—much stronger. Escape him—possibly. Escape herself—never.

As their legs intertwined and she welcomed him into her body, she knew that she would soon succumb to that melting feeling, until he erased all conscious thought by the force of his manhood deep within her. It did not matter that these feelings were so much more than desire, so intense that she could not hope to control the outcry of her passion and delight, nor her pleasure when his answering growl freed her to experience a sunburst of sensations.

It only mattered that he had proven to her that, beyond physical desire, he had laid claim to her very soul.

Chapter 9

While William, Duke of Normandy, waited in his camp outside London, a large complement of his men built a fortress in the city. Here William would prepare for his coronation, but only when he had been assured that the city was secure. He had not come this far to be assassinated.

London seethed with unrest. Though the witan, the Anglo-Saxon elders of the country, in keeping with William's design, had begged the duke to accept the crown, there were still dangerous Englishmen who would try to wrest that power from him with force of arms and stealth.

Blaise and D'Arcy left for London at dawn. Though Morgana knew that traveling, pregnant, at this time of year would be difficult, she summoned all her strength for the journey.

"Do you think she should ride such a distance in her condition?" D'Arcy asked the first day.

"The girl is strong," Blaise retorted.

"But she might lose the child."

"Methinks you worry overmuch about *my lady,* sir knight. Several times this day you have ridden the length of the garrison to inquire of her health."

"Well, someone must inquire, since you do not care."

"Aye, I care enough to warn you not to dally with my— leman. 'Tis not her health you should be worried about, but your own."

D'Arcy spurred his horse onward. Blaise resented this situation that William had passed off onto him. D'Arcy was a thorn in his side, and always would be. There was unfinished business between them, and to join them at the hip as William had done was to invite dissension.

Blaise reined his horse in and fell back until Morgana rode up next to him. "Why do you dally with that man?" he asked, shooting her a penetrating look.

"What man?"

"D'Arcy."

"Dally? I am indifferent where that man is concerned."

" 'Tis not the gossip that comes to my ears," he insisted, his impatience growing. "They say you are attracted to him."

"*They* say. Who are 'they'?"

"Why do you always avoid answering a question by asking one?"

"I am not attracted to him. Could I be attracted to the man who raped and murdered my brother's betrothed?"

"How do you know about that?"

"Gossips will talk. 'They' told me."

" 'Twas not among my men you heard this—so where? I have forbade anyone to speak of the ill deeds done at Hartley."

"Many from Hartley live in our village now, my lord," she replied casually.

"When we return, you will point out this person to me."

"Why? So you can have him beaten?"

He stiffened as though she had struck him. "Though I *threatened* to beat you, when have I ever had anyone beaten? Have I ever been other than just? Have I treated these people with less than the utmost consideration?"

"Why do you want to know?"

"Because I suspect that your lover in the wood has filled you with these horrors."

"These nightmares really happened."

"So! You do not deny it." His lips thinned with anger as he urged his horse forward to the front of the line.

When the caravan pulled to the side of the road, the men pitched a sleeping tent for Blaise and Morgana. She sat on a boulder as D'Arcy pressed a cool, damp cloth to her forehead and neck, all the time whispering soothing endearments.

"I can take over now, if you do not mind," Blaise said.

"Not at all." D'Arcy handed him the cloth and went to seek out a horn of ale.

"Where is your mother?" he asked casually.

"Resting."

"This job is more properly done by her, or Elvina, or even me. I do not want that man to touch you again. Do you understand?"

Morgana nodded and snapped the cloth from him. "I can do it myself, thank you."

Inside the tent, Blaise spread three thick wolf pelts on the ground. "Come, little wildcat. You shall be comfortable on these." Morgana lay down, and Blaise lay next to her, fully clothed in his chain mail, with only the helmet and gauntlets removed. "I do not like this, Kirsten, exposing you to danger this way." She moaned slightly as she adjusted her position. "What is wrong?"

"My back aches. Little twinges down across here, and here." She pointed out the sensitive areas.

" 'Tis the babe." He went to his saddle, and returned with a jar of herbal liniment. "Your mother said that there would be some discomfort, and gave me this jar of olbas oil." He pressed her over. "Lie upon your side, and I shall rub it in."

Through his careful ministrations, her body relaxed. She curled into him, and his arm stole around her in a protective motion.

"You are very quiet, my lord."

"I am wondering if 'tis truly my babe."

She sighed. "I am weary of this subject."

"If I could just be sure, then—"

"Then what? Would all be put to rights? Would you wed me in a church to assure legitimacy for your bastard?"

The silence was thicker than castle walls. "We can never marry, Kirsten."

Morgana bit her lip as she lay still for fear that the pain

would burst forth in uncontrolled sobs. She steeled her heart, and found her voice.

"Marry? You presume too much if you think that I would ever marry you, or any other Norman, for that matter."

"You would have your child born a bastard by choice?"

"Bastardy means naught to me," she lied, remembering how painful it had been, growing up thinking herself a bastard.

"In Normandy, it means quite a bit."

"It could not mean much. William soon ascends to the throne of England."

"I will repeat again, my love. Never mention William's bastardy in London. He is most thin-skinned on the subject."

A pall fell over the conversation, until he turned her onto her back. His voice was thick with tension and unspoken meaning. In the pitch black of the tent, she could sense his eyes piercing into her. "If I knew that this was my child, I think that I would be well pleased."

She could no longer control the tears that streamed down her cheeks, falling into her ears, and chilling her. She shivered, and he misunderstood her reaction. "Do not be frightened, Kirsten. I have had time to think on this. If you tell the truth, I promise that I will not hurt you."

"My lord," she began, barely suppressing the sobs, "who was she who played you so false that you prefer to see a lie in all that I say, rather than accept the truth?"

His breath, indrawn, was caught and stifled into silence. Instead of answering her, he sought her lips and kissed the salt tears away in gentle nibbles.

"I have done everything I could to avoid these feelings, but I know now that the battle is impossible. I—am fond of you, Kirsten."

"Do not say these words that you do not mean."

"I would not say it if 'twere not so. Something in you has touched me. I care for you deeply. I shall always take care of you and the child, even though 'tis not my child."

"I do not wish to be taken care of. Will you never understand that?"

"What do you wish, my little shrew?"

"Shrew?"

"Aye! You seek to wear me down like a shrewish wife with one or two utterances a minute from your vinegar tongue."

" 'Tis your own guilt that wears you down."

"What do you want from me?"

"I have never asked anything of you. I—I truly want only one thing."

"Do you want me to love you?"

"Nay. If you should love me, and I you, we would surely meet with unrelenting pain and disaster. We both know that it can never be. You are a Norman, and your murderers have degraded and devastated my country. I am but a mere Saxon maid. I cannot fight you, nor have I tried. You and I both know that we are victims of our lust for each other. Let us not play the fool and think that it could ever be more than this between us."

"Your lips say one thing, but I think you have something else in mind. Is it your mother's plan to dangle you in front of me—make me think that you do not want me so that I will want you?"

"My mother's only plan is to survive."

His voice turned deadly serious. "I would marry you if I could, Kirsten."

"Again you speak of marriage? I have told you that I do not wish—"

"We are handfasted, Kirsten. You would speak the vows in church tomorrow if I commanded you to do so."

"I would not," she replied quietly as she turned back onto her side. No matter what, she would never speak words of love to him, never admit that she might, under the right circumstances, accept him as her husband. She would never admit this because it could never be.

Morgana rested fitfully in his arms, waking several times throughout the night. Each time he pulled her close and gentled her. As she drifted back to sleep, safe in his arms, she wondered if fate always played such evil tricks on its unsuspecting victims.

Blaise left Morgana and Father Jerome to rest at an abbey on the outskirts of London while he finalized arrangements for their stay. A virtual multitude pressed toward the city, some invited, some not, all curious to see this man who had subjugated England by sword and fire.

The muddy, rutted roads lengthened the travel, and Morgana, in her condition, was not feeling very well at all on this, the last day of their long, arduous journey.

"I shall not move one step from this chamber," she informed Blaise when he came for her. "I am tired—and I ache, and my body knows the dip of every rut in every road between here and Retford."

"We must go. William has arranged a bedchamber for you at the home of a rich Norman merchant. He has asked for you, and plans to meet you there this eventide."

"I cannot. Truly I cannot move one more step without rest in a proper bed. Even these hard pallets are preferable to that rocking motion. And I have been in this clothing so long, it smells of walking death."

"I will strike a deal with you, my love. You will eat a good meal. Bathe. Rest a few hours. I will leave your mother with you—"

"And Elvina?"

"And Elvina," he agreed. "And then, tonight, I will take you to see William."

"In a litter?"

"Have mercy, demoiselle. 'Twill take us all year to reach William by foot."

"I refuse to ride. I cannot ride."

"You will ride with me, in my lap. I will hold you as tenderly as a newborn calf."

She thought about it. "And my mother?"

"Kirsten! I cannot carry both of you." He considered other solutions. "Mayhaps Sigvald—"

"I will ride, my lord," Astrid interrupted. "These bones may be getting old, but they are still strong."

"You see." He smiled as if dealing with a simple-minded child. "All has worked out for the best."

"You shall be in full battle armor tonight?"

His smile faded. "Of course. Under the circumstances, I think it wise. I did not come this far to be cut down outside the West Minster."

"In that case, I will ride by myself."

He gaped at her, baffled by this quick and circular turn.

" 'Tis the babe, my lord,'' Astrid explained as she ushered him toward the door. "It makes her confused. She must needs rest."

"Wait!" Morgana called. "I have sewn a new tunic for you—with your colors—and a cover for Reynard."

Blaise fingered the white and gold material. "I recognize this. 'Tis the silk I gave you to make a gown for the coronation."

"I had some left over." Her face beamed. "Mother helped me. I am not very good at needlework."

"Are you admitting that there is *something* you do not do well?" he teased. "Nay! You are too modest. 'Tis beautiful work. I am well pleased. And my horse shall be the most finely caparisoned animal at the coronation."

Morgana's mood suddenly uplifted.

The Norman merchant, Rainolf, was actually an Italian with a strange accent that Morgana found difficult to follow. He was short, like Sir Guy de Boulogne, but his hair was longer and styled like a Saxon, and his face was hidden behind a full, thick beard and mustache.

Morgana and Astrid were settled together in a bedchamber across the hall from D'Arcy. Blaise, who slept in a different section of the house, paid a brief visit.

"I see that they have taken care to build a fire. Do you need anything?" he asked as he walked to the hearth.

"I have all that I need."

"Good! Good!" Silence hung between them like a sword. He seemed preoccupied, and she wanted to ask if something was the matter, but she kept her counsel. He would tell her in his own time.

"Did you rest?" he inquired.

"Nay! But I feel less weary. Mayhaps the excitement of meeting William tonight?"

"Mayhaps." He opened his lips as if to say something more, but stopped. Another long pause turned into minutes wasted.

"Did you wish to speak with me about something, my lord?"

When he drew her to him, his fingers gripped her upper arm until she cried out in pain. He acted strangely, and she sensed that the demons of hell stood at his back, ready to separate them. "I want you to remember tonight that I have tried not to love you and failed miserably."

She pressed his chest so that she could see his face, so distressed as he regarded her. "What is wrong? Why do you tell me this now?"

More pain was etched in his golden eyes. "No reason. I— Do you love me even a little?"

"Mayhaps a little," she admitted. " 'Twould be most difficult to feel naught for a man who beds you with such passion," she quickly explained. "I am not a whore, even though you have tried to make me so."

"You are no whore because you enjoy caresses without benefit of marriage." He lifted her and crushed her against him. "You are the wife of my heart, Kirsten. I will never let anyone separate us. Never!"

She wanted to ask why he did not make her his wife in deed, as much as in word, but she could not debase herself. If he loved her, he would marry her, once he was secure about the child, and her—love. My God! Did she love him?

"Something is wrong. I feel it. What is it? What was your purpose in coming here, my lord?"

"No more 'my lord' between us. I want to hear my name on your lips." He drew her into a crushing, bruising kiss that spoke not only of his need, but of a desperation akin to violence.

"You frighten me!" She shivered as a shaft of fear traveled the length of her spine. "What is it?"

He merely shook his head and left her.

D'Arcy came to escort her and her mother to dinner.

"Where is my lord Blaise?"

"I am to escort you this eve, demoiselle," he replied with an unusual glitter in his ice blue eyes. "If you are ready." He motioned toward the archway, and she preceded him.

As Morgana walked alongside him to the dining hall, she tried to quell her confusion. If Blaise did not want D'Arcy near her, why was he now her escort?

Mayhaps it was because of propriety's sake? Yet the more she thought about it, the more it rankled her. How could he speak of her as the wife of his heart, and then allow another to escort her to dinner—a man whom he hated?

"I feel like a victim being led to the block."

"Do you indeed? How perceptive you are for a Saxon."

Morgana nearly tripped, certain now that something was afoot, but she recovered quickly and walked straight, her chin lifted with dignity. "I did not think that Saxons were particularly lacking in intelligence, my lord D'Arcy."

"They are like little children, demoiselle, easily led and more easily deceived."

Morgana stopped midstep. "You have something at the back of your tongue. Mayhaps you would feel better if you allowed it to roll out."

" 'Tis not for me to say, demoiselle. I would advise only that you keep your head held high and your tongue in check this night."

"Come, Kirsten," her mother said as she took her forearm. " 'Tis not the time to be wasting words on a fool."

D'Arcy's humorless laughter followed her down the hall, until he sprinted to catch up to her.

"We shall see who is the fool."

It was not long before Morgana understood the true meaning of D'Arcy's cryptic words.

The hall was gaily decorated with evergreens and holly strung across the walls. Morgana noticed that there was no mistletoe, as there would be in Maude's hut. Mistletoe was a favored plant of the Druids, who burned it as a sacrifice to the Gods. The Church forbade its use, for through the ages it had also been associated with Roman and Viking fertility rituals. These Normans would never have mistletoe.

At the archway of the great hall, D'Arcy drew Morgana closer, winding his arm in hers, as if they were together. When she made to pull away, he whispered to her, "Stay, lest you put your life in peril, demoiselle." She was confused, but heeded his words. As they entered, Morgana quickly searched the hall for Blaise, and saw him upon the dais, a few seats from William.

How would he react to this open assault by D'Arcy? she wondered. She thought that she saw a momentary flame of anger burning brightly in his eyes, but then a mask fell over his face, and he turned to talk to a knight seated next to him as if nothing were amiss.

D'Arcy moved her to sit diagonally across from Blaise. "My liege—" he bowed to William "—my lords, I beg your forgiveness. The Saxon maid sleeps overmuch these days, with the babe in her belly."

Heat rose from Morgana's neck and flushed her cheeks. She was discomfited, but Blaise said nothing as the guests made ribald jests that told her they believed her D'Arcy's woman. Why would Blaise let her be subjected to such abuse?

D'Arcy filled her cup most solicitously and introduced her to all around them. Morgana wondered at the game D'Arcy played so viciously. "And, of course, you know *mon seigneur,* Blaise, Vicomte de Rouen—" she nodded to Blaise, her lips poised to speak, "—and Lady Gisele, his *wife.*"

Morgana for the first time noticed the woman who sat next to Blaise whose hand stole over his forearm in unmistakable possession. The blood drained from her face, and she clutched the edge of the table to keep from swooning. D'Arcy *had* said wife. But Blaise had claimed that she was dead. Yet no words of denial passed his lips, and she could not escape the import of his silence. This was Blaise's wife, alive and breathing, and Morgana truly *was* nothing better than his whore.

It was now quite clear why he could never marry her—why there was torture in his eyes each time he mentioned marriage. She had been an amusement, easily won, easily taken. Gravitating between hurt and anger, she needed an explanation, and D'Arcy was quite willing to give it to her.

"You are shocked, demoiselle. He never mentioned that he had a wife—did he? I knew, of course, but he swore me to secrecy, and 'twas not worth losing my life over. I could say naught to you without breaking my oath."

Morgana's pain was boundless, and despite Astrid's suggestion that she be silent, she sought some explanation from D'Arcy. "What happens now, my lord D'Arcy? Who do I go to now that my lord Blaise has his wife to warm his bed?"

"Me—I hope. Although the child—"

"Blaise's child."

He trailed a hand across the silken smoothness of her shoulder. "I believe you, demoiselle." He brought her hand to his lips. "All one need do is look into your eyes to know that 'tis so."

"Aye! A fact of which I am most certain."

D'Arcy poured her a measure of wine. "Drink, demoiselle. Forget him tonight. Forget that he presented himself as a man of honor. He has no honor where women are concerned."

"Take heed, child," Astrid warned, but to no avail as Morgana took large gulps of the beverage, caring naught about the consequences.

Gisele's eyes followed her for half the night. She sensed the scrutiny and wondered if the woman knew about her. Morgana likewise studied the woman. Chestnut brown hair framed a heart-shaped face, and dark, inviting, almond-shaped eyes completed the picture. She laughed easily, her voice deep and throaty. Morgana had to physically restrain herself from scratching the woman's eyes out.

D'Arcy ripped a leg of roast fowl and placed it upon her trencher. "Eat. You must be starving."

Morgana glanced around the hall. "I cannot eat of such plenty when my people starve in their huts. 'Tis not right that Norman tables overflow while my people die."

"Your words are prideful and arrogant, but remember that you bear a child. If not for yourself, then surely for the babe—eat."

Morgana ate reluctantly, taking meager portions, and concentrating on Duke William, soon to be her king. She had caught bits and snatches of the conversation, and knew him to be clever—witty. He was of medium height with dark hair and a firm chin, and eyes that saw beyond the obvious.

For the most part, she avoided Blaise and his lady. During the few glimpses she stole, she noted that he drank overmuch, his fingers gripping the goblet so intensely that she thought he would crush the silver. She was well pleased.

Gisele, Vicomtesse de Rouen, scrutinized the Saxon girl. Christian had told her about Blaise's whore. A mere girl was not capable of stealing Blaise from her, although she could see what had attracted him to the chit. She *did* have beautiful hair, and a certain voluptuousness that would appeal to a man who had spent many a year among monks. Starved for passion, he had been easy prey to the first maid to raise her skirts.

There would no longer be need for this Kirsten of Retford, Gisele assured herself. Through Duchess Matilda's intercession, she had been released from the nunnery. She had braved the Channel in winter to be with her husband and make amends for her adultery. Having had many years to ponder her stupidity, Gisele was confident that she could now be a good and faithful wife to Blaise. He had once unsuccessfully sought a dissolution of their vows, claiming that he would never again be husband to her, but the pope had turned his suit away. Divorce would mean excommunication, for by the precepts of the Church, they were bound forever.

She had not understood the importance of discretion. She had wanted to hurt Blaise, to strike at him for his indifference. Even if her marriage had been a meeting of fortunes, there was no reason why he could not love her. It had angered her that he had never really tried.

Of course, he had told her that he loved her, but she had never believed him. He was away on endless jaunts for the duke. If he loved her, he would have tried to stay home more often. Had he really expected her to await his return whenever he chose to grace her with his presence?

So she had taken Christian to her bed. He was a most inventive lover who kept her from boredom by introducing her to the pleasure of pain. In his arms she had reached new and dizzying heights of ecstasy.

Blaise had found out, and sent her away. Thank God her cousin, a lady-in-waiting to Duchess Matilda, had pled her cause.

And Blaise's fortunes were bright, for not only did he have the lands in Rouen, but tonight, before dinner, William had assured him that upon his coronation, Blaise would receive the charter to Retford and Hartley. She must remain his wife.

And that would mean forever, till death do they part.

Morgana, wearied by the tension of the night, left the

dinner table early. D'Arcy accompanied her and Astrid back to her bedchamber. Astrid, after helping Morgana undress, went to the kitchen to steep some herbs to settle the girl down.

Morgana sat by the window, watching the courtyard with unseeing eyes. Although she had told herself that she would never have married Blaise, somewhere in the back of her mind she had secretly wanted to wed him. Now, when it could never be, she could admit that to herself.

Could God have really planned this for her—to be trifled with, a mere plaything for an invader who would take her by force should she say him nay?

But she had never said "nay" to Blaise. She had fallen in love with him from the first moment—as if the matter were predestined . . . beyond them. She had been drawn to him like a moth to the flame, and her wings had been duly singed, until she wondered whether she would ever fly again. She had lost her heart, for all her cool words, to an uncaring lout who had taken her to his bed repeatedly, knowing full well that their relationship could never be legitimized. He had taken no care to protect her, though she had never been, could never be, more than his whore.

Her heart throbbed dully at the sting of her thoughts. She could have loved him. She would have protected him from her people, her own brother, who sought to kill him. When Brent found out how falsely Blaise had played her, there would be no hope of staying his hand. He would surely murder the Norman now.

She would have gone anywhere with him—even to Normandy after the rebels reclaimed England.

"Ninny!" she chided herself. "To be gulled so easily. All he had to do was thrust between your legs, and your good sense flew upon the wind. How could you be so foolish, to give your love to an unscrupulous murderer?"

She sat by the window, tears flowing freely onto her white and gold shift. It had been much easier being the granddaughter of a midwife, a child of the forest picking herbs and berries for Maude and Alyson. If only she had never known her true heritage, she would have never met that vile, evil, faithless bastard.

After a time, Morgana lay down to rest, but her sleep

was so fitful and disturbed that Astrid soon realized that she was slightly feverish. She sat at Morgana's bedside, mopping her brow, as the hours turned into a day.

Morgana was still too weak to attend William's coronation, but Astrid retold the events in detail.

" 'Twas like an armed camp—the abbey church. At the conclusion of his crowning, the Normans inside raised such a hue and cry that the soldiers outside believed them to be under attack. Some stupid bastard gave the order to burn the houses, and all houses around the church were quickly put to the torch. 'Twas a fit coronation for a murderer. I was not . . ." Astrid's voice trailed off.

Morgana sensed that he had come, and the hair on the back of her neck prickled. "What are you doing here?" she asked calmly. "Finished with your wife, and ready for your mistress?"

"Such statements are beneath you," he whispered.

"Are they?" She turned away from him. "I am weary, my lord. By your leave, I wish to sleep."

"Leave us," he ordered Astrid. He barred the door behind her and traversed the bedchamber, but as he drew nearer, Morgana crossed to the other side. "We must talk," he insisted.

"There is naught to speak of. Is it *speaking* that you have on your mind, or are you looking for a quick tumble?"

"I know that you are hurt. I meant to tell you—"

"There is no need to explain. Your are your own man, *mon seigneur,* Vicomte de Rouen, Lord of Retford and Hartley." Her words were chips of ice, the dullness in her voice echoing her pain, draining him as it did her.

"I want to explain—"

"Nay! I want no explanations. I will not listen!" She covered her ears and clenched her eyes tightly shut, but he loosed her hands.

"You must listen. You must understand."

"Take your hands from me!" She slapped him away, pounding upon his chest, and pushing him from her. He drew her into his embrace, heedless of her many cuffs, and lifted her easily to lay her upon the bed. "Loose me, my lord, or I shall scream the walls down."

"Be silent, you little fool! I shall not harm you. I merely want to talk to you—to explain."

"Ah! Is the Lady Gisele indisposed? Mayhaps with an aching head? Will you take a moment to lay your Saxon wench?"

"Do not do this to yourself and to me. Do not malign yourself so. I love you, Kirsten. You are the only true wife of my heart." The intensity of his words, combined with his gaze, took her off guard for a moment. She tried to speak, but no words came, for deep within her was a pain sharper than she imagined the stabbing of a dagger would be.

"Take pity on me," she begged through tear-filmed eyes and quivering lips. "Loose me."

"Nay, I shall never loose you. Can you not fathom the depths of our love? Can you not understand that you are mine? You tell me on the one hand that my babe grows within you, and on the other hand, ask that I would free you?" He put his palm over her belly in open possession.

Under other circumstances, this most tender and loving moment would have pleased her, for he had almost admitted that he was the father of her child. But now thoughts, edged with unreasoning fear, darted through her consciousness. If the fault was not his, as her belly could attest, then his wife was surely barren. Would he take her child from her to be accorded its proper birthright? Would she give life to her child only to have Blaise and his wife wrest the child from her arms? Was this his plan, now that he had reconciled with Gisele?

" 'Tis not your babe." She barely whispered the lie born of desperation.

"What?" He sat back. "What say you?" There was a most perilous glint in his eye, but she refused to abandon her chosen course. He had taken her love, had taken her very heart. He would *not* take her child.

"I said 'tis not your babe."

He tensed, the muscle in his cheek twitching. She tried to remember a time when he had been this angry, but could not. She feared he would murder her, that his fingers that flexed on each side of her chin would curve around her slim neck and snuff out her life. "You lie," he hissed between clenched teeth.

"Nay," she answered calmly. " 'Tis time for truth telling for both of us."

"Whose then?"

" 'Tis not your concern."

He wrenched her upright to face him. "Who? Your lover in the wood? I shall burn the wood down to find him. I shall kill him, I swear it."

" 'Tis not him." She could ill afford to have Blaise scouring the wood in search of a nonexistent lover, endangering her brother and his men. "He is not of the wood."

"Who then? His fingers left an imprint on her upper arm, and she winced. "Who? D'Arcy?"

She evaded his piercing eyes. He interpreted this motion and her silence as guilt. This was why she had insisted she hated D'Arcy. This was why D'Arcy conceived the story of the man in the wood—to hide his own betrayal. They were lovers. "How could you have bedded with D'Arcy? How could you lie with that knave?"

"Release me. I have admitted nothing."

"You need not say a word. I read you well." His hands clasped her face, drawing her close to him. "And to think that I loved you. I trusted you. I believed that you were mine alone, that we were blessed, that what we had was more than an appetite for each other's bodies. What an oaf I have been! But it makes perfect sense. D'Arcy has always coveted my women. Surely he told you how he seduced my wife. Mayhaps you two have compared bedding tales." As he rose from her, his fingers trailed through her hair.

"How dare you act the injured party. At least D'Arcy has no wife to prevent our marriage."

"Keep away from me, witch," he spat as he raised a restraining hand toward her, "or I swear I shall kill you and your bastard babe. Your lover is not here now to save you from my wrath."

He flung open the door and bolted from the bedchamber. He passed Astrid in the hall, but did not acknowledge her. Instead he propelled himself through D'Arcy's door as if all the devils of hell were at his heels.

Christian D'Arcy lay abed with Elvina as Blaise burst into his chamber.

"Begone!" Blaise swore at the girl through clenched teeth, and the terrified girl plummeted from the bed, snatched up her clothes, and ran from the chamber, stark naked.

" 'Twas quite a lively piece you just chased from here, my lord Blaise. I hope your justification equals the loss."

"Why would you bed that sow with your mistress available across the hall from you?"

"What say you, sir?" D'Arcy sat upright, his amusement fading swiftly.

"Kirsten has admitted all to me. You will not squirm out of these circumstances as easily as you did with Gisele."

"I do not understand—"

"You understand, all right." Blaise flung his clothes at him. "Clothe yourself."

D'Arcy slowly dressed. "Mayhaps you can be more specific in your claims."

"You thought to win at this game again, but I have you in check this time. I will not play the fool as easily as I did when you bedded my wife. I am not that same love-struck lad. I have pondered this matter of you and the bitch, and I know now what you are."

"Where does this talk lead us?"

"To the altar for you."

D'Arcy choked. "The altar? Kirsten and I? 'Tis too absurd for words."

"You will right the wrong this time."

"You think to pawn your whelp off on me, and you talk about righting wrongs."

Blaise's sword was at D'Arcy's throat before he could expel another breath. "You will marry her, or I will cut you to pieces. Is that plain enough for you?"

"Already you have too much control over my life. You will not force me to marry your bitch."

"Finish dressing and we shall see what I can force you to do."

As soon as D'Arcy locked his belt over his waist, he backed away from Blaise and drew his sword from its sheath. Blaise fought with the power of three men, but

D'Arcy had the advantage of a cool head. The clang of metal against metal rang through the halls, yet none dared enter the chamber. Not even the devil himself would get between two such fearsome knights.

Morgana, despite her supposed indifference, cringed at each clang of weapons. If D'Arcy wounded him, or, God forbid, killed him, it would be her fault. She could have avoided all of this if she had told the truth. But she could not tell the truth and risk losing her child.

Her feet moved of their own accord toward D'Arcy's bedchamber. She could see snatches of movement through the crack in the door. The sounds of impending death echoed endlessly, and just as she pressed through the door to halt this barbarity, she was wrenched back and flung aside by the personal guard of the newly crowned King William.

Only William could halt this duel, for the two men were so enraged that only blood would satisfy them. He stationed his men at the door, and locked himself in with the two knights.

"Lower your voices, sirs. You are guests in this house." He saw the sword in D'Arcy's hand. "You would raise arms against your *seigneur?*"

"I started the quarrel, Your Majesty," Blaise admitted.

"Surely there are better ways to deal with disagreements than to draw blood. I need my knights alive, and working their fiefs. Neither of you are of worth to me in the grave."

" 'Tis a matter of honor," Blaise advised the king.

"Honor? Whose?"

"Lady Kirsten of Retford."

"The old king's goddaughter? The young woman that I bid you invite to these festivities?"

"Aye, Your Majesty," D'Arcy said. "I escorted her to dinner last evening."

"A very lovely girl."

"And my lord Blaise's mistress," D'Arcy said.

"My former mistress, sire. The girl now graces Lord D'Arcy's bed, and carries his child."

"Is this true?"

D'Arcy's eyes narrowed. It was on the tip of his tongue to deny Blaise's accusations, but then, when he thought about it, his chest heaved as if it would burst. It was the perfect revenge. He would have Blaise's lover *and* Blaise's child.

"I will not deny it, sire."

At first Blaise wanted to shout his success in unmasking D'Arcy's debauchery, but a pall that approached mourning veiled him, dulling any pleasure that he may have derived from the moment.

"I see how it is now," the king said. "Sheathe your weapons. All will be set to rights."

Morgana fled to her bedchamber on swift feet. What would the king do? William was a man of little patience— a man who wielded power mercilessly. He considered himself a moral man. What would his response be?

Morgana did not have to wait long to find out. Within the quarter hour the king and his interpreter were at her door, insisting that she receive him alone. Astrid, after issuing a warning to Morgana to keep her counsel, waited outside.

Morgana curtsied at his entrance. The king motioned her to the chair by the window, and she sat in stiff discomfort. Although she scorned the king, she was a pragmatic person.

"Arise, demoiselle."

"To what do I owe the honor of this visit, Your Majesty?"

"I am told, Lady Kirsten, that your father was Harold's well-respected thane. Also that you were King Edward's goddaughter." Morgana nodded. "You have been well treated by your new lord, my friend, Blaise?"

"Our village has fared well, by most measures."

"What of you, and your child?"

"Your Majesty?"

"The vicomte has discussed your, ah—condition with me."

She blushed. "My condition?" She would kill that arrogant bastard. It had been ill mannered of D'Arcy to joke about her pregnancy at dinner, but for Blaise to bring her to the king's attention—she would kill him!

"I have spoken to the man involved, and he has agreed that you should not continue in this state much longer."

What exactly was he telling her? What state? It did not

make a bit of sense. "I am sorry, Your Majesty. I do not understand."

"He has agreed to marry you."

"But that is quite impossible."

"He is willing to say the vows. When one is king, girl, nothing is impossible." He motioned toward the doorway with a negligent hand, and the guards brought D'Arcy in, now dressed in the vibrant crimson and purple velvet of his colors.

Morgana could hardly wait for the interpreter to finish before she fainted dead away.

"Quite a response to you," the king noted.

D'Arcy sauntered to where Morgana lay senseless and plucked her from the carpet like the fairest flower in the field. "She is overwhelmed by her good fortune, no doubt."

" 'Tis to your advantage to put the matter to rights. You must learn responsibility for your actions, D'Arcy."

"I am more than willing to do my duty, Your Majesty." His mouth smiled, but in the corner of his right eye there was a slight twitch. Blaise would deeply regret the day he had dared put off his bastard onto him. And the girl was more the fool, for by naming him the father, she had unwittingly played right into his hands. Once she was his, she would pay for her rash behavior, for she would submit, or pay the penalty for her recklessness.

Chapter 10

You cannot say him nay, Morgana. 'Tis by royal decree. If there were any other way—"

Father Jerome, clearly distraught, adjusted his cowl as if it choked him. "Your brother will be furious when he finds out. Blame me, no doubt. He wanted to attack the caravan, but I reminded him of his oath to you, so he stayed his hand. Mayhaps, if he had followed through—"

" 'Tis too late now," Morgana agreed as she twisted her braid into a chignon at her neck. "But I will not yield so easily. Surely the Church will save me from this— Ow! The pin stuck in my head."

"Give it to me," Astrid said as she whipped the hairpin from Morgana's fingers and deftly finished her hair. "You must wear this headdress. The king sent these rosebuds."

"I do not want to wear roses—" she ripped the braid from her neck "—or these pins." She threw the hairpins to the floor.

"They are a gift from your betrothed. You must wear them. Amethysts and rubies. He has insisted."

"I hate them. They chill me almost as much as he does."

"They look lovely. Lord D'Arcy only wants you to look your best on your wedding day."

"I am sick to my stomach," she wailed as she hung out the window and breathed in the cool night air. "How can I be expected to look my best?"

"Come in here!" Astrid exclaimed. "You shall catch your death of cold. Pinch your cheeks. There! At least now you have some color."

"Father Jerome, I cannot be forced to say the vows, can I? The Church would never agree to that."

"No, Morgana, you cannot be forced," the priest admitted, "but think, girl. Once William has set his mind to something, he brooks no refusal. Besides, if you do not marry D'Arcy, Blaise may later lay claim to your child."

"But do I want D'Arcy to have control over me and my child? Do I reject the wolf only to find the jackal at my door?"

"You leave England in the spring, Morgana. D'Arcy will not come after you. Blaise would follow you to the ends of the earth if he knew for certain that it was his child, and he had a legal claim."

"I am so confused." She sat on the edge of the bed.

"If you marry D'Arcy, you will stay at Retford Hall. Lady Gisele will pose no threat to you, for as D'Arcy's wife, she cannot conspire to have you sent away. We need you at Retford, Morgana."

"Now I see your strategy. You have all the arguments at the ready, priest, because you do not want to lose your spy. Do you know what kind of a man he is?"

"Morgana, you are under the king's protection. The king obviously favors you, to have taken such an interest in your well-being, and D'Arcy needs to curry that favor. D'Arcy would not dare harm you."

"As always, your argument is compelling." She mouthed the words merely to comfort Astrid, for in truth Morgana was convinced that this marriage was cursed.

Not so with Christian D'Arcy, for while Morgana bemoaned her fate, he was quite delighted with the turn of events. His wife would be a fitting helpmate, and within the year, if all went as planned, he would be back in the king's good graces. Mayhaps the king would even serve as godfather to the child, as had King Edward to Kirsten.

D'Arcy now had full rein to execute his plot for revenge against Blaise.

Was it only two days ago that the king had betrothed him to the girl? Every moment that he waited to bed her was an eternity. The bedding would finalize matters—consummation of the marriage would make her his forever, or until he tired of her. Mayhaps, at first, he would make an effort to be faithful.

No doubt she was worth it, for there was a fire in her that he had never known in any other woman. Under different circumstances, he could even have loved her, had Gisele not ruined him for love and twisted his devotion into something evil until, in the end, he had hardly recognized himself. He would never love again. What did it matter? Gisele was the past. He would not dwell on her now. Kirsten of Retford was his future.

Morgana was not as encouraged about this forced wedding. She would have been quite happy to remain a maid. Instead she found herself dressed in a wedding gunna and kirtle of crimson and purple silk—a gift from the king himself fashioned in the latest style in her betrothed's colors.

With the hour at hand, and having discussed her plight for hours on end, she suddenly found herself rendered mute—a jangle of nerves. There was no room for fear; she would not falter, for such action would put her family, indeed her entire village, in jeopardy. King William was a man who sought extreme payment for even minor wrongs, real or imagined.

The ceremony was a blur, and directly afterward, Morgana remembered only that a Norman bishop had officiated. She mouthed the words through wooden lips, and stared at the wall with lifeless eyes. Ultimately a manacle—D'Arcy's signet ring—was placed upon her finger.

She was too numb to cry, too numb to perceive anything beyond her overwhelming melancholia. She knew few of the attendants, for they were William's knights and their ladies. It was therefore not expected that she be congenial or expressive.

In the great hall, she and Christian were seated upon the dais to the right of King William, who offered a toast and retired to his chamber.

Caryl Wilson

Blaise, as Christian's overlord and at the king's request, hosted the wedding feast, but nary a word was spoken by him.

Morgana alternated between fatigue from her condition and anxiety that increased as night approached. D'Arcy remarked that she had not touched the paltry portions of food on her trencher, and finally, when nausea welled up in her throat, she welcomed the excuse to leave the table.

"I am unwell, my lord husband." Mayhaps, in deference to her illness, he would leave her alone this night. Mayhaps, but not bloody likely.

"The last few weeks have been burdensome for my wife, with all the excitement of the king's coronation and our trip," D'Arcy announced as he rose and bowed. "We are to our chamber to—rest." He escorted her from the hall amidst lewd teasing and lascivious jests. Blaise glared at her, his eyes mirroring an anguish that tore apart her soul. Why had he let his jealousy steer them along onto this wave of tragedy? she wondered.

D'Arcy was unusually solicitous as he ushered her to his bedchamber. "A stroke of luck—your taking ill. Otherwise, I would have had to devise an excuse." Morgana turned rigid in his arms. "I have no taste for the bedding ritual this night," he explained. "I want no other man to bask in your beauty."

"I really am indisposed, my lord."

"You are a high-strung lass, but I will put you at ease soon enough." His humor and unspoken intent served only to increase her panic.

At the door, he left her in Elvina's care. After the servant girl removed and carefully attended to her clothes, Morgana climbed into a sheer silken shift. Elvina brushed her hair in long strokes as the fearful bride tried to hide her concern.

"It shall not be so bad, my lady. Your husband is a skillful lover, if you do not fight him."

"I know that you have lain with him. Why are *you* sent to assist me?"

"Your mother thought it wise, since I know of what I speak." She hesitated. "If you had any loving feelings for Lord D'Arcy, I would not be here, my lady."

"If I fight him, I risk injury to my child."

" 'Tis not as bad as all that, my lady. He is quite handsome. The king could have married you to some doddering old fool."

"The king has married me to a murderer. Right now I would prefer an old fool, were he gentle. My Lord D'Arcy will expect more from me than I am willing to give. What shall become of me and my babe?"

There was a light knock at the door, and Christian entered unbidden. "My lady is not ready," Elvina said.

He took in Morgana's dishabille. "She is ready enough. Leave us."

The servant girl squeezed and patted her hand, and withdrew. Morgana traversed the chamber to the bed, slipped beneath the fur coverlet, and tugged it to her chin. She affected a proud mien and regarded her husband as he undressed. She would face the devil head-on. Now was not the time for false modesty.

He was lean, where Blaise was broad, yet not so lean as to be thin. Though his bone structure was smaller, his wide shoulders tapered to a tightly muscled waist.

"Explain to me, if you will," he said as he removed his chausses, "why you told Blaise that you carried my child."

"I never told him any such thing," she insisted.

"Aye! He assumed 'twas me, but you could have convinced him otherwise."

Morgana moved closer to the edge as D'Arcy lay next to her, hovering like a hawk.

"I grew weary of trying."

D'Arcy's eyes were opaque with an unreadable emotion. "It *is* his child you carry?"

"Aye, my lord."

"Swear it." A fearful darkness masked his features as he clamped his hand over her shoulder and pressed her into the featherbed. His hand moved her small palm until it rested over her heart. "Swear it upon your babe's immortal soul." As he pinned her to the bed, a fleeting anxiety ripped through her.

"I swear it."

Her lips quavered, and she flinched as he sat back on his haunches, drew down the pelts, and inspected each inch of her. She trembled as D'Arcy's fingers tore her shift. "Do you fear me?" She could not find her voice, so merely nodded. "Never fear me." His lips followed the line of her shoulder down to one swollen, tingling breast. "I could never mar such perfect skin."

The slight pressure of his touch shocked her senses. She pressed his chest to stay him. " 'Tis most strange that we find ourselves wed," she mumbled. "Would you not say so?"

D'Arcy raised a brow in mock concern. "Are you regretting so soon that you spoke vows with me this day?" His lips brushed the nape of her neck. "I will have to take special care to convince you that you have bargained well."

"Can we talk awhile, my lord husband?"

"You may talk only as long as your mouth can form the words, for I mean to make talking most difficult for you. Truly, how could you expect me to resist you?" he asked thickly.

"I need to talk first, my lord."

"Christian."

"Christian. I need to discuss what being wife to you means."

"It means pleasure."

"I want to be a good wife to you."

"I have seen the grin upon Blaise's face when he comes from your bed each morningtide. I think that you shall do quite nicely."

"But I do not love you, my lord—Christian."

"This match is not built upon love, but necessity. Many similar matches have grown into love." His tongue flicked at one darkened rose nipple, closing upon it, drawing it taut, while his hand carefully caressed her other tender breast.

Morgana pressed her palms against him. "One thing, my lord."

He crushed her into the featherbed, his tongue piercing her lips. She gasped as he ravaged her mouth, plundering, leaving her breathless. "I grow weary of these questions."

"Be gentle with me, my lord. For the child."

He held his breath, and for a moment she feared that he would strike her. She buried her face in the thick mat of hair on his chest, then placed her hands on his shoulders and shyly coiled them around his back. His muscles rippled under her palms as he shifted position. When he spoke, there was a vulnerability in his voice that she had never expected to hear. " 'Twas the child who brought us together. I would never hurt it. 'Tis Blaise's child now, but mine to raise—'twill carry my name. My seed will be planted soon enough. In the meantime, can we cease this prattle and commence this marriage?" His tongue traced her lips lightly, and Morgana shivered with alarm.

Despite his assurances, she sensed that he would harm her if he knew that she loved Blaise. She would have to be very careful, for her child's sake.

Not even D'Arcy's expert lovemaking could overcome her deep concerns. His approach was cool but lusty, and she yielded to him, thrust for thrust, no match for his skill and experience. He led her to dizzying heights, but her thoughts would allow her no surcease, and in the end her response was feigned as she pressed her wrist against her lips to quell her fear and loathing.

"Aye!" D'Arcy laughed mirthlessly. "You shall soon forget that you were ever bedded by that pompous ass, Blaise."

The mention of *his* name sent ice water coursing through her veins, but D'Arcy's face loomed over her no matter how tightly she closed her eyes. "My God!" he gasped as he held his weight on his forearms. "You are a witch! I shall have to guard myself well, or surely you shall cut out my heart." She turned away from his diabolic grin, terrified that he might read her contempt and harm her.

Yet she had come through the fire without being burned. He could never touch her—never reach inside to steal her soul. She knew that now, and in the knowing, his power over her was diminished. There was no danger of giving in to D'Arcy's seduction—as there had been in Blaise's arms.

As Blaise checked Reynard's reins, the horse brushed against him and neighed. "I can always count on you, my faithful friend," he said, his breath a foggy mist.

"The men await us by the postern gate, *mon seigneur*," Sigvald said as he brought Blaise his weapons.

Blaise belted the sword around his waist as he watched

the early morning sun rise in the horizon. "Where are D'Arcy's men?"

"In the hall."

"And the Lady Gisele?"

"Awaiting your summons."

"And you shall summon me," Gisele whispered from her window. "You will take me back to Retford and install me as your chatelaine. And then you shall take me to your bed."

He would not dare leave London without her. Blaise had not spoken more than two words to her beyond his initial greeting of "What the devil are you doing here?" No matter. She would insinuate herself into his life. Already she sensed a weakening of his resolution.

Sigvald left his lord's side, and soon was pounding at her door. Even after all these years, she recognized his knock. How often in the past she had dreaded that sound, for it inevitably meant that Blaise was leaving her bed for one or another of Duke William's escapades. She was never meant to be the wife of a knight in active service. She should have married an older man, a man done with warfare, a man who would stay by hearth and home. As Blaise would want to do now. She sensed it in his mien. And he would have to stay at home at Retford, to build and hold his fief by force of arms against the rebellious Saxons.

She had no regrets about crossing the Channel in winter. Her father had doled out much gold for the king's cause; and Gisele had exhibited much courage—or recklessness. 'Twas better than rotting away in that prison, surrounded by the daughters of God. By royal decree, Blaise must accept her as wife. Yet even now it would be a great victory to elicit the bare bones of a conversation from his pursed lips.

"*Mon seigneur* awaits you, my lady."

As she had come straight from the nunnery, she had not engaged serving women. No matter. There were plenty at Retford, no doubt. She could barely control her excitement at the thought of facing her new life. She had never before left Normandy, had never been to a holding that her husband had received by right of conquer. She had never been in a position of power among a conquered race, and the thought of such control thrilled her. Only one blemish upon the lot of it, beyond her husband's aloof attitude. That Saxon bitch had stolen her lover.

Seeing D'Arcy had brought to mind all the passionate feelings suppressed these many years past. D'Arcy, as her husband's page, squire, and loyal knight, had been easily enticed into her bed. Mayhaps, since he and the bitch would be at Retford, mayhaps—

"Now, my lady."

On her way to Retford, she would plan her husband's seduction, and failing that, D'Arcy's. She would take redress for those lost years with exuberance. Both men would pay her price of vengeance—Blaise for locking her away, and D'Arcy for leaving her there to survive without her.

She would bide her time. She had learned much at the convent about patience.

Chapter 11

Shortly after returning from London, Blaise abandoned his wife and left for Hartley. When D'Arcy and Morgana returned to Retford, Blaise summoned D'Arcy to join him.

The January chill coated the land with frost, but the weather was no match for the cold hearts at Retford Hall. Toward the end of the month, Blaise supervised work on the stone palisade, which was being elevated six feet to afford more protection.

"The Saxons built their palisades to keep out robbers," Sigvald said, trying to engage Blaise in conversation, for he had been unbearable these past few weeks. "The Normans build palisades to keep out Saxons."

"I am sick to death of politics. Where is D'Arcy? He was to awaken at dawn to supervise the work. I cannot be at both sides of this fief at the same time."

Jests flew among the men as D'Arcy's disappearance was attributed to his beautiful wife.

"Silence, you knaves!" Sigvald exclaimed. "You will have no need for wives or mistresses should this work remain unfinished when the rebels marshal their forces."

"Lord D'Arcy returned to Retford Hall?" Blaise asked. At Sigvald's nod, he swore an oath. "Without my leave?"

There is work to be done and he thinks of bedding his woman?" The thought of D'Arcy touching Kirsten enraged Blaise. She was *his*. How dare she act the proper wife to that ruthless savage?

Blaise kicked his horse's flanks, and the beast whinnied. "Reynard, my friend, I am impossible to live with these days, eh?" As if in response, the horse snorted and shook his heavy head.

"Leave only a light guard," Blaise continued. "We return to Retford until the ground thaws. Someone we can trust to watch over these simpletons." He pointed to D'Arcy's men. "They have shown their ability to tear down fortifications. Now let us find out if they can build and protect them."

Blaise spurred Reynard onward, arriving at Retford shortly after D'Arcy. The moment he rode through the gate, his eyes flew up to *her* chamber window. Was he lying with her, their bodies joined? he wondered.

Blaise refused to dwell upon this foolishness. She *wanted* him to think of her—to regret his choice. He would never do so. She had dared to be unfaithful to him—had allowed that maggot to touch her. He had offered her so much more than his body or love—he had offered a joining of their souls. How they must have laughed behind his back.

Blaise dismounted and stood beneath her window. "Lord D'Arcy, are you going to stay abed all day?"

He saw movement at the window, and D'Arcy stuck his head out, clearly bemused. "You arrive close upon my spurs, *mon seigneur*. I have not made it to the bed yet," D'Arcy retorted. The men in the courtyard guffawed loudly until they spied Blaise's darkening scowl. "I shall be down presently," he continued.

Morgana, aroused from a deep night's rest, sat up and arched her back. She caught her husband's hawklike stare and hesitated, rubbing the sleep from her eyes. "How long have you been standing there?"

"A moment or two. I did not want to wake you. How goes the battle with Lady Gisele?"

"I have kept to my chamber," she replied curtly.

"Do not let Gisele think that you are cowed. She preys upon the weak." He perched on the edge of the bed.

"Come, slugabed. The *seigneur* has returned to the manor; can the chatelaine be far behind?"

Morgana groaned and tried to hide under the pelts. Her head peeped out. "You would not believe what that woman has done to this household. She has turned it this way and that. The servants stare at her as if she were addlebrained. They do not speak a word of Norman French, and yet she chatters constantly. 'Tis really quite humorous to watch."

"Do not underestimate her," he warned as he removed his scabbard and hauberk and laid them across the chair.

" 'Tis very difficult for Mother to watch the witch destroy in a matter of days a household that she has devoted her lifetime to building. But what can she do?"

"Gisele had no use for a chatelaine's skills in the nunnery." He stoked the fire and stretched his tensed muscles. His brow puckered in thought as he sat next to her on the bed.

"D'Arcy! Are you going to break your fast today?" Blaise called impatiently from the stairway.

"The man is persistent, if nothing else," D'Arcy muttered into her hair as he gave her a light kiss. " 'Tis your fault, you know. You entice me with the slightest movement, and I dream of staying in your bed and spending the morning coaxing the sleep from your eyes—and your body. If I could, I would indulge in the pleasure of you several times a day, but *mon seigneur* is determined to keep us apart." He leaned on his elbow and drew her into the crook of his arm. "Ah, Kirsten," he mused, "who would have believed it? 'Tis most queer how you and I have found this happiness."

A fragile existence, she thought. Certainly *not* happiness. She sensed that, although he might be capable of great loving, he was also capable of even greater violence, for she had glimpsed a side of him that she preferred never to see again.

"I never thought to find love in this squalid country in the arms of a Saxon wench."

"I think that you mistake lust for love, my lord."

D'Arcy appeared sorely vexed as he curled a tendril of her hair around his finger. "Not even in jest should you say such a thing. I have known lust, and I know this to be more." He drew the coverlet away from her breasts and undid the drawstring of her shift. He touched the peak of one swollen nipple, circling the darkened tip until she gasped, biting her lip. He misread her consternation for passion as he moved his mouth to where his finger had been, kissing a path from breast to navel.

Panic held Morgana in thrall, and she seized his head to stay his movement. "I wish that this was my child within you," he said as he kissed the soft mound of her belly. "But we have a lifetime."

Sigvald pounded on the door and called his name.

"Bah!" D'Arcy gave her a virtuous peck on the cheek and bounded from the bed. "I thought to leave Blaise at Hartley, but he followed me."

"How goes the rebuilding?" The moment the words left her lips, she wanted to call them back. They had never discussed the village, for it was a potential point of conflict between them.

"I am sorry about what happened at Hartley," he began solemnly, ignoring Morgana's distress. "My men were out of control. The fever of the battle at Hastings clouded their judgment. I tried, but could not stay their assault. I never meant for the village to be put to the torch."

Morgana read the lies in his eyes. She had heard each gory detail of the truth from the villagers in the wood, but she resolved to keep this knowledge to herself. "I accept your explanation."

"I want naught to come between us."

She wanted to scream at him that there was much to come between them, but she bit her lip and chose to deceive him. "It shall not."

"Was your lover from Hartley?"

"My lord husband, to speak of a nonexistent lover will only lead to harsh words. Besides, I would avoid arguments—"

"Avoid? Avoid at all costs?" He pressed her for a response, his temper seething. "Do you think I fail to notice the fear in your eyes?" He clenched her wrist and jerked her to him. "Have I ever injured you?"

"Nay, my lord husband," she replied too quickly as she moved back.

He wrenched her toward him until their faces were mere inches away. "Christian! I told you to call me by my name."

"Please—Christian!"

"Who at Hartley then? Who has captured your interest?"

" 'Twas the Lady Alayne. She was betrothed to my brother."

He flinched as if he had been struck, but before he could respond, the familiar pound of Sigvald's fist sounded at the door. *"Mon seigneur* commands your appearance in the great hall, my lord D'Arcy. Now!"

"Blaise takes to command naturally, does he not?" He rose from the bed. "We shall discuss this later." D'Arcy released her and, in mock courtesy, bowed and left.

Morgana rubbed her wrist. She had been a fool to mention Hartley. In the future she would take care, for D'Arcy could be truly dangerous. It would not help to have the king's protection if her husband was beyond reason.

Blaise plotted to take any action necessary to keep D'Arcy from his wife's bed. During the day, Sigvald piled one enterprising task after another upon D'Arcy's shoulders to keep him from the hall.

After dinner, Blaise dismissed Gisele and swigged wine and ale with D'Arcy until well past the witching hour, when the younger man excused himself and fairly crawled up the steps to fall into his bedchamber.

Morgana pretended sleep as D'Arcy lifted her from the bed, wrapped her into the fur coverlet, hoisted her over his shoulder, and removed the torch from its wall bracket. He traversed the hallway, then bounded down the back steps through the kitchen and out to the mews.

"Where are we going?" she finally asked.

"I want to be alone with my wife," he explained thickly.

He laid her on a mound of hay while he expelled the stable hands and drunken men-at-arms with the flat of his sword. He barred the doors behind them. Morgana wrapped her arms around her breasts and shivered in the night air as D'Arcy tightened the skins over the windows, lit a small candle to stick into the dirt, and doused his torch. She stood trembling as his hot breath burned her neck.

"Remove your bedclothes!" he ordered dispassionately.

"I am cold."

"Remove them, wife," he growled, his upper lip drawing back in a sneer.

"I do not want to be bedded here in the mews, Christian. I am not an animal—"

"Damn you, woman, you talk too much." She stood her ground as he ripped the shift from her. "Are all Saxon noblewomen overly proud? You will come to me where and when I please. Do you understand that?"

Morgana observed the stubborn set of his jaw and nodded, fighting back tears of frustration. His breath was sour with wine. He was drunk. It would be impossible to reason with him in this condition. "I just thought that we would be more comfortable in our bed, my lord husband."

"With Blaise at our door, ear pressed to hear your every moan."

A red blush suffused her face with heat. "I am sure that he would not resort to such childishness."

"He will do anything to keep me from you. Tonight I had to listen to one boring tale after another while he plied me with drink. He thinks to make me unable to perform with you. Little does he know, it makes me harder." He led her fingers to his manhood to prove his point.

"Christian—"

He drew her down and lay next to her, covering his hardness with her hand. "Feel. Like a rock for you." He rubbed her hand up and down its length.

"Stop!" Morgana withdrew her hand.

"You are so unbending; how could he prefer you to Gisele? She was hot and wanton, always ready to open her legs." He moved over her and pressed his hard thighs between her legs, forcing them apart. "She was always wet here—" he touched her intimately "—always ready. It takes so much work to get you ready, 'tis a wonder I can remember what I am about."

Because he was drunk, it was a relatively simple task to catch him off balance and knock him to the side. Once that was accomplished, she raised herself on her knees. "Do not expend the energy, my lord. I am not interested in your lusty attentions."

"You lie. You are interested. You pretend not, but I

heed your breathing, and your muffled moans." He intercepted her and laid his leg over her thighs, holding her immobile. "You are like all of them," he slurred, "saying no with your lips but beckoning with your open thighs." He dug two fingers into her woman's place, causing her body to jerk. "Alayne said 'no,' but the cream between her thighs said 'yes.' " Morgana stiffened at the mention of Alayne's name as D'Arcy yanked his swollen manhood from his chausses. "But she is dead, and your brother is dead. Mayhaps I did her a favor, dispatching her as I did. She would be despondent now without him, would she not?"

Morgana lay stunned by this revelation. What kind of creature would utter such words? When and how had he gained that callous air, and how many innocents had fallen victim to his evil ways?

As if he realized his slip of the tongue, he answered arrogantly, "I cannot let each death bother me, wife. I am a soldier. I live and breathe death."

"Say no more," Morgana begged as she put a finger to his lips.

Unheeding, he continued in a caustic tone. " 'Tis the truth. Look at my foul deeds. Look at Lady Alayne."

"You claimed to have been innocent of that assault."

" 'Tis what you wanted me to say," he whispered in her ear as he pressed her into the hay. "I laid her." He nudged between her legs. "I raped her, taking her time and again, ruthlessly disregarding her cries for mercy."

Morgana tried to squirm from under him, but he lifted her buttocks and rammed into her, the perversity of his confession increasing his arousal. "I did this to her, and she liked it. She moaned, and drew furrows of skin across my back, as you do now." Morgana pummeled his back, trying to force him to release her.

"I tell you this, my lady wife, because I will not have lies between us."

He was not himself—or maybe he was more himself than she had ever seen before—a madman excited by pain. Her clever wit considered several rejoinders, but she bit them back in favor of a more restrained approach.

" 'Twas your first command, Christian. You reacted—"

He halted in his assault, clearly confused. "Damnation, woman! I bare my private pain to you, and show you who I am, in all my ignominy, so that you may accept me as I am. I want to love you, Kirsten, but I must cleanse myself first. I am not fit to—"

"You killed Alayne?"

"I did not slit her throat, but my men acted upon my orders."

"And the people."

"All. All on my orders. They were lined up, and swarms of arrows cut them down, like wooden targets. They had dared to resist me when I was bone-weary and sought sleep."

She turned her face from him, knowing that he lied. There had been no resistance at Hartley—no time for resistance. She remembered Brent's vengeful words and understood why her brother hungered for D'Arcy's blood. D'Arcy had no compassion for his victims, or their relatives—only indignation that he had been defied. And anger because he had been caught, like a child with its finger in the sweets bowl.

Morgana turned from him to face the flickering candle. She would never cleave to this man as the vows had said—for he was truly her enemy. One day soon her brother would see to his quick dispatch, and she would be widowed—and still a young woman. What had happened to Alayne, and to the people of Hartley, was too hideous, too gruesome to be forgiven, or forgotten. Brent never would—nor would she.

"Do you forgive me?" When there was no answer, he grew impatient and twisted her face so that her eyes met his. "Do you forgive me?"

Morgana's lips could not form the words of forgiveness. In his rage, he tore himself from her and rolled away. The weeks of comfort were over. Now she would plot in earnest with her brother to rid herself of D'Arcy at all costs.

When the first signs of spring came, she determined to escape the compound and venture into the wood. She had not attempted to do so for months, so the watch had grown indolent as of late.

She had not visited Brent since her return from London. She would have to tell him of her marriage to his hated enemy. She looked upon this talk with some consternation. How would he react? she wondered. Surely he already knew? He employed spies in her household.

" 'Tis a warmer day than we have had of late, my lord husband," she said during the noonday meal. "I have decided to walk in the wood to pick wildflowers."

"It may not be wise to go outside the palisade, Kirsten," D'Arcy advised.

"Go outside the palisade?" Gisele asked in her halting French, shocked that she would consider doing so. "Is your wife touched?"

"The rebels are very active," D'Arcy insisted.

"I have nothing to fear from my people. 'Tis spring, and I must visit the midwife, Maude, to replenish my herbal stores. I have tended many sick in the past few months."

When D'Arcy translated for Gisele, she smiled wryly. " 'Tis only right she should tend her people. I cannot be expected to do so. She lives off our bounty, after all."

"This was her home," D'Arcy pointed out.

"And now 'tis mine."

"She is my wife. 'Tis only fitting."

Morgana wanted to scratch Gisele's eyes out, but instead looked to her mother. Astrid had taught her much about biding her time. A cool mind would serve her well in the coming days as they conspired to escape. True to form, her mother spoke volumes with her eyes.

"Your men will watch her," Gisele offered.

"Of course," D'Arcy readily agreed. He turned to Morgana. "My men will accompany you. I will have the chestnut brought out—"

"I prefer to walk."

"You will ride," he insisted. "If you choose to walk part of the way, and are feeling well enough—"

"You treat me like an invalid, my lord." She knew that he wanted her on horseback because his men, in full chain mail, would move slowly on foot should she choose to flee. Her pregnancy had not yet progressed far enough to slow her down. "Do you mistrust me?"

"My heart would break should anything happen to you,

my sweet love." She knew that he said this more for Gisele's benefit than hers, for she was not blind to the lightning that crackled between them. He was trying to make Gisele jealous, and from the woman's sneers, he had succeeded.

As he helped her on with her light woolen mantle, he avoided answering the question.

As Blaise returned from Hartley, Morgana was making her way across the field outside the palisade. Gisele watched from her bower as Blaise dismissed his guard and rode toward the girl.

D'Arcy's men, thinking that Morgana had no knowledge of their language, snickered and jested about the frequency of Lord D'Arcy's bedding of his wife. Morgana held her tongue and listened.

"Did you see the way Lord Blaise looks at her?" said the first soldier.

"Like she is a sweetmeat," replied the second soldier.

"I would bet she is sweet, with lips like currants, and eyes that see through you. I bet her thighs are strong—"

"One can understand why the *seigneur* of Retford is enraged every time he thinks of her in Lord D'Arcy's arms. Goes to London his woman and returns as D'Arcy's wife."

"Well, what could be done? He has his own wife waiting in her bed each night—patiently."

"But look at the Saxon bitch. He's to be pitied to have lost such a plum."

"I think the Lady Gisele is made more to a Norman's taste. At least she knows how to act like a lady."

"Rumor has it that she was not quite the lady in her youth, before he locked her in the nunnery. Then she opened her thighs to Lord D'Arcy with alarming regularity."

"I have heard those rumors. And now D'Arcy has taken this Saxon girl from Blaise. You have to wonder at his purpose." They failed to notice that Morgana fell back from them. "The Saxon wench is too wild, given too much license. No man could hope to tame her. And yet—" the first soldier winked "—I can see the excitement one would have trying to do so."

Morgana hid behind a giant oak, and when they had

rounded the bend, she galloped off toward the edge of Andredeswald—toward Brent—quite pleased with herself until Blaise appeared from out of nowhere.

He held his helmet in the crook of his arm, and she could see where the sun had reddened his cheeks—almost like a little boy's.

"Where go you, my lady?" His eyes swept over her, sharp and assessing.

"To Maude's hut," she replied smoothly.

"You venture the wrong way, Lady D'Arcy." He grabbed her reins. "Come! Methinks your escort will be missing you."

"No! I am not going to Maude's hut right now, but rather for a walk in the wood. I—I want to be alone."

"That would not do. 'Tis too dangerous. I shall accompany you."

"But, my lord—"

"I insist." He continued to the edge of the wood, entered, and stopped at the first copse.

Blaise's nearness made Morgana conscious of the quickening ebb and flow of her pulse, but her pride kept her lips pursed. Although they broke bread at the same table, they had said precious little to each other since that night at the merchant's house in London—a few cursory words in almost four months since he had given her away to another in a moment of unreasoning ire.

"You gather wildflowers?"

"Sunday next 'tis Easter."

"I did not realize . . ." His voice trailed away.

"Lady Gisele has sewn a lovely tunic of crimson and purple for you."

"Yes." His lips thinned in marked displeasure. "She has so informed me."

"You are angry?"

"They are D'Arcy's colors, not mine. Am I supposed to be pleased?"

"I—I suppose not."

They continued through the copse to the edge of the wood, where the flowers sprouted in wild disarray. He dismounted and tethered Reynard, then took her reins and tied them to a tree trunk. He removed his gauntlets and circled her thickening middle with his large hands and lifted her down gently.

The grass was high, and thick, and still scratchy from the cold winter.

"We have not talked much of late," Morgana said.

"We have said quite enough."

"Why do you ignore me?"

"Kirsten, I have not ignored you—I—" He leaned back and closed his eyes, then replied, in a controlled voice, "I have naught to say."

"There is much I can say. The people in the village are starving."

"Some of them. I offered a full extra measure of food for those who would help us build. If they were foolish enough to turn it down . . ." He shrugged his shoulders.

"A good lord takes care of his people."

"I know my duty, Kirsten. What would you have me do, take the food from those who work to feed those who shun me? Take it from my men, mayhaps?"

"Why are the people kept from hunting in the forest?"

"They are the king's royal hunting grounds. Poachers will be punished by loss of limb, and if they persist, death."

"That is unjust."

"This is the king's law."

"Is this why you accompanied me—to advise me that William will kill my people if they feed their children?"

" 'Tis not my doing, Kirsten." His mouth tightened into a grim line.

"Would William be king without the men that put him there?"

"Would William be king if foolish Saxons had not succumbed to silly superstitions that damned them more than any might of arms could?"

"I am sick to death of hearing you blame the Saxons for being vanquished. I do not expect you to understand. You are a barbaric animal—an assassin without a conscience."

His eyes narrowed. "You mistake me for your husband, madame."

She lifted her skirts and walked away from him, but he cut off her retreat, and took her into his arms. She wrenched free. "Nay, my lord! You have no right to touch me now. I am no longer your paramour."

He pressed her against him, his hand rubbing her buttocks, the mail cutting into her slightly protruding belly. "You may try to convince me that you are *his* now, but I know differently. I know that you have not forgotten me— could never forget me. We can never truly be parted, my love."

"You arranged the deed by your own lips."

"I was sorely wounded. Jealous! Angry! I spoke venom in my grief. I have had time to regret my impetuous words."

"Regret is all there can ever be between us, my lord. I am wife to another now."

"Wife? To that impudent pup? You can never be wife to another. You can mumble all the damned vows you want; you are mine. Then. Now. Always."

Something in his eyes frightened her. There was a truth to his words. He had branded her his more surely than if he had laid a hot poker to her breast. No other could truly possess her after him.

When he tried to grip her wrist to draw her to him, she flung his hands from her and slapped his face with her open palm. "Aye." He grinned as he released her and made to remove his chain mail.

Morgana saw his intent and fled across the field, her movement hampered by her long skirts and the high grass. Her breathing turned ragged, and before she had gone too far, he pounced upon her and rolled with her, careful to cushion her body against him.

"Kirsten!" He growled her name, his voice murmuring low, guttural endearments as she twisted in his grasp. He rolled her over him and onto her back, his body following and one thigh over her legs to press her down.

She squinted in the midday sun, until his face blotted it out, to be replaced by a new and dizzying inner brightness. He threaded her fingers with his, and their eyes met and held. Hot blood surged through her veins as he tenderly brushed a hair from her cheek with his lips. He murmured love words against her temples. His lips stole closer to her mouth, closer, until he barely breathed above her and she sucked her breath in.

He kissed her slowly, leisurely, as if they had a lifetime in which to make love. She tried to control her breathing, but her body conspired to outwit her, and moved in unison with his. She strained against him, remembering how naturally they joined with each other. Despite her resolve, there was no way she could remain passive this close to him. It was not fair that he should have such a hold over her— such ability to enthrall her.

His tongue invaded the hollows of her mouth, seeking— seeking, until it found the response it sought. As her own tongue parried and thrust, his lips blazed a trail along her neck. "Jesu! I want you still. You are in my blood. I have tried to banish you from my thoughts, but you haunt me yet—the specter who hangs over each moment of my tortured existence. You truly are a sorceress!" He tasted the salty wetness of her tears with the tip of his tongue, and brushed them away with his kisses. "Do not cry, my little love."

She nudged him with her elbow, and he lifted slightly from her. "Do you think me such easy prey that I shall lay you right here for all to see? You have always preferred to believe lies about me. Now you seek to make me an adulterous whore?"

" 'Twas no lie that you carry D'Arcy's brat."

"You are a fool. Could it ever have been anything but a lie? Until you and William put me in his bed, I had lain with no other man but you. I swear it upon the child's soul."

Blaise sat back upon his haunches, clearly distressed. "You led me to believe—"

"I never led you to believe other than what I have always told you. From the moment of its conception, I have known that I carried your child. I knew that I carried this child when I gave you my vow." She sat up and moved back from him. "But you were not free to give your vow, and then you forced me to swear in front of witnesses and the bishop that I would be wife to D'Arcy. Now you have much to think about, my lord, as I have these many months. Despite my distaste for D'Arcy's attentions, he

has taken care of me when you chose to forsake me. I am
no longer yours. I can never again be yours. I will not lie
with you and put horns on my husband's head. 'Tis not my
way, despite what you have always believed about me.''
She rose and took a step back. " 'Tis not D'Arcy's child,
but it can never be your child either. 'Tis my child—that
is the only reality that exists within the void that my world
has become. A child does not become yours by a careless
dropping of the seed. In that sense, D'Arcy will father this
child, wipe his tears when he falls, teach him to ride, to
hold a sword, take him falconing. D'Arcy shall be my son's
father.''

She turned resolutely and walked back to where her
horse grazed in the midday sun. "Then it really is my
child?'' he asked, his voice losing its steely edge.

Heated words rose to her lips, but she took a breath and
held them back. " 'Tis the child of the devil, conceived on
All Hallows' Eve on the rock of sacrifice.'' She choked
back the tears that came unbidden at the memory of that
most wondrous of nights—that night when *something* had
happened.

Chapter 12

She is to make a tea of this, the day she wishes to conceive," Alyson advised as she handed the herbs to Gisele. Minna, Gisele's serving girl, had formerly attended a Norman lord, and was therefore able to translate the midwife's instructions. "And this is for my lord Blaise. Powdered dandelion root. Mix a pinch with hot water and flavor it with honey to hide its bitter taste."

"This shall harden his rod?" Gisele asked.

"Aye," Alyson assured her, "though, to the best of my knowledge, my lord Blaise has never needed such aid in the past."

Gisele ignored this last barb as she watched at the window. Blaise returned from the wood with D'Arcy's whore wife. She looked to have been tumbled, for her braid fell loose down her back, and there was grass on her clothes. Gisele swore to herself that she would rid herself of that wench at all costs.

"Get out!" She swept Alyson and Minna out the door as if they were bothersome flies, and barred the door behind them.

"Slut! Taking my husband when she has her own. She thinks to capture him with the babe. She shall be sorely nettled, for she shall have no hold over him when his legitimate child grows within my body."

Gisele was beside herself with hatred for Morgana and the child she carried—Blaise's child. No doubt about it, according to Christian. Then why did she continue to steal into the wood? Certainly not to meet Blaise, for she could not have known that he was on his way to Retford. Another lover, mayhaps?

Gisele dragged her chair to the window, and sat watching out of sight as they trotted to the gate. When they were near the entrance to the hall, she picked up her embroidery hoop and pretended to be busy at needlework. But he did not come to her, and when she looked out the window for him, she saw him approach the midwife, his lips moving quickly in the Saxon tongue.

Gisele tried to control her reaction to this development. Surely the woman would be discreet? Or would she? She was friend to the Saxon witch.

Gisele had her answer a short time later when Minna came to fetch her. "My lord Blaise wishes an audience with you, milady."

Visibly shaken, Gisele flung the hoop against the wall, and railed at Minna for her stupidity. "Get your ugly face out of here, you filthy slug, before I have you beaten."

Minna hastened from the chamber and down the back stairs to the kitchen. "She be at it again," she told Elvina. "Better keep away from her."

"A vile-tempered harpy, that one. She be needin' what my lord Blaise better be giving her, before we all suffer."

As Gisele forced herself to remain calm, Blaise entered her chamber, Alyson in tow. Her breath caught in her throat, and she swallowed, forcing her breathing into a slow pattern. " 'Tis interesting, what the midwife has told me," he said, his quiet tone belying his anger.

Gisele's eyes were guileless, a look that she had cultivated well during her many years of confinement. "My lord husband, I do not know what lies she has told you—"

"Silence! Do not compound your perfidy with more falsehoods. You claim to have found God in the convent—to have done your penance. No more lies."

"Are you so surprised that I would seek a potion to

conceive? Have you not yearned for a son these many years?"

"Yea, but when you failed to conceive year after year, you blamed me. Now I find the truth of the matter. Alyson has told me that you admitted taking a potion to prevent my child from growing in you—a potion whose effects you now seek to reverse," he snickered, "although it may not be possible."

" 'Tis true, my lord," she cried, her weeping too loud to be sincere. " 'Twere actions of my wild youth. I have had many years to ponder upon them—to regret them. I want a child now, Blaise. Verily I do."

Blaise kicked over the chair near her, and the midwife took flight. He picked Gisele up by the fleshy part of her arms and shook her until her teeth chattered. "You have no idea what you have done, do you, woman?"

"I did it all for you, *mon seigneur*. I have never loved anyone but you. Not even D'Arcy. I sought him out because you spurned me."

"I was William's man, Gisele. I could not spend every moment fawning over you. 'Tis something you could never understand. Now 'tis too late."

"Too late?"

"Leave Retford, Gisele. I shall never be husband to you again."

"I will not leave Retford so that you can lie with your slut. Never! Even were I no longer your wife, you would have D'Arcy to contend with, and he shall never let her go."

"She carries my child, Gisele. My son."

"Yours in blood; D'Arcy's in law."

"You are jealous?" He was surprised that it should be so after so many years.

"She is younger, and you yearn for her—would kill for her. You think I fail to notice the hunger in your eyes. I remember that all-consuming look." She sidled up next to him, her eyes flashing. "I remember what it was like to feel your hands on me, to feel your body joined with mine." She insinuated her fingers into his hair. "Why would you wish for that cold fish, when you could have me?"

He loosed her hold. "I would not want you were you

the last woman on earth. The mere sight of you sickens me. Years wasted in the monastery, wondering how God could have punished me so. I never truly understood until this moment what kind of woman you are. You could never be satisfied with one man." When she began to protest, he held his hand to her lips. "D'Arcy was not the only one, but the one who lasted the longest. I knew about the many others."

"I have never loved another," she replied petulantly.

He walked to the door. "Go back to Normandy, Gisele— to our manor house in Rouen. You always liked it, and will be comfortable there. Take a string of lovers, for all I care, for there is nothing for you here."

"You would give it all up for that bitch? Who will carry on your name? Who will inherit your fiefdom? For what do you work, if not to leave it to your son?"

"I shall have an heir, but I would rather die childless than to father a child on a she-demon like you."

As he slammed the door behind him, Gisele whispered, ruthlessly, "That could be arranged."

A few days later, two days before Easter, D'Arcy returned from Hartley. Gisele had spent long hours contemplating her revenge and had determined that she needed to enlist D'Arcy's aid in order to be successful.

She sought him out as he tethered his horse in the stable. "You have returned—and not a moment too soon."

"Why is that, Ladyfair?"

She smiled at his use of her pet name. "Your wife was in the wood with my husband on the day that you left for Hartley."

"My men were with her—"

"She eluded them and met Blaise, I tell you. Ask them."

D'Arcy hesitated for a mere second, then looked at her— his eyes dark, unfathomable. "And what conclusion do you draw from that?"

"They are lovers still."

"I doubt it." He affected disinterest.

"She returned disheveled, with grass in her hair and clothes."

He considered this for a moment, his eyes conveying the

fury within. "Go to your bower," he said brusquely. "I shall come to you after I attend to some matters."

Gisele knew that if she lured him to her bower, he was hers. Like the spider, she would draw him into her web of intrigue and devour him—once again.

As Gisele concocted her schemes, D'Arcy inquired of his wife's whereabouts, and was told that she was visiting Father Jerome at the chapel. From his bedchamber window, he could see her and the priest deep in conversation. What had driven her to seek him out? Were she and Blaise lovers? Mayhaps they were plotting to flee. Did they often meet when he was at Hartley? Was she cuckolding him as he had cuckolded Blaise? If so, she would pay with her life.

D'Arcy quaffed a horn of ale and returned to Gisele, pleased that she had finally approached him. She still had the power to stir his blood, as she had many years before—exhilarating—a vibrant, living thing. He grew hard at the thought of possessing her once again.

And Gisele was ready for him, dressed in a silk shift so sheer that the dark hair of her mound and brown nipples showed through.

"Do you always dress thus to converse?" he asked as he barred the door.

"Only with you, my love," she replied as she rubbed her breasts against his back.

He faced her. "Why now, when I have waited these many weeks?"

"Because I need you." Her voice was deep, throaty and velvet-edged.

He drew her hand to his hardness. "You need this."

She nodded quickly, voraciously, and fell to her knees, rubbing her cheek against his burgeoning rod.

D'Arcy swore an oath, swept her into his embrace, her legs circling his thighs. "Why should I give you what you want?" he teased.

"Because you remember how good it was between us."

"Aye, 'twas good, but I have a wife now who is your equal in bed."

"You lie. She cannot possibly meet my passion. She cannot do for you what I have done for you."

"But I love her."

Gisele laughed. "You would not be such a fool as to love her." She clawed at his clothes like a she-wolf, until he was naked. She removed her gown and rose on her knees to grasp his upthrusting manhood and rub it against her breasts. His moan thrilled her, and her tongue snaked out to caress his flattened nipples in a circular pattern, lightly flicking until they stood erect.

"I do love her," D'Arcy insisted as Gisele continued her caressing motions. He carried her to the bed as she tried to impale herself on his organ. "Not yet, Ladyfair," he murmured as her voracious lips searched for and found his manhood. He drew the leather from his garters, and rolling her onto her stomach, lashed her hands. Gisele's eyes glittered. "You have been a very bad girl, and must be punished first."

"Please, my lord," she beseeched with insincerity. "Please spare me."

He hovered over her and rolled her onto her back, scoring each upthrust nipple with his teeth. "Sparing you would make you most unhappy, vixen." He bent her legs and pinned them beneath his chest, then lifted her bottom to press into that other place, meeting at first with incredible tightness until she relaxed and allowed his entrance. As he drove mercilessly into her, she nearly swooned from the pleasure-pain of his movement, and her climax, when it came, drove them jointly and swiftly into peaceful oblivion.

"Tell me that *she* does this for you," she whispered with satisfaction.

"If I want her to, she shall," D'Arcy groaned.

Morgana, unaware of her husband's tryst, dined with Father Jerome and returned to the hall midevening. Upon her return, Astrid took her aside and warned her that D'Arcy lay with Gisele in the witch's bedchamber. As Morgana passed the chamber, she could heard the unmistakable sounds of passion.

"Go to your brother! Now, when he will not miss you," Astrid suggested.

Morgana drew on her woolen mantle and stole down the back steps and through the empty kitchen. She crossed the yard back toward the chapel. In the distance the dogs yelped in their pens as she hastened her movement. Blaise lay asleep at the dinner table—drunk.

She cared naught that D'Arcy bedded Gisele. Indeed, it was a relief. They were evil beings whom the devil had fashioned for each other. Mayhaps D'Arcy would keep from her bed now that Gisele had finally opened her legs to him.

She found Father Jerome at his prayers, but he put the beads aside, and he and Morgana soon crossed the lake in a small skiff. Brent would be waiting on the other side, as he had waited all day since her earlier fruitless attempt to meet him.

"Does he know about the child?" Morgana asked as she dragged the boat onto the sand and tied it to a rock.

" 'Twas not my place to tell him," Father Jerome replied.

They skirted the trees. "What of my marriage?"

"He has heard."

Brent appeared as if out of nowhere, his black-clad body meshing into the night. They walked together through the wood, until they came to a clearing lit by a bright shaft of moonlight. He removed his mantle and laid it upon the ground so that she could be seated in comfort.

"You are grown thin, brother."

He embraced her, and felt the unmistakable bump in her waist. "And you are grown thick." She tried to turn from him, but he drew her back. " 'Tis no doubt a Norman babe, but which Norman?"

"Blaise's child, of course."

"Why 'of course,' Morgana? You wed that vermin, D'Arcy."

"He is my husband, Brent, but not by choice," she sighed. "I do not wish to discuss him. We were to talk of escape—"

"Your marriage shall bring everlasting shame upon our house. Of course, you did not grow up in our house, and could not understand the responsibilities of a noble Saxon."

"There was no choice, I tell you. 'Twas by royal decree. The king himself—"

Brent slapped her face, and she fell back against a moss-covered tree trunk, stopping midsentence, stunned by this sudden violence.

"Royal decree of an evil king! You have married with the devil himself to please *that* king?"

"I had no choice."

"You had death. I would rather you killed yourself before allowing that murderer to take you to wife."

"Fie, Brent! Watch your tongue, lest God punish you for these ill-spoken words," Father Jerome exclaimed, moving Morgana out of the enraged outlaw's range.

"Yea, I am at heart a peasant," Morgana retorted, her chin raised, "but when I saw my duty, I did it. What of you? You leave me and Mother to the whims of Norman bastards. You glean your information from me, and now, when I am victim to their passions, you berate me. 'Twas not I that deserted my mother. Though I may have suckled from another's breast, I am a true daughter. You forced me into Norman beds."

"Enough!" Father Jerome exclaimed.

"Aye! Enough!" Morgana agreed. " 'Tis spring now. Will you keep your word and take us from here?"

"Where can you go with the Norman's brat in your belly?"

"Are there none among your men whose women bear the results of rape?"

"Aye! Many were tortured by the Norman scum at Hartley. Many bellies swell."

"Am I to be treated differently?"

"You welcomed the seed of that spawn of the devil. Do not lie to me. I have always known that you lusted for him, and even now it sickens me."

"I love him."

He slapped her again, and she was saved from a third blow by the priest's intervention.

"Mayhaps your words reflect anger at yourself," Morgana accused. "Is your guilt so deep that you must blame me?"

Brent sat at the bottom of a tree and ran his fingers through his hair. He pressed on his forehead, and grazed lightly across it, as if the pain within could disappear, magically. "It tortures me that you wed that monster."

"I understand," she murmured, her hand upon his shoulder.

"He killed my Alayne, and you lie with him."

"Brent, I feel naught for the man. What is done is done—I cannot change that—but together we can defeat the Normans. We can turn this horror to our mutual benefit."

"I want D'Arcy's head, and you shall help me get it. We will watch the crows peck his eyes out and eat his brain."

"He is my husband before God. I cannot plot his death."

"What use are you then?" He flung her from him, and she fell over a rock, bruising her knee.

As she rubbed the area, she came to a painful realization. "You care naught for my welfare, or even that of Mother or your people. You place us all in jeopardy for vengeance."

"You shall never understand me, Morgana. You live at Retford. You have seen naught of the sadness that covers this land."

" 'Tis not true," she insisted. "You think 'tis easy to watch small children in soiled clothes eating scraps thrown from the hall? We feed and clothe Hartley's poor as best we can. They live in tents on our land, and each day their stench rises to greet me upon my rising."

"No doubt 'tis a source of humor to you that I am reduced to the life of a serf while you are raised to the hall."

"How can you think that of me? I have begged you to rescue me from the hall, and now you chide me for continuing to live there at your insistence. I crave my simple life in the wood—my freedom to go hawking, or to stalk a deer with bow and arrow, or mayhaps fashion a snare for a rabbit."

"Your life is gone, Morgana," Father Jerome offered. "As for you—" he turned to Brent "—you will cease this unseemly behavior immediately. Where would you be without your sister? She has been of immeasurable assistance, and has safeguarded your mother at her own peril."

"It did not require her becoming D'Arcy's whore," Brent insisted stubbornly.

" 'Twould be interesting to see how you would fare if

you were a woman. 'Tis easy for you to speak your mind from your vantage point—free in the wood." Morgana fled back to the shore—to the boat. Determined to flee her brother at all costs and blinded by her tears, she was not aware that she was being observed until she ran straight into a hard, muscular body.

Her heart plummeted, and her pulse beat so wildly that she was certain she would keel over any moment.

"What are you doing out here?"

Morgana wiped her tears and composed herself. "My lord Blaise. What are you doing here? You were asleep when I left the hall."

"No doubt you assumed you left Retford undetected, but I am not as drunk as you would believe me." He sighed. "But enough of this! I am asking the questions. What are you doing here across the lake?"

"There is a special mushroom that may be picked only at night."

"And you were compelled to search this night alone?"

Father Jerome called her name loudly. "See," she said, "I am not alone."

Blaise's hawklike glance pierced the wood, and his hand automatically went to his sword hilt, wrist bent, at the ready to draw and thrust should it be necessary. Despite her claims, clearly there were two men, although the one dressed all in black slipped back into the wood.

Morgana feared that Brent would confront Blaise. As angered as he was, he might harm him, for Blaise had left the hall without his mail.

As Father Jerome approached them, Morgana asked, "Did you find any of those mushrooms, Father?"

"I regret having agreed to escort you on this jaunt." Father Jerome yawned. " 'Tis way past both our bedtimes."

"Aye!" Blaise agreed. "Were the Black Outlaw to happen upon you, you would wish you had kept to the hall, for he would gladly slit the throat of D'Arcy's wife."

She feared for Blaise. As long as the Normans believed the Black Outlaw a commoner, they would take no special efforts to bring him to justice. If they knew him to be a noble, and the rightful Thane of Retford, he would become a special quarry. Blaise would want no noble lord who could muster men to challenge his authority, no matter how bedraggled they might be.

Noble women, of course, did not count. She could be raped—taken as the spoils of war. She could be recast into the mold of a Norman "lady." Change her dress, force her to speak Norman French, feed her Norman foods prepared by Norman chefs, and fill her hall with Norman minstrels singing of Norman exploits and values. It happened around her, and she was powerless to stop it. But she would retain her identity at all costs. She would not be stripped of her self to be replaced by the ideal Norman wife. Not for any man.

She hated that men controlled the smallest details of her life. Soon she would escape. Her son, half-Norman, would be born in Ireland and grow up a Saxon, hating the Norman conquerors who had enslaved his people.

"Did you hear me, Kirsten?" Blaise asked. "I asked where your basket was."

"I did not bring one. I was going to put the mushrooms in my mantle, like so." She demonstrated, but could tell that he remained unconvinced.

"Come with me. Father Jerome will follow." He helped her into his boat.

The return journey proceeded in silence, and at Retford he accompanied Morgana to her bedchamber. He slammed the door back on its hinges, and pushed her in before him. "Where is your husband?"

"Surely you know with what mare that stallion ruts."

Blaise understood. "I care not if D'Arcy seeks Gisele's bed." As if to prove the truth of his words, he dragged Morgana down the hall to his own bedchamber and tried the door. It was barred. They returned to her bower and he lit a torch at the fire, then entered the secret passage, Morgana in tow. When had he found it? she wondered. How long had he known?

Once inside, they could see from behind the tapestry that Gisele lay bound to the bed on her stomach, D'Arcy laboring over her in a profuse sweat. Blaise pulled Morgana against him, until their bodies met, and after a snicker of triumph, he turned on his heel and left. She lifted her chin, desperately trying to salvage her pride, and followed down the passage, sickened by the sounds behind her as each pleasured the other.

Once in her chamber, she told herself that it did not matter, but it did matter. Not because she loved D'Arcy, for clearly she bore him no love. It was her condition that upset her—the fact that Gisele could so easily usurp her position.

She barred her door, determined to turn D'Arcy away. Blaise had known when he dragged her down the secret passageway that he would be setting her free, and he had gloried in the moment. She would never forget that smug look of satisfaction on his face.

Blaise had returned to his drinking when D'Arcy confronted him. "What happened to Kirsten's escort today?"

"They lost her, and I found her."

"You lie! You removed the guard I set to my wife?"

"Christian, do not, as usual, think with your ballocks. There is naught between Kirsten and I any longer, only because she respects her vows, though why, I shall never understand." He shrugged. "If your wenching with my whore wife does not drive her away, then no doubt she will put up with anything."

"You dare to plot against me?" Before Blaise could answer, D'Arcy stormed up the stairs and sought entrance to Morgana's bedchamber.

"I shall break the door down," he assured her. "You shall regret it should I have to resort to such measures."

She unbarred the door, and he flung it open. "What do you want?"

"What is there between you and Blaise?" he asked as he wrenched her toward him.

"Go to hell."

"What happened with Blaise today in the wood?"

"Nothing happened."

D'Arcy was unconvinced. "You were seen coming from the wood with Blaise, your appearance unkempt."

"By who? Your whore? There is naught between us."

He placed his hand upon her swollen middle. "Really? Can you ever be free of him?" He pressed her to the floor, and stood over her, threatening to thrash her. "Your shoes are wet and muddy. Where were you tonight?"

"I went to the wood to pick mushrooms."

"Alone?"

"With Father Jerome."

"Without your escort?"

" 'Tis more dangerous for me to be escorted by your Normans at night in the wood."

D'Arcy removed his tunic. "Mayhaps you should come to bed, and I will help you ease this excessive vigor, so you shall be less likely to wander off to dangerous places."

"I will not sleep in the same bed as you after you have been with that woman."

"Come, Kirsten. That woman has not sapped all from me. 'Tis likely that I shall have a bit left for you."

"I shall never lie with you again."

"Never?" He laughed humorlessly.

"If you refuse to leave my bower, I shall go elsewhere."

"If that is what you want, I am too weary to fight. That woman is a wildcat. Ah," he sighed, "I do need to gain my strength."

"If you try to make me jealous, 'tis useless. I care not whether you lie with one hundred such whores."

"There is only one Gisele. Ask Blaise." As Morgana turned on her heel, his mirthless laughter chilled her heart.

Chapter 13

You work yourself too hard," Morgana chided as Astrid mended the household linens. "Look at the hollows under your eyes and the swelling over your lids!"

" 'Tis our *chatelaine's* fault. She resents my former position, so puts me to menial tasks."

"I will talk to Blaise."

"Nay! Keep your distance from him. She is evil. She will harm you and the child if she believes you a threat."

"No doubt she would gain much should I lose this child. That is why I prepare my own meals."

"She has no shame to lie with your husband in Blaise's bed."

"I am eternally grateful, for now I no longer need pretend to be wife to him. She has freed me." Morgana lay across the bed on her side and rubbed the small of her back. "I ache so."

"I will prepare a bathing tub with cider vinegar."

"I hate the smell."

"We shall scent it with rosemary. Rest, and I will wake you when all is ready."

Morgana undressed. "My seams must be let out."

"I will tend to it immediately." Astrid grinned. "The household linens will have to wait."

"I can help."

"You have enough to do in caring for the villagers. You must not overtire yourself." She lifted Morgana's chin. "You look so pale. Are those bruises on your cheeks?" Morgana did not respond, but removed all but her sleeveless shift. "You bruise too easily. Look at you. Who marked you so? D'Arcy?"

Morgana shook her head. "Brent does not know his strength. He frightens me sometimes."

"He did this to you?" She stepped back, her hands on her hips. "The matter is settled then. I must see him."

"Not now, Mother. I doubt that you would recognize him."

"Life's experiences often make one bitter," Astrid agreed. "Today lady of the hall, tomorrow little better than a serf. That is no reason to take it out on one's family."

Just as Morgana climbed into the bathing tub, D'Arcy entered. "Are you coming down to dinner, or are you going to continue to sulk in this chamber?"

"I prefer sulking to your boorish company."

"There was a time you thought me charming." He grinned lasciviously.

"Never—not even for a brief moment," she responded with obvious displeasure.

"What is this?" He pointed out the bruises on her arms, the bruises left when Brent had held her arms too tightly. "Did Blaise dare lay hands on you?"

"Would you care if he had?"

"Not really. 'Tis only that 'tis not his right to beat you." He hesitated. "You know that I would kill you if I knew for certain that you still lie with him."

"I am not Gisele."

"If not Blaise, then whose fingers made these bruises? You should not have such skin, my love. It speaks volumes." She flinched. "Why do you do that? Do I beat you? Do I give you reason to fear me?"

"Your hands are soiled with that bitch's odor."

"You could learn much from her."

"I prefer to remain uneducated, thank you."

"Mayhaps you were excited by last evening."

"I was sickened to the pit of my stomach."

D'Arcy lifted her, dripping, from the bath and brought her to the torchlight. "If I wanted to take you now, I would. You would not be able to stop me. You know that, do you not?"

"I would fight you."

"You would get hurt, or mayhaps the babe—"

"The king would be the first to hear of your ill treatment of me, provided that Blaise allows you to live, for indeed, he has vowed to kill you should you harm a single hair upon my head."

"You still love him?"

"Did you think otherwise? You are pathetic. I could never love you. You are unfit to shine his spurs."

"You lay with him yesterday," D'Arcy accused.

"Nay! But I wanted to."

"I *will* kill you if you do," he said seriously. "I vow it. Your cheeks are bruised. Someone has beaten you. Mayhaps your lover can shed some light on the matter."

He loosed her and strode from the chamber, slamming the door behind him.

In the meantime, Blaise brooded over the twists his life had taken in the past year. He had been comfortable, sheltered in the monastery. No need to make decisions—to serve anyone but God. He could forget that he was a living, breathing man with needs and desires, capable of dealing out death.

Now Kirsten carried his child, yet was wife to his greatest enemy, and Gisele flaunted her adultery for all to see, all the more excited that he knew.

Blaise, after years of steeping himself in guilt over his failed marriage, was confused. Kirsten had taken him out of his foul moods—had given him a sense of completion that he had never before experienced. But it was not to be. They were ill fated; he had known it from the beginning of their affair. He had no right to take her to his bed, for he could never marry her.

And yet he would not take back a single moment, for he had found joy and love in her arms.

He had to contend with Gisele's latest adultery. He could force her to return to Normandy and consign D'Arcy to Hartley, but the gossips would whisper that he did this only because he coveted D'Arcy's wife. Though the hall buzzed, none dared approach him with tales. D'Arcy, however, boldly pulled up a chair next to him as if the events of the previous night had never occurred.

"Why does my wife look like she fought off William's guard?"

"Have you asked your wife?"

"I ask you how she was bruised from picking mushrooms."

Blaise remembered the dark shadow at the edge of the wood—the man clothed in black. The Black Outlaw? Had he bruised her? If so, why would she go to a man who would hurt her? Was he her lover, or was there another, more sinister motive?

"You fret overmuch. You have more important matters to consider."

"I want to wear this kirtle tonight," Morgana said as she held up the emerald brocade.

"Mayhaps you should eat dinner in your bedchamber," Astrid suggested.

"I will not let Gisele intimidate me. 'Twould suit her purpose were I to hide like a timid mouse. I have no shame. Besides—" her eyes glittered, "—I hear there is a new minstrel come from Normandy to play for us this eve."

"Stay away from Lady Gisele. I have a premonition."

An answering chill coursed down Morgana's spine.

Dinner began as a rather solemn affair, but at twilight the knights returned from their work on the motte, some bringing women with them. Morgana noted that women were appearing in the hall more often, as alliances of both expedience and love were formed. Many of her father's noble knights, cut down in battle, had left behind widows and gently reared daughters—women who, unless they made such an alliance, might likely live in near poverty.

"What do you think of the new minstrel, Lord D'Arcy?" Gisele asked halfway through the performance.

"A fine voice and wit," Christian replied smoothly. "He speaks Saxon well."

"Master Corbett has entertained the queen herself."

"Well, at least he is not boring."

"I am told that your wife prides herself on her wit. Master Corbett would give her a contest. 'Tis said that he can tie up the tongue of any Saxon strumpet.''

The hush of the hall was broken by heads that nodded into each other with whispers. Lady Gisele had never openly attacked the Saxon woman.

Morgana kept her chin firm in calm defiance as Gisele chuckled vindictively. It would mean disaster to lose her temper and betray her knowledge of their language.

D'Arcy threw back his head and laughed contemptuously. When a tense hush fell over the hall and all faces turned to Morgana, she lifted questioning eyes to D'Arcy, who gladly hurled the translated taunt in her face.

"Master Corbett, the story of Uther Pendragon," Gisele began, "in Saxon, in deference to our guests."

"Uther Pendragon," the troubadour began, "was the father of King Arthur, a valiant Briton warrior who, 'tis said, defeated the Saxons. At the feast following the battle, the wife of Gorlois, the Duke of Cornwall, Ygerne by name, caught Uther's eye. He bespoke his passion to Ygerne, but she was a faithful wife, and told her husband of Uther's desire for her. When Gorlois fled the court with his wife, Uther made war on him at his castle in Tintagel. As the duke rode out to meet Uther—and his death—Uther was changed into Gorlois's image by the necromancer, Merlin. Uther bedded Ygerne and she begat Arthur, who eventually succeeded his father to the throne."

Morgana held her tongue.

But Gisele sought to press a point. " 'Tis most distressing when a man allows himself to be ruled by passion, is it not? To lust after another man's wife," she continued with a touch of venom, "even to the point of killing that man to gain her hand?"

Blaise, evidently used to Gisele's ways, had learned to ignore her. It was not so easy for Morgana. Would Gisele increase D'Arcy's jealousy and suspicion? His neck grew taut, the pulse spot throbbing, standing out like a thick cord as lines wrinkled his forehead.

And yet, two could play this game. "Although I am most familiar with the Arthurian legends, my lady, another tale springs to mind. Master Corbett, tell us the tale of King Arthur, his wife Guinevere, and her lover, Launcelot.

Surely you know this tale, my lady? 'Tis the one where the king's vassal and most trusted knight covets his wife. For many a month his knights tell Arthur that she deceives him, but he refuses to believe the meddlers until he finds them together, entwined naked in the forest. So he shuts her up in a nunnery." Morgana relished Gisele's embarrassment as she drew a long, rasping breath.

"You have the gall to speak against me, Saxon slut?" Gisele rose in her seat and leaned over the table.

Morgana responded with constrained ire. "I will not stay at table to be humiliated." She made to rise in feigned disgust, but D'Arcy caught her wrist and pulled her into his lap, hard against him. "Mayhaps you seek a gentler sport, wife." As his mouth swooped down to claim her lips, the hall echoed with hoots and howls of encouragement.

Morgana shuddered in revulsion at his touch and his ale-soured breath on her neck. She twisted in his arms and caught Blaise watching her expectantly. He seemed on the verge of reacting, then sat back in his chair, a mask of indifference falling over his features.

Before D'Arcy knew what she was about, Morgana drew his dagger and held it to his throat. "Take heed, husband. If you are looking for a good night's toss, yon 'lady' will oblige." She threw a contemptuous glance toward Gisele as she wrenched free of her husband's chafing embrace. A murmur rumbled through the hall, and the men looked as if they would devour her flesh with their feasting eyes and smacking lips. They all sickened her.

With amazing agility, she threw the dagger across the length of the hushed hall to land between the eyes of a boar's head, then sped away to her bedchamber.

"I should have warned you, D'Arcy. The girl is dangerous around knives." Blaise smirked as D'Arcy's features darkened with ill-concealed anger. "Something to think about, eh?"

Gisele leaned in and whispered to her lover. "She is a silly Saxon girl, Christian. Make merry, and forget her," Gisele cajoled. "You have all night to devise a fitting reprisal."

An evil leer twisted D'Arcy's lips. " 'Twill have to be something especially original."

"Why bother devising plots. Mayhaps 'tis time to think of ridding ourselves of her—permanently?"

Although Astrid could not hear their conversation, she knew by the tone of their voices and the look upon each face that they plotted against her daughter. " 'Tis the child, my lord," she said from her seat next to Sigvald. She rose to follow her. " 'Tis the babe that makes her peevish these days." She started up the steps. "Not enough rest, I think."

"Your prattling begins to annoy me," D'Arcy snapped back. Gisele's eyes were smoldering black coals of anger as they followed Astrid. How could she provide a legitimate heir if Blaise refused to bed her? Were he to die tomorrow, she would inherit a pittance of his worth. She must rid herself of the whore, with or without D'Arcy's aid. She glanced nervously around, fearful that Blaise had observed their conspiracy. She need not concern herself, for he stared pensively at the upstairs hall which led to the bedchambers.

Gisele smiled in relief.

Once in her bedchamber, Morgana found it nearly impossible to control her temper. "Why does she goad me?" she asked as she wrung her hands in dismay.

"Your mere presence is a sore nettle in her side. She wants you away from Retford." Astrid sat on the bed.

" 'Tis my home! She can return to Normandy. Who invited her anyway? Her husband rejects her. Is that my fault? Is it my fault that I am the innocent victim of the licentious *Vicomte de Rouen?* He is the wrongdoer—not I. Why am I to be blamed?" Morgana worked herself into a frenzy. "I have been wronged a thousand times more," she continued, swallowing back a rush of tears, "because I let myself love that—that cloddish ass." She stuttered in her rage.

"You are hurt, Morgana, because Blaise did not rise to your defense."

"Nay!" she disagreed.

"But surely you understand that he would have come to blows with your husband had he interfered. 'Tis not good for their men to see them fighting, for dissension among the ranks could result in evil conspiracies against Blaise."

"D'Arcy would not dare to plot against him." Morgana knew a sudden prickling of fear, and her heart gave a sickening lurch.

Astrid rose from the featherbed. "The man treads on the path to madness. I would not expect him to do what is right."

In the hall, the continued taunts of D'Arcy's men were cut off by the entrance of a messenger from Hartley. There was a momentary lull as the men ascertained what had happened, then they called loudly for retaliation.

The man limped in, a broken section of arrow sticking out from his thigh as he swallowed convulsively and retold the night's events.

"The fortifications that we built at Hartley, my lord—all the outbuildings—have been put to the torch by the Black Outlaw and his men. The fire spread from the compound to the thatched roofs of the new cottages, until all went up like kindling wood."

D'Arcy gave a snort. " 'Tis clear that these Saxons prefer the wood to our Norman-built huts."

"Damn! These people test me sorely." Blaise raked his short-cropped hair. "Begone, D'Arcy! We shall never rebuild Hartley if you stay at Retford. As underlord, you must live on the land and protect it."

D'Arcy considered arguing the point, but kept his counsel. "I shall leave first thing in the morning." He stumbled from his chair and reeled across the hall to the stairway. "I shall tell my wife to pack her belongings—"

"The woman stays here under my protection," Blaise commanded. D'Arcy tried to dissuade him, but to no avail.

"If he wants to take her with him, 'tis his affair," Gisele offered as she tugged at Blaise's sleeve, "or is this the biblical tale of David and Bathsheba? Do you send Christian out to die because you covet his wife?"

Blaise ground his teeth in anger and bellowed loudly, "Lady D'Arcy stays, and there will be no more said about it."

A silent battle raged between the two knights. Venom spit from D'Arcy's ice blue eyes. He would slice Blaise in two and slit his gizzard—but not now. His time would come soon enough.

D'Arcy climbed the steps two at a time to his bedchamber. He brutally kicked a hound that cowered outside Morgana's bower, and its yelp rent the night air.

Morgana opened the door at the sound, and D'Arcy

thrust his foot in the doorway before she could shut it against him.

"How did you accomplish it?"

"Accomplish what?"

D'Arcy took hold of her slender throat. "Come hither." He wrenched her toward the window and flung the shutters open with such marked impatience that they banged back against the outside wall.

Morgana struggled to free herself. What was he after? Why this new burst of violence?

D'Arcy's jaw grew rigid. "Look! There!"

Morgana surveyed the quiet night. In the horizon beyond the watchtower was the bright yellow-gold of blazing flames.

"My God! Fire!" she whispered.

He settled an accusing glare upon her. "Your ploy did not work."

"I had no hand in this."

"I can see it in your eyes—smell it in your fear. You are in league with him. The Black Outlaw!" He grabbed at her but only succeeded in pulling off her headrail. "You set the Black Outlaw on Hartley? Why? To rid yourself of me so that you could have Blaise?" He struck her a stinging blow and flung her away from him.

"You are raving, my lord husband. I know no *Black Outlaw*, nor do I know anything about Hartley."

"Leave be! For the love of God!" Astrid wailed from the doorway as D'Arcy cornered Morgana on the floor. The girl's arms automatically covered her belly in a protective motion as he laid the flat of his palm against her face in a stinging slap. He arced his foot to kick her, but as he stood poised in this vicious motion, Morgana rolled away from him on the rush-covered floor and took the blow on her forearm, shrieking as if all the devils in hell had descended upon her.

Astrid's clawed fingers ripped at him from behind, but he whipped around in a fluid motion, slammed his fist against her cheek, and thrust her away from him with a jerk of his foot to land on the floor with a sickening crack.

An icy rivulet of fear coursed down Morgana's spine as she watched her mother's limbs flail about reflexively, then—with a shudder—lie deathly still.

Morgana crawled to where her mother lay and tried to drag

her away. Astrid lay unmoving. A wail rose in Morgana's throat and tore from her lips. The chamber swam around her in a maelstrom of morning mist. She ceased to feel the overwhelming pain of loss only when she fell unconscious.

At her mournful cry, Blaise slammed down his horn and bolted from the table, taking the steps two at a time and pushing the servants away from the chamber door.

"Jesu! You crazed fool! What evil have you wrought now?" Blaise asked as his gaze shifted around the bedchamber. Morgana lay on the floor partially hidden under the heavy mass of her unbound hair. Astrid lay nearby—motionless. As Blaise faced D'Arcy, his fist whitened around his sword hilt.

"It was an accident. She attacked me," D'Arcy insisted.

Blaise knelt at Astrid's side, then cast an uneasy glance toward Sigvald. "Send the swiftest messenger for the women—Maude and Alyson." He gathered Astrid's broken body and carried her gently to her bedchamber, where he laid her upon the bed. "And send for the priest," he continued as an afterthought.

He returned to Morgana. Her breath was weak, but even. "Stay with your mistress," he bade Elvina as he laid her upon her bed and covered her with the wolf pelts.

D'Arcy stood in the hallway dressed in full mail. He pulled on his helmet and gauntlets and followed Blaise to Astrid's bedchamber. "I go tonight to Hartley."

" 'Tis for the best," Blaise agreed, eyes cold with loathing, "for if you stay, I may kill you."

D'Arcy's fists clenched as Blaise bent over the ominously silent woman. "You may try."

Blaise threw him a frigid glance that sent ice up his spine. "I would succeed."

D'Arcy left the chamber in irate strides, but Blaise cared naught, for Astrid's well-being was of paramount importance. D'Arcy could be dealt with later.

Gisele withdrew from the shadows of the hall where she had observed the exchange between Blaise and D'Arcy, then ventured quietly into Astrid's bedchamber.

"How may I aid you?" she inquired of Blaise.

"Escort Lady Gisele to her bedchamber," he called to Sigvald, who stood outside the door.

Gisele, heedless of his rising anger, approached him yet again. "But I want to help—"

"Leave be, Gisele," Blaise replied. "You hate the woman, so why help her now? Have you not wrought enough damage this day? Do you think I fail to recognize your hand in all of this?"

"My hand? You whoremonger!" She scratched at his eyes until his palm cracked mercilessly across her cheek and she sprawled backward on the rough wooden planks of the rush-covered floor. Sigvald picked her up and flung her over his shoulder like a deer carcass.

"See that she keeps to her chamber. I want no more interruptions by that ignoble shrew."

Blaise sat holding Astrid's hand until Father Jerome arrived. The priest knelt beside her, mumbling prayers in Latin and anointing her with oil.

Morgana awoke shortly after the midwives arrived, just as Alyson examined Astrid, whose eyes were dazed, the pupils dilated, her breathing shallow.

"Will she heal?" Morgana asked.

"Only time will tell, for 'tis difficult to predict the course of an injury to the head."

"But my head was injured, and I am perfectly well."

"True. But you are much younger. We must wait and see."

"She cannot die when I have just found her," she whispered insistently as she reached for Astrid's hand to press it against her wet cheek. " 'Tis not fair." She turned to Father Jerome, and knelt, pleading in her despair. "God must do something, Father. He will not gainsay me now, not when I have sacrificed so much for my people."

"Shush, girl," the priest said as he enveloped her in his arms. "The Norman will hear you."

Morgana strained away from him, her back straight. "Do not fear, Father. I never forget my duty."

" 'Tis not good for you or your child. Come away," Blaise said as his hand slipped under her knees to raise her into his arms.

"Put me down!" she said in firm decision as she tried to squirm out of his grasp. She fought him until he crushed her to his chest and shredded her resistance.

" 'Tis not good for the babe," Alyson agreed.

"Rest in your bedchamber for a moment, and I will have a pallet moved in here for you." It was a compromise. Morgana nodded absently, and he carried her to her bedchamber. "Maude will give you something to help you rest."

"I need no potions. I want my wits about me."

Alone, Alyson and Maude stared over Astrid's quiet form at each other. "We are surrounded by death," Maude observed. Alyson merely nodded.

Blaise, true to his word, had a pallet brought into the bedchamber upon which Morgana could lie. All night the women tended Lady Astrid, forcing potions between her dry lips and placing poultices of thyme leaves and olive oil upon a lump the size of a goose egg to draw out the poison.

Morgana grew more distraught as time passed and there was no change in Astrid's condition. Despite their tender ministrations, her head continued to swell. Morgana finally weakened and drank an herbal drink that Alyson prepared. Within the hour, she succumbed to sleep's seduction.

As the gray dawn crept through the shutters, Morgana awoke from a wild dream in sore disarray.

"What is it, love?" Blaise asked softly as he wiped the sweat from her forehead.

"My dream," she whispered. "Somewhere in the distance there was weeping." She yawned, and flung her arm across the pallet to stretch her aching muscles.

"She wakens, Mother," a familiar voice said.

"Alyson?" Morgana asked thickly, trying to remember what it was that stood poised in her consciousness.

"Aye, 'tis me."

"My mouth is likely filled with straw. I can barely move my lips."

"Sleep, girl."

"Ummmmmmm!" She drifted off again.

When she next woke, Blaise still sat at her bedside. Her mind unclouded quickly this time, and with the lifting of the veil of forgetfulness, her memory returned in sharp relief. "Mother?" She sat up straight and realized that she was in her own bedchamber.

"Pay me heed, sweet one," Blaise began in low tones of

gentle understanding as he grasped her fingers. "Your mother . . ." He hesitated, reluctant to bear such ill tidings.

"Your mother has gone to heaven, girl," Father Jerome finished.

Morgana's breath seemed to suffocate her as she rose on trembling limbs and stumbled out of the chamber and down the hall, toward the bed where the now-covered form lay silent. She drew back the linen sheet, and relief flooded her features. " 'Tis not my mother," she said with chattering teeth. " 'Tis not—"

"Kirsten," Blaise began, but Morgana put her fingers over his lips as if to hold back the words. "She looks different because there was swelling, but 'tis her."

Morgana looked again at the body, and knew the truth of his words. She bent to kiss the cool, rigid cheek, and knelt to press her head against Astrid's thigh as tears welled forth. Blaise motioned everyone outside.

"What day is this?" Morgana asked when she finally exited the bedchamber.

"Easter," Blaise answered quietly. She had lost days.

"Was she in any pain?"

"Nay! She never woke."

"Does Christian know?"

"He has been at Hartley since . . ." his voice trailed off.

"I will be wife to him no longer."

"I would never force you to bed with the man."

So much grief! Morgana thought. All for jealousy and vengeance. Vengeance! Its venom pulsed through her veins, bringing the gorge to rise in her throat.

"What will you do to him?"

"He claims 'twas an accident."

"He beat me. She tried to come between us, and he pushed her." She waited for his response, bewildered that she did not hear the expected words.

"I can do naught. D'Arcy is a Norman knight, my vassal."

"You are his lord. You have the power."

"Your mother was a Saxon."

"Does her life mean less than that of a Norman lady? If 'twere Gisele, would his punishment be different?"

" 'Twas an accident."

"I hate you! Do you hear me? I hate you!" She pummeled her small fists into his muscled chest. " 'Tis all your fault. I would never have been forced to marry him if jealousy had not gnawed at your gut." Blaise winced at her sharp, brittle words. "I will never return to him—ever. Not even if the king himself wills it. I would rather kill myself."

Blaise steeled his body against his desire to crush her to him. "You will never be wife to him again. You are mine."

"I shall never be your harlot again either, Norman cur."

"You carry my child, a half-Norman child. You spoke the words from your own lips."

"I lied in the wood."

"You did not lie," he stated flatly. "You repeated the words while under the potion's effects."

She tensed. What else had she told him? What other secrets had slipped from her lips while she lay helpless?

"I will not be your whore, you shallow-witted fool."

"We are handfasted. You are my wife in all but name. I swear, your child shall inherit—"

"He is D'Arcy's son. You have seen to that."

"He will never be D'Arcy's son, even if I have to kill the man."

Morgana was appalled at his words. He would seek no rightful payment—no wergeld—for her mother's death, but would kill her husband to gain her. Did he truly believe that she would ever return to him? Did he think so little of her?

She sat upon the pallet and laughed ruefully. His very presence set her stomach aquiver. Caution stilled her lips, and a single tear slipped down her cheek to be dashed away with a negligent hand. 'Twould do no good to sob out her sorrows—no good to fight Blaise with words. He suspected that because she was in a weakened state, she could be easily bent to obedience. Let him continue to think that she could be controlled. She would keep to herself that she had felt the first movements of their child. She would keep to herself her plots and schemes to leave him.

A strange sense of foreboding washed over her.

Chapter 14

True to his word, Blaise kept D'Arcy at Hartley as Morgana set about burying her mother in a manner befitting the wife of a Saxon thane. "These will do." She pulled out fine garments of blue and gold silk brocade and handed them to Elvina. "We will attach the overtunic at her shoulders with my emerald brooches."

"You would not waste such exquisite jewels on a corpse, would you?" Gisele stood on the threshold.

"What are you doing here? Get out! Out!" Morgana forced Gisele back through Astrid's chamber door.

"Who do you think you are?" Gisele shrieked, taking a foothold. "I am mistress here."

"What mischief do you make now, madame?" Blaise demanded as he came upon them.

"The witch dares to cast me out."

"She has no right," Morgana began, biting her lip in an attempt to control her ire.

As Blaise snapped a curse, Gisele quailed in fear. "Begone!" he ordered as she aimed an angry glance at Morgana, tossed her head, and left.

"I expected no less from her." Morgana paused. "I wish

to bury my mother in the wood, in the copse near Maude's hut.''

" 'Tis folly, Kirsten. I cannot protect you in the wood.''

"*I* have no need of protection,'' she pointed out. "I want to bury her in the wood—alone.''

Blaise saw that she was determined, and his emotions played havoc with his reason. He wanted to take her into his arms—console her—wipe her tears away and tell her that this pain would pass. But he could not. He had not the right—even though his heart would break at any moment for her—even though her pain ebbed and flowed through his veins as if it were his own.

Though he feared for her safety, he wanted to give her free rein, as if he could somehow set this great wrong aright.

"Then so be it,'' he reluctantly agreed.

Morgana now plotted her escape from Retford in earnest. There was no reason to remain. Gisele had hounded her mother into her grave. Surely Morgana and her child would meet a similar fate if she did not escape that petty, jealous she-wolf.

And if Gisele's threats were not reason enough, there was Blaise himself, who daily hinted that, with her estrangement from D'Arcy, she should now welcome him back into her bed. Undoubtedly he thought little of their respective marriage vows. Yet it could never be. Though her passion for him may never die, she must escape him or risk losing her very soul. Her marriage may be over, but she would not be an adulteress. She sensed his eyes boring into her as she bent at her tasks. He would bring her to his bed— child or no. Just this morning, as she prayed at the prie-dieu Father Jerome had moved into her bedchamber from the chapel, his eyes had rested upon her with ill-concealed desire. Though he had not spoken the words, he would have her again.

Once her mother lay in the hard ground, who would protect her? Not the Church, for when she had gone to Father Jerome before, he had sent her back to Retford Hall.

Nay! She must escape to the wood—to her brother.

Surely Brent would not expect her to continue her spying now—to return to Blaise's bed as his mistress until he cast her off like an old gunna and took her child. Not even Brent would expect that of her.

These concerns continued to nettle Morgana right through the burial, which was attended only by Morgana, the midwives, and Father Jerome. Blaise, out of respect and at her request, kept his Normans to the edge of the wood.

Halfway through the solemn ceremony, Morgana noted that three figures stood in the distant shadows on her opposite side—unseen by Blaise. Brent, Gareth, and Cedric. Father Jerome had sent word to them of Astrid's death, and now they were there. Her heart called to them, and it was all that she could do to keep from hastening the short distance to their side.

But she could not. She would not endanger another of her loved ones, so she turned away, trying to concentrate on the service, which was marred by confused images and empty words. She snorted disdainfully as Father Jerome beseeched God to accept Astrid's soul into heaven, and when the priest stared at her with perceptive eyes, her sense of hatred swelled anew. "Mouth no pleas for me, priest. I want nothing from a God whose mercy is so lacking that he would take a woman like my mother and leave that sow Gisele to yet walk upon this earth."

"Morgana, now is not the time."

"And when, Father? They have stolen everything from me—my home, my country, my family. I have been provoked beyond endurance, and yet you would have me turn the other cheek?"

"I have not said that. God has not forsaken you, Morgana," he whispered intently.

" 'Twill be hard for you to convince her," Alyson offered. "Mayhaps when the shock has worn thin."

Morgana watched as the gravedigger shoveled dirt upon the enshrouded body. "You expect too much from me," she sobbed. "Too much!" She turned away to lean against a tree.

The priest gave the gravedigger a measure of wine at the conclusion of his work, then came to her side. "That villein performed his job well," the priest said. "He brings news from your brother. Tonight, by the mews, when all is still and at the greatest moment of darkness, he will come for you. Take heart, girl. You will soon be in Ireland, with your sister."

"Hush!" warned Alyson. "The Norman approaches."

Morgana lifted her eyes toward the wood. The outlaws had disappeared. Praise be!

Morgana returned to Retford Hall in silence. Blaise, mindful of her dark, forlorn spirit and concerned about her drained, haggard appearance, entreated her to rest before the midday meal. As she lay across her bed, excitement flooded her body, for the child moved in earnest. She must plan her escape—flee this evil place where murderers lurked behind each shadow. Murderers. Adulterers. No place for a simple girl—a midwife's granddaughter in all but blood.

Elvina brought her food, but she pushed it away.

"Lord Blaise said that you must eat."

"I want nothing."

Elvina took the food away, but Blaise returned with the trencher. "You must eat. Now. For the child's sake."

"I will eat when you leave. I wish to be alone."

She nibbled at the fare to prove her good faith, and he left. She sighed in relief. He confused her and, she feared, could cause her to waver from her purpose. This she would not do.

Finally, through an effort of sheer will, she slept in dreamless peace. When she awoke, it was eventide and Blaise slept in a chair at her bedside. She had dreamt of him—dreamt that she lay in his arms, her passion spent. As she stirred, he roused and bent over her, cooing soft words, his eyes clouded, unreadable as he brushed the tendrils of hair from her forehead. Half-asleep, her supple body burned with a heat that she recognized, yet had successfully forsworn for months. Not so now. She needed him—needed to feel his cleansing love, needed his body joined with hers to drain her of this pain and renew her—to give her life. Life. She needed life—not death.

Yet—he wanted a commitment. He wanted more from her. He wanted her love—her understanding. He wanted her soul. She could not—did not dare to give in to the summons she read in his eyes.

But then, when his lips grazed her forehead, she could no

longer think. She looped her arms about his neck and drew him to her, her fingers entwining in the ebony thickness of his hair. She would have this one last time—this one last memory to sustain her for a lifetime of emptiness. For years to come, during those cool, damp nights in Ireland, she would remember this parting with sadness, and with joy.

He captured her lips with his own, igniting a fire within her that left her limp and moaning, sapping the small shred of resistance that was left. She was not an adulteress—for in her heart he was her *true* husband, the father of her child. They had been joined for all eternity by the old gods upon the high stone. For that reason alone, she could never truly belong to another, no matter how many kings or priests spoke.

It was right that she lay in his arms as he gently suckled her swelling breasts. She craved him as she did her next breath. It made not one whit of sense, but she yielded to him, spreading herself, each inch of her ripening body yearning for his touch.

Neither of them spoke lest they awaken to reality. When his lips pressed a light kiss on the mound wherein the child slept, she grasped his head to her in soft regard, loosening only when his tongue moved between her ivory thighs and he raised her hips to his wild caress. Her release came swiftly, not truly a release, for it was soon followed by another, and another, until she thought that she would surely die if he did not enter her, and told him so.

At their joining, he drove into the depths of her, Morgana quivering to his fiery strokes. That familiar, tremendous passion knotted deep within her, twisting like a bow, taut, until she matched his shuddering movement with her own, grasping him tightly, rhythmically, her pleasure heightened a hundred times because her ecstasy was reached in conjunction with his.

And at the very moment of her greatest joy, she whispered in his ear her parting gift. "I—I love you, my lord." He seized her to him as if he would hold her so forever, and her breasts heaved as her mind tumbled in swift images that bewildered her.

" 'Tis the sweetest moment of my life. You have yielded all to me. Do not be sad. You know that this was our destiny. None shall ever part us, even unto death. I would kill any who tried."

Morgana averted her eyes, forcing her tears back, for she knew that, contrary to what he believed, this had not been a commitment, but rather a fond farewell.

She swept back a lone tear and hardened her heart as she poured two horns of wine. They toasted their future and savored the sherry, and when each horn was empty, she said, "I wish to be alone, my lord, to think upon this day—and our future."

"Not now," he protested.

"Now, my lord! *Mon seigneur,* surely you know that I have the strength to endure even the horror of this day."

He nodded and kissed her forehead, stroking her hair. "If you must—then sleep alone. But should you need me—"

"I know that you will be here for me in a twinkling."

She bit back the lie. He would be of no assistance should she need him, for she had taken care to lace his horn with a powerful powder that would take him swiftly to the land of dreams.

In the middle of the night, she crept down the back stairs dressed as a page and slipped out through the kitchen door. A horse stood saddled and waiting behind the mews, its feet covered with cloths to smother the sound of its hooves, and its mouth muzzled. She adjusted her dagger at her waist and led the horse, a gentle, swift bay, toward the beckoning wood. A tall man stood outlined in the moonlight.

Morgana recognized the housecarl as he exited the shadows. "Make haste, my lady." She glanced up at the watchtower, unable to drag her eyes away from the sentry. "He shall be no bother to anyone ever again," Cedric assured her. As they passed the tower, a drop of thick liquid splattered on her cheek. The sentry's blood dripped from his severed throat, soaking the ground beneath the tower, and driving her onward.

The drawbridge was already down, and once over, she sprinted through the fields to the wood beyond. Once in the wood, she slowed to a trot, feeling safe, as if she had returned home. And she was safe—finally hidden from the prying eyes of all Norman vermin.

Except for one.

Gisele watched the girl's retreat, her head reeling giddily as Morgana disappeared into the dense wood. "Begone, Saxon whore! Now he *will* turn to me."

She mixed the powder that Alyson had given her with a glass of wine, donned a peach silk night shift so sheer that her nipples showed through, and went to Blaise's bedchamber.

Sigvald, who slept on the floor just inside the doorway, woke as she came through the door, but did not stop her. Blaise could handle this one easily enough, he warranted.

Blaise lay on his back, a thin linen sheet covering him to the waist. Gisele's hot, greedy gaze took in the outline of his body, and her whole being filled with lust for him. She removed her shift and climbed in next to him, her thigh burning where they touched.

In the darkness, Blaise drifted back from sleep, drawn out by Gisele's insistent ardor. His lithe form unfolded to cover her, and her body tingled at each place of contact. There was a dreamlike intimacy in his kiss as his lips slowly descended to meet hers. "Kirsten—Kirsten," he murmured.

The kiss stopped as Gisele heard his gasp, and his body stiffened. He lifted his head to peer down at her.

"Gisele?" He rolled from her in sore aggravation, braced for battle, as the passion that had quickened in his loins swiftly waned. "Your stupidity knows no bounds, wife."

As he stood, Gisele flung herself from the bed to grovel at his feet. "Do not send me away, *mon seigneur*."

He loosened her grasping hands. "Be gone!"

"I know you are angry. Punish me, if you want, but do not turn from me. You need a child—an heir."

"I shall have a child."

Gisele's heart gave a sickening lurch, but then she remembered that the girl had escaped into the wood. "D'Arcy will never let you have her," she taunted.

He lit a torch by the fire's embers, and she could see that mockery twisted his handsome face. "I do not plan on asking his permission."

"She shall bring you naught but trouble."

"More trouble than you have brought me?"

"She is a Saxon," she whimpered.

"And you are a Norman whore," he threw at her, his eyes skimming her closely, "and an old one at that."

"Not too old," she said with more than a small measure of confidence. "Definitely not too old."

"She pleasures me well, better than you ever did, or could." He put the shift on over her head, then lifted her in his arms and carried her back to her chamber.

She spoke heedlessly in her rising anger. "The girl makes a fool of you, Blaise. But then—" she shrugged as he kicked open the door and dropped her onto the floor with a loud thud "—you always have been a fool." A sudden chill hung on the edge of her next words, and she spoke without thinking, spoke to hurt—to destroy. "That is why I never wanted to carry your child—that is why I killed your babe."

He suspended movement and twisted toward her in a rage. "What say you?"

She pressed on, heedless of his outrage. " 'Tis true. In those days, when you begged my favors, I did conceive your child. But you left me for Duke William, and you knew not how long you would be gone or when you would return. I was not about to sit and bloat like a stuffed pig. D'Arcy wanted me—enjoyed looking at my slim body. I could bring him to my bed, but not if your child grew within me, so I rid myself of the brat."

"You murdered my child—my heir—for that man!"

She threw back her head, and her eyes gleamed. "Aye! Just as I did his child for you a few months later. After all, you had been gone for months, and would have known that it could not possibly be your child."

"Two—two murders on your conscience? Does D'Arcy know?"

"Nay! He is as much a fool as you. But at least he knows how to fulfill my needs."

"That is because you are two of a kind." He sneered contemptuously. "Make haste and pack your belongings. You leave on the morrow for Rouen."

"Good!" she shrieked. "There are many young men more to my liking in Normandy."

"I care not whether you fuck your way through Normandy—Brittany—the whole of France."

He walked away with nary a backward glance. Gisele slammed the door behind him and threw herself across her bed, pummeling the pelts and screaming with unbridled fury. After a while she dissolved into tears, and finally into writhing as the potion she had taken took effect.

Her thoughts were confused, jumbled, as she wriggled in her bed, her legs convulsing, her eyes tightly shut. Her fantasies placed man after man between her legs—Blaise, Christian, the falconer at their manor house, Sigvald, several men-at-arms—one after the other, she drained them.

Her fingers stroked each inch of her skin as she arched and twisted, seeking to free herself of this almost painful need within her. She was burning up, squirming under her own touch, probing herself knowingly, as she had learned to do in the convent.

She rubbed her sex swiftly, continuing until her moment of climax was upon her, when she thrashed upon the bed, her head whipping back and forth upon the pillow. The moment lasted an eternity as she rolled onto her belly and pressed herself rhythmically into the pallet. When it was done, she lay, bathed in sweat, unable to move, gasping—gasping—her eyes bulging in terror—

Above her a cloaked, hooded figure lay on top of her, a knee pressed into the small of her back, hands encircling her delicate throat. Soon she no longer struggled. The figure remained over her, ensuring that it was not a faintness, but death that had stilled her breathing. One swipe of a jeweled dagger, and blood seeped from her throat to soak the pillow. Finally, certain that she no longer lived, the robed figure rose from the bed and disappeared back into the shadows.

Brent was late in meeting Morgana. From the edge of the wood, he led her horse by its tether, so that she would not be thrown.

"Where do we go?"

"You shall see," he replied tersely.

Morgana ceased to care where she went, giving herself completely into her brother's capable hands. He would protect her. It was his duty. It was her right.

A long silence hung taut between them. "Why do you take such a tone with me?" she asked.

"Mayhaps I do not trust you," he replied.

"Have I done aught for you to deny me your trust?"

"My mother is dead, and you carry the Norman's bastard in your belly."

"*Our* mother. I am a victim. You accuse me of betrayal?"

"How can I be sure that you do not lay a trap for me?"

"I prayed," she retorted icily, "that you would stir a measure of compassion for all that I have endured, but it appears that you no longer have any to give. I will not be burdensome. As soon as you can arrange passage, I will be gone from your life." She bit her lip to restrain the tears at the corners of her eyes. "What have I done to you, to warrant such cruelty?"

Feeling duly chastened, Brent, in a brusque manner, urged his horse forward while Morgana fumed in silent rage. "Do you want to rest for a moment?" he asked after a quarter hour.

"Why? So you can accuse me of delaying you until the Normans find us?"

He leaned toward her in his saddle. "I am an unfeeling lout. Forgive me."

"I want to go to Ireland. I ask no more of you," she replied curtly.

He slowed his horse and circled to draw up next to her. In the moonlight, he could see that a single, silent tear glistened upon her cheek. "I have become a churlish oaf in the wood. No manners. Please forgive me, Morgana." He brushed her cheek with gentle fingers and pressed her face to his chest as Morgana wept out her torment. "I should never have let you talk me out of attacking the caravan on the road to London. Damn D'Arcy's soul! Will he slay every person I love?"

" 'Tis not your fault, or mine. D'Arcy will meet a violent end. I have no doubt of that."

"Aye! At the end of my crossbow."

They continued on, winding in and out until they stopped at a hut in an area she did not recognize. "I had this built for you. One of my most trusted men, Ethelbert, and his wife, Anne, will live here with you, to serve and protect you. He is a tanner, and the shed behind smells to high heaven—" he twisted his nose—"but 'twill serve its purpose."

He lifted Morgana down from the horse just as Cedric

reined in behind her. "Cedric is in charge of your security."

"What if Blaise or D'Arcy should come for me?"

"The Norman lord is not a fool," Cedric offered. "He knows that it would mean sure death for him to try and find you in Andredeswald. And as for D'Arcy, I can only hope that he will search you out, for we await him."

The hut was sparsely furnished—three beds, three chairs, a stool. Cedric moved one of the pallets from the wall to reveal a wooden platform hidden under a large woven rush carpet. When he lifted the platform, Morgana could see a deep, black cavern inside.

"Should anyone come, you will remove this rug and climb into the cellar. 'Tis lined with wood planks and rushes for your comfort. Ethelbert or Anne will then cover it over. There will always be one of them here with you."

"How long will I be here?"

"If I arrange passage for you from Brigstoc, you will get safely across the Irish Sea," Brent assured her. "The soonest would be a month, for I go north the end of this week to seek assistance from the Northumbrian and Mercian earls, Edwin and Morkere. Do not fear, little sister. You shall be rid of all of them very soon, one way or the other. I promise."

She was torn by the disparate feelings that her impending freedom evoked. On the one hand, she wanted to flee this sad, unhappy place—to leave Astrid's death behind her. And she wanted to escape D'Arcy and Gisele, both of whom presented a threat to her very existence.

On the other hand, this was her home—her people. And Blaise was here. All the more reason to flee, for she could never be his slave—never warm his bed and bear his bastard children. She would not spend a life of pain, heaping one humiliation upon another.

" 'Tis a good plan, brother. I thank you for keeping your promise to me."

"You and the child shall be safe," he decreed resolutely. And she believed him.

As Blaise sat at table the next morning to break his fast, he noticed that neither Gisele nor Kirsten had come down to eat. He picked at the food on his trencher, and planned Gisele's return to Normandy.

Although the general din of the great hall muffled the scream somewhat, Blaise's head shot up at the high-pitched squeal. There was a lull in the conversation at table, and he knew that others had also heard it.

Elvina screeched as she scrambled down the hall of the upper landing toward the stairway. "Murder! Murder!"

Blaise dashed from his seat and took the steps two at a time. He scowled at Elvina, who sat on the top step, mumbling incoherently. He yanked her to her feet by the elbow and pulled her along behind him as he thundered down the hall.

Elvina followed reluctantly, her feet lagging, until she stopped outside Gisele's bedchamber. Blaise continued with purposeful strides to Morgana's bedchamber, a cold knot in his stomach, and his chest close to bursting as he tried the door. It was not bolted, and opened slowly on its metal hinges.

It appeared empty. Confused, he searched, but found no one. He wavered, trying to comprehend what he saw—or did not see. Where was she?

"Mon seigneur!" Sigvald called from the hallway.

Blaise backed out of the doorway and turned to see Sigvald outside of Gisele's bedchamber. The retainer cocked his head and stepped back from the doorway so that Blaise could enter.

The stench of death assailed him, overwhelmed him. He had smelled it most of his life, but this was no rotting corpse on a battlefield, this was his wife. He had once loved this woman, though not for a very long time had he held even the slightest regard for her.

Yet he did not wish her dead, and in such a ghastly manner. She lay on her stomach on the bed, naked, her throat slit. Large clumps of clotted blood dotted each side of her. When he tried to turn her over, he noted that her head had nearly been severed from her shoulders.

"Send for the priest," Blaise said solemnly as he rose from the bed.

Outside, a horn sounded an alarm. Sigvald went to the

window. *"Mon seigneur!* Look! 'Tis not the only treachery wrought last night."

Blaise strode to the window in time to see his men removing a body from the watchtower. At the bottom, in the new dawn, a pool of blood had formed.

"What does this mean? Were we attacked last night? Find out what has happened." As Sigvald moved swiftly to do his bidding, Blaise returned to Morgana's bedchamber, but she was nowhere to be found.

"Where is Lady D'Arcy?" he asked as he gripped the servant girl by the shoulder.

Elvina shrugged. "I have not seen her today, my lord."

He went through her trunks. "The ungrateful bitch!" His eyes gleamed as he turned with calm deliberation and went to where Sigvald stood questioning the men.

"What news?"

"No word. Two horses are missing."

"Two?" So someone had assisted her. "How many dead?"

"Just the sentry, and your lady."

"Do you think they are connected?" Blaise asked.

"An unusual coincidence."

" 'Tis what it is, a coincidence. The Saxon bitch goes to the forest. Though she may have disliked Gisele, she would not murder her."

"I agree." Sigvald nodded. "Mayhaps she merely went for a walk," he offered.

"Nay! She has fled. Her coffers are gleaned of all she owned of worth." He pressed his hands to his temples, and rubbed his forehead. "What evil has been wrought here?"

"I know not, *mon seigneur.*"

"The men will whisper that I killed Gisele for the girl." Sigvald looked away toward the wood. "Well, I wished her dead on many occasions. Who cares what these louts think? And who among them would dare utter such suspicions?"

"None would dare say a word, *mon seigneur,* except possibly—D'Arcy. But we cannot stop them from thinking it, and should D'Arcy use whisperings to his advantage, as he has in the past, it could mean calamity."

Blaise had Gisele buried behind the chapel in a private ceremony.

Her bedding was burned. After the chamber was aired and scented with herbs, Blaise returned and barred himself in, as if the walls would speak to him of their secrets.

Kirsten's escape gnawed at him as he freely drained a flagon of wine. His sense of loss was even more acute than when she had married D'Arcy. It was an almost physical pain. How desperately he needed her, even if she was to be at a distance, as long as he could see her, drink in her beauty, watch the sun as it caught the highlights of her hair. Nay! It would never be enough. He needed to hold her—touch her—lose himself within her softness.

"Are you going to eat, or are you going to stay here all day, pouting like a child?" Sigvald asked later that day.

"I do not pout."

"You pout. Like a child."

" 'Tis only . . ." he began, but the words were difficult to express. "How can she leave me this way?"

Sigvald sighed. "Your men think that you grieve because of Gisele."

"She has not been my wife for many a year."

"And the other was never your wife for a day. At a time like this, even after she has betrayed you, you love her?"

"She did not execute the sentry."

"The men do not see it that way. She plotted with whoever did it. The seax cleaved his skull in two, and opened his throat."

Blaise crouched forward, his head in his hands. He massaged his temples as a painful pressure built. "God! What have I become? Would that I had stayed in the monastery, reading my books, searching for God."

"You would not have met the Lady Kirsten."

"And would never have known the pain and mystery of love. I cannot be grateful for a quirk of fate that has resulted in so much pain for all of us." He threw a log on the fire to chase the evening dampness from the chamber. "I still cannot believe that she has fled me," he said miserably.

"She loves you. Women differ from men."

"And yet she married D'Arcy? She would allow him to father my son—that swine?"

"*Mon seigneur,* if you would but remember, you were the one who told the king that she carried D'Arcy's child.

You were the one who urged the king to force D'Arcy to accept responsibility for his actions.''

"I was crazed with jealousy. I thought—''

" 'Tis your damnable pride that has cost you the girl *and* your child. Your pride." Blaise tried to deny it, but Sigvald would not give quarter. "Gisele was right. You sent D'Arcy to Hartley so that you could have his wife to yourself. Hartley holds special danger for D'Arcy, and it would not be unusual for him to end his life skewered by a Saxon arrow. The Black Outlaw wreaks havoc on the village nightly. He steals foodstuffs, burns houses, tears down the palisade walls. He toys with D'Arcy, but one night he shall kill him.''

"D'Arcy sowed the seeds of dissension. 'Tis only right he should reap the whirlwind.''

"But look, *mon seigneur,* at how the pieces of this puzzle fit together. Your wife dies—D'Arcy dies—and you and she can be together.''

"Damn you, man! You are my friend, and I see the disapproval in your eyes. Do you think that I have purposefully sent D'Arcy to his death? Do you?" He grasped Sigvald's forearm. "The truth, man.''

"Is it not the only way that you can have her and your son?''

"I have not thought much of this matter. 'Tis true that I want him away from her. 'Tis true that I covet her. But I have not consciously planned his death." He raked his fingers through his hair. "I will go to Hartley—tell D'Arcy that she has flown. I will send him back to Retford and supervise the work myself.''

"And you will comb the wood for her?''

"He cannot harm her, now that she has fled the compound.''

"But you will seek her out?''

Blaise thought long and hard about this. "Nay! Mayhaps 'tis best that I leave be. She asked for her freedom. I told her 'twas not in my power to give her, and now she has taken it. Letting her go to D'Arcy was one of the most difficult decisions of my life. Now that she has escaped him, I will not again enslave her.''

Chapter 15

Blaise, accompanied by a small party of his men, rode to Hartley with demonic fury. Upon his arrival, he strode into his tent and summoned D'Arcy.

"What are you doing here?" D'Arcy asked casually, his smile growing serious when he beheld Blaise's sour temper. "What is it? What is wrong?"

" 'Tis Gisele—she has been killed."

"Surely you jest? It cannot be. You!" he gritted between his teeth. "Your obsession for my wife is so strong that you would kill Gisele?"

"Curb your tongue, or I shall cut it out for you." Blaise cut him a murderous glare, and D'Arcy knew that he should tread lightly, for Blaise was clearly distraught. "Besides, there is no woman to gain any longer."

"What?" D'Arcy asked, in anticipation, and dread.

"The little bird has flown to the wood."

Blaise was not certain what D'Arcy's reaction would be, but he was not prepared for the gleam of obvious satisfaction in his eyes, nor the laughter that floated up from his throat—scornful and triumphant.

"I see the game now. You think to spirit Kirsten away, hide her, and thereby keep her for yourself."

"Nay! She wants naught of me, or you."

"That did not stop you in the past."

"I have abandoned her and the child, and you have killed her mother. Do you blame her for fleeing?"

"I heard that her mother had not survived. 'Twas an accident."

"Kirsten saw you in bed with Gisele. Was that an accident, too?" D'Arcy cocked a brow. "Aye! We both saw you, so cease your ranting. 'Twas folly to bed my wife, but you never were very clever."

"You will never have Kirsten or the babe."

"I know that she carries my child."

"I never said she did not. 'Twas your own stupidity that put her in my bed. Remember that."

"Do you never tire of taking my leavings?"

"Kirsten enjoyed my touch. Ask her when you find her."

"I do not plan to look. The search is your responsibility, not mine."

"I will find her, and drag her back to Retford." D'Arcy smiled wryly. "She will pay for this foolish act."

Blaise scowled. "You care naught for either of them, do you?"

"What say you?"

"You claimed to love Gisele, and now she lies dead, and you have not one word to speak of it."

"Gisele was a faithless harlot, as you well know. She is not deserving of even one word." D'Arcy turned crimson with resentment. "But you are so righteous, *mon seigneur*. Whose wife were you bedding while your own lay in my arms? You think me a fool? I know you took Kirsten."

"Your communications travel quickly," Blaise noted.

"Aye! Even here in this godforsaken hell, I am told the truth of the matter."

"And what is this? Do you plead my bad influence to explain your actions?"

"I am a rogue, no doubt, and shall answer for all of it on Judgment Day." He paused. "But you are perfect. Mayhaps my wife fled to the wood to escape you, not me. Have you thought on that, or do you blame all of it on me?"

"I will accept a measure of the blame. You destroyed

her family and loved ones, and I destroyed her and drove her to do things . . ." his voice trailed off.

"Do you suspect that she killed Gisele?"

"Nay! She does not have murder in her."

"Not even if in a moment of recklessness? Once acted upon, she would flee instead of risking retaliation."

"Do you know naught of your own wife?"

"I know that she held a knife to my neck not too long ago. I know that she wielded it with the expertise of a man-at-arms. The sight of it sticking between that boar's eyes still raises the hackles on my neck."

"She does not have murder in her, I tell you. I could never have lain with the girl and not known this about her," he replied brusquely, "nor could you, I imagine."

D'Arcy paced back and forth with a menacing step. "Well, when I find her—"

"I have reconsidered, and I forbid it. You are to return to Retford. I shall stay at Hartley and complete this job."

"But the child—"

"The woman is frightened senseless by your ill treatment of her and her mother. You shall not harm her, or my child—"

"How conveniently you claim the child."

"Gisele admitted that she took potions to prevent conception. 'Twas foolish of me to ever think that Kirsten would have laid with you. I forced her into your arms, and now you two are properly wed. But the child is mine, and I will have it. I swear it."

"She will never give over. She *would* kill for the babe."

"I am the lord of this demesne. I will have my son."

"The law makes him my son. I will ride to the king to plead my case."

"Try, and you will never reach William alive. You have my word on it."

"You are mad!"

"That may be true. I have just seen the wife that I once loved slaughtered like a lamb. The mother of my child has fled to the wood with the only babe I am likely to ever sire. I have lost much this day, and no one shall take more from me—leastways you. Keep the woman if you find her, but I want my child." Blaise took a flagon of brandy from the table and poured himself a stiff jolt. "I have a theory about where she has gone. I believe the Black Outlaw has given her refuge. I am told the man hates you. He harries Hartley nightly to repay your treachery. To get Kirsten, you would have to enter the dragon's lair. Do you still want to seek her out?"

"It would please you to have the Black Outlaw do what you are too weak to do yourself."

"I never had to kill you, D'Arcy. Locking Gisele away in the nunnery was the perfect redress for the wrongs done me. Death was too easy; leaving you alive was so pleasurable."

D'Arcy turned on his heel and took his leave, while Blaise completed his tour of the fortifications that had been rebuilt. "The next time these churls venture forth from the wood, will we be able to stave off an attack? What say you, sir?"

Sir Guy de Bologne scratched his head. "If Lord D'Arcy had listened to me in the first place, we would not have suffered the losses we have. I wanted to build the motte first, but he insisted on heightening the palisade."

"You have torn down the charred remains of the structures?"

Sir Guy nodded. "We need to build in stone if we are to hold this village."

"Is there enough at the quarry for both villages?"

"Aye. And 'twould be a wise defensive move."

"Why did D'Arcy not suggest this himself?"

"He does not explain to me why he acts as he does. Just last night I sought his opinion on the location of the barn, and he was nowhere to be found."

"Lord D'Arcy was gone, you say? For how long?"

" 'Tis not the first time, *mon seigneur*. He often goes off into the wood for long hours; I know not where."

Blaise mulled this new information over in his mind. Could D'Arcy have returned to Retford last night? Could he have killed Gisele? It was too wicked to think, but he was capable of it. But how to prove it?

"I will stay until the work is completed," Blaise assured the little man. "But I want crews to work throughout the night—every night—and rest only on Sunday. This job must be completed before the rebels attack."

When Brent left for the north, Gareth came to live with Morgana. Time moved more slowly in the wood than at Retford Hall, where she had spent each day catering to the needs of the refugees. Each day meshed into the day before it; weeks turned into months. The child within her grew, and when Brent's man returned with the news that he had not been able to arrange passage for her, Morgana resigned herself to her fate. She breathed a sigh of relief, for as her time grew nearer, she knew that she would not be able to travel without jeopardizing the child's life.

The babe had asserted its existence with a vengeance, reminding Morgana of every detail of her relationship with the father. Separation from Blaise had confused her. At times her mood was light, buoyant, and she was certain that she had found new strength in her pregnancy—or at least less despair. At other times she was restless, irritable—a terrible tension crippling her thoughts. She could be composed one moment, and thunderous the next. Anne attributed it all to her pregnancy; Morgana attributed it to her loneliness and loss of her mother—and Blaise.

She thought of him each day—the man who had so easily deserted her and his child, who had driven her away from him. When she would see a man with black hair, she watched to see if it fell across his forehead, just so, reluctant to obey, as did his. At night, when she lay on her pallet, bereft and desolate, she would remember the touch of his fingertips as they slid lightly over her bare arm, and down her thigh. And when the child moved within her, she remembered the first night that she lay with him upon the great stone, shrouded by the thick night mist, as their babe was conceived. Had she loved him from the beginning? Had she seen in those brilliant gold eyes something else besides a flicker of interest in bedding her? Had she known then, in that first moment, that he was her destiny?

For what purpose? It had all fallen apart like a poorly made mantle, this ill-fated love of theirs. But when would it truly end—when would she be free of him? He spoke of obsession. Was she herself obsessed with him? Despite what he had said and done to hurt her, did she want him still? Could she love him still? Could anything quell her doubts?

One morning, in mid-June, Gareth skipped into the hut, sucking the sweetness from a softened honeycomb. "Where did you get that?" Morgana asked.

"A priest gave it to me in the wood."

"Near here?"

"Aye, very near! Do you want some?"

Morgana craved the sweet honey. "Nay! You eat it. Was there more?"

"Sure. He only broke off a piece for me, then went on his way. Can we go and get the rest of it? Huh? Can we?"

She tousled his hair. When he grinned, he reminded her of Brent. Had Brent been like this once, seemingly happy, with a smile totally lacking in artifice?

She brought out her basket. "Where are you going, my lady?" Anne asked as Morgana pulled on her new leather shoes that Ethelbert had fashioned from pigskin.

"To gather honey in yonder wood. Gareth saw a hive."

"You will be harmed."

"Nay!" she replied as she draped herself in thin netting. "This shall protect me."

"Well, then, wait a moment, and I will come with you." Anne removed her apron and made to follow.

"Nay! I know you fear the bees—"

" 'Tis only that when I was stung, it blew up so fat. I saw someone choke to death once from just such a sting."

"I will be all right. You need not attend me. Stay here with Gareth."

"But if anything were to happen to you, your brother would never forgive me."

"Nothing will happen. I am safe here with you and Ethelbert. And Cedric sees to our welfare. All is as it should be."

"I am not sure—well, all right." She handed her a horn. "Should you come to danger, blow this. The men in the wood will come on swift feet, my lady."

Morgana, certain that the woman was being over-cautious, reluctantly tied the thong of the horn around her neck. Draped in her netting, she looked like an apparition as she made her way through the quiet wood. As she passed through a clearing, she saw the bees and peeked to her right and left. She was alone. The sharp, white light of the noonday sun slanted through the trees as the morning mist rose from the swamps beyond. She stepped gingerly through the bushes toward the hive, and knew a moment of uncertainty. It was much too quiet for this time of day, in this place. She fingered the dagger at her belt, slung low over her belly, as an unexpected wind whipped up the netting.

"Those who tarry too close to a beehive are wont to get stung." Blaise was right behind her, his hand on her arm, turning her to him.

Morgana, despite her pregnancy, moved with an agility he did not expect. She lunged beneath his arm to escape.

"God's mercy, girl! Stay close upon my hand before you slip into the bog."

She stood back on her heels, and presented a defiant mien to the knight who hid behind the garb of a friar. "What are you doing here?"

"Paying you a visit, my love."

"How came you here?"

"Do you truly believe that I would let you go and not know your every breath?"

"Have you yet yielded to madness in my absence, or is it only that your needs are sorely wanting, and you thought to tumble me on a summer's afternoon?"

"Are you well?" he asked the railing maid.

"Can you not see that I am?" She gave him a withering look. "You, on the other hand, look like the devil's own."

"I do not sleep well these days."

"Too much guilt to clutter your thoughts, eh?"

"Not enough jovial bantering now that you are gone."

"There is no one left with enough wits to best you in a fight." She gloated. "Certainly not your lady wife."

He removed his helmet and gauntlets, and released the catches on his coif. It fell back and draped his neck. He raked his hair as sweat poured down his forehead in rivulets.

"You look like you are going to collapse in your mail,"

she suggested. "Mayhaps your man should help you out of it."

"I came alone," he whispered as his eyes slid over her— leisurely, hungrily—until they rested on her face, delving deeply into her own. Relief was evident in her expression. "You have nothing to fear. I merely want to converse with you."

"About what?"

"Help me out of this mail, and I shall tell you."

Morgana hesitated, and against her better judgment, assisted Blaise in removing the armor. "Do you stay in that netting? I give my word I shall not sting you."

She whipped the netting from her in one fluid motion and turned away from the slow, unhurried caress of his regard.

He laid his mantle on the ground, and bade her sit upon it.

"I hope 'tis not a romp in the grass you seek this day, for surely you have come to the wrong maid," she said, indicating her belly.

"I seek only to make amends—to speak with you about the past, and the future."

She bristled at him as she jumped up. "We have no future." She tried to pass him, but he blocked her path. "Let me go!"

"Not right now," Blaise admitted. "I would speak first." He stood a hairsbreadth from her, his bold, unblinking stare taking in each contour of her body.

Morgana raised her chin in defiance. "I daresay, if you feel so passionately about speaking your mind, then do so."

"You know where my passions lie, and 'tis not in speech."

"Yea, you have left me a bold reminder." She patted her belly. "But I see now which way the wind blows, my lord. You think to come here, after all these months, and assume that I await your pleasure."

His breath seared her earlobe, and unconsciously, she brought her fingers up to protect herself, to press against the broad, rock-hard expanse of his chest. "You pleasured me well, I must admit. Even now, to think of you beneath me sets my very being afire."

"God knows, there have always been a dearth of ladies willing to spread their skirts for you. Gisele, for one."

"None compare to you, my love." He pressed toward her and was brought up short by her dagger at his throat.

"Nay! Norman feet have tread upon my heart often enough."

As an arrow whizzed by their heads at lightning speed, Blaise reacted as a seasoned warrior and laid her flat. He covered her, and when no shower of arrows followed, he lifted from her, sword at the ready in his hand. He admonished himself for having removed the glistening mail. 'Twould be of no use to him today, he warranted. He had foolishly let his guard down, and would no doubt pay the price of such folly.

They were under attack. This fact slowly penetrated Morgana's consciousness. But by whom? For what reason?

Blaise rolled and dragged her along the ground behind a rock, hunching forward to escape a volley of arrows. Whoever it was toyed with them, for the arrows merely formed a makeshift wall on each side of the stone.

"Blaise of Rouen, lackey of William the Bastard, allow me to introduce myself."

Brent! He had returned from the North, and as Morgana peeped over the boulder, he came forward, accompanied by at least a hundred yeomen. "The Black Outlaw at your service." Morgana blanched and bit her lip.

This reaction was not lost on Blaise. In that moment he knew that they were acquainted—mayhaps well acquainted.

"Come, girl." Brent beckoned her to him. She gained a small measure of composure and, with grace and bearing, lifted her skirts and climbed over the arrows, her eyes rebuking Brent sternly for frightening her and putting her in such danger. He gave her his hand, which she freely took, and he drew her into his arms and hugged and kissed her in brotherly greeting. "Look what I brought you." He removed a gold filigree girdle from his sack and tied it high on her waist, to lie over her belly. "Why do you enter my wood?" Brent asked, as if he had just noticed Blaise.

"No doubt you know why. I want my woman—my child."

Brent mused upon the stubborn set of the knight's jaw.

"Only a very brave, or very foolish, man would enter the wood to challenge me. Which are you?"

"Mayhaps both," Blaise quipped.

"She has sought, and I have granted her, sanctuary. She is no longer your woman, sir. Besides, she was wed to your underlord, Christian D'Arcy, at your insistence, I am told."

"D'Arcy is at Retford. I bring her to Hartley."

"Not to Hartley or Retford," Brent retorted disagreeably. "I want the woman, or by God I shall burn down every tree in this wood to get her."

Brent smirked. "An idle threat, sir. 'Twould not please William to lose this wood. We have the finest hunting grounds in all of England. Besides—" he raised a taunting brow "—methinks you are in no position to make threats."

Seemingly out of nowhere, Sigvald swooped out of the tree above Brent and, in mere moments, had a thong of leather around his throat and a dagger at his neck.

"Not as bad a position as one would think, sir outlaw. Have your men put their weapons down," Blaise demanded as Sigvald tightened the thong and scraped the well-honed blade against Brent's neck, flaying the skin slightly so that crimson rivulets of blood seeped through the cracks.

"Go back, my lord," Morgana railed, moving toward him, now livid with rage. "Back to Hartley, or Retford. Ease your anger, and leave me in peace."

Despite his precarious position, Brent tried to wrench free to stop her, but Sigvald held him fast. "Stay away from him! Argh!" Brent's voiced choked off, and his face reddened.

Morgana continued onward until she was just in front of the stone. Blaise came from behind the boulder now, his brooding eyes showing the pain of betrayal.

"I will not return without you." His voice was firm, determined—final.

"Loose me" she begged. " 'Tis the only way. Surely you cannot continue to blind yourself to that fact? I will never be your leman—your chattel." She licked her lips, cursing their wretched dryness.

"Gisele was murdered," he replied simply.

Surprise gave way to reproach. "You would go to such

lengths to have me—commit such a heinous crime? And who is your next victim—my husband?"

It rankled him that she knew so little of his morality. "You have such little faith in me to think such a thing?"

"To make me your whore, you would do anything."

His extraordinary eyes blazed, and she was unable to drag her gaze away from their glow. "Never my whore," he admonished. "Always my love."

"Such an obsession puts your soul in peril, my lord." She fought to control her breathing. "The Black Outlaw has sworn to murder *you* should you touch a hair on my head. His vengeance knows no bounds. He survived Stamford Bridge and the carnage of Senlac Ridge. He metes out death with chilling efficiency." She halted, her speech stumbling as he brushed his knuckles gently along the line of her cheek.

"Fickle maid." Blaise laughed ruefully as he leaned to her, his snarling lips a hairsbreadth away. "Tell me, then. Are you the price for your 'sanctuary'?"

Morgana balanced as Brent struggled, but Sigvald jerked the tether, and she heard the grumbling of Brent's men as they discussed what to do about the situation. "Your insolence would arouse a saint's ire, my lord Blaise. But you have always thought me less than a possession," she reproached. "Well, I am nobody's possession—not yours, or D'Arcy's, or the Black Outlaw's. But I have chosen to be with him, over both you and my husband. Free will. My own decision."

"Then our fate is sealed."

She faced him squarely. "It was sealed many months ago, upon the rock, in the high place." She turned on her heel and strode to where Sigvald and Brent stood. "Call your men away," she ordered Brent. He stared agape at her as she turned to Sigvald. "Loose him, I beg you." She fought back tears. "Your lives for his," she whispered.

"His word first," Sigvald grunted.

Morgana's burning eyes searched Brent's, and saw the hatred blazing there. "Your word," she urged, but he bit his lip, fangs drawn like a cornered animal. Morgana prostrated herself at his feet. "Please, my lord, he is the father of my child. I am pledged to you. I stay with you. Leave be!"

There was a spark of some indefinable emotion in Brent's eyes, but he quickly masked it over, and nodded in agreement. Sigvald loosed the tether.

"Back! Back to the wood!" he ordered hoarsely.

"But, my lord—" Cedric began.

"I have given my word, and my word is my bond. Leave us!" The men, who had stood at the ready, bows pulled back, eased off and removed their arrows. As quickly as the swarm had come, it was gone.

Sigvald backed toward Blaise, sword in hand, as Morgana tended her brother's abrasions. Blaise watched as she ripped a length of muslin from her shift and dabbed at his neck. Over her head, their eyes met, each smoldering with a fire that would not be denied.

Blaise whistled, and Reynard galloped from the wood, Sigvald's horse in tow.

Morgana turned to face him, to drink of his countenance one last time—the man who, even now, threatened to snatch her will with the promise of a kiss.

Sigvald motioned, and the wood around them filled with mounted knights and men-at-arms. Morgana's chest rose in uneven breaths as she clenched her brother's hand, but the knights did not raise arms, nor in any way menace them. This was merely a show of might. At any moment, Blaise could have called forth his men, and slaughter would have ensued. He wanted Brent to know that he, too, could have exercised his strength, but had chosen not to do so.

"I will have my woman," he shouted to Brent as he shifted in his saddle, "but not over the blood of her people. 'Tis between you and me, and when next we meet, I will kill you."

"Return to Normandy, Blaise of Rouen. The wood is my place, not yours, and should you find your way here again, you will never leave alive."

Blaise nodded and took his leave, but there was no aura of defeat about him. He had learned an important fact about his enemy—the man had compassion. Brent could have given the order, could have cut Blaise down at the outset, but he had refrained, no doubt for her sake. He was a fool. Warfare could not be tempered with sympathy. The blending of the two could only lead to one's downfall.

Blaise would remember this the next time.

Chapter 16

"You will not kill him. You promised."

"Morgana, he has my word that I shall try if he returns. You cannot expect to fight the Normans without casualties."

"You promised to spare the father of my child."

" 'Tis war, Morgana. War! Stop thinking with your heart and use your head. If he returns, I must kill him, or surely he will kill me."

Fear pricked her anew. True, she did not want to be Blaise's possession, but neither did she want him dead. "Let me send a message to him, then."

"What message?"

"I will tell him that I have left the country. If he thinks me gone, he will not come for me again."

"Morgana, think! Your child comes any day now. You cannot board a ship so close to your time. No seaman will take you aboard. It may be a month before you can leave."

"Too close to the equinox. Should something go wrong— I would not be able to leave until next spring."

" 'Tis nearly Lammas night. Let us plan the celebrations, and forget this tiresome talk. What if Blaise harmed you— what if something is wrong with the babe—"

"Hush! Naught is wrong with the babe. She is a strong

lass—kicking and stretching—anxious to greet life." She looked up into the approaching night. " 'Tis said that one life is born as another goes to heaven. I miss Mother."

"She was dedicated to our father—a graceful helpmate—and now she is with him. You never knew him. He was strong-willed, and difficult—sometimes very difficult. But Mother knew how to influence him most artfully."

"Yes," Morgana agreed. "I could see that about her. I knew naught of him; indeed, saw him only from afar in my girlhood."

"And what are you now—an old woman?"

"Old beyond my years. Life was much simpler a year ago. I was—content. Oh," she admitted, "I had none of the comforts—no furs—no silks—no jewels," she sighed, "but I was—"

"Free?"

"Yes, free. I could do what I wanted, when I wanted."

"I have seen you handle a bow, a seax, and a dagger with an ability better than half my men. You are not a common Saxon lady." He smiled slyly. "I warrant the child shall put an end to your illustrious calling."

"All the more I shall try to set an example of strength for her." She paused. "I think often of her—dream strange dreams. Sometimes . . ." Her voice trailed off.

"What?"

"Sometimes I see her as if she were before me in the flesh."

"Some women have a sense of such things, I am told."

"Blaise wants a son."

" 'Tis best it should be a daughter. Normans do not treat their male bastards well."

" 'Tis not a bastard. You forget my vows to D'Arcy."

"Ah, yea," he sighed. "And if all goes according to plan, you shall be widowed before the year is out."

"A daughter of mixed heritage might do well in a conquered England; would you not say so?"

"A girl will be afforded all privileges of her rank, and hopefully D'Arcy would ignore her. If a boy, he could make matters difficult for you. Blaise cannot claim the boy, as D'Arcy is his legal father. And D'Arcy could decide at any time to disclaim him and declare him a bastard."

"I go to Dubh Lin, so no matter. Vikings care naught about legitimacy, I am told. Our own King Harold had several children with his handfasted bride, Edith of the Swan's Neck."

"William the *Bastard* considers the matter of slightly more importance."

She sat at his knee and laid her head in his lap. "You will protect me, whatever happens?"

"With my life." He patted her hand as if she were an errant child. "It cannot have been easy for you—all of this. So much for such slight shoulders to bear. I should have gotten you out before all this happened."

"No recriminations—you gave your word."

He nodded and stroked his chin thoughtfully. "Look in that sack. I have brought you a gift."

She dug into the sack and removed a red mantle lined in wolfskin. " 'Tis lovely." Her joy turned cold as she realized that it was bloodied.

"I took it from a Norman who had no further need of it." He shrugged and handed her a golden brooch. "You may wash it a bit—but the red hides the blood well." He saw that she was disturbed. "I am sorry—'tis all I have to offer you."

"It matters not," she answered, turning her face away from him as she pulled the cape around her neck and secured it, trying not to remember that it had graced the neck of a Norman knight, perhaps one of Blaise's comrades.

"Come! You look tired. I shall escort you back. Rest, for tomorrow night we shall celebrate in the wood." He took her hand in his, and they strolled back to the hut. "The Feast of Bread. *Hlaf-mass* night. Lammas night, the Normans call it. The old ones called it *Lugnasad,* or Games of Lug. In one of the games, you could marry by ancient rites on Lammas night, and stay married for a year and a day, and then, if you wished, you could separate."

" 'Tis sad," she mused.

"Sometimes 'tis better to have a year and a day than to have nothing at all. I would have settled for such with Alayne," he said in an oddly muffled voice, "rather than what I gained—nothing."

"Come for me tomorrow?"

He gave her a grudging nod, and walked briskly away.

Morgana tried to rest the next day, but was driven by a sudden burst of energy to scour the hut. Much to Anne's dismay, she changed the rushes. "They were changed only last week," the woman insisted, but Morgana would brook no refusal.

In the afternoon she sat behind the house, her nose twisted away from the smell of the tannery, and pounded the muslin bed linens with smooth stones.

"You overdo it, my lady. Here." Anne pushed Morgana gently to one side. "Let me."

Morgana sat back on her haunches and searched futilely for a comfortable position.

"What is it?"

"My back aches."

"See! You *have* overdone it," the woman chided. "Go sit down!" She pointed to the hut. "I will come put on the new linen that milord Brent brought as soon as I hang this to dry."

As Anne struggled with the wet sheet, Morgana put the new linen on the bed and promptly fell asleep upon it. Anne let her rest well on into the night.

When she awoke, she could make out, in the pale glow of the candlelight, a gunna of lightweight mauve cotton hanging on a hook near her pallet, along with a garland of wildflowers for her head. " 'Tis from your brother," Anne said. Unbidden, memories of the bloodied cloak came to Morgana, and she grimaced. What poor maiden had lost her life to give up these clothes?

"Do not fret," Anne said. "These were made especially for you by a seamstress in his camp—a woman of *many* talents, I am told."

This eased Morgana's mind considerably as she snatched the kirtle over her head, and then the gunna. "How do I look?" She postured saucily, and it rankled her when Annie broke out into bursts of laughter. "I am fond of you, but should you continue to laugh at me—"

" 'Tis not you, but your manner. I fear you are much too pregnant to be batting your eyelashes at the lads tonight."

"I do not plan to bat my eyelashes at anyone," Morgana

assured her. "Look at me! I look like a sow ready for the headman's ax."

"Nay! You are lovely, as always," Brent assured her from the doorway. "Make haste!" He tipped his hollowed bull horn. "The ale awaits, and so do the maidens." He winked and she faced him, arms akimbo.

"You are not going to take me to this feast so that I may witness your wenching, are you?"

"I had not planned it, but I have earned the right to indulge some of my brutish delights."

"Men!" she scoffed. "You are all the same."

Brent lifted her into his arms. "Come, little sister. It cannot be easy to carry all this weight on those tiny feet all night. I shall carry you there, for Lord knows, I shall most likely find it hard to stumble back."

In the music and the feasting, she found a cleansing sweetness, a joy, a rhythm of life so primitive and natural that it swept away all the sorrows of the past year. Her soul skipped lightly along, as it had on All Hallows' Eve.

She clapped her hands to the music as the others danced. Ale flowed freely, and the sky filled with so many twinkling stars that it looked like a jeweled curtain.

Despite her rest that afternoon, she tired quickly. She knew that she had driven herself much too hard for a woman in her condition. Brent had disappeared into the wood with a maid, and she wondered if it was the same one who had sewn her gunna with a delicate hand. When she had left, Ethelbert and Anne were swimming in the pond, their naked arms holding each other in a fond embrace.

Morgana remembered a night Blaise had made love to her in the wooden tub, and she flushed, heat stealing into her face as she saw his eyes as she had last seen them— glittering in repudiation. Reluctant to bother anyone, she quit the feasting and returned, alone, to her hut. She was bone-weary, and it was time to put the revelers and their music aside. It was cooler in the wood, the leaves crisp and crackling in the night breeze. She pulled her mantle tighter about her neck as she reached the door of the hut. She thought that she heard a sound, and glanced down the pathway, her ears pricked to listen to the night. Cedric's men were perched high in the trees. No one would breach the sanctuary of the wood this night.

Inside, she quickly doffed her gunna and lay down to sleep in her kirtle, covering herself carefully with the blanket of squirrel pelts. Someone had lit a fire, and the hut was cozy, warm enough to chase away the chill night air.

Sleep eluded her. She rebuked herself for having overdone it this day—cleaning and feasting with no thought to her eventual discomfort. She rubbed her lower back, lying first on one side, and then on the other. Finally exhausted, her body began to slacken, and sleep claimed her just as the first pain ripped through her belly like a bolt of lightning.

She breathed in shallow, quick gasps until it subsided, then she pressed her heels into the bed and sat up, a thrill of frightened anticipation shuddering through her. This was it! The child was coming. Well, 'twas not so bad as other women had led her to believe. 'Twas not constant at least.

Her relief was short-lived as another pain followed by a mere two minutes upon the first—a cold knot within her begging for release. She tried to control her breathing, as she had watched Alyson do with others, but her fear cut off her breath, and her chest felt as if it would burst. She moaned, and when the contraction had subsided, screamed, certain that the sentry would come to her aid. But no one came. Had they heard her cry? Would they know that it was not a riotous merrymaker?

She dragged herself from the bed and opened the door. Grasping her belly, she padded down the pathway toward the sentry, but she halted when she saw at the base of the gnarled tree the sentry's silent, broken body.

Her gorge rose in her throat, but she choked it back and hastened back to the hut, heedless of the new tightening at her middle and stopping only for a moment when water gushed down her legs.

She knew what this was. The sack wherein the babe lay had burst—there would be no turning back now. She bit her lip to keep from screaming, but ignored the taste of the salty blood. Blood! Some women bled, she knew. Usually those who died—whose children died. She looked at her legs to make sure that it was not blood that drained from her body, and was relieved to see that the liquid was clear.

A screech owl swooped by her window, and she jumped almost out of her skin. She must hide—she must hide. She opened the trapdoor to the cellar and, dousing the candle, slid in—turning her ankle in the process—and waited, her lips moving in silent prayer.

Almost immediately the pain intensified, the period of ease shortening as the pain fell close upon the one before it. She heard muffled voices outside, but did not grow terrified until she recognized one as D'Arcy!

He would kill her—he would steal her child and kill her. He could use the child to taunt Blaise, but he would have no need for her any longer. He never really wanted her, only the child—Blaise's child. She was as good as dead if he realized where she was. But how could he not? He knew that she was in the hut—that she had extinguished the candle. No doubt he had been watching.

She steeled her body for the next pain, and it came with such intensity that her breath quit in shock. Above her, she heard footsteps and the clank of a knight's spurs. One of the men lit the torch in the iron sheath upon the wall. As if he knew exactly where she was, he strode toward the floor panels and opened the trapdoor.

'Twas indeed D'Arcy who leered above her, the torch in his hand. A piece of pitch fell and burned her arm. She hissed at him as he yanked her to her feet and lifted her none too gently out of the hole.

"You son of Satan!" she hissed.

He smiled a crooked smile. "One would think you were not happy to see me, wife." He caught her as she reached for her knife next to the bed, and twisted her hand until she dropped it. "Kirsten, are you still trying to lay me low?" He bent a cold, ruthless gaze upon her. "I am aghast at this behavior," he mocked sternly, and his men chuckled behind him.

Morgana was rooted and unable to move as the next pain washed over her.

"Hah! Methinks the child comes, eh?" He lifted her none too gently and sent her sprawling upon the bed, until she scrambled back and sat cross-legged. "I have never taken my ease of a breeding woman. 'Tis said to be especially exciting. Should I ride between your thighs and find out?''

Morgana fought the need to swoon. She must keep her wits about her. "Touch me and you shall surely die, lord swine.'' She spat at him, and he slapped her so soundly that her head snapped back.

"Mayhaps you do not understand your predicament, lady wife. What would you do if I tethered your ankles together so tightly that these lovely limbs could not open? Your child would die. You would die.'' He affected a mien of sickly sympathy. '' 'Twould no doubt be a tragedy—the loss of one so young in childbirth.''

As he leaned over her, Morgana saw thick blood on his mail, and she trembled in revulsion. How many men had he murdered to get to her? She would retch if he touched her.

He grasped her kirtle and in one rending tear held it in his gauntleted fist. Guffaws filled the hut, and an icy tendril of fear slashed through Morgana as he doffed his helmet. He would not dare. 'Twas an idle threat.

"Well, *chérie*, I admit that I have been a wayward rogue—wenching my way from one woman to another in your absence—but I am here now, most penitent, and willing to give it another, ah, *bloody* go.'' He looked around him. "Of course, I would have chosen our bedchamber, but since you clearly prefer this filthy hovel, I suppose 'twill have to do.''

"Your brutish wit falls short, as do you, my lord husband. In all ways.''

One of his men helped him out of his armor. "I have something for you, my lady, that is sure to quell your rebellious nature.''

"I want naught from you save to be left alone.''

He eyed her closely as he stripped off his leather tunic and chausses, and stood in his brief loincloth, the extent of his excitement evident. Morgana whimpered as the next pain held her in its thrall.

He rose defiantly over her, naked now, his manhood rampant. "Leave us!'' he ordered, his eyes intense as a beast in the hunt. His men griped, but he threw them a scowl and they withdrew into the shadows of the night. Morgana's breath came rapid, uneven. "I could have loved you, Kirsten. I—I did love you—in my fashion."

"My lord, if you ever felt a bit of love for me, do not do this evil deed."

"My pledge to you was true—"

"Nay! You lay with that harlot."

"It meant nothing to me. She meant nothing to me. I could have *loved you*." His voice grew shrill, impatient. "But you loved *him* instead. You wanted *him* between these thighs." He covered her mound and she arched away from him, her humiliation past bearing. " 'Tis your own fault, Kirsten. You goaded me into such unreasonable action. You set me aside for my enemy."

"You caused the breach. For the love of God! You killed my mother!"

"You know 'twas an accident, though I must say I am not sorry to see the meddlesome bitch go."

"And now you are intent upon my punishment?"

"Someone must mete it out. I am your husband. 'Tis my right—my duty." He pressed her down into the pallet, his chest cutting off her breath as the next contraction tore through her. Her lips rounded in a scream, but D'Arcy was too quick, stuffing her torn kirtle into her mouth until she could only moan.

Morgana thought that she saw a movement behind him in the dim light. Had his men returned? "Shift, and I shall skewer you upon this sword." D'Arcy froze at the sound of Blaise's voice, and the ruthless hands that had pawed at her skin were snatched back as if burned. "Arise!" Blaise raged.

"Ho! The hound is on the scent—eh?"

"If you are wise, you will move quickly, but carefully, or you might find that prick you are so proud of at your feet." Blaise slapped him on the back with the flat of his long-sword, raising a series of welts. "Pick up your clothes. My men shall escort you from here—back to Hartley."

"She is my wife—"

"Not when you abuse and debase her. The king put her under my protection. You will not harm her—or my child."

"My child, you mean. Once again I must remind you that the law makes it my child."

"I would free her before I let you have her, or my child."
As Blaise levied another blow, D'Arcy bounded from the
hut, swearing an oath, and heaping vile threats upon them
both.

"How do you fare, my love?" he inquired in a soothing
tone.

Morgana, sweating, grasped his hand and kissed his
palm. "Thank you! Thank you! Thank—ah!"

"What is it? The child?" Morgana nodded, unable to
talk. Blaise knew naught of birthing. "How much longer?"

"Soon," she replied hoarsely. "Too soon."

He swore an oath. "What—what do I do?"

Morgana concentrated on the contraction, and once it
had subsided, she quickly related what she knew. She
helped him remove his mail, and he washed the grime from
his hands in the water from the cauldron that sat over the
fire. Next he removed what was left of her shift, bathed
her, and dabbed at her face with a cool cloth, pausing only
when another pain took her attention.

"I know naught of birth, Kirsten. I know only of death—
not life."

"We shall learn together, my lord. Together." Tears
flowed down her cheeks in wide streams.

"I will send for the midwife—Alyson."

"No! Your man will be caught in the wood, and *they*
will come for you. He will kill you—the Black Outlaw. He
has sworn it. My God! I could not bear it—not now." He
saw the wisdom of her words. "Besides," she continued,
"there is no more time."

The pains came now one on top of the other, one meshing into the other, until she could not tell where one ended
and the other began. She panted quickly, then blew out,
knowing that she should not push if the child was not ready
to come. "I think—I think I see his crown," Blaise said
excitedly. "Yea, 'tis the child's crown, to a certainty."

Morgana pushed in earnest now, for with the crowning,
the time was right, and as the child slipped from her body
in the wonder of birth, Blaise reflected that this was truly
what it was all about—life, not death. Birth—not severed
heads and split skulls. As he lifted his squalling daughter
over Morgana's belly, he swore that he would do all in his

power to protect her from the curse and destruction of war that he and her mother had known.

" 'Tis a girl," he whispered, almost reverentially.

"I know," Morgana murmured. "I am—sorry."

"I am well pleased," he assured her as he counted the babe's fingers and toes. "She is perfect. I am not certain, but I think her hair is your color. 'Tis still damp and hard to tell—but there is a gleam in it when the firelight hits it, like yours." He held her up. "She is of length—strong and tall, like you."

His tender ministrations swelled her spirits as he completed the birthing process, washed her gently, and held her when her limbs trembled uncontrollably. Later, as he swaddled the babe in linen, she remarked on his gentleness. "One would never know you to be a battle-scarred knight, to listen to your cooing," she teased.

"I have produced a beautiful child," he remarked.

"Conceited lout! I had something to do with it."

"Aye!" His brows knit as he thought about it. "I chose to breed with a quality female."

She slapped at him playfully, and he captured her hand in his own and brought it to his lips. "I thought for certain I would die in that stinking hole tonight," she said, suddenly serious. "Then, when D'Arcy came and drew me out, I wished I had." She quivered as the pain of the memory became intolerable.

Blaise embraced her. She might well have died. The child might have died. "Do not think on it now. You are safe. All has turned out for the best. D'Arcy is far from here by now."

"If you did not come, he would have killed us."

"Hush, my love. Hush!" He pulled his fingers through her loosened plaits. "Look at your hair—a mess."

"He would have murdered us—he threatened to tie my legs together, so they could not open, and the child—the child—" She yielded to the deep sobs that racked her body, even as he crooned to her, and told her that he would always protect her.

"Sleep," he whispered. "Sleep. I love you, Kirsten. I love you."

Morgana, exhausted by her ordeals this night and secure in his love, fell swiftly into a deep, untroubled sleep.

Blaise sat in the chair next to her bed, holding the baby, his thoughts disturbed. What would he do now? What could he do?

She was beautiful, his daughter. Yet *all* would conspire to separate them—the church, D'Arcy, even William.

The babe whimpered and her mouth sought food. "I am afraid I do not have what you need, little one." She stared at him, as if she saw him, then pounded his face with her tiny fist and screeched.

Morgana roused and sat up in the bed. "Bring her to me," she said, her arms outstretched. The child knew instinctively when she was in her mother's soft arms, and she rooted around until she found and clamped on to her nipple.

" 'Tis amazing," Blaise remarked as he brushed her cheek with his palm. "I have thought much on what to do. I shall go to Rome. When the pope hears of D'Arcy's perfidy, he cannot help but annul your marriage."

"I am wed to D'Arcy by royal decree."

"Then I shall seek the aid of William's man in Rome. The king has taken an interest in you."

"And if he refuses?"

"Then I care not. I will give up all honor—all rank and privilege. I must needs have you. I must—"

"My God, Blaise, then verily we are damned. Will you never see the true nature of things? This cannot be. It never was meant to be. You are William's man first—you told me this yourself. And I shall not be consumed by the 'firebrand' of the king."

"What of our love?" he asked hoarsely.

"For how long may we love? A year? Two years? Five years? And how will we live? You are a knight—'tis all you know."

"I can get work."

"As a mercenary? A hired killer for money?"

"I am no better than that for William."

"You are his man. You made a vow of fealty to him. You would hate me—eventually—for causing you to break that vow."

"You argue like a priest."

"I am Saxon. You are Norman. Our worlds are separated by blood—and death. The invasion has ended, aye! But the inner battle continues."

"Do you expect me to look at my child, the child of my loins, and not want her near me? Do you expect me to release you so easily? Do you care naught that I love you?"

"I care," she admitted, "to my everlasting shame. Though I may love you with my heart and soul, it changes naught. Fate conspires against us. Will we become as evil as D'Arcy to feed your obsession? They will excommunicate us. Would you kill our souls with your desire for me? Will you kill my husband to gain my hand?"

"Why do you think he yet lives?" He moved his mouth so close, his breath burned her lips. "Because I could not know for certain whether I killed him for his ill deeds, or because I *am* obsessed with you." He kissed her first with his eyes, and when her lips opened slightly, his mouth covered hers to drink of her sweetness. She returned his kiss with a hunger that belied her words. "You cannot leave me. You cannot say me nay." His words were a hypnotic, leaving her weak, confused. "You are not his—will never be his. I truly *would* kill him before I let him touch you again, for I love you."

"Nay! 'Tis only obsession. You Normans have slaughtered my family, my people; you have conquered my country, and ravished my body. But my soul is my own—and 'twill be free."

"You think to lie under me, and bear my child, and turn from me so easily. You are more a fool than I."

" 'Twill not be easy. Never easy. I have loved you longer, and harder, than ever you loved me." He shook his head in denial, but she put her fingers to his lips.

"Has this experience of the birth of our child—has it meant naught to you?"

"It has meant everything, and is a memory that I will long cherish." She shook her head decisively. "But that is all it can ever be—a fond memory."

"Enough of this. I take you from here—tonight. Prepare the child."

"I will not go with you willingly."

"Is it your lover in the wood—the Black Outlaw? Does he bind you to him?"

"He is not my lover."

"Not yet, but now that the child is born—"

"He will never be my lover." She saw him look at the child. "She *is* your child."

"Make ready."

There was a rustling outside, and the sound of swords clashing until she heard her brother's voice. "You never truly learn, do you, Norman warlord?"

Blaise stood at the ready, sword drawn.

"Hold! For pity's sake," Morgana pleaded.

"Your men will not be much help to you this time, Blaise of Rouen. As you can see, should you look outside, we have them surrounded. The lord of the manor has come once more to retrieve his possession—" The eerie silence was broken by the lusty yell of the babe. "Or is it possessions?"

"Move aside, sir, or die."

"Please," Morgana urged her brother. "You swore."

"He brought us to this," Brent insisted, "not me. I told him that I would kill him should he return for you."

"He saved my life. He saved my child's life. Have mercy, my lord. Mercy!" Morgana held the sleeping child out to him, and he gawked at the little bundle, uncertain of what to do next. "See! Take her! See how beautiful she is—the first grandchild of Lord Wulfrid and Lady Astrid."

Brent threw Blaise a questing glance, and the Norman laid down his sword. He moved past Blaise, to Morgana's bedside, and she spoke quickly, leaving out no detail of D'Arcy's visit and the subsequent birth. "You must spare him, my lord. He has saved my life and that of my child."

"Again you have managed to escape retribution," Brent said as he laughed mirthlessly. "No doubt D'Arcy plots now to pay you back in kind." He turned to Morgana. "Gather your things, and the child."

"She cannot travel now."

"You spoke of taking her yourself. I heard you. She comes with me—and you stay behind."

When Blaise moved toward them, Brent had his dagger at his throat in one swift movement.

" 'Tis for the best, my lord," Morgana said as she pulled on her clothes. "I am not a possession—shall never be a possession." She strapped on the leather shoes, and stared into his eyes, her own pain clearly mirrored. "I cannot be more to you. Do not come for me. I leave the country within the fortnight. If you love me, let me go."

"Aye!" Brent added. " 'Tis foolish for you to keep searching for her, when she does not want you. I shall take her far from here, where neither you nor D'Arcy can find her or the child."

"You are mine, Kirsten," Blaise rejoined. "I shall follow you to hell if need be. What I take, I keep."

"My God!" Morgana whispered in bewilderment. "Will you never see? Because of your pride, you have lost me forever. Forever! And each day that I look upon my child, I shall hate you for not holding us dear when it mattered."

Chapter 17

The spring of 1068 crept quietly into Andredeswald, greeted enthusiastically by Morgana and her daughter, Aline. Though Brent had been unable to secure passage for them to Ireland before the equinox, he was now in Brigstoc arranging for her and Aline to leave and join her sister in Dubh Lin.

Morgana wondered whether it was wise to leave. She had found comfort in her life deep in the wood. No Normans. No intrigue. Brent shielded her from the fighting and plotting, but could he do so forever? Yet what awaited her in Ireland?

As she planted her garden, she wondered whether she would reap the vegetables, or whether they would go to seed.

She had brought Maude with her, as much for the woman's health as companionship. She enjoyed this solitude. It gave her time to ponder the many twists and turns her life had taken.

And if there was no love—no passion—then that was as it should be, for passion had brought too much pain in its wake—more than a lifetime's worth.

She tended the people's ills and wounds, and wondered

how the refugees at Retford fared. Her mother and Gisele were dead. Would Blaise care for them?

Somehow she knew that he would. Alyson was often called to the hall. Her gifts for healing were known far and wide.

As the months passed, Blaise took great pains to fortify his lands. Hartley was completed in late autumn, and the larger village of Retford the following spring.

Despite numerous raids carried out by the Black Outlaw and his men, the Normans set about filling their storehouses with enough foodstuffs to feed each village through the winter, and word came to her that the people were well treated and content with their lord.

The refugees were reluctantly returned to Hartley, and D'Arcy was installed as underlord, though Blaise left one of his most trusted knights at D'Arcy's side at all times.

One spring day, as the sun tried to decide whether to stay out or relinquish its spot to clouds, as Blaise pored over his ledgers in the solar, Sigvald announced that the midwife, Alyson, wished an audience with him. Blaise motioned her in, and she closed and barred the door behind her.

"How fares my lady?" he inquired.

"Well, my lord."

"And my daughter?"

"Beautiful! The picture of her mother, with her red-gold hair, but your eyes."

"Does she walk? Talk?"

"She crawls and says 'mama,' but 'tis all so far."

Blaise sighed, and rubbed his knuckles along the binding of his ledger. "Wine?" he offered. She declined. "Why do you come?"

"My lady is determined to leave the country."

" 'Tis the same plan she has always followed."

"But this time she may succeed. The Black Outlaw has arranged passage from Brigstoc to Dubh Lin."

"When?"

"In two months time."

"Much can happen in two months."

"I know," she admitted.

"She may even change her mind and return to me."

" 'Tis possible, but not likely."

"What game is this you play? Why do you keep coming to me to let me know each step she makes?"

"Because you love her, and she loves you. You would never harm her. I know that, if she does not."

"If I brought her back to Retford, she could be harmed."

"Someone murdered your wife, and until the culprit is unmasked, Kirsten and the child would be in danger."

Blaise sat back in his chair, watching motes of dust climb a ray of light, twirling and twirling—

He sighed. "I have a brace of hare for you when you leave."

"You do not need to pay me."

"They are for her, too. And your mother."

"Thank you."

It began to rain in earnest now, and Blaise closed the outer shutter of the window. When he turned back to her, he caught reluctance in her glance, and her lips were parted as if there were more words to be spoken. Yet she held back. "Tell me."

"Nay! There is naught else."

"If she is in danger—"

"There is naught else, my lord."

Though her words were insistent, she had lied. He would find out why.

His concern was not ill conceived, for although Morgana fared well in the wood, there was a plan afoot of which Alyson was aware that would surely endanger her and the child.

It had naught to do with her everyday survival, for truly she was gifted with clothes and fur pelts fashioned by Ethelbert into fine cloaks and blankets. Brent sent one of his men daily to make certain there was enough wood, that the fire always roared in her hearth, and that there was food in the storehouse. Much of what she ate was stolen from Norman tables—the wine, the marinated venison, the partridges—so she wanted for naught, and never allowed herself to think of from whom the bounty had come.

In the spring, word moved like wildfire through Andredeswald of a most uncommon Saxon knight who lived in the marshy fens on the Isle of Ely. Hereward by name, he was called the "Wake," for he had been outlawed when he had refused to bow to the Norman yoke, preferring to be ever watchful of the Normans who plundered his land.

Hereward was also the most successful Saxon rebel. It was rumored he was the son of Leofric, Earl of Mercia, and his lady, Godiva, and had been out of the country when his lands were confiscated by William. Upon his return, he raised a banner, and loyal Saxon knights from all of England were anxious to join his cause.

Morgana sat with Brent eating roast venison in a clearing one evening when a good friar wandered into their camp accompanied by a Saxon minstrel. The minstrel sang of Hereward's exploits as the friar blessed his good deeds.

Brent sent an envoy to arrange a meeting with this Hereward. Mayhaps they could join forces and drive the bastard king and his Norman executioners from England once and for all. Within the month, his messenger returned with a date, time, and location for a meeting. London—in one month's time. 'Twould be simple enough to lose themselves in that large city of more than fourteen thousand inhabitants. They could be right under the king's nose, and he would never know.

Morgana insisted on accompanying Brent.

"But your days as a spy are over. You have Aline to think about now."

"Aline and I will be fine—as safe with you as we are in Andredeswald."

"You will jeopardize yourself needlessly."

"I want to meet this man—to talk with him."

"You are not going to stop until you get your way?"

"Consider this. If Aline and I are with you, we can pretend to be a family of peddlers on our way to market. Otherwise, as a man traveling alone, you shall be suspect."

"I would not put your life in peril."

"You shall not, I assure you."

On the day that they started out for London, the heavens opened as if all the angels were weeping. "This rain be damned!" Brent cursed. "How can we be expected to get anywhere in this mud?"

Ethelbert pulled up on the reins and looked to his left.

The wheel had stuck in the rutted road, finally sliding in such a way that half the cart lay at an angle in a gully.

"Out. All of you," Brent ordered. Morgana handed Aline to him and helped Anne out of the rig. She pulled her mantle about her, but she was already soaked to the bone.

"Normans, milord," Ethelbert mumbled as Brent removed a stack of straw and sprinkled it into the rut.

"From Retford, by their colors," Morgana offered.

Brent grinned at her, his grin turning foolish as he twirled toward the men.

"Good day, sirs knights," Ethelbert mumbled.

"Trouble on the road?"

"Aye, sirs. My cart slid in the mud."

"Where go you?"

"To market, to peddle my skins." One of the men glanced inside the wagon. "Leather tunics for William's knights."

"Who are these people?" another of the men inquired.

"My wife, my widowed daughter, my son."

"S-s-son—son." Brent danced around them, and peered over at the driver.

"What is the fellow, a fool?"

"He injured his head as a child. He has never been the same. Has never grown up, I fear."

"Can I see sword? Can I have sword? Are you bad men?"

"Go away, fool," the first knight said as he kicked Brent down onto the ground.

"Father. He hit me, Father. He hit me."

Ethelbert came down and helped Brent back onto his feet. Anne brushed him off and cautioned him as if he were a naughty little boy.

Morgana noticed that the first knight stared at her, and fearing that he might recognize her, went to the cart to feed Aline. When the man followed for a second glance, he blushed profusely and closed the flap. Had he recognized her? True, she had put a vegetable dye in her hair to darken its color, and had caked mud on her skin to dull its creamy smoothness.

No, he had not been able to tell. If he had recognized her, he would have taken her there and then.

That meant that they were safe—for now.

Or so they thought, for they did not reckon with the prowess of the king's firebrand, nor of the quick wit of his men, for though she played her part as well as any performer, the young man had seen through her ruse.

"Where did you say you saw her? On the road to London?"

"Aye, *mon seigneur.*"

"You are sure it was her?"

"Her hair was dark, like chestnuts, but I would remember those eyes anywhere. And she had a babe, of a size and an age, with red-gold hair, and eyes—eyes like yours."

"Damn her! Is she daft? What foolery is this?"

"Speaking of foolery, the man pretended to be a fool."

"The Black Outlaw, I wager. He is a clever one. Pretended at one time to be a hunchbacked shepherd." And at another time, Blaise thought, he played at being her lover—or was he?

"Certainly looked the part of the fool. The man who claimed to be his father said his head was injured as a child. And he did have a scar on his face—"

"Aye, 'tis him." He pondered this information for a moment. " 'Tis not meet that he should drag Kirsten to London. Much could befall her on that road—much more than a mere splattering of rain. Fetch the midwife, Alyson. She knows something of this, I warrant."

A complement of Blaise's men sped to Alyson's hut, and returned with Alyson, clearly befuddled as to why he had summoned her.

"Why did you not tell me Kirsten goes to London?"

"To where?"

"Stop this pretense," he spat, his temper sorely raging. "She could be in danger."

"I know naught of what you speak," she insisted.

"Was this the information that you withheld?"

"I am not your spy, my lord, despite any notions that you may have to the contrary."

"But why to London? Why now?"

"Surely I have no idea."

"Begone then, woman! Do you fancy yourself my only spy in the Black Outlaw's camp?"

"You are a fearsome knight, but a mere child where the girl is concerned. She has run loops around you—"

"Only because I let her."

"If you tell yourself that often enough, you may begin to believe it."

"I will stop her."

"Use your head, my lord Blaise, for more than a place to perch your helmet. Do you think that they travel alone? The wood on either side of them teem with his yeomen. If you go near her, you are dead. Plain and simple."

"What is so important that she would risk her life and that of the child?" He considered all the facts. "London is on the opposite side of the country from Brigstoc, so she will not be leaving for Ireland from there."

Alyson stood obstinately silent, confident that he would figure it out eventually. 'Twas not her place to interfere. Fate had a hand in all—his and Morgana's fate. Alyson had no place in it at all.

"What would be so important that she would undertake such a journey?" He thought of the parties involved, and where they ventured, and suddenly all was crystal-clear. "Rebellion! The fool girl goes to plot rebellion."

Alyson carefully masked her reactions, her eyes keen yet dispassionate as Blaise silently cursed the Black Outlaw.

"That is it, is it not? She plots against the king." He flung a horn of ale in the corner at his falcon, and the bird screeched and swooped around the hall before settling down. "And you thought this too unimportant to mention to me? Should William find out, her life is forfeit. Do you love your mistress so little—"

"I love her more than you could imagine—like a niece—like a child of my own."

"Then help me, for pity's sake."

"I know nothing more than you have guessed. 'Tis up to you now to do what you think is best with the information."

"I will find out where they have gone and stop her," he whispered sharply as he gave Alyson a slight shake. His hand dropped away as they stared at each other across the silence. He pressed on his aching forehead and raked through his hair, his eyes rolling back from lowered lids that shut tightly. "She will be the death of me yet."

"Somehow I rather doubt that," Alyson replied.

Blaise and his men departed Retford under cover of darkness, dressed as Saxons. It was easier to accomplish now that William had ordered the Saxons groomed in the Norman fashion—shaven faces and short hair. They rode until they caught up with Morgana's party. On each side of the road, as Alyson had guessed, the Black Outlaw's men followed in parallel lines of defense.

Blaise purchased a cart from a tinker and followed close behind.

"Do you think that this Hereward can help us?" Morgana asked her brother.

"He has learned much about defense. Although the lay of the land at Ely *is* different. 'Tis surrounded almost entirely by water. Mounted knights entering the area must know where each bog and crag is or they might find themselves sucked under the watery sand."

"William is a bright man—and no stranger to treachery himself. He shall not be waylaid by marshes, I warrant."

"Nature always wins out, little sister. Take Andredeswald. The Normans have the power, but we know how to use the wood."

"But they will make an effort to find out. War is their lifeblood."

"You have lain too long with Normans. You begin to believe that they will succeed in this invasion."

"Why do you speak this way to me? I am faithful to the truth. Are you angry because I choose not to gull myself with empty hopes for success? Hope is all we may have to drive out the Norman vermin, and we shall find it sorely lacking."

" 'Tis treasonous to speak such words. The blood of King Aelfred runs in our veins. Our father was a much-loved thane of the murdered English king—"

"The *last* English king, I fear."

"The Normans shall never succeed in conquering our souls, Morgana. They may be able to control our bodies with chains and whips, but our souls will remain free—and Saxon."

As the cart plodded down the road, Morgana remembered just how Blaise had controlled her body, and flushed with guilt. There has been no need for chains and whips.

Within two days, Blaise knew for what town she was bound, and whom she was to meet. Hereward! The Saxon outlaw and rebel leader. But what was he doing in London? And why would the Black Outlaw meet with him, if not to join forces? And if that was accomplished, would there be any doubt that Kirsten would be enmeshed in it all, her life and that of his child endangered, and—when William found out—forfeit?

"They have taxed my patience, taking Kirsten and my child on the road, with danger lurking on each side of them."

Sigvald nodded in agreement, and Blaise swore an oath as he sat back in a makeshift chair in his tent.

"The only saving grace is that D'Arcy has no idea, or he would surely take this opportunity to rid himself of her and my child." He stood and took an abrupt step toward the flap of the tent. "Call the men together." He tore off the Saxon clothes. "And burn these rags. I want my chausses, my tunic, my mail, and my golden spurs. We ride for London tonight to await her." His dark brows slanted into a frown. "I shall speak with William, and let him know what treachery is afoot. If she is found out by another, I shall not be able to save her. Mayhaps I can convince William that the girl was unaware of her companion's ill deeds—that he used her." He lifted a brow. " 'Twould be a plume in my cap were I to present William with Hereward the Wake *and* the Black Outlaw. He might even intercede with the pope to annul Kirsten's marriage as a reward." His mouth twisted wryly. "The plan is brilliant—to gather all rebel forces under one banner. But these Englishmen are a diverse lot. 'Twould never work, and Kirsten could end up dead."

"Aye, *mon seigneur.*"

Blaise poured wine into his horn. "Tonight we will drink hearty, stuff ourselves with some fine French food, and loose the men for a bout of wenching." He took a long sip of the wine. "Then we will sit and wait for my little hare to jump into the snare."

Chapter 18

They will take the old Roman road that passes within sixteen furlongs of where they are now," Blaise said as he pointed to the map.

"Aye. But the river lies between them and the road," Sigvald pointed out. "They can cross by boat, which they are not equipped to do, or go down forty furlongs to the newly built ferry. 'Tis where you crossed when you went to London for William's coronation. A good shallow place to ford the river."

"Aye! And we must be there to greet them," Blaise said, his mouth turned up in a wry grin.

"They travel in a cart, so we have the advantage."

"Yes." Blaise nodded. "We shall be waiting when she reaches London." Wistfulness stole into his expression, to be soon replaced by pity.

Morgana suspected naught when she arrived in London, but she would have gladly surrendered herself into Blaise's control if it meant that she would have a clean, soft pallet beneath her for a change. "Only one thing can be said of this trip," she remarked as they passed through the gate into London. " 'Twas only slightly less uncomfortable than the last time I entered this town." She rubbed her callused derriere.

" 'Twas you who insisted on coming. Try to remember that when these complaints roll off your lips."

"Just bring me to a place where they will take mercy on me and provide me with a warm bath to ease my aching muscles."

"You take more baths than a fish," Anne said.

Morgana sniffed the air. "We all could use a bath, I would say." She looked at the woman meaningfully.

"I am for a brew to warm my belly," Ethelbert suggested as he searched for Tanner Street.

"And a wench to warm my bed," Brent chimed in.

Morgana was surprised. In almost two years, no female had caught her brother's attention, but she sensed that someday soon, when he was no longer so obsessed with executing D'Arcy, he would be able to love again.

Perryn the Tanner, their contact, was not only a young man, but a powerful assistant in the rebel movement. He welcomed them into his home, and after quaffing a quick draft of ale, said, "The one you seek is not in London yet. He was delayed, but is expected tonight."

"Good! 'Twill give my sister time to eat and rest."

"Yes, my lord. Though I am a humble tanner, I make a good wage at my trade. Did you know that the Bastard's mother was a tanner's daughter?"

"Yon Ethelbert mentions it every chance he gets." He gulped down the ale. "No doubt the stink of the tannery never deterred William's father from his purpose."

Perryn's wife giggled in a high-pitched nasal whine as she showed Morgana to a chamber off the kitchen. "Thank you," Morgana whispered. "The child is hungry." The young woman watched with a curious frown. "What is it?" Morgana asked.

"Are you a lady or a serf?"

"Are there any Saxons left who can truly call themselves 'ladies'? The Normans have come and we have all become their slaves. 'Tis no difference now between cottager or villein—we are all the same to the Normans." Morgana looked about her. "But you do well." The girl nodded.

"Count your blessings, for the mighty have fallen on hard times."

" 'Tis said that Hereward is of noble blood, too."

"I have heard as much. 'Tis good for my brother to believe that England may yet shake off this yoke and chain—"

"And you do not?"

"I do not know what to think any longer. I have seen the enemy, and I know his might and strength of purpose. 'Tis not that I would deprive my brother of this moment . . ."

Her voice trailed off as Brent entered the chamber with a wolf pelt. "I brought this from the cart. The night may be cold." The tanner's wife excused herself. "Are you settled?" Morgana nodded. "Everyone thinks that you are either very brave or very foolish to have ventured forth with me on this trip."

"Mayhaps a bit of both."

"I suspect you have come to still the wagging tongues that name you traitor. Some think that, because the Norman has bedded you and got a brat on you—"

"A brat! Your niece is a brat now?"

" 'Tis what the gossips say, not me. I love the babe."

"As Aline's uncle, I expected better from you."

"I am sorry. I never meant to hurt you." He hung his head sheepishly. "I have left my manners and my tact on the battlefields and in the wood. War changes one, I am afraid."

"Our lives have changed. We cannot keep looking back."

"Hereward will lead us out of slavery—"

"As Moses did the Israelites? I think not. Our land is well taken."

"If you value your life, Morgana, never let my men hear you speak thus. We will drive the Norman swine from this land," he stormed, "and at the head of my list are your husband and your lover."

"You will not hurt Blaise." At his hardness, she grasped at his sleeve. "You have become a shell of a person."

He shook her loose. "Be still, you Norman who—" He caught himself, but he saw that her eyes turned opaque with pain.

"Whore! Say the words. Whore! That is what you think of me. Say it!" She pummeled her small fists upon his chest. "Whore! Whore! Whore!"

He slapped her, and her voice caught, her disbelief evident. "You frighten the child," he said.

"Call me whore. It matters not. Your bitterness is a sickness. So you lost much. I never had much to lose, except my mother and my virtue. I can be no man's wife ever again. But I have my child to love. And I have loved a man, and—Norman or not—I do not regret it."

"Do not speak of your love for that man."

"I will not deny him. Each day apart from him has been my private hell. I see him in my dreams—in my child's features. How can I deny him, when I know my own heart? You would have me lie and pretend that I feel otherwise. I have tried. Lord knows I have tried." She burst into tears.

"If you were not married to D'Arcy, you could take a Saxon husband." He considered this. "If I kill him—"

"You want to wed me to a peasant to soothe your pride?"

"A Saxon lord, my sister."

"Do you hear naught of what I say? William is a man of singular purpose. Even his men fear his wrath. He was yet a child when he became Duke of Normandy, and he killed his fair share to keep his title. He gained the respect of those who owed him fealty, and the fear of those who opposed him. A man of his fighting ability—when once he has gained the advantage—would not give ground."

"Hereward shall lead us, Morgana."

"The only ground we will gain back from William is the plot that we shall be buried in." She lay back and turned to her side. "I am weary. I would sleep now."

"After you have slept, I am certain that you will see the error of your thoughts," he muttered as he quit the chamber.

Blaise was kept abreast of all developments. "The man Hereward is outside the gates of London Town at this very moment, *mon seigneur*," Sigvald whispered as they stood overlooking the Thames River.

FIREBRAND'S LADY

"Good!" Blaise replied. "What do you think?"

" 'Tis a clever plan. The men are near the gates, awaiting word of the meeting. We have narrowed the locations down to two streets—Tanner or Miller Street—and the section along the waterfront."

"I have thirty of the king's men at my disposal. That brings our force to sixty. Separate in groups of twenty and begin the search—dwelling by dwelling."

"He will choose the area near the waterfront in order to effect a quick escape if necessary. What do you think?"

"What I think does not matter. What the Saxon thinks is important. His methods are different."

" 'Tis a good plan, *mon seigneur*. We can only try."

"Nay! We must succeed. I have promised the king the heads of the Saxon outlaws, and should they escape—it shall mean my hide."

Morgana, knowing nothing of these plots and schemes, awoke to muffled voices outside the curtained door of the bedchamber. Aline slept peacefully in her cradle, but had kicked off her blanket. She covered the infant, then parted the curtain and entered the room.

The room was dimly lit by candlelight, and she rubbed the sleep from her eyes to focus. Seven men, two women. At her entrance, there was a noticeable lull in the conversation, and Brent nodded toward her. "Lord Hereward, my sister, Morgana."

She could not see the man's face, for he was shadowed, but she knew that he was golden-haired, with a full beard. He swiftly glanced the length of her body. "She is charming, Lord Brent. Even a man who plots rebellion would take note of such beauty. Lady Morgana—" Hereward nodded to her—"your brother has told me much about your inner strength and your work for our common cause. A formidable ally, I am told."

"I am but a mortal woman much like any other."

"You underestimate yourself. You are learned, and you read and write Norman French. These and other talents you possess are most unusual for a woman."

"My village priest saw that I had a gift for languages, so he trained me as a spy."

253

"And you wield a knife and bow like a yeoman, I am told."

Morgana nodded, uncomfortable as he sang her praises, in light of her recent argument with Brent. She kept her counsel. No sense in saying anything that she may regret. Hereward would speak to her brother, and they would plot, and Brent would return to the wood of Andredeswald and dream of the day he could overthrow the Normans. The minor battles and skirmishes would continue until William burned every acre of England and left it all behind him—scorched earth.

"I go to seek the aid of Swein Estridsson, the king of Denmark," Hereward continued. "He has a claim to the throne through Canute the Great, the Danish king who ruled England and brought the Godwins to power."

Ale passed freely as the men discussed their plans. As the conversation grew more tedious, she sat next to the hearth, thankful for the fire's glow on this damp night. The fog lay thick upon the streets, and she could see no farther than the front gate.

There was a lull as Perryn's wife paused while refilling horns. Something was wrong. Morgana sensed it, too. She glanced out the window—but saw no one.

She stared at the door, but there was no one there. A moment later, one of the sentries posted at the end of the street burst through the door, winded and gasping for breath.

"My lord Hereward, the Normans. By their colors, the Bastard's men, and a banner I do not recognize—white with a gold torch. We are betrayed."

Blaise's banner! Blaise here in London? How? She breathed deeply to ward off a faint.

All eyes turned toward Morgana as she shook her head in negation of their thoughts. Hereward looked at her, then Brent. "How could they have known, unless—"

"Hurry! This way!" Perryn lifted a wooden wall rack on leather hinges to reveal a series of tunnels. "In here. Be silent, for even if they find this and try to follow us, they shall be lost. 'Tis a maze. Come now! Hasten away!"

The men grabbed their goods and slipped into the tunnel. Brent reached for Morgana, but she shook herself from her trancelike state. "Aline! There is no time. Go! I will close off the tunnel. Go!" She shivered in horror as the Normans pounded at the door.

"Hereward will think you betrayed him. They are *his* colors, Morgana—white and gold—Blaise de Rouen's colors."

"He would not hurt his child. For pity's sake—begone!"

Brent gave her a slow, deliberate stare. Would he ever be able to fathom the depths of her mind? She was as changeable as the wind. "Your life is in danger. Would you do this just to see him again?"

" 'Tis not the reason," she assured him, but even as she spoke the words, she wondered at her motives. "With me alone, they can prove nothing. If you are captured—"

"Do not despair. I will not desert you, Morgana." He disappeared into the tunnel.

"Godspeed," she whispered as she moved the rack back into place and went to quiet the baby who now screamed.

The iron-bound door of hard oak gave way with a crack and a thud as it fell forward on its hinges. Morgana sat in the bedchamber, crooning a sweet song to soothe the child. They would show her compassion—Blaise would protect her.

At their bidding Morgana rose and walked, undaunted, to the table and sat upon a rough-hewn chair. Soldiers swept through the small house, upending furniture and overturning vats of tanning fluid in the process.

"How did they escape, woman? Where do they go?"

Morgana stared ahead, knowing full well that her resistance warranted crushing, and that these men—William's men—would most likely oblige.

"I know naught of whom you speak. I am a visitor from Retford. I came to purchase a fur mantle."

"A likely story," a familiar voice said.

She sensed his presence even before she had heard the words, burnt by the blaze of those golden eyes, until he turned her toward him and searched her face. His eyes locked onto hers. "Where is your leader?" She remained silent. He turned to a young man, scowling. "Who gave the order for the men to enter?"

"I—I did. I thought—"

"You thought? Were you charged to take orders from me? I am the one to do the thinking. Your rash behavior has cost us much this day. The rebels are far away by now."

"Aye! but—"

"But? But what? There are no excuses. And I shall not be the bearer of ill tidings to William. Do you want to tell him that we lost them?"

"We have this one, *mon seigneur.*"

"This one? Oh! 'Tis rich!" He chortled in mock glee. "This girl? Does she look like a rebel to you? A pig maiden more likely. She is no rebel, but the wife of my underlord, Christian D'Arcy." He propelled the soldier to the door. "Get out and find the rebels, fool!"

Sigvald stood at the door, his mouth twisting in derisive humor as he waited for William's men to leave. "A weedling youth anxious to bring himself to his king's attention."

"Well, his plans have gone awry." Blaise turned toward Morgana. "But he was right in one thing—we do have a rebel here, do we not, Lady D'Arcy?"

Morgana shifted the baby over her shoulder and patted her back rhythmically. "I have no idea of what you speak."

"Do you not?" he replied with a slow, secret smile that discomfited her. "Where are they?"

" 'They'? Who are 'they'?"

"You know full well, Lady D'Arcy. The Black Outlaw, for one. Hereward, the rebel known as 'the Wake,' for another."

Morgana knitted her brows and shrugged in feigned ignorance, and his frown deepened. When a twitch began in his left cheek, she turned away, knowing the measure of his wrath and preferring not to meet it head-on. "I know naught of rebels, or others of whom you speak."

"You cannot thwart me to no ill effect, my lady. Do not count on my good nature to keep you from harm." His lips thinned.

Morgana sat the baby in her lap facing Blaise. He stared in awe. "This man who threatens us is the Vicomte de Rouen, Lord of Retford and Hartley—your father, Aline."

Blaise colored fiercely, his anger deflated. "We—we have met. She has gotten bigger. She is quite—remarkable," he stuttered. "And lovely." He flicked a tendril from her face, and Aline grabbed his gauntleted finger to draw it toward her mouth. Blaise turned crimson and peeled the gauntlets from his hands. "I would hold her, but the mail—"

"Yes. We have taught Aline that a proper lady never greets a knight until after he has divested himself of his mail." The humor escaped him as he stared at his child.

His eyes swept Morgana's body, taking in each luscious curve. He cleared his throat. "This is not the place to discuss these matters. Bring the child and let us be gone."

They proceeded to his quarters in total silence, but once she had settled into her chamber, he pressed her for information. "The king has no loyalty or weakness where you are concerned, Kirsten. He deals harshly with traitors."

Morgana consistently kept her counsel throughout the many hours of interrogation, increasing his annoyance. "Damn! You cannot be such a fool as to think that this is a coincidence? I knew your every step—followed you and that damned peddler, and the Black Outlaw, who thought himself so clever when he disguised himself as a fool."

Morgana squinted, but quickly regained her composure. "If you know it all, there is no need to question me. My child and I shall be on our way home—to the wood."

"You are so stubborn that 'tis a wonder I have not throttled you before this."

Morgana rose from the table and adjusted her kirtle. Her breasts were swollen—tingling—and soon they began to drip. "Where is my child? She will be hungry."

"I have sent for a wet nurse."

"But I must feed her. The milk must be released, or it shall cause me pain. See?" She stood a handsbreadth from him as his fingers gently grazed their wet tips. The child's screams rent the silence. "Not even you would seek to punish me in such a ridiculous manner. Aline and I need each other."

Blaise pondered her words, then sent for the child. As Morgana sat in a corner and nursed the babe, he sat back in a chair, one foot resting on the table in front of him, watching her until he was interrupted by the young inept knight from William's guard.

"We have discovered a secret door with a series of tunnels that run out to all sections of the town. We split up and each followed one."

"Did one lead to the river?" At his nod, Blaise smiled with smug satisfaction. "So now we know how they escaped, but to where?" He stared ominously at Morgana and the smile disappeared. "Where have they gone?" And why had she not escaped with them? If she had known it was he, would she still have stayed? Or did she know and stay to see him? Did she feel what he felt—this unseen force that even now drew them together?

"Well, Lady D'Arcy, your conspirators have eluded us, but you are left behind to pay the minstrel."

"I have no idea of what you speak. I am here of my own will, my lord," she responded evenly.

"Your new lover could not have loved you well, to sacrifice you as he has." He poured a horn of wine. "He cares naught for you and the child."

"He cares deeply," she disagreed. "He would give his life for us." She adjusted Aline to her other breast, and the child continued to gnaw greedily. Blaise was trying to frighten her or spur her on to make a costly mistake. The air crackled with tension, but Morgana remained cautious.

"Leave us!" The sentries vacated the chamber, and Morgana became even more constrained, as if at any moment she expected the worst and was preparing for it. He bided his time until Aline was fed and sleeping in the safety of her mother's arms.

Blaise had the child removed once again to the care of the nurse. Morgana's careful control flew out the window.

"You cannot take her. Even you would not be so cruel."

"Nothing will happen to her, Kirsten. She is my child, for God's sake."

"She needs me. She will cry when she awakens."

"The moment she awakens, she will be brought to you. We have matters to discuss."

"You want to fill me with wine and veiled threats in hopes that I shall confess to you. I know full well that you prefer to barter from an advantage."

"I do not wish to barter with your life, but I must." He strode to her side and knelt next to her. "Kirsten, use your head. You know what William is capable of. Do you think that an irksome girl can best him?"

"I have naught to do with it all. I was in the wrong place at the wrong time."

"Many have died a violent death for much less, my lady." He hunched over, one arm resting upon his thigh, and looked up into her face. "If you think me cruel—you have no concept of cruel. William will imprison you, take Aline from you—"

"And you would let him," she reflected bitterly.

"Never by choice, Kirsten," he said huskily. His fingers bit deeply into her trembling shoulder. "But this dilemma must be solved. I sought William's assistance in the Black Outlaw's capture. Now I have no man to deliver, and he shall not be pleased with that turn of events."

"I have oft thought of you these past months, but never as my executioner."

"Do not speak this way!" He shook her vehemently until she tore herself away with a choking cry.

"I have not lost enough? What else do you want from me? You want my child? You want my very life's breath?" She took a step toward him. "Did I not lose enough when I lost you?"

Blaise's eyes glowed with unspoken pain. He closed the distance between them, crushing her shamelessly against him, pressing her against the wall, his palms flattening to frame her head. "You have betrayed me, and plot with my enemies, but God's blood, woman, I still desire you." The fierceness in his eyes alternately frightened and thrilled her.

Her breath came shallow as his lips moved down her earlobe, to her neck. She was being sucked into a whirl-pool—pulled down—down—

"For pity's sake, cease this assault," she begged.

"Assault? You do not know what assault is yet, my lady," he whispered against her lips. "William would not think twice before flaying this ivory skin from your delectable body." His lips brushed the tops of her breasts, and he swore an oath as a knock sounded on the door.

"Go away, damn you!" He dragged her by the arm to the door, bolted it, and pressed her slowly into the rough-hewn wood. "Kirsten," he mumbled, as he reached for her and lifted her into his arms, pressing her against his hard body.

"Nay! You just want to possess my body—not *me*."

He showered her with kisses and stroked her hips, clutching her skirt until it rode high upon her thigh. "Aye! I want your body, but I want much more. I want all of you—all. Your heart. Your soul. Your every thought. All. You are mine—shall always be mine."

He backed away as her breath came in gulps, her breasts straining against her bodice, and tried to regain his control.

"You are comfortable?" He finally asked.

Her fingers clutched at her throat. "As comfortable as can be expected, under the circumstances."

"Damn! You were more comfortable in that damned hovel in the wood with that cranky old woman?"

She turned to him, slowly, realizing that he knew where she was—had probably known these many months past.

"Yes, I have known your every movement. Did you really think that I would allow you to elude me completely with my child? I have had to pay off several sea captains to thwart your escape to Ireland, although of late there is one that I did not bribe in time. He was not in port, but he shall come around before the time for leaving."

"You? You prevented my leaving England?"

"Do you really think that I would let you take my child from me forever?"

"The child that you chose to deny?"

His eyes darkened ominously. "That was in the past. Have I not regretted my actions a hundredfold since then?"

"What do you plan to do with me now?"

"More to the point, what does William plan to do? Can I keep that pretty little head on your shoulders?" His finger drew an imaginary line at her throat, and she shivered involuntarily. "I can see that you think the same thoughts." He frowned and dropped his fingers, his hands clenching and unclenching at his sides. "I truly do not know what William shall do. He is a hard man. I will bring information regarding this futile attempt to Winchester. I must convince him that you were a pawn—that you are of no real use to us." Sigvald came forth with her mantle. "You are returning to Retford. You will be locked in a chamber in the new keep.

You will see no one—not even the servants. Sigvald is the only person who will have access to you besides Aline's nurse." He wrapped the mantle around her. "Pray, Kirsten, that William is in good humor, for if not—" He shrugged.

At the riverbank, the renegades boarded several small boats, split up, and made their way along the shoreline, hidden in the thick mist from prying Norman eyes. Brent and Hereward sat together—silent and brooding—as Ethelbert rowed.

"How did she know about the Normans?" Hereward asked.

"My sister is a child of the old ways. She has a certain—sensitivity to things."

"She is a witch?"

"Not a witch. She has gifts."

Hereward's eyes squinted and a brow arched. "You make excuses for the girl. She betrayed us to the Normans—"

"Never! She would not!"

"She is married to a Norman. Her child is a Norman bastard. How can you proclaim her innocence?"

"She hates her husband. He killed our mother."

"But the other. 'Tis rumored she does not hate him."

"In truth, she loves him more than she is willing to admit. But she has fled him. I vouch for her, on my honor."

" 'Tis not your honor in question. The fervor of the Black Outlaw for our cause is legend."

"No less than your own. Morgana did not betray us; yet someone possibly whispered too much in the Norman's ear."

"Why did she allow herself to be caught then?"

"Did you expect her to leave the child behind?"

It troubled Brent, but he kept his counsel. Would he use the child to reach Morgana? Would Blaise employ such methods—his own child? Could the Norman be so evil?

Chapter 19

Morgana spent more than a fortnight locked in Blaise's chamber at Retford with not one visitor allowed, other than Aline, whom the nurse brought in for feedings and short visits, and Sigvald, who spoke to her only once to remind her to remain as quiet as possible and stay away from the window. "No one can know that you are at Retford. D'Arcy will come for you when *mon seigneur* is not here to protect you."

"He would kill me," she had responded quietly.

"Take heed, then, and curb your callow temper. It could very well mean your life and that of the child."

More than a fortnight of waiting—for what? What would her fate be? To be whipped? The block? Could any punishment meet the pain of estrangement from her child?

Morgana surveyed the chamber. Ledgers. She scanned them and memorized their contents. When and if she returned to her brother's camp, she would have information to bring him.

And books. Most of them were classics written in Latin. She vaguely recognized the names—Ovid, Cicero, Virgil. She liked Ovid's poetry about love. The pages were dog-eared, as if he had often read them. What a strange man he was.

One afternoon, as she sipped wine and read a *chanson de geste,* she lay back upon the bolster and fell promptly asleep, the open book across her stomach.

Outside, in the corridor, Blaise pressed his ear to the chamber door. Not the slightest sound. Mayhaps she slept, he told himself as he removed the bar and slipped in. Reluctant to wake her, he crossed to the bed. She had fallen asleep while reading—reading? Reading what? He glanced at the title. A book in Norman French?

The wench could read? He picked through the other books. Latin, too? He pondered this information as he divested himself of his clothing and pulled the skins across the window slits. If she could read in Norman French, she could speak it. As he lit a torch, he thought of the many times he had spoken in her presence. She had been privy to all his plans.

He slid in beside her and dropped light kisses on her eyelids, cheeks, and lips. The brush of his lips was delicious. "Have you drank enough wine to let me make love to you?" he asked in Norman French, his voice thick and silky.

Morgana, in her dream state, knew not where the reverie ended and reality began. He had been a muse, and suddenly he was there, in the flesh, his fingers drawing the response he would always be able to elicit from her—immediate excitement. "Aye, my lord. Too much, I fear," she responded in Norman French, his language husky on her tongue. The heavy lashes that shadowed her cheeks flew up as she fought the fog, trying to gauge his reaction. He stared at her, eyes narrowed. He knew. There would be no turning back. But how had he found out? He held the book up, and she groaned, cursing her stupidity. She tried to sit up, but he forced her back into the featherbed.

" 'Tis time for a bit of truth-saying."

"I will explain all, if you move away from me and let me rise." Her response chased away any doubts that he may have had, for her accent was flawless. "Heed me, my lord, before your anger overshadows your reason. Let me clothe myself."

Blaise sat back on his haunches and turned in the bed to lie back against the bolster. For more than a year he had unwittingly revealed his strategies to her, and she had—what? What had she done with the information? Was she a spy?

"Why did you pretend to not understand?" he asked coldly.

"You are a warrior. You have to ask that question?"

"Nay! 'Tis an effective tool—knowledge cloaked in ignorance." He looked around his chamber. "And there was so much for you to find out. You *do* work for him, do you not? You are his—spy?"

Morgana nodded, wishing that she could call back the words that caused such pain and anger.

"I trusted you." His fingers laced in her hair as he drew her to him. His thumbs pressed into her cheekbones. "You slept with me to gain knowledge, pretended what you did not feel to glean information from me? You are worse than a whore." Unspoken pain glowed brightly in his golden eyes.

"Nay, my lord! 'Tis not the way of it." In the back of her mind she knew that it was not quite true, but what could she tell him? "Yes! It may have started that way. You wanted me—would go to any lengths to have me. And I—I had special gifts, abilities. It seemed natural—"

"Natural?" He flung her from him and drove his fist into the wall, heedless of injury. " 'Tis the most unnatural alliance of which I have ever heard. I thought that you came to me joined by a force greater than either or both of us. All the time you were sent to me by that fiend to—what? Seduce me?"

He turned from her, and she placed a restraining hand on his forearm. She knelt before him and took his injured hand into her palms, her soft lips kissing the torn flesh, her tears washing away the blood. At the feel of her wetness, he lifted her in his arms and carried her to the bed.

"Why?" he asked as he pressed her into its softness. "How could you betray me, yet claim to love me? Talk to me, Kirsten, or I shall not be responsible for what happens—"

"My name—it is Morgana—not Kirsten."

She heard his quick intake of breath as he stared at her.

"Morgana?" He thought about this for a long moment. "And when I found you running from the midwife's hut, 'twas because you lived there?" he guessed. As she nodded, his body stiffened, and he rolled away.

"Why, then, did you parade as Kirsten of Retford—as the daughter of the former thane—when you were merely a lowly wench of the wood, the granddaughter of the midwife?"

"I did what I did to protect the people of the village. 'Twas my duty. Should I have shirked my duty?"

"So you were not only a whore—but a common whore."

"Dare you name me so, you—my first lover?"

"A common serf! What did you hope to gain by your charade? Did you hope to catch an unwary Norman vicomte in your web? And the woman who pretended to be your mother—she championed your cause well. Had I not already been wed, she might have snared me in your web of deceit."

His words cut her to the quick. Things were not as she had planned. He was angry because she was not of noble blood. He had loved her—given her his child—yet all that mattered was that she was not who she seemed to be, but rather a serf.

She should tell him the truth, but indignation sealed her lips. To hell with him. Let him believe that he had loved a woman so far beneath him that he could never hope to raise her to his level. William, sensitive about his own mother's humble beginnings as a tanner's daughter, would never allow Blaise to marry a lowborn wench.

Now he would have to let her go.

"I swear upon my immortal soul that I never wished to wed you when I came to your bed." Only a half-truth; yet it was all she was willing to give him.

"What did you hope for then? What *was* the point of your lies? Did you think me such a simpleton that I would not care when the truth—" He was overcome by fury, and his yell resounded off the rafters. Could these thick stone walls withstand his ire? He held her in a crazed grip, shaking her with such force that her hair fell from its loosened braid to cascade along her shoulders and bathe her in its red-gold glory. She saw his intense pain—and desire.

An answering call welled up within her, but she dared not free it. She struggled within his grasp, but his fingers constricted her, manacles of flesh around her wrists.

He lay heavily over her. "I have hungered for your ruby mouth and the sweetness that is within you, the passion that I can unleash. One minute I want to lose myself within your softness, and the next I want to choke you for your lies."

She tried to move him, her body trembling against his own. Hard, harder than she had remembered him. "How bright the luster of your hair, even now after being confined to this chamber for almost a month. You have fared well for a serf. Maids to tend your needs. Beautiful gowns. Jewels." He framed her face in his battle-roughened palms. His voice was a painful, hoarse gasp, and his eyes wild as they held her own. "You never missed me one whit, did you? Did my love mean so little that you could turn away from me so easily? How could you plot against me?"

Tears pricked her lids, begging to be let free. She blinked them back and bit her bottom lip. There was an answering ache within her at the knowledge that there was a schism between them of such proportions that she would never be able to remove the dagger's edge that tore into her heart.

She wavered. Their love was never an illusion. She loved him—completely—wanted only him, on her and in her. They were one. His pain was her pain—his loss her own.

"Who turns you against me? The Black Outlaw. Who is he?" he asked gruffly.

"I—I cannot say. I am honor-bound—"

"Honor! You have no honor, whore." He nudged a knee between her thighs. "Who plots against your king?"

"I will not say. Let me rise." She tried futilely to move him.

"You shall tell me, or so help me, I shall drag you to William by your hair and swing the headman's ax myself."

"You play a foolish game, my lord, to use threats where a light touch would accomplish twice as much." Her legs clamped shut and she tried to unseat him, bucking like an unbroken mare. "You will have to kill me, for I shall not succumb to your evil threats."

"You will couple with me—"

"Nay!"

"You will accept me—now—as your lover, or I swear, I will give you over to William with nary a second thought."

Blaise watched her face as the soft kitten changed into a wildcat. "I will kill you first. I hate you. I hated every moment I lay under you."

He pushed her from him, snorting in disgust. "Did you now? Well, sheathe your claws, little cat. I would not take you in this bed or any other. It would mean both our heads, for William frowns on adultery, and your husband, pitiful wretch that he is, still walks upon this earth. Although not for long, I warrant, if your protector, the Black Outlaw, has anything to say about it. He has toyed with your husband for nigh on to two years now. Mayhaps, with this change of events, he will see fit to swat that bothersome gnat and concentrate on me. What do you think?"

"I think that you are addlepated. I live a simple life. I know naught of the Black Outlaw's inner thoughts."

"A quiet life among thieves, outlaws, and murderers. For what purpose were you in London Town if not to foment unrest and plot rebellion?"

" 'Tis not your affair."

"Not my affair?" He smirked. "You are my serf, and at the very best, the wife of my vassal. How dare you question my authority? And to expose my child—"

"D'Arcy's child."

"*My* child, to whom I gave life on Lammas night, or did you so conveniently forget all these facts? Am I expected to care naught for the child—to let it be brought up as a serf?"

Morgana thought of Lord Wulfrid. "You would not be the first sire to forget the careless dropping of a seed."

"Careless dropping," he replied with heavy irony. "My memory was that it was most purposeful. I sought you out that night. You remember?" He mocked her. " 'Twas when you slipped into the wood and awaited me on the rock, the night of the pagan feast." He drew her and pressed her hips against his throbbing hardness. "We were brought together by a force—to seek each other out, though we wished we could escape." He lifted her and laid her at the edge of the bed.

"You said that you would not force me."

He smiled humorlessly as she tried to elude his advances. "You should have escaped when you could, Morgana. No more. I loosed you once, when Aline was born. I want you now—though it may cost me body and soul. I would take you in the lair of the devil himself, my hunger is so great."

"You are William's man—remember? Do you thrust yourself within me now only to forswear me in the morning?"

Blaise rose from her. "You are right. I am William's man, and I will not lie to him. You are a traitor. I would fuck you now and turn from you tomorrow."

She fought to control her voice—to deny him the pleasure of her fear. "I am a Saxon, and you are a fool if you ever expected anything else from me."

Blaise turned his back and quickly donned his clothes. Outside, a trumpet sounded. He glanced out the window, then swore an oath. "Clothe yourself! 'Tis the king. Tell him naught of your identity." She did not acknowledge his words. He gripped her chin and forced her to look into his eyes. "Do you hear me, foolish girl? Tell—him—naught!"

"Aye!" she agreed, then roused herself from the bed, her pulse racing as she pulled her kirtle and gunna over her head. Not a moment too soon, for as Blaise opened the chamber door, the king stood upon the threshold.

Morgana slipped to her knees, taking the time to rearrange her clothing as she curtsied. "Your Majesty."

The king stared first at Morgana. She prostrated herself at his feet as he circled her. "Lady D'Arcy, 'tis beyond my ken that you would ever dare to defy me or plot against me when I raised you from certain poverty to the Norman nobility." He turned to his men. "Escort the vicomte to his solar. I wish to speak with Lady D'Arcy alone."

"You need an interpreter—" Blaise began, but William pointed to his retainer and waved Blaise away. He hesitated, words of defiance straining to pass his lips, but he swallowed them back. His oath of fealty meant strict obedience. Besides, no one had ever succeeded in influencing William by defying him. Indeed, William reacted most negatively to such a strategy. Legend had it that William had beaten his own queen, Matilda, when she was yet his unwilling fiancée—had pulled her from her horse, beaten her, and dragged her through the mud by her hair.

Blaise nodded to Morgana, praying that she remembered his words and kept her counsel.

"Arise, Lady D'Arcy." The king sat at Blaise's desk and motioned her to a seat across from him. She held her head high, refusing to cower, but did his bidding.

"I thought to find you much distressed, my lady."

She kept her chin straight, knowing that William appreciated courage, but not stupidity.

"Instead I find you looking lovelier than I can remember. 'Tis not hard to see what drives Lord Blaise to the edge of madness."

She blushed profusely, but kept silent. William would get to the point of his visit soon enough.

"I highly prize women of your mettle. You remind me of my wife, who has recently come from Normandy."

"I am honored by your visit, Your Majesty. Thank you for considering this matter of such importance as to warrant your personal attention."

"Lady D'Arcy, your honeyed words do not hide the fact that I preferred to be elsewhere at this moment, but you surely must understand that I cannot countenance disloyalty."

"Aye, Your Majesty." Morgana licked her dry lips. "I understand well the call of duty."

"Then what is to be done about this matter? If you were me, what would you do?"

"I would do what duty required of me."

"You say so much, and yet so little. Is duty not a malleable thing?"

"For kings mayhaps, for who would say nay to a king?"

"True. And as king, can I not design my own duty?"

"There are things, my liege, that even a king must bow to."

"Such as?"

"Treason. When one plots against the king, he plots against the people that the king represents, does he not?"

"You are a very perceptive young woman. A shame that

your husband does not share your gift for politics." He paused. "So then, 'tis clear what must be done about you?"

"Aye!" Morgana swallowed. "Death."

He nodded and began to say something, but held back because there was a light knock. "Enter!" he called, and the nurse brought Aline to Morgana's arms.

"I—forgive me, Your Majesty," Morgana whispered, her love for her child visible upon her face. "She hungers." There was a weak whine as Aline twisted in her mother's arms to see more of the stranger.

William watched the bobbing red hair. So much like her mother. As Morgana turned from him to nurse her child, he asked, "Can a king not be merciful?"

Morgana's heart lurched as she sensed a glimmer of hope. "A good ruler tempers justice with mercy," she replied.

The king was silent. After Aline had eaten a bit, she fidgeted in her mother's arms and tried to look over her shoulder at the king. Morgana adjusted the tie of her bodice, and turned to him. The king walked to where they sat and held out his finger to the babe. Aline grabbed the long, strong digit and tried to bring it toward her mouth.

"Your child much resembles her father." Clearly William knew the truth. "Well, I could have you brought to the block at the first light of dawn. Yet, I have asked myself, what would it gain me? You would be a martyr to your people—a cause around whom to rally. I do not wish to help them organize their rebellions."

"You have never had such considerations in the past, Your Majesty. You have easily laid low those who fought against you, burning whole villages, blinding—"

"I must say, Lady D'Arcy, you have a strange sense of appreciation. This is a matter with political implications, is it not? You are the wife of a Norman knight, by royal decree. You are the mother of the future—a generation where Normans and Saxons will be one English people." He twined his hands and tapped the thumbs on the desk. "But even more, you are the beloved of one of my favorite nobles. I need your lover, Lady D'Arcy—plain and simple. He is a key vassal; he holds a primary piece of defensive property at Retford. He is a fearsome warrior and a learned man—a prize amongst my knights. He shall rise to great power in this country, with the right woman behind him. So you can see, Lady D'Arcy, that he had pled your case well. Quite well, indeed."

"I am married to another, Your Majesty."

"If you approve, I shall send an envoy to Rome—to the pope himself. We are well acquainted. Of course, my messenger will bring many gifts for the Church."

"On what basis would the Church agree—"

"I have executed an affidavit stating that you were married under duress. Further, that Lord D'Arcy lied when he led me to believe that he was the father of your child."

"It—it cannot be."

"What? It cannot be?" William was totally bewildered by the girl's response. "Would you prefer to stay married to the man? I was led to believe that he is not to your liking."

"He murdered my mother. I can never be wife to him again."

"Good! Then all is in order. You have only to give me your vow that you shall never again plot against me."

"I—cannot."

William cocked a brow and suppressed a perceptible twitch in his cheek. "You try my patience, madame." He pressed in at his temples. "I would have to execute you if I ever found you plotting treachery against me—godchild of Edward or no. Do you understand that?" Morgana nodded, and there was a long silence during which the king weighed the matter. "If you refuse the vow, your movement shall be severely curtailed. We will take temptation away from you." Aline squirmed from her arms and began to toddle toward the king, holding on to the furniture, and sitting down when there was naught else to hold her up. "When I came here today, your life was forfeit. So when you think to plot and scheme, lady, remember that child of yours. You have a responsibility to her, too." William rose and went to the door. "Oh!" he said as an afterthought. "There is one other requirement. Once your annulment has been granted, you will marry Blaise, and his child shall be legitimized by royal decree. As the Vicomtesse de Rouen and Lady of Retford and Hartley, you will accomplish more for your people than all this plotting has netted you. Blaise is kind and just."

She pursed her lips, trying not to betray the feelings warring within her. "As you will, Majesty." She curtsied.

"Good! That is more like it." He left with a flourish.

Morgana lifted Aline and crushed her to her breast. William could posture all he wanted. She would not be told whom to marry. She would never marry such a callous man.

Blaise returned a short while thereafter in a fit of pique. He paced the floor, flung wood into the fire, and cast fearsome glances upon Morgana. She finally handed the babe to the nurse and faced him.

"Why this mood, my lord?"

"With what did you bargain, my lady?"

"I do not understand."

"To have gained a pardon from William in the face of such treachery—with what did you bargain?"

"I had naught to bargain with, except possibly an affection that he believes you have for me."

"We are to be wed. How did you accomplish so much behind the closed door of your bedchamber?"

"I do not appreciate the suggestion of your words. I therefore shall not answer that question."

He gripped her arm and wrenched her against him. She sensed his anger in the tension of his sinewy arms, the clenching of his teeth, and the blazing flames that flickered in his eyes. "What did you give to William for your life?"

She struggled in his iron grip. "How dare you!"

"I dare anything. Answer me, or I will wring your neck."

"And risk disfavor with the king?" she taunted.

"I will not let William foist off his whores on me."

"You bastard!" she spat, slapping him soundly on the cheek. "You wretch!" She kicked his knee. "You foulmouthed whoreson!"

His fingers curled around her neck, as if to snuff the life from her, but they never pressed in. "Have a care! Do not push me, Morgana. Your life hangs tenuously in my hands."

"Kill me, then! 'Tis easier than this purgatory you have

left me in." She shook her head slowly, tears brimming in her eyes. "The king told me 'twas your idea."

"Aye! But when I approached him with it, he turned me away."

"He is the king. He is allowed the luxury of changing his mind. Can you not be thankful that he has seen fit to show me mercy? Must you always see plots and conspiracies in everything? Must you always think the worst of me?"

"He does not know everything, *Morgana*. Not all."

"Must he know more? Must he have every detail? Will you be happier if my severed head rolls at your feet?"

Blaise's anger evaporated at the thought, leaving confusion in its wake. He drew her into his arms and kissed her neck. "My jealousy moves me to say things better left unsaid." He led her to the bed and laid her back, gently. "Why is this anger always between us?"

"A foul trick of the fates," she mumbled.

He flicked a tear from the edge of her slanted eyes with the tip of his finger. "Not quite so foul, since we are to be wed. For whatever reason, William finds favor with you."

" 'Tis not what you think."

"Do not speak. Our words are weapons in our hands. We play the game too well. No more words."

Their need for each other was so great that they both were out of their clothes in a matter of moments. He laid her down where they stood—on a bearskin rug. A force higher and stronger than both of them brought them together. His first tender touch sent a thrill through her, and she felt an answering tremble in his arms.

She opened her mouth to his questing tongue as he grew more insistent, his leg stealing over her thigh, pinioning her to the fur. He sat up and drew her to him, and unraveled her braid. It fell in a red-gold cascade around her shoulders, like a precious silken mantle or threads of gold that fell across her nipples. He lifted her hair and brushed her breast. The nipple tightened in answer, puckered, begged for his lips to surround its heated mass. On the tip a dot of bluish white liquid beckoned him.

Morgana watched his eyes, and saw his intent, and hesitation. She wrapped her arms around his neck and drew him toward her. " 'Tis all right," she whispered, as she lifted her breasts to his lips.

Blaise flicked the liquid from the tip, then surrounded the aureole in a swirling movement, finally drawing it into his mouth and sucking. Morgana felt the release of the milk as Blaise tasted of her. " 'Tis sweet—like sugar." He massaged her breasts, fascinated by their engorged state, thinking them the most beautiful he had ever seen, or touched.

Morgana's legs opened invitingly. His mouth traced a line from breasts to belly, moving lower, to her navel and the slight curve of her abdomen, and finally down to where her thighs joined. He separated the peach-colored lips of her cleft, and inside the skin was a darker pink, slick with her love juices. The core of her pleasure, that little nub that rose, erect, from between the folds, beckoned his lips and tongue. She bucked when he touched her ever so gently, for she was exquisitely sensitive there, and the rhythmic ravaging of his tongue drew her body out of itself as her hips rose to meet his wet thrust, her whimpers of need changing quickly into screams of primitive rapture as he rapidly took her to that precipice and flung her to the depths below.

But it did not stop there—could not stop there. She wanted all of him. She was consumed by the need to feel him—to taste of him as he had of her. She pressed him back into the furs, and when he tried to lift her onto him, bade him be patient as her fingers traced a swirling pattern on his thighs, to each side of his rampant thickness. She cupped the bag from whence her Aline had come, and kissed it fervently, wondering how a man like him, of such intense masculinity, could ever have believed that he could not father a child.

Her tongue dropped a line of light, feathery kisses up the wall of his thrusting manhood, until at the top, she whirled around and around until he thought that he would surely die—dissolve into spasms of nothingness. Even then she would not stop, as she took him into her mouth, turning so that she could take more of him in, bit by bit, deeper and deeper, until, in his fierceness, he once again found her soft woman's place, and with tongue and fingers, brought her swiftly to her own completion. As her lips moved rhythmically, she never paused, not even when the unending ripples of their mutual climax drained them, and they drank, unashamed, each of the other's bodies.

That, too, would not be the end, for they were driven to make up for their separation. The only thing that was certain was that nothing was certain. Each moment could be their last together. They had to take what they could *when* they could. Consequently, even after she had drained him, Blaise remained hard, covering Morgana as a stallion does a mare, bringing her onto her knees to enter her from behind.

She could not remember when he had been so deep within her. He touched places that she had not known existed. Yet she offered herself to him, pressing into his surge, doubling her efforts as his fingers found her jewel and rubbed it and his rod rammed into her. Wildfire swept her body, consuming her as he pierced her softness again and again, his tongue licking her neck, her backbone. When he heard her low cry of triumph, he spent his seed, dropping it right at the door to her womb.

Chapter 20

Afterward, as Blaise and Morgana lay on the bed, he held her. "Is this the first time we have made love for love's sake—not because we are enemies, or spies, but because we are lovers?" he asked.

"We have always been lovers. I fought you, and ran from you, because loving you is too painful. There was never any pretense between us to the contrary. And yet I have loved you—even though I tried to ignore or deny my feelings."

"God's splendor, but I thrill every time I hear that word upon your lips." He trailed kisses down her throat, then returned to her beckoning mouth. "Those most petulant lips."

Her breath caught in her throat. "My breasts tingle. I must cleanse my nipples. Aline will want to suckle soon."

Blaise brought her a cloth dampened with warm water from the caldron over the fire. "Have you had your monthly courses since the child came?"

"Nay! But Alyson says that a woman will most likely not conceive while she nurses."

" 'Twill suit our purposes for the moment. There must be no stain upon my son's legitimacy." Morgana nodded, oddly quiet. "It shall only be a few months, for William has promised to offer the Church a princely sum for a quick resolution to your annulment."

Aline screamed outside the door. Blaise retrieved her as Morgana bathed her breasts. Aline promptly wet the front of her father's tunic.

"Here. Let me," Morgana insisted as she cleaned the child with considerable expediency. He cherished the moment. She had always been the wife of his heart—always would be—even should the pope refuse to dissolve her union with D'Arcy. But he would not even consider that eventuality.

"Why the scowl?" she asked as she lay on the bed and put Aline to her breast.

"The annulment is all the more reason that D'Arcy must not know you are here. He will plot against us in earnest now." Aline fretted and grasped at Morgana's breast. "I think she is much like you," he said. "Demanding. A wild thing."

"How do you know that I was not a shy, retiring maid before you came along to win me?"

"Win you, you say? Was it not you who jumped from the stone, dagger in hand, a Celtic goddess bent on destruction?" He chuckled at the memory of that wild witch whom he had taken from the wood so long ago. "Aye, and you were magnificent. But you are always magnificent."

He threw a log onto the fire and, when Aline slept, renewed his lovemaking until Morgana begged for sleep as dawn dipped over the horizon and spilled through the slitted windows.

Blaise finally relented. "Though you may have a short respite from this, for I have to be within you." He held her against him long after she slept.

Yet it was impossible for him to sleep, for he could not help thinking that their love, their very existence together, was as fragile as a silken thread.

And Blaise was accurate in this thinking, for D'Arcy was indeed bent on vengeance. It ate at him like a growth. His hatred was a palpable thing. He could almost taste it—so real and alive it was.

No matter what schemes he hatched, they overcame all. And why had William seen fit to champion their cause? Why did no one see what D'Arcy had wanted them to see—that Blaise was capable of murdering his wife to gain his mistress?

It irked him sorely that they slept together. When she had left them both, that was one matter. But to return to Blaise's bed—

Mayhaps he should have hesitated before dispatching Gisele to the netherworld. True, he had not planned the act. He had merely returned to fuck her. It had been her own fault—taunting Blaise about aborting the babes, one of whom was *his* child. She had known that he had wanted that child—and had killed it. So he had crept from the secret passage and killed her. 'Twas fitting. A life for a life.

And now his wife slept with Blaise, cuckolding him, caring naught that his men knew. How clever they thought they were. What a fool they thought he was.

But he would have the last word—would wait until they made a mistake. Mayhaps he could get them together. Then it could be made to look like the work of the Black Outlaw.

Father Jerome sat in Morgana's chamber, pounding upon the table. "For the love of God, girl, make up your mind. Your brother has expended a lot of time and money to arrange your escape. You told him that was what you wanted. Why suddenly do you change your mind?"

"William knows of my spying, and has pardoned me. An envoy goes to Rome to seek my annulment. My place is with the father of my child."

"Morgana, do you hear yourself? Will you accept the Norman yoke on your shoulders?"

"*You* are not listening. As my husband, Blaise will not seek to enslave me. He already thinks me a serf, and is willing to raise me up to the nobility."

"Your brother will be sorely disappointed."

"I have not seen him since my return from London."

"He fears for your well-being."

"And I for his, for he lives in the past. 'Tis time for him to think of his future."

"He does not have a future until England is free."

"More's the pity then," she murmured, "for I fear that England is well and truly taken. William is a man of purpose. He gained his dukedom at a young age, and learned early about treachery and power. 'Tis why he is such a formidable enemy—because he has already anticipated any minor skirmish we may devise, and countered it."

Father Jerome stared at her in shock. "I never thought that I would say this, Morgana, but methinks you are a fool. I will tell your brother that you have stopped thinking with your mind, and are now thinking with your heart. I only hope that you do not live to regret this decision. Is it really you he wants, Morgana, or the child?"

As Lammas night drew closer, Morgana remembered Aline's birth the year before. She stood at the window, looking out at the dense wood, and wished that she could be feasting with her people, and not a prisoner in her fancy, well-appointed prison. True, she was not in chains in a dank, sweat-walled dungeon, but she was fettered all the same.

Prisons were a Norman invention. At night she often thought she heard sounds rising from the dungeon, but it was her loneliness and confinement that distressed her. If she did not get out soon—

Aline was her only amusement. The child grew taller each day, but this was no way for Aline to live—stuck away in a chamber, her only sun from the solar. She should be running in the fields, picking flowers, but as long as D'Arcy was in the area, they would be in danger. Then why did Blaise refuse to send him away?

"Aline reminds me of you when you were little," Alyson said one day on a visit. Morgana merely nodded and poked her needle into her tapestry. "What is wrong?" Alyson asked.

"All is well."

"Then why do you look that way?"

"I was thinking of Mother, and how much I miss her." She sighed. "And of D'Arcy, the devil take his soul."

"As long as he lives, he will never let you go."

"Aye!" Morgana agreed. "He has killed my mother without impunity. He thinks that he is above the law, and so he is, since Blaise will not rid me of him."

"You are still angry about this?"

"Should I be otherwise? The mere thought of that man walking around free while I am forced to keep to this chamber—should I not care that Blaise considers the needs of that hateful knight before me and Aline?"

After a long pause, Alyson took Morgana's hand. "Why did you ask me to come?" she asked.

"I never could hide anything from you, could I?" Morgana smiled crookedly. "I think that I am with child again."

Alyson clucked with excitement as she quickly went about examining her. "Midwinter," she finally said. "All looks well."

"All is not well—cannot be well while that monster D'Arcy lives to stalk me like an animal." Morgana dissolved in racking sobs, refusing to be consoled. Alyson, at a loss, finally sought out Blaise.

"What do you want now?" he asked the midwife as he scratched in his ledgers.

"Morgana needs you. She is ill. Go to her."

Blaise reluctantly put his work aside and went to his lover. "Alyson says that you are ill. What is wrong?"

"I am not ill—except maybe in here." She pressed against her heart. " 'Tis this chamber," she exclaimed, bursting into tears. "I am sick to death of this prison."

"I thought that you understood—"

"Nay! I do not understand. If D'Arcy is a threat to me, then throw him in your dungeon."

"His men will rise against us."

Her hand went to her dagger. "Then let me kill him."

"Morgana! You are a bloodthirsty vixen, but we will rid ourselves of him my way. What is wrong?"

"I cannot continue like this."

" 'Tis only for a while longer."

"I will never be able to leave here while D'Arcy lives."

"Are you uncomfortable? Some new books mayhaps."

"I will not birth my child in captivity. He *will* be free. *I* will be free."

Blaise stood agape at her words.

"See! You are not pleased. I knew that it would be so. You should have kept your seed to yourself, my lord, and not planted it in such fertile ground if you wanted no more bastards.'' She flung herself on the featherbed and pounded her fists into the furs.

"Morgana, I—I am pleased. You do not understand—''

"Get out! Out!'' She backed him through the door and barred it against him.

"Morgana, I am well pleased,'' he insisted.

"Go to the devil!''

Blaise returned to his solar and thought upon the matter for a long while. What was to be done with Morgana? He really was thrilled that she carried his child—a son, mayhaps. She had read so much into that one infinistesimal moment of pause.

Of course, she had also been easily upset the last time, and true, he had not much experience with breeding women.

Blaise summoned Sigvald to him. "Morgana is with child again. I want her released each day, and taken for a walk around the bailey.''

"Do you think that wise?''

"She must needs be free for a portion of each day.''

"I will take care of it.''

Within a day of Morgana's first walk, Christian D'Arcy knew that she was at Retford—and with child. Now he determined to move in earnest, before she escaped his revenge.

An opportunity presented itself within the week.

It began with Morgana's visit to Father Jerome. "I have given the matter much thought,'' she told the priest. " 'Tis best if Aline and I go to Ireland after all.''

"Morgana, again you change your mind?'' the priest asked, clearly exasperated.

"I cannot live like this—a prisoner on my own land, terrified that D'Arcy will harm my child—or me. I cannot eat for fear he has poisoned my food. He will come for me, and Blaise would have me do naught to defend myself.''

" 'Tis hardly credible, Morgana—''

" 'Tis true, I tell you.'' She burst into uncontrolled weeping. "There—there is more. There will be another child—another bastard of Blaise de Rouen.''

Father Jerome shook his head in disbelief and sighed.

"Now 'tis a difficult task, Morgana. Blaise has me closely watched. When first I approached you, the plan was in place. Now 'twill be more complicated." He thought on the matter. "I will consult with your brother."

He returned within a few days with a plan. "You must somehow leave the keep and clear the drawbridge."

"Blaise will stop me."

"Prevail upon him, Morgana. Tell him that you want to see the midwife—that you want to pick flowers—"

"He has heard each excuse before."

"I have every faith in you, Morgana."

Indeed, she did not need to wait long until a ruse appeared, for Maude died shortly thereafter.

Blaise, concerned about Morgana's well-being, cradled her in his arms and wiped her tears.

"I want to bury her—with Astrid," she said as they lay side by side, her head in the crook of his neck and her fingers twined in the hairs upon his chest.

" 'Tis not wise that you leave Retford Hall."

"I want to attend to her burial."

Blaise opened his lips to say her nay, but she lay across him, her flaming hair a scarlet mantle over them both, and pressed her lips to his. "A boon, *mon seigneur*. A boon for your ladylove." She drew her legs up and sat upright, abruptly impaling herself upon his burgeoning manhood. Within moments he was beyond all thought as she rode him. "A boon?" she inquired as she slowed her movement. He tried to buck beneath her to keep the pace, but she started to dismount.

His stared at her through slitted eyes as she pinioned his wrists to his sides. "What say you, my lord?"

He loosed his wrists with a growl and gripped her buttocks, and in an instant he had her upon her back and he was within her to the hilt, each movement calculated to tease—to bring her close upon the precipice and then draw back. Morgana, however, had a trick or two of her own, and by contractions within her woman's place they both soon fell, together, into that oblivion that they sought.

"Aye!" he exhaled at her ear in a ragged breath. "You have your boon."

She held him to her and stroked his back, memorizing

every scar, every sinew of his muscle, reluctant to loose him without filling her mind with memories that would have to stay within her heart for a lifetime.

As Morgana made her preparations the next morn, Blaise determined to do all in his power to insure her well-being. There was a problem, however, for he was summoned to William's side in a most urgent matter. "I must go," Blaise insisted. "Mayhaps 'tis the annulment." He commended her to Sigvald's care.

"Godspeed," she whispered as they embraced, assuming that this call to the king was part of Brent's plan. She kissed every plane and angle of his face, and caressed his body. She would remember her Norman warlord on those cool Irish nights. Verily, could she ever forget his glorious body and how it felt joined with hers?

She unconsciously embraced her belly.

After he had departed, and so as not to call attention to herself, Morgana rode out with a small party in the company of the priest and Aline in her arms. At the copse, all went smoothly. As when she had buried her mother, the Normans held back so as to not impose upon her grief. When they were at a distance, she, the child, and the priest were replaced by impostors.

Morgana mounted the steed provided, and with Aline strapped to Father Jerome's back, sped through the wood toward the high stone with all due haste.

Something had gone awry, however. When they arrived at the stone, there was no one to meet them. "Are you sure of the place?" Morgana asked the priest. At his nod, she continued. "Tarry here a bit while I look around."

Morgana climbed upon the stone and scanned the area. No one. Where were Brent's men? Surely this was the place. Initially he had said the pond, but the place had changed—

Or had it?

"My lady wife, returned to her husband."

Morgana's heart froze as she turned toward D'Arcy, now standing at the opposite end of the stone. A dozen men quickly surrounded them. She whipped her peasant's shift off, and he saw that underneath she was dressed in breeches and a chainse. Her dagger was out of its sheath and in her hand as she wrapped the material of the shift around her other arm.

"Why this defensive posture, my lady? I have no need to raise arms against you. I have the child." He nodded toward Father Jerome, who was now held captive by D'Arcy's men.

"Not even you would dare kill a priest and an innocent child."

"Would I not?" The vile truth gleamed in his eyes. He would enjoy every moment of it. "Put your weapon down, Kirsten, or I shall skewer the babe on my sword." Morgana dropped her weapon to her side. "Get down now!" He motioned to the ground as Morgana eased from the rock, her fingers bleeding as they scraped along the rock's edge.

"William will kill you if you harm me," she said evenly.

"He would have to find me first."

"This is not war, Christian. There is no excuse to kill me such as you used when you murdered Alayne."

"I need no excuse. Because of you I have fallen out of favor with the king. He wants to send me to Sicily."

"Do—do you want me to come with you?"

"Come with me?" He laughed shrilly. "You are too late."

"No! We can go away together—I am your wife, after all."

"You should have considered that before you opened your legs so freely for the Lord of Retford. Now he has gone and sired another bastard on you—" His voice whined, and before she could gauge his intent, he punched her stomach. Morgana doubled over with pain, but held her chin stiffly as she gasped for breath. He pulled her off her knees and pressed her face to his, one hand fondling her breast.

"Take the priest and child from here," he ordered as he removed his hauberk, gauntlets, and helmet. He ripped open her bodice and pressed her back into the grass. His lips locked on to her nipple as he suckled loudly, slurping, sickening her.

Morgana kept her wits about her as she planned each movement. She must escape. Now that he had sent the men away, she had to contend with only him. She could best him. She could do it. Their lives depended on it.

He fondled the round globes and drank hungrily of her, heedless that his teeth scored her tender nipples. She opened her legs, enticing him, and began to undulate ever so slowly in a familiar rhythm.

"Yes, you are like all the rest of them—certainly more like Gisele than I thought."

Morgana felt his hardness growing along her thigh, straining for release. She ripped at his crotch and he loosened his breeches. His rampant manhood burst from its loincloth. He tore at her breeches until she was fully revealed to his glazed eyes. He brought his mouth to her sex, and she arched into the touch of his lips, moaning.

She would not be ready for him if he chose to enter her, but at least she would be wet. You can get through this, she told herself. A man in his passion is weak. A man in his passion can be overcome. Draw him into you, and then—

She entwined her fingers in his hair and moved faster to his laving tongue, urging him pleadingly to bring her ecstasy.

He stilled his movement. Morgana moaned, disappointed. "You must earn it first." He stood on his knees and raised her up, pushing her face between his legs.

She smiled wickedly as she brushed her fingers along his shoulders and ran her tongue along his lightly furred chest. She nipped at his nipples as he had hers. His manhood grew and pulsated. She pushed him back and pinned him beneath her body, her sex at his mouth, his hardness at her own lips, as she brought him to the point of vulnerability. When he stood poised on the precipice—she moved like a wildcat, all muscles and grace, and bit his shaft mercilessly. His blood dripped as her hand crushed the sac below and she kicked his face.

She rolled away in a fluid movement, glorying in his snarling moans. She picked up his sword, but it was too unwieldy for effective use. He growled loudly as she retrieved his dagger. She heard a noise and saw him stand, poised gingerly atop his feet. "I shall kill you, bitch, as I killed that other one—Gisele." He chortled in maniacal glee as he adjusted his breeches and started toward her. "You shall be most sorry you ever let blood."

He limped slightly, recovered, and swaggered toward her. She backed toward the high stone and climbed atop, seeking her own dagger. Her torn shift covered her nakedness as she tied it around her thighs for easier movement. "Come down from there. If I have to come for you, your life will be forfeit."

"I am no foolish lamb like Gisele to be led easily to your slaughter."

"You could have avoided this, but you played me false."

"You filthy swine! From the moment of our marriage, this has been coming. You killed my mother—you killed Alayne."

"One cannot coddle the vanquished."

"When you are dead, my lord, I will cut your body into a thousand pieces and scatter them to the wind. You do not deserve a decent burial. No priest would bless your grave."

"You need not worry about the manner of my burial," he assured her as he climbed the rock, "for you shall not be around to attend to the details." He stood now at the opposite end of the stone from her, sword pointed. Her brow rose as she saw the blood on his breeches.

His eyes followed hers. "Aye! You have injured me sorely, bloodthirsty bitch, but you shall pay. I shall cut the nipples from those impudent breasts—"

"You will die trying, lord husband." She faced him, legs apart, her weight evenly distributed, a dagger in each hand.

He stalked her, teasing her. "I think that I shall put you to the lash first. It would be interesting to see your hide flayed, the flesh hanging—"

His words fell unheeded, for she knew this tactic—a maneuver much like those used by the Roman general whom she had read about, Julius Caesar. She watched every step he made, and to his point provided a counterpoint.

"Why prolong this, Kirsten?" He stood, his legs spread. "You could not hope to venture a defense. You have no sword." As if to prove his point, he flicked his wrist and sliced a shallow cut through her shoulder. "Had you been a wifely maid, this all would have been avoided." A dimple flirted at the corner of his mouth, and she swore that she would cut it out before the day was through. "All that you shall get for your trouble is blacked and bruised."

"I shall see you to hell with my dying breath."

He was pleased at her reaction. "You will submit. Mayhaps I will not kill you—at least not until you have met all my whims. You do know how to stiffen a man's staff." She made a dash, but he was quickly on her. "Yield the day."

"Why, husband, have you found cause for dissatisfaction with me?" she crooned.

"Properly tethered, you will do just fine."

He was too close. She neared the edge of the stone. She must not let him back her over it, to take the slight advantage that her intelligence gave her.

"We have dallied too long. This stops now!" His enraged bellow chilled her as he flexed his sword arm at her.

She stepped back at his thrust, and went over the edge of the stone to land in a crumpled heap. D'Arcy stood over her in a reddish haze, a rock ready to crush her skull.

"I think not, sir."

D'Arcy swung on his heel. "The Black Outlaw, I presume."

Brent nodded at him, and tapped his long-sword to his head in mock salute. "This tryst in the wood has been a long time coming."

"Before we engage," D'Arcy said, "I must know. Who are you anyway?"

"Brent, son of Lord Wulfrid of Retford, your wife's brother, and betrothed of Lady Alayne of Hartley."

D'Arcy's sick leer aggravated Brent's anger. "She was a lively piece for a virgin. Hot and saucy. She creamed for me by the time I tore into her."

Brent's swing of his long-sword was easily parried by the Norman. D'Arcy was an able warrior, and could have come far in William's ranks if not for his grievous faults. He taunted his quarry, crazed and untiring.

Brent tried to remain dispassionate as he wielded his sword with the pent-up fury of the last two years. He envisioned his Alayne at this swine's feet, pleading for mercy from a man who had none to give. His sword arm took on a life of its own, driven forward by the deep, tormenting knowledge that this man had enjoyed torturing his beloved, that even now he besmirched her character and memories of her sweetness.

"But your sister is a better tumble. Have you tried her yet? You really should. She has been well trained by our good friend, Blaise de Rouen." Brent continued to thrust, but D'Arcy easily warded off his blows. "He thought you her lover. Too bad! She does things with her mouth—"

"Be still, you filthy pig!" Brent spat as he pressed forward, his anger taking him off his stride for one moment. One moment was all that D'Arcy needed. He landed a blow to Brent's shoulder, and another to his thigh. They were deep—not meant to kill, but to disarm and cause pain.

Brent fell back, and the stone cut into his shoulder. Blood streamed down his limbs, and his breath came in gulps.

"Such an impasse, *Lord* Brent. You see how women can affect one's life? A minor squabble between us has resulted in your death and my dishonor. Did you have to harry Hartley nightly?" He punctuated his question with a shallow cut above Brent's scarred cheek. "To ruin my career?" Cut, Cut. "To cause William to strip me of my fiefdom?" Cut, cut.

"You can kill me, D'Arcy," Brent gasped, "but with my last breath I curse you and all your kin. I vow you shall be made to pay for your evil, spiteful ways."

D'Arcy stood over him, prepared to mete out the punishment that he believed the Black Outlaw so richly deserved—death. "Mayhaps," he said as he lifted his sword with both hands above the Saxon's heart, "but not by you."

"Nay! By me!"

"Blaise!" D'Arcy swung around.

"I see that, as usual, you have managed to get yourself into mischief during my absence."

"But you were called to William's side."

"Yes, well, I started to go to William, but thought it too convenient. In truth, I thought that it was a plot to free your wife by the Black Outlaw. I never expected you to be behind this."

"You always did underestimate me. She was indeed escaping you." D'Arcy hesitated, hoping that he had served Blaise's pride a hearty blow. "With his aid. Her brother."

"Brother?"

"Lord Brent of Retford was *not* killed at Stamford Bridge, but has been masquerading as the Black Outlaw." D'Arcy turned back to Brent. "I was just about to dispatch him to the Almighty when you appeared."

"Aid her, I beg you, my lord," Brent gasped. "She is gravely injured."

"Hold your assault," Blaise bellowed.

D'Arcy faltered. "I will remove this hindrance once and for all. This man had bedeviled me for the last time."

"Hold! I say."

"No more!" D'Arcy screamed as he swung at Blaise. "I am sick to death of you—of your being given freely what I have had to take—my women, my fiefdom. No more."

But Blaise was ready for him, and without a moment's hesitation, thrust his sword into Christian's blackened heart. D'Arcy fell upon it like a rag doll, then fell back, the sword sticking up out of him like a road post. Blaise held the body down with his boot, retrieved his sword, and wiped the blood on D'Arcy's chausses. "You should have kept your mail on, as I had taught you," Blaise admonished coldly.

"Morgana!" Brent crawled to where she lay, unconscious. "Morgana!" His words fell, unheeded, as Blaise knelt by her side. Her chest barely rose and fell, but when he put his blade to her mouth, there was a scant fog from her breath.

"She lives, though barely."

"I thank you for my sister's life," Brent said.

"You are the former Lord of Retford?"

"The rightful lord," Brent retorted.

"This is your sister?"

"Morgana, the twin of my sister, Kirsten, who was taken across the sea by her betrothed, Eirik Einar. Morgana was raised in the forest by the midwife, and when the Conqueror came, it was revealed that she was the lord's stolen child."

Blaise understood now—at least part of it. She was

noble. Her resemblance to Astrid was more than chance. She had been raised a serf, but had proven that she could survive well in both worlds. Their children would be well bred, provided he could save her life.

"Well, you are lord of the wood now, sire. Return to your camp. Your sister must be tended while there is breath, however slight, in her." He lifted her gently and wrapped her in his cloak. "I fear for her and our unborn child."

Blaise whistled for Reynard, and when the horse came, he handed Morgana to her brother as he climbed onto the saddle. "I pray that her life is not the penalty we pay for moving her without a litter. But time is her enemy, and I will not leave her here to die."

Brent kissed Morgana's forehead and said a swift prayer as he handed her over to Blaise. The Lord of Retford cushioned her, lashed her to his chest, and held her in the crook of his arm as he sped toward Retford, all the devils of hell at his heels.

Chapter 21

Death hovered over Morgana for nearly a fortnight. When she returned to awareness, her first thought was of her babe.

"There was nothing to be done," Alyson said. "You have healed well. Your injuries should not affect future births."

"There will be no future births," she replied weakly, and drifted back to sleep.

Alyson plied her with potions, but there was nothing to be done about the sickness in her heart, which only time could heal. She refused Blaise an audience until, exasperated, he one day burst into her chamber.

"We must talk about what happened in the wood."

"Why? Do you want the details of my humiliation?"

"We must talk and put this behind us."

"Do you want to know how I played upon D'Arcy's lust to gain the advantage?"

"We must talk about D'Arcy and *your brother, Brent.*" She stared in dismayed silence. "What is your last memory?"

"I fell from the high stone, and then—all went black."

"Your brother saved your life. He fought with D'Arcy, but D'Arcy proved too much for him. He wounded your brother, and was ready to deal him the death blow when I came upon them.''

"*You* killed D'Arcy?''

"Only after he attacked me." Her lips moved in wordless prayer. "You are safe, Morgana—and free." He brushed wisps of hair from her forehead. "Free to do as you please. We are free to marry, or if you choose not to, I will respect your choice and escort you to your brother when you are fit. You need not decide now." He studied her, and when she did not speak, turned to leave.

"Blaise!"

He spun around and grasped her hand and brought it to his lips. "Morgana, I know that you yearn to be free, but would marriage to me be such a poor plight? God wants us together. He has removed all obstacles. Besides, you yourself have admitted that your old gods have plotted for our union from the first.''

"I was running from you when D'Arcy found me."

"I know, and I will not pretend that it does not distress me. But now we must needs look forward to our new life together as lovers and friends. Our children—''

She looked away from him in shame. She had cost him the son he wanted. He would never forgive her.

As if he read her mind, he sought to assure her. "Morgana. I am saddened by the loss of the child, but 'tis not your fault. We can have another child when you are well, but if you want no more children—I will try to abide by your wishes.''

She was trembling now, her emotions unrestrained. She had sought freedom for so long—but what would it be without Blaise there to share it? Was there freedom outside of his embrace, or would she spend her lifetime steeped in regret for having lost the only man she had ever loved?

"You are so pale, my sweet. When I thought I would lose you, I was crazed. Not even Sigvald dared approach me.''

Something in his manner soothed her, and she wanted to assure him and lessen his pain. "Whatever I decide, I want you to know that, even though I sought to leave you—I do love you.''

He nodded. "In my heart, I have always known 'tis so.

Your love is only the other half of my love." He placed her hand upon her lap and rose to leave, but her wistful voice stayed him.

"I wonder whether we can ever be happy together. There is so much that has come between us." She paused as if searching for the words. "But—I am willing to try—for Aline's sake."

"For Aline's sake," he repeated, disappointed. "Of course. That is all any husband and wife can do—try."

They were wed on All Hallows' Eve amidst joyous revelry. The hall was opened to all the villagers from Retford and Hartley for three days. Brent negotiated a truce for the duration of the wedding feast. His gift was a matched set of jeweled daggers that he had commissioned for he and Lady Alayne. The gift brought tender tears to Morgana's eyes, and she hoped that her brother would someday find love and peace, as she had.

Morgana and Blaise sought their bedchamber. They had fasted, and abstained from lovemaking, and their appetites were whetted for food, and each other.

Their first joining was explosive. She needed no coaxing as he pressed through the soft petals of her womanhood, laving her nipples until she gasped her passion and exploded.

"It only gets better between us," he rasped throatily as he brought her urgently to another peak, plunging within her over and over.

When Morgana marveled at her husband's unflagging strength, he replied, " 'Tis difficult to satisfy a wife who is insatiable."

She laughed, and drew him into her. "You do quite well, my lord husband. I think that I shall keep you—this year."

Later, as they lay abed stuffing themselves with assorted fruits and nuts, she remarked on the length of his hair.

"I have decided to keep it long a bit. 'Tis too unruly short. Besides, it grows so quickly."

Morgana pondered this. Saxon hairstyles and customs? Her Norman husband, in deference to her, was accepting more of her ways. Was that how England would fare? The English would never truly bend—Brent knew that. With intermarriage, there would be a strong and proud new race of children like Aline.

And someday—peace. The rebels still plotted in many shires of the realm, but there was harmony in their small fiefdom, for Brent had agreed, in deference to his sister, to move his rebel camp. Blaise had proven an honorable man—a man to whom her brother owed his life. This was his payment.

Gareth stayed at Retford with his sister. She wondered if, when he grew to manhood, he would know freedom, or would still be fighting oppression. Only time would tell.

Cedric chose to accompany Brent. "I have lived too many years serving the Saxon lords of Retford. I am too old to change my allegiance at this late date."

She said a silent prayer for her brothers—and the sister she had never known and had heard naught of these many years—as she drifted off to sleep in her husband's arms.